# SUSPICIOUS BEHAVIOR

"I asked if I should take him to the police. He nodded. I took his hand, brought him to my car and...and...and I drove him here. He didn't say nothin'."

"And, sorry, I've forgotten. Why did you think he needed to go to the police?"

Alex's face burned redder than a vine-ripened tomato. "I...I don't know."

"What was Nicholas wearing when you found him?"

"A white shirt, blue jeans, white sneakers an—" Alex stopped.

Tain waited, then tried to prompt him. "And?"

"That's it." The squeak was back in Alex's voice.

"Could I get your cell phone number again, just for the record please?"

After a false start, Alex corrected himself and finally rattled it off. "I don't see why this is so important. The boy was lost. I brought him here. It's not against the law."

"You don't understand why we're interested in Nicky Brennan?"

The blond head shook and then the finger reached for the glasses again.

Tain pulled out the newspaper he'd had folded underneath his notepad, the one with the headline about Taylor Brennan missing and Isabella Bertini's body being recovered. He tossed it down in front of Alex Wilson. The red cheeks blanched.

"Do you understand me now, Mr. Wilson?"

# SANDRA
# RUTTAN

---

# WHAT
# BURNS
# WITHIN

LEISURE BOOKS  NEW YORK CITY

A LEISURE BOOK®

May 2008

Published by

Dorchester Publishing Co., Inc.
200 Madison Avenue
New York, NY 10016

ISBN 10: 0-8439-6074-4
ISBN 13: 978-0-8439-6074-7

Printed in the United States of America.

10 9 8 7 6 5 4 3 2

Visit us on the web at www.dorchesterpub.com.

*For Ken Bruen, a god walking amongst mere mortals.*

# AUTHOR'S NOTE

Coquitlam, Port Coquitlam and Port Moody are the Tri-Cities, and do share many services, such as a fire department. However, Port Moody does have its own police department. For the purposes of this series, I have given the RCMP (who police Coquitlam and Port Coquitlam) joint jurisdiction in Port Moody.

The Lower Mainland of British Columbia is a challenging setting, because it is comprised of several cities that exist side by side. The actual city of Vancouver has Vancouver Police. The Vancouver Airport is actually located in the city of Richmond, which has RCMP. Jurisdictional issues have, in the past, hindered investigations and still present challenges.

Once married to a firefighter and trained arson investigator, I'm aware arson investigations are often misrepresented on television and in works of fiction. People do not go traipsing through burned-out buildings hours later. Hot spots can produce flare-ups hours after the fire is technically considered "out" (and I have been on scene to witness this myself) and whoever has authority in the jurisdiction has to consult a structural engineer regarding the safety of the building. Where I live in Canada, the RCMP do not have final authority on an arson scene. That rests with the arson investigator, who can order them off the premises and have the building destroyed, regardless of the status of any criminal investigation.

This is a work of fiction. Not all places referred to within the book are actual places. School names, recreation centers and some of the fairs referred to do not actually exist.

For more information about how I try to balance realism and believability in a work of fiction, visit my Web site at www.sandraruttan.com.

# SATURDAY

Her brother's fingers slide against her palm as the damp pool of sweat causes her to lose her grip on him. She relaxes her hold and grabs his wrist, yanking his arm. "Come on."

The force of her pull causes Nicky to jerk backward. He lands on his backside on the pavement. "I don't wanna go."

"Look, we're not wasting time at the silly old carousel." Taylor wipes her sticky palms on her jean shorts. "It's just plastic horses for little babies to ride. I want to win a big tiger. And get a new charm for my bracelet." She reaches down and helps him to his feet.

"But, Taylor . . ."

"But nothing, Nicky. I'm in charge."

He screws up his face, cheeks puffing out in a pout, breaths coming hard and fast, like they always do when he's about to cry. "I wanna play at the park." Nicky's lower lip starts to quiver.

"You're such a whiner." It's one of those days when adults talk about frying eggs on sidewalks, and even their mother had nagged them about sunscreen and drinking water.

It's one of those days Taylor would rather be at the ocean or at least a swimming pool. Her best friend, Angie, had invited her, and she'd begged and pleaded, but her mom had refused.

Instead, she got stuck babysitting, at some dinky little mobile fair, surrounded by crowds, concrete and candy, listening to the carousel drone over and over. Even with her hair up in a ponytail her neck burns and there's a pool of sweat making her shirt stick to her back.

She drags her brother through the crowd, pushing a damp strand of hair out of her eyes, weaving between the clusters of people. The tinny sound of the carousel is overtaken by the bleeps of electronic games and shouts of enticement to try your luck to win a stuffed bear, unicorn, SpongeBob, or Pokemon knockoff.

*That's, like, so yesterday,* Taylor thinks.

Taylor spots a vendor's display filled with shiny, metal necklaces and charm bracelets and steps forward. Her brother's fingers slip until she's holding nothing but sweat and air. She wipes her palm on her shorts and turns to grab him.

The crowd fills the gap between her hand and Nicky's. He disappears into a forest of legs whizzing by. She stretches up on her toes and then squats down, peeking through the gaps between the people, trying to catch sight of him.

"Come get your face painted," a clown calls to her.

She's tempted to forget about Nicky, let him have a real good scare, but the thought of her mother prompts her to turn away from the clown. *Stay with your brother. Don't you dare take your eyes off him for one single second.*

There are women with babies in strollers, toddlers hoisted on the shoulders of adults, groups of children dragging weary mothers, mothers juggling balloons and cotton candy as they yell at their kids to stay together.

But no Nicky.

"Here, have a seat. Come on, doll." The clown moves forward, grabs her arm, tugging her toward the chair.

Taylor spins around and wrenches her arm free. She darts through the crowd, bumping backsides and taking an elbow for her trouble, muttering apologies under her breath as people curse at her, tell her to watch where she's going. She brushes hot tears away from her eyes.

"Nicky, Nicky . . ."

The tune of the carousel beckons. Taylor sprints across the pavement. The music repeats. Her body trembles, her legs shake, and she swallows against the sob rising in her throat, then splutters a cough.

He isn't there.

*What have you done, Taylor? What have you done?* She bites her lip so hard she tastes blood, trying to think where Nicky would go, where he'd be.

"The park," she whispers. "That's it. The park."

With knees like Jell-O she moves toward the green space behind the carousel. *He's there, he's there, he's got to be there. Please Nicky, be there.*

*Be there so Mom won't ever need to know.*

She wasn't the type of woman he was interested in. Constable Tain knew that before he even set eyes on her. Everything from her tone of voice to her abrupt manner to the way she hung up the phone before she heard what he had to say bothered him.

Paranoid. That's what his friends would call him, if he had any left he could talk to. It had been a while since he'd checked, but he knew what they would have said before. That he'd been thinking like a cop for too long.

That if he saw a smiling toddler with a lollipop he'd assume the kid stole it.

His gut told him the woman had probably had her share of run-ins with the law, at best a negligent parent, at worst . . . Well, he wasn't sure yet. Despite that, he noted the store-bought blonde might have been a looker if the layers of makeup hadn't cracked under her snarl.

"I'd better not hear you've been taking things," the woman hissed at the child, who cowered on the edge of the bench as she clip-clopped by on her three-inch heels.

Tain wondered how she could move in clothes that tight. He gestured to the open door as he identified himself. "Right this way, Mrs. Brennen."

She tossed her head, causing her multiple dangling hoop earrings to clink together, and marched past him. Once she reached the table inside the small, bland interview room she turned on her heel.

"Well?" Her right hand landed on her hip.

"Well?" Tain echoed, staring back. With heels she was about an inch taller than he was, and that was saying something. In bare feet she must have been 5'11".

The woman blew out a deep breath. "What's he done?"

Tain sat down on a chair. "He was found at the park near the fair just off the Lougheed Highway. Wandering around alone."

She blinked, and the lines around her eyes softened, but only for a split second. Everything about this woman bothered him, from the fact that her first instinct had been to assume her son was in trouble to the fact that she acted more like a suspect than a parent whose child had been found unattended at the fairgrounds, brought to the police station by a stranger.

"Mrs. Brennen, what—"

"Jesus, what do you take me for? Is that what you're after, some sort of trumped-up neglect charge? Who are you anyway? Quota filler so the RCMP can look like an equal opportunity employer for Indians too? Oh, I mean native or aboriginal or First Nations or whatever the hell you people call yourselves."

Tain stared at her. No look of regret even flickered across her face. Her upper lip curled, and everything from the toe-tapping to the way she blew out her breath hinted at nothing more than annoyance and impatience. No trace of concern for her son.

Or evidence she felt any responsibility for the situation.

The woman finally dropped the hand from her hip, sat down and exhaled audibly as she crossed her legs to the side of the chair, her gaze leveled at the door instead of at the police officer across from her.

"He was with Taylor. His sister. When I get my hands on her . . ."

She froze. After a moment the scowl slipped from her face. Tain started counting and hit five before she looked him in the eye.

"Where's my daughter?"

"I tried to explain when I phoned—"

She sprang from the chair and was across the room and out the door before he had a chance to stop her. He ran into the hallway.

"Where is she? Where's your sister?" Mrs. Brennen grabbed her son's shirt and shook him, lightly at first, then forcefully. Nicky's head snapped back dangerously close to the wall.

The boy started to cry as Tain pushed his way between them. "Let him go!"

She did just that and slapped Tain across the face, his skin burning from the blow. He grabbed her wrists.

"Take your hands off me." She jerked her arms back as soon as he released her. Tain unclenched his jaw and nodded to the officer who'd been watching Nicky.

"Please take Mrs. Brennen to an interview room."

"I'm not—"

Tain lowered his voice. "I can charge you with assaulting a police officer. You can cooperate, or you can cool off in a cell." He turned back to the officer. "And please find this young man a snack once Mrs. Brennen is settled."

Nicky had slid down under the bench, curled with his arms wrapped around his knees.

The next ten minutes were spent painfully watching the officer try to coax the boy out from under the bench. It was a curious thing to Tain. Sims was a clean-cut guy. He had an easygoing smile and looked sharp in his uniform, but the boy kept looking at Tain, wiggling back against the wall whenever Sims reached toward him, pulling his knees up to hide his chin.

Sims stood up, looked at Tain and shrugged. "Do you want me to pull him out?"

Tain wasn't great with kids, but he wasn't eager to have one dragged kicking and screaming down the hall either. Especially when the child was a witness he was responsible for.

He squatted down beside the bench and tried to offer a reassuring smile. "My friend will take you for cookies and find you something to play with." Nicky remained in a ball.

"We need to talk to your mom. It's okay. My friend will take good care of you."

For a moment they were locked in a stare. Tain wondered

what was going through the boy's mind. If his own brief encounter with Nicky Brennen's mother was anything to go by, the child probably didn't have much of a reason to trust adults. Tain reached out his hand slowly.

Nicky unclasped his hands, unbending his legs one at a time. His eyes were huge.

"Are you gonna find my sister?" Nicky pulled himself out from under the bench. He looked at Tain's hand for a moment, his mouth twisted, and then he stood.

Tain pulled back his hand, his heart sinking just a bit as he contemplated what experiences would cause a child to be afraid to trust a police officer. He took out his wallet and handed Nicky a five-dollar bill. He whispered, "Make sure he takes you to get a treat."

Tain watched the boy glance at his mother, who had her back to them, arms folded across her chest, not moving. A hint of a smile curled the boy's lips as he clamped the money in his fist. He didn't take the other officer's hand either, but followed without argument.

As they walked away, Nicky turned back to look over his shoulder, those big eyes meeting Tain's gaze. The smile was gone.

Tain drew a deep breath. From the corner of his eye he saw someone approach him.

Sergeant Steve Daly was a little shorter than Tain, with sandy hair just starting to turn gray at the temples. Daly nodded at the boy. "What's the situation?" he asked.

Tain didn't have a great track record of getting along with his superiors, or pretty much anyone for that matter, but he respected the way Daly operated. The man was available without being intrusive. It didn't feel like Daly checked up on him, so much as checked in with him.

Most other officers would have punted Tain sideways, put him on desk duty or some marginal unit without much stress, tried to keep him out of the way. Instead, Daly had pulled him up for this case, getting him away from the routine humdrum assignments.

He'd even let him work alone. It had been the only thing

Daly had hesitated over. In the end he'd agreed, as long as Tain understood that at the first sign the case was snowballing he'd have to deal with a partner.

Tain had hoped that wouldn't be necessary, although he had to admit it didn't look good now. He filled Daly in on how Nicholas Brennen got to the police station.

Daly's eyes narrowed. "Some guy drove him here?"

"Apparently he didn't want people to think he was abducting the boy. He didn't come inside. Just wrote this note and gave it to the boy. Kid came in on his own. We'll have to check the tape and see if we can get an ID."

"Now I've heard everything," Daly said.

"Not quite." Tain told him about the missing girl.

Something about the way Daly's cheeks sagged made him look like he'd aged ten years in that moment. "How old is she?"

"I was just about to ask when Mommy Dearest flew off the handle."

"Do we need to bring in social services?"

"Already called them."

Daly blew out a deep breath. "Talk to the mother. I'll have Sims handle the background check. Report to my office as soon as you're done."

Tain nodded as he went to interview Mrs. Brennen for the second time.

When Tain reached Sergeant Daly's office twenty minutes later, Inspector Hawkins was already there. "Sir." Tain nodded.

Hawkins had a few years on Daly, but he was as fit as any man on the force. He was the poster boy for the respectable RCMP officers, the kind of man who embodied confidence and authority. Clean cut, with nothing more than a few laugh lines around his eyes and his rank to hint at his age. Few things rattled the inspector, but the fact that he was in Daly's office suggested to Tain that he was worried.

The inspector didn't acknowledge Tain's arrival. "What's the status?"

Daly answered. "Patrols are out canvassing now. We've got uniforms at every exit point from the fairgrounds, taking statements."

Hawkins frowned. "And the girl is the right age?"

Daly glanced at Tain, then nodded.

"Shit." Hawkins muttered the word under his breath, but not so far under that Tain didn't hear him.

Tain looked at Daly. "There's usually a news crew on the grounds filming, right?"

Daly nodded.

"We should get their tape, double-check it. Look for any known pedophiles, any sign of these kids in the background, anything."

"I'll call the patrols."

"I think we should reassign this case," Hawkins said.

"Respectfully, sir, I don't think that's a good idea," Daly said.

Hawkins turned to look at Tain. "Last month we recovered the body of Julie Darrens from a burnt-out shack at the industrial park near the Mary Hill Bypass. Isabella Bertini is still missing. The press will have a field day with this."

"I decided to have Tain respond to every arson fire since we found Julie Darrens," Daly said. "He's been working 'round the clock on the Bertini girl. No solid leads."

"Just crackpots and dead ends," Tain said. "We'll be getting more of the same when this hits the news."

Hawkins kept his gaze on Daly. "You can have Tain assist, but I don't think it's in the best interest of this department—"

"What about the best interest of this case?" Daly's eyes pinched with uncharacteristic anger. "Tain has been working in conjunction with Burnaby. He knows all the particulars. Pulling him off—"

"I didn't say to pull him off."

"No, just have him take a backseat so that Burnaby will think we softballed them, gave them a body just to shut them up because we don't take finding dead kids on our patch seriously."

Hawkins pointed at Daly. "Julie Darrens and Isabella Bertini may have gone missing from Burnaby, but Julie was found here, in Coquitlam, and now a child's been snatched from within our borders. I want our department handling this case."

"Then Tain will take the lead."

The two men stood staring at each other for a moment, until Daly's phone rang and he grabbed it. "Yes. No, I . . . Thank you."

He hung up the phone and leaned against his arms, his hands planted firmly on the desk in front of him before he looked up again. "Industrial area just south of the Trans Canada Highway, right on the Fraser River. Not far from the fairgrounds where Taylor Brennen went missing. Another suspected arson fire."

For a moment the room was silent, Hawkins and Daly still locked in a match of visual chicken, waiting to see who would blink first.

It was Hawkins who turned, glanced at Tain, then looked back at Daly. "I sure as hell hope you know what you're doing."

He crossed the room, pulled the door open and slammed it behind him.

Constable Craig Nolan was familiar with the image of his partner, all business, from the straight skirt to the pressed shirt, straight brown hair clipped back in a ponytail looking like it knew better than to dare fall out of place, the touch of makeup that somehow emphasized the icy eyes.

She stopped at the steps to the house and turned to look at him. "You should let me handle this."

Craig unclenched his jaw. "Did I miss the memo?"

Her forehead wrinkled for a second. Lori Price was as pushy as she was tall, and she met Craig's gaze steadily.

"The one about your promotion, putting you in charge," he said.

Lori folded her arms across her chest. "It might be better for her if she deals with a woman. I didn't know you were so touchy."

Craig shook his head as he watched his partner turn, march up the steps, pause, then yank the door open. He counted to ten before he followed her silently, clenching his fists.

"I already told them," the low, hollow voice murmured from just beyond the hallway where Craig stood.

"Yes, but I need you to tell me now." Lori's voice failed to sound sympathetic. Instead, it sounded pushy. As usual.

Her words were met with silence.

"Mrs. Parks, it really would be best—"

"No. I don't think so."

Craig heard movement, which told him that either Mrs. Parks was preparing to flee or that Lori was trying to corner her. He walked into the living room.

Mrs. Parks was standing, but Lori towered over her. Craig's partner looked like she was ready to tackle Mrs. Parks if the woman tried to leave.

Craig stopped just inside the room. Mrs. Parks looked at him and blinked.

"For a second I thought you were Carl. Except your hair's a bit longer."

A quick glance at the prominent wedding photo on the mantel showing Mrs. Parks and a blond, fit man was all Craig needed. "Your husband?"

She nodded. "Three years. He's at work."

"Would you like us to phone him, have him come home?"

Mrs. Parks nodded again. She sank back down on the sofa across the coffee table from where Lori Price stood, arms now crossed.

"Perhaps you could locate her husband." Craig glanced at Lori. Her eyes pinched partially shut, and her nostrils flared. He turned his back to her, approached Mrs. Parks slowly and knelt down until he was below eye level with her. When he finally heard Lori march out of the room he spoke. "Is there anything else we can get for you, Mrs. Parks?"

"Cindy."

Craig frowned, glancing back at the photos for a clue. "Cindy?"

"Call me Cindy. Please."

"Okay. Is there anything else we can do, Cindy?"

She continued sitting rigidly, her hands clasped together on her lap, her face long and cold, without a trace of a spark in her eyes. Then she lifted a trembling hand to wipe away an unbidden tear that had escaped, before tucking her blond hair back behind her ear. She looked at Craig. "You can find the man who did this to me."

Craig swallowed. He felt like he'd been punched in the gut, winded. The look in her dark eyes sent a chill down his spine.

*How's she supposed to look? What do you know about how it feels to be raped?*

"We're going to do everything we can to catch him and put him away, but I'm not going to lie. This won't be easy."

Her face didn't move, but her gaze shifted to the right, as though something on that side of the room had caught her attention. Then she took a deep breath and looked him in the eyes. "You need me to tell you what happened."

He nodded.

"Carl got a call just before four PM."

"From his work?"

"From the fire department. He's a volunteer." Cindy Parks leaned back against the sofa, pulling her cardigan tight as she wrapped her arms around her body.

Craig eased himself onto the couch across from her, listening as she told her story.

Constable Ashlyn Hart parked her vehicle, the sting of smoke already burning her eyes. She flashed her ID and ducked under the barrier. With the spate of arson fires in the area lately the police weren't taking any chances. They were being cautious about protecting the scenes.

Not that it had done much good. Officially no leads. Arsons were notoriously hard to bring to trial, and so far their arsonist hadn't given them much to work with. That was the reason she was handling every scene personally. She had to find a different way to pinpoint the culprit.

"Maybe we should get you some gear, have you work out of our station."

She looked up and offered the firefighter who'd spoken a smile as she accepted a helmet from him. Ashlyn recognized Adrian Vaughan, the man under the layers of soot, but he'd barely stopped to offer the remark and hat before he disappeared again. She watched him move toward the thick plume of smoke billowing from the building. Flames were already licking the exterior from windows on the upper floors.

"Not much we can do now but hope to contain it."

She turned. Paul Quinlan, the battalion chief, was standing beside her. "Arson?" she asked.

"What color's that smoke?"

Dense dark clouds swirled out of every opening she could see. She'd been getting an education in fire ever since she got this assignment, but Ashlyn still hadn't learned everything. "And black smoke means what?"

"Petroleum-based accelerant. Likely gas."

*Gas. Not too helpful. Only about a thousand local places where someone could get their hands on that.*

Paul passed her the object he was holding. "We found it on the door, just like before. Could this help you?"

Ashlyn pulled a bag from her pocket, wrapped the angel quickly, then put it in the trunk of her car. "Generic materials found in hundreds of stores in the province, virtually untraceable, handmade. We haven't turned up anything so far."

"What the hell?" Paul raced forward, toward the door. She tried to follow him. Other firefighters started running, and one grabbed her arm.

"Stay there." He glared at her as he backed away, watching until she stopped moving before he turned around. The man disappeared amidst the sea of turnout gear each firefighter wore for protection on the job.

Ashlyn moved her head from side to side and up and down until she could see through the smoke and men to what had caught Quinlan's attention.

A firefighter was racing down the front steps carrying a child.

The paramedic repositioned the stethoscope and paused. It had been at least twenty minutes since the girl had been pulled from the building, and the paramedic's shoulders sagged. She shook her head.

"Fuck." The firefighter who'd found the girl turned and kicked a garbage can. His dirt-streaked fingers clenched into a fist beside his head as he walked away.

Ashlyn pulled plastic gloves from her pocket, stepped forward and knelt beside the body. She tossed the helmet she'd been given aside. The girl's hair was darker than hers. Careful not to touch her unnecessarily, Ashlyn surveyed the victim visually until she got to her hands. Then she reached into her jacket pocket, pulled out a pen and used it to nudge the loose shirtsleeve up, revealing black and purple skin mixed with partially healed wounds. The gashes and bruises stretched out like an overgrown tattoo, covering the girl's arm.

A voice cut into Ashlyn's thoughts from above her. "Can't you cover her up and get her out of here before the reporters start shooting photos?"

She shook her head. "This is a murder investigation now."

"For Christ's sake, she's already been moved. What difference does it make?"

Purple shirt, green pants . . . It kept playing through Ashlyn's head as she studied the girl's face. There was a shiny metal pendant around the girl's neck, and she reached for it.

"What the hell do you think you're doing?" A different voice this time. One she'd describe as demanding, unapologetic . . .

Familiar.

"My job." She pulled out her ID as she turned around. For a moment she crouched, jaw open, then dropped her hand and put her badge away. He was tall, athletic, dark hair, a face of stone, and he never let anyone call him by his first name. She frowned as she realized she didn't even know his first name herself. That was the kind of distance he put between himself and even the people he worked closely with, but she knew he had a warm smile when he let his guard down and was a good person. "Jesus."

"Well, I am back from the dead."

"Your penance is over?"

One curt nod. "Sorry. Didn't know you'd been called out on this."

"I wasn't. I'm working the arsons."

The skin between his brows puckered. "Wasn't that Robinson's case?"

"Not anymore. He died." Ashlyn was still crouching between him and the girl, obscuring Tain's view.

She almost couldn't believe it was him. They'd worked together once, on a tough case. One she tried hard not to think about. At the end of the day they'd solved it, but it seemed like Tain had managed to piss off every senior officer from Vancouver to Halifax in the process. It had taken a toll on him.

It had taken a toll on all of them. Maybe that's why she'd found herself making excuses when it was over, picking up the phone and setting it down without dialing the number . . .

Willing herself to forget. Willing herself to believe they all had forgotten and that nobody wanted to hear from her because it would bring it all back.

"What have you got?"

"Likely the reason for the fire." She stood up and stepped back so that she wasn't in his way.

"Purple shirt, green pants . . ." Tain's eyes turned down at the corners. With him, the expressions were all subtle, but she knew him well enough to see it.

"And a charm on a necklace."

"Shit." His fingers pushed through his short dark hair and into his skull. "It's Isabella Bertini."

Tain leaned back against the truck. "It never gets any easier, does it?"

Ashlyn shook her head. She was still reeling from the shock of seeing him, wondering about so many things but not knowing how to ask. "But you'd better pull yourself together."

His eyes narrowed.

"There are uniforms all over this place. Don't you have an image to maintain?"

The ghost of a smile flitted across his lips, but it failed to reach his eyes. She made the mistake of turning away from him too soon, jumping as his hand smacked her backside.

He leaned toward her as he walked by. "Just protecting my reputation."

"Smartass."

"Yours is pretty tight. You been working out?"

She pointed a finger at him. "I swear I'll break—"

"Hey, is that the guy who found her?"

Ashlyn nodded. She sprinted ahead of Tain.

"This is my case, Ashlyn."

"Carl, we need to have a word with you." She ignored Tain as she took the lead.

"About the girl?"

"We need to know where you found her," Tain said. "If there was anything near the body, anything you remember at all."

Carl paused and stared at Tain for a moment.

"And you are?"

"Constable Tain." He pulled out his ID and held it up as the firefighter removed his helmet and wiped his brow with the side of his hand, a futile gesture that only resulted in smearing soot across his forehead.

"I thought you were working the arsons," the firefighter said to Ashlyn.

"Tain's working the child abductions."

His eyes widened. "You mean that's the girl? The one they've been looking for? Shit."

"We need you to keep that to yourself, Carl. We need to notify her parents before the press gets wind of it, okay?" Ashlyn said.

Carl took a breath and nodded. "Sure. Sure, I understand."

"Anything you can tell us could be critical to the investigation," Tain said.

Carl shook his head. "I was just concentrating on getting her out, you know? I thought she might be alive."

"Where did you find her?" Ashlyn asked.

"Fourth floor. Back right-hand corner, lying on a table by the window. I just grabbed her and started running. There was smoke pouring out the window. I almost didn't see her when I went in there."

"The window was open?" Tain asked.

Carl froze, then shrugged. "It must have been."

"Any chance you guys broke the glass, trying to get in off a ladder?" Ashlyn asked.

Carl's eyes narrowed as he shook his head, slowly at first, then emphatically. "We didn't have a ladder on that side of the building. You can check that with Quinlan yourself, but I don't think we broke the window."

"Okay," Ashlyn said, making a note. "Do you remember—"

A uniformed officer stepped between Ashlyn and Carl. "Excuse me. I need to speak to Mr. Parks."

"Can't it wait?" Tain held up his ID again, his eyes narrowing as he glared at the officer, who offered only a fleeting apologetic glance.

"Mr. Parks, that woman right there—" he pointed to the tall woman in a straight skirt, brown hair pulled back in a ponytail, pacing by a dark sedan—"she needs to speak to you right away."

Tain and Ashlyn exchanged a glance. As soon as Carl Parks was out of earshot, Tain turned to the officer.

"He found a murder victim. A child, and we—"

The officer held up his hand. "Look, I was just following orders."

"You and the Nazis."

"Tain!" Ashlyn turned to the officer. "I'm sure that girl's parents will be thrilled to hear we couldn't interview the person who found her body because you were doing your job."

The officer blew out a deep breath. "Look, I'm just—"

"Following orders." Ashlyn watched Carl get into the car with the woman. "What the hell is going on?"

"Constable Price is taking him home to be with his wife," the officer said. "She's been raped."

Ashlyn watched the officer walk away, her shock overriding her frustration for a moment. She couldn't imagine the hell that Carl Parks was about to find himself in. Talk about a bad day. A fire, finding a girl's body, having to go home to deal with his wife after she'd been violated.

And there they were, pissed off because he couldn't answer their questions. As though their dead kid trumped his raped wife.

She turned to Tain. "I see you're still winning friends and influencing people."

He responded with a thin smile. "One out of two, anyway."

There was something about his mannerisms, his facial expressions, that made her suspect it was all veneer. That beneath the surface he was as fragile as a soft-boiled egg. Strike him in just the right spot and everything would come spilling out.

She didn't think he'd ever really put what had happened behind him, but she hoped she was wrong.

Craig felt the icy stare on him when he pushed the Bruce Cockburn CD into the player, but he ignored it. It was as certain as death and taxes: whatever he liked Lori Price would loathe.

Either that, or she derived some perverse pleasure from being difficult, which he had to admit was a distinct possibility.

Bruce sang about screaming police cars, drunks, tunnels and bike paths while Craig drove through his own beat. His RCMP detachment covered Coquitlam, Port Coquitlam and Port Moody, three of the twelve cities that, in conjunction with a few villages and municipalities, formed the Greater Vancouver Area, or GVA.

This part of the city suited him. Vancouver felt pressed in, the coast on one side, the Fraser River to the south and

Burrard Inlet to the north, with more condos than trees and more people per square inch on an average day than shoppers in the mall on Christmas Eve. At least, that's how it felt. The entire GVA was caught in the pre-Olympic boom, with skyrocketing housing prices and construction everywhere. Every vacant lot was being eyed for development. The Tri-Cities, as Coquitlam, Port Coquitlam and Port Moody were known, were no exception, but they had redeeming qualities, with the provincial parks hemming the north side, offering easy access to Burke Mountain to the northeast. Port Moody was a haven within the urban sprawl, hemmed by the Burrard Inlet but serving as the gateway to Buntzen Lake and Belcarra Provincial Park, miles of wilderness with hiking trails and waterways to satisfy kayakers and hikers alike. Coquitlam itself was a city, no question, but it was one that nestled against the backdrop of Mother Nature. It wasn't unusual for hikers to encounter bears on the trails at Rocky Point, or even the odd cougar, and the number of coyote attacks on pets and people alike had risen in recent years.

Although the GVA was made up of several cities Coquitlam lacked the heart of a central core where people strolled from shop to shop. Instead, residents flocked to malls and, in Craig's opinion, "downtown" remained a term more for appropriate for Vancouver than anywhere else in the lower mainland.

The Tri-Cities had their share of traffic problems and congestion, though, with commuters from Pitt Meadows, Maple Ridge and even some from as far as Mission crossing Coquitlam on route to Burnaby and Vancouver. As a result, it wasn't a quick drive back to the station.

Once they returned it didn't take long for Sergeant Daly to track Craig down for an update.

"Shortly after her husband left she went to the bedroom to fold linen. There's a back entrance by the laundry room, which opens up to a bathroom that has a second door to the master bedroom. I'm guessing that was the point of entry, because she said she had her back to the bathroom door when the lights went out and she felt someone grab her from behind."

"You're guessing?" Daly asked.

"There was no sign of a break in. Not even dirty footprints."

"And she didn't hear him approaching. Thick carpeting?"

Craig shook his head. "Beech tile in the bathroom and laundry room, and hardwood floors in the bedroom and entrance."

Daly arched an eyebrow. "He took off his shoes? What about the rest? Does it fit?"

Craig nodded. "He slid a blindfold over her eyes and held a knife to her throat while he forced her to bite down on a gag. Then he pushed her facedown on the bed, tied the gag, tightened the blindfold and bound her hands behind her back."

"And raped her from behind."

"Anal and vaginal penetration."

Daly winced.

Craig studied his notebook for a moment as he sat back in his chair, feet up on a box of overflowing paperwork on the floor. Then he looked up. Daly was leaning back against the desk.

"He broke in during the day. He's getting confident," Craig said.

Daly frowned. "What if her husband had been home?"

"Then we could be looking at an escalation to murder. This guy is organized, efficient. He wears a condom. He comes with a blindfold prepared, and something to gag and bind the victim. He's armed. And he doesn't personalize the victim in any way, which means he sees these women as objects. He goes in, gets what he wants and gets out."

"And if he doesn't get what he wants, he could get violent."

"As though being raped at knifepoint isn't bad enough."

"I'm not disputing that. This is victim number three?"

Craig was looking across the room. Lori Price pulled on her coat as she walked out the door.

"Uh huh." Craig shifted his eyes to look at Daly and flinched when he saw him turn from looking at the doorway where Lori had just disappeared.

"Is this going to be a problem?" Daly asked.

"If I have to have a partner, can't I have one with a personality?"

"Craig." Daly folded his arms across his chest.

"Look, I'm sure deep down she's a decent person and I'm not saying she's stupid, but she almost completely shut the rape victim down this time. She refused to let me participate in the interview. I only got in there after Cindy Parks tried to leave."

Daly sighed. "Lori is tough."

"Well, she's trying too hard to prove herself."

"I'll talk to her."

"Don't bother. I don't need people thinking you're going to play dad and come to my rescue every time I have a problem."

The only response from Daly was silence, but Craig could imagine what Daly was thinking, and it was worse than having him say it. It was a moment before Craig could look up. "You know what I mean. But you have to let me stand on my own two feet."

"I didn't want to—"

Craig's neck started to burn as he put up his hand to keep Daly from saying more. "I—"

"Daly, we need you," Inspector Hawkins called from across the room. Daly stood automatically, but paused before he left.

"At least I don't need to worry about any unprofessional involvements between you and your new partner."

"You got that right," Craig muttered, swiveling in his chair as he watched Daly walk away.

Daly's office was a decent size. Even with Hawkins standing beside him, Tain didn't feel crowded, for the moment. Still, he had to wonder if the news about Isabella Bertini would prompt Hawkins to force Tain to take a backseat on the case. He'd radioed in, so they already knew about the body.

"Do you have a positive ID?" Daly asked once he'd closed the door to his office.

"Her parents need to confirm it, but she matches the circulation photo. Green pants, purple shirt, a charm on a necklace with her name on it. There's no doubt in my mind," Tain said.

"Where was the body found?" Inspector Hawkins asked.

"The building was in the industrial area south of the Trans Canada, near the Fraser River. She was on the fourth floor in a room at the back, lying on a table under an open window."

"Anything relevant found with her body?" Daly asked as he sat down at his desk.

Tain shook his head. "I can't tell you much more than that. At this point I don't even know if I'm going to be able to get inside and check the room. The fire had engulfed the building by the time I arrived, and they were just trying to contain it. Damn lucky they even found her and got her out."

"Who was the officer assisting you at the scene?" Hawkins asked.

Tain felt the skin between his brows pinch. He had deliberately not mentioned Ashlyn when he called in. "Which officer are you referring to? There were several—"

"A plainclothes officer was seen questioning the firefighter with you."

Tain wondered how the hell Hawkins knew that. "Constable Hart, sir. She's investigating the arsons and was on the scene when the body was recovered." He noticed Daly's head snapped up, but the sergeant didn't say anything.

"You know Constable Hart, don't you, Daly?"

"Yes, sir."

"Good on the job, competent?" Hawkins turned back to Tain. "She worked with you last year, didn't she?"

Tain glanced from Hawkins to Daly, who was looking

down at the desk now, face unreadable. It wasn't hard to guess what was going through Daly's mind. If Tain wasn't up to the job, working with Ashlyn might be enough to send him over the edge, to bring it all back. . . .

"Constable Tain?"

"Sir? Yes, sir. I worked with Ash . . . Constable Hart last year."

"Maybe we should consider reassigning her to this case. You wouldn't have an issue with that, would you, Tain?"

Before Tain could respond, Daly's head snapped up again. "Ashlyn took over Robinson's case when he died. I don't know if it's such a good idea to pass that case off again. She's been building a rapport with the fire department, getting to know the system. There's a lot of man hours invested there, and they seem to like working with her."

Tain thought of the way that at least half a dozen firemen had eyed the willowy brunette at the scene and tried to suppress a smile. They seemed to like working with her. Yeah, who wouldn't? Ashlyn had silky hair, enormous dark eyes and a smile that could take your breath away, not to mention that she was smart, funny and more than capable of handling herself on the job.

Not that he'd ever admit as much to her.

"I'm not suggesting we pull Ashlyn off the arson case," Hawkins said. "She was part of that task force last year. Multiple cases, simultaneous investigations. Right now, the arsons seem to be connected to the child abductions. It makes sense to me that the officers investigating those cases work together."

"Some of the arsons."

"Pardon me?"

Tain flinched as Hawkins stared at him. "Some of the arsons seem to be connected, sir. Five fires have been linked, but we only have two bodies."

"It's still the best lead we have." Daly leaned back in his chair. He ran his fingers over his short brown hair and shrugged. "I don't have a problem with Tain and Ashlyn working together. She has an empty desk across from hers. You can move your stuff there. Just as long as we don't pass the arson case off. Ashlyn needs to keep a handle on it."

Tain looked at Sergeant Daly. "I'm fine with that."

"Excellent. I'll go speak to the staff sergeant." Hawkins turned abruptly and left the room, letting the door clap shut behind him.

Tain glanced at the desk where Steve Daly sat.

"Do you have a problem working with Ashlyn?" Daly asked him.

"No." Tain took a breath. "I thought you—" Tain did the sensible thing, for once, and shut his mouth.

"I don't have a problem as long as you both behave like professionals," Daly said.

"That won't be an issue."

"For her, perhaps. Your reputation precedes you."

"I'll be a perfect gentleman."

"I'm not asking for miracles, Tain. Just a bit of restraint."

Tain smirked as he walked down the hallway, still thinking about Ashlyn's reaction when he'd slapped her ass. Daly would have had a stroke if he'd seen that.

Ashlyn was waiting for him by the front door, dangling a set of keys from her fingers.

"I see somebody told you the good news," Tain said.

"Good news? I was told I was stuck on babysitting detail. Nobody told me I was being pulled off it."

"Babysitting me? The real question is: can you keep up, sweetheart?"

"Oh, you expect me to do something other than make you coffee and wear tight jeans?" She followed him outside.

He snatched the keys from her hand. "If you feel it's your womanly duty to inspire the hard-working men of this station, I'm not going to stop you."

She shook her head as he held the door open for her, gesturing for her to get inside. "I was wrong about you."

"You've realized I'm not the completely heartless bastard you thought I was when you first met me?"

Ashlyn waited until he climbed into the driver's seat. "I

thought you'd changed. I just realized you still are a heart-less bastard, and I'm inclined to add sexist pig to the list."

"Careful, Ashlyn," Tain wagged a finger at her. "There could be a protest over such an offensive comment. A lot of pigs wouldn't like it."

"Clearly your penance is over and mine is just beginning. What did I ever do to piss off the powers that be?"

"I don't know, but you've clearly caught Hawkins's attention."

She turned to look at him, and he met her gaze with a solemn expression for a moment before turning back to the road. It never surprised her when he got serious. Quiet, in-trospective, completely focused. It was his obsessive person-ality and dedication that made it hard for him to let go of the job. Some guys drank. Tain's poison of choice was work, and it had come close to destroying him once.

The only thing that surprised her was when he relaxed and joked around with her. Something he'd done readily so far, and it had only been a matter of hours since they'd been reunited at a crime scene. Months before she might have thought he was more sociable than the rumors inferred. Now she knew better. It was his way of burying his hurt. But he'd only joke with someone he felt safe with.

Someone he believed would understand his pain.

She pushed that thought aside as she considered what Tain had said about Inspector Hawkins.

"This was his idea?"

Tain nodded. "I don't think Sergeant Daly was too keen on it."

"Steve will get over it."

Tain snuck a glance at her. "How do you know him?"

"Platonically."

"Seriously."

"He was one of my instructors at the Depot." The Depot was the common term for the academy where all RCMP of-ficers completed their training.

*So Ashlyn has known Daly since her training to be an RCMP officer, when she was just a cadet. And Craig . . .* Tain tapped the steering wheel with his thumb.

"What are you thinking about?" Ashlyn asked.

"If Daly thinks so highly of you, maybe you'll help give him a good impression of me."

"Wouldn't I need to have a good impression of you first?"

He braked at the intersection and glared at her. She smiled innocently.

"See, Tain, when it comes to putting you in your place, I can keep up."

Tain laughed. "You know what I was really thinking, Ashlyn?"

"Enlighten me."

"It's nice to have a partner who isn't afraid to tell me off."

"Wish I could say the same."

"Huh. You know me. I've never been afraid to give you a piece of my mind."

"I know. I almost have the complete puzzle. You really should stop giving those pieces away."

He saw her grin as he turned back to look at the road. "Feels good to laugh, doesn't it?"

"At your expense? Absolutely."

"That's not what I meant," he said as he parked the car.

He watched her smile fade, her mouth twisting. "I know."

"You ready for this?"

She glanced at him sideways as she unclipped her seat belt and reached for the door handle. "Are you ever ready?"

"Probably not, Ashlyn. Probably not."


"Constable Nolan," he said into the phone.

"Ye . . . need . . . ort . . . rime."

"I'm sorry, I can hardly hear you," Craig said as he held his hand over his right ear, although he knew it wouldn't do much good. The room was almost as still as a church on a Friday afternoon. Craig reached for the volume dial on the phone.

He heard the caller clear their throat. "I . . . I need to report a crime."

Craig rubbed his forehead. "Okay. Did you call dispatch?"

"They redirected me."

Craig paused. "What do you need to report?"

Silence.

"Ma'am?"

"A rape." The voice coughed and sputtered, and then Craig heard the sharp intake of breath. "I was raped."

Crossing the threshold into Isabella Bertini's bedroom made Ashlyn feel like she'd stepped back more than a dozen years in time. There were books and stuffed animals and posters. Different icons, but the same generic style as the ones she'd hung up on her bedroom walls when she was a kid.

The room was tastefully done, with sunshine yellow walls and crisp white trim. There were murals on the far side, above the bed, depicting butterflies in flight. To her left a mirrored sliding door concealed the contents of the closet, but exposed the stickers and decals the girl had used to personalize the cold metal that intruded on this space.

On her right a long bookshelf overflowed with novels. *Anne of Green Gables* was stacked on top of *This Can't Be Happening at Macdonald Hall*. Beside the other Montgomery and Korman titles was a copy of *The Call of the Wild*, and behind them were rows and rows of books about dogs and horses.

Ashlyn turned in the other direction, scrutinizing the artwork on the wall. It looked like pastel to her untrained eye.

She turned again and stifled a gasp. Ashlyn knelt down.

"Hi there."

The little girl with silky, dark brown hair and enormous black eyes smiled, partially concealing her mouth behind her blue stuffed bunny. She was a smaller version of her sister.

"My name is Ashlyn."

The girl smiled again and then spun on her toes. She stepped right into her mother's legs.

"Time for bed, Sophia. Go on to your room."

Ashlyn stood, smiled and waved as the girl glanced back at her and then trotted down the hall, almost tripping over her pajama pants.

Mrs. Bertini blinked. "Would you like some tea, juice, coffee?"

"No, thank you. I'm fine."

The woman stepped inside the room, her arms folded in front of her. She nodded at the mural behind Ashlyn.

"Isabella loved to draw."

"She was very good."

"I suppose we might as well leave things as they are. Sophia has always loved this room. Maybe in a few years . . ."

Ashlyn offered what she hoped was a supportive smile. "It's still a bit soon to worry about that. You have plenty of time to decide what you want to do."

"And yet we must decide. We must decide where we will bury our daughter. We must decide if the flowers should be pink or purple, whether to put a cross or a sacred heart on her tombstone."

Ashlyn's breath caught in her throat. What could she say to that? That the room was at least one less thing to worry about? "Do you have someone, anyone who can help you? I can give you the number for—"

"Victim's services." Mrs. Bertini brushed tears from her cheek with her left hand in one efficient motion, looking at her dampened fingers as though they were a curiosity, nothing more. "Yes, I have their number. And we have our church."

A baptismal certificate on the wall caught Ashlyn's attention. Infant baptism. Stickers adorning the frame of the mirror. A crucifix, the Easter lily, the dove, the fish.

"You're Catholic?"

"Yes."

Ashlyn nodded. "Well, if there's anything we can do, please call us."

Mrs. Bertini stood with her lips slightly parted for a moment.

"There's only one thing I wanted you to do, and you failed. All that's left is a small consolation."

She turned on her heel and walked away.

Ashlyn exhaled. She wanted to defend herself, defend Tain, point out they'd done all they could, but that was her pride talking. Could she really blame Isabella Bertini's mother?

Ashlyn switched off the light, shut the door and followed Mrs. Bertini down the hall.

"We should have someone from victim's services check on them in a few days. Get someone to talk to Mr. Bertini," Tain said.

"Did he fall apart?"

"No." Tain backed into a driveway to turn the car around. "He took it like a man."

"That is cause for concern," Ashlyn said, but she knew what he meant.

He glanced at her. "Seriously, he just bottled it all up, like it wasn't really happening to him. When it hits home with this guy he'll take it hard."

Ashlyn sighed, thinking about the tight bun Mrs. Bertini had her hair pulled into, the neat skirt, dress blouse, the modest heels, even in the house on a Saturday night. Was it strength or madness that had enabled her to hold it together in front of her daughter and the police officer nosing about her dead child's room?

"I take it you have some concerns about the mother?" Tain asked.

"It would be a good idea to have someone check on them. Since it's summer it's not like the little girl has a teacher or someone we can rely on to notice if the family starts to fall apart."

"We'll need to interview Isabella's teacher anyway. Maybe we can sneak her sister's teacher onto the list, just so she knows. Can you imagine going back to school in a matter of days after all of this?"

"I can't imagine any of it. Living this nightmare, trying to decide what to put on your child's tombstone."

Tain was silent for a moment. "Not the first parents who've had to deal with that," he said quietly.

She felt his eyes on her for a split second. When she finally did turn to look at him he was staring straight out at the road, his lips mashed together. "It doesn't make it any easier for them."

They drove in silence. Ashlyn could see the Burrard Inlet and wished for a moment they could just pull over, feel the breeze off the water, shut their eyes to the world and listen to the caw of gulls, the waves lapping against the shore. They weren't far from their next destination, and it was a visit she wasn't looking forward to.

"So, we've dealt with hopelessness. Now we get to face unknowing desperation?"

He glanced at her. "That's one way of putting it."

When they arrived, they got out of the car and started walking up the front steps. Loud voices spilled through the windows, and Tain quickened his pace.

He rapped three times, barely paused and rapped three more times.

Ashlyn looked at him and started to reach back for her gun.

"Goddammit, what the hell is it now? More bloody . . ." The door was yanked open in front of them. The man's face morphed from a scowl of annoyance to a worried frown when he set eyes on Tain. Then he turned to look at Ashlyn, and his jaw dropped. He blinked.

"Ashley Hart?"

"Ashlyn."

"Right, sorry. I, uh . . ." His eyes narrowed for a moment, and he glanced over his shoulder and then turned back around. "Did you need to talk to me about the fires?"

She glanced at Tain and shook her head. "No, Mr. Brennen. We're actually here about Taylor."

"What? You've found her?" A woman pushed forward then, her silk blouse partially pulled out from her tight skirt, wisps of hair falling out of the clasp that pulled most of her long blond strands back, her thick makeup smudged and tear streaked.

Tain answered. "I'm sorry, Mrs. Brennen. We haven't found Taylor, but we'd like to ask Mr. Brennen some questions."

"How will that help? You should be out there looking for my daughter instead of wasting your time."

"Mrs. Brennen, please. We have uniforms covering the fairgrounds and the surrounding area. Everything that can be done is being done. Can we come in, Nick?" Ashlyn stepped forward, hoping Nick Brennen wouldn't resist. It sounded as though things had been on the verge of getting out of hand when they'd arrived. A domestic assault charge might have been understandable, but it wasn't going to help anyone.

Nick Brennen stepped back and held the door open, gesturing for them to enter the living room.

"What did you want to ask me?" he said as he sat down across from them, barely balancing on the edge of the couch, looking like he was prepared to jump up at a moment's notice.

"How often does Taylor stay with you?" Tain asked.

"She's here every other weekend with her brother. It's in the custody agreement," Mrs. Brennen said, returning to the room with a drink in her hand.

"And every weekend when you can't be bothered with her because you're screwing the aerobics instructor or the pool boy or some drunk fool you picked up at a bar or whoever else you can get your hands on."

"I didn't ship them off to you this weekend, did I?" she snapped back.

Nick jumped to his feet. "Because I was working and Mom couldn't watch them, so you sent them to the fair. The fair. What the hell were you thinking, Connie? Maybe you'd pick up some vendor for a quick fling while the kids were entertaining themselves?"

She flung the drink in his face, and he slapped the glass out of her hand, sending it crashing to the floor where it shattered, sharp pieces scattering across the hardwood.

Ashlyn jumped between them. "Separate corners, now," she said, pointing each in opposite directions.

"Waste of a good drink," Connie muttered.

"Daddy?"

They all turned toward the hallway where Nicky Brennen stood wearing Blue Jays pajamas. He had tousled blond hair, a brown teddy bear in his hands.

"Hey, sport." Nick took a step toward his namesake and knelt down. "Let's get you back to bed, okay?"

"Actually, do you think I could talk to Nicky for a minute?" Ashlyn asked, glancing at Tain, who gave her an almost imperceptible nod. She crouched down beside the boy. "Would that be okay?"

He looked up at his dad, who said, "What do you want to know?"

"Can you think of anyone unusual you might have seen around recently, maybe when Taylor was staying here? Anyone who showed a lot of interest in her?"

Nick frowned for a moment before shaking his head, tossing a hand up in the air. "No."

"Had Taylor gone to any sleepovers or parties lately, anywhere unusual?"

"What has that got to do with anything?" Connie stomped across the room from the corner Ashlyn had sent her to and sat down on a chair. "She was grabbed at the fair."

"Mrs. Brennen, we have to consider every possibility," Ashlyn said, glancing at Nicky. She wished she didn't need to say this in front of him. "Someone may have been watching Taylor. They could have been waiting for an opportunity to take her. And it's still possible that Taylor wasn't taken by anyone, but that she's wandering in the park and we just haven't found her yet. It's too soon to say anything for certain."

"Come off it," Nick Brennen said. "We all know what's happened. This selfish bitch sent her ten-year-old daughter and eight-year-old son to the fair by themselves, and my little girl has been snatched by that sicko who's been taking other girls. Remember that one, they found her body a few weeks back? And the other one, Isabel, I think her name is? She's still missing, right?" Nick stared at Tain, who didn't meet his gaze.

"Oh my God. You have . . . Is she . . . ?"

"I can't comment on an ongoing investigation."

"Like hell you can't! The same sick freak has my daughter. He has my little girl." Nick Brennen's body convulsed as he sank down on the couch and choked back a sob.

"It's not going to make you sleep better," Tain said quietly.

Nick lifted his head, his eyes bulging, red-rimmed. "What the hell makes you think I'll be able to sleep at all?"

Ashlyn had asked Nicky to show her his room, in part to get him away from his parents. She'd been listening to Nicky identify every model car he owned. He had antiques and current cars, trucks and sedans of all shapes and sizes, and he knew his vehicles better than she did.

"You know the name of every single one. I'm very impressed," Ashlyn said as Nicky finished labeling the cars that lined the bookshelves in his room.

He jumped into his bed and pulled the covers up over his head.

"Oops, you forgot somebody," Ashlyn said, holding out the teddy bear, which was incredibly soft. The covers inched down slightly, revealing big puppy-dog eyes blinking up at her.

She sat down on the edge of the bed.

"I need to ask you something really important," she told him.

His eyes got a little smaller. She suspected his smile had disappeared beneath the blanket.

"Was anybody talking to your sister, or maybe you saw someone following you around at the fair?"

Nicky scrunched his whole face up like a raisin and shook his head. "No."

"How did you get separated?"

"I wanted to play at the park."

"So you went by yourself?"

"Taylor wanted to get a charm and play games. I didn't want to. I pulled on her hand, and she pulled on mine, and then people came and got between us."

His eyes had gotten big again, but this time they were sagging down at the corners.

Ashlyn smiled. "I think I would have rather played at the park, too."

Nicky looked down at the teddy bear in his hands. "But it's my fault. I should have listened. Now Taylor's gone."

"Oh, no, it isn't your fault. It was an accident that you two got separated. Accidents are nobody's fault."

"But Mommy said so. She said—"

Ashlyn shushed him softly. She tucked the covers in around him as he lay back against the pillow. "Your mom is just upset right now because she's scared. Did you know grown-ups get scared sometimes?"

He seemed to think about it, his lips twisting with uncertainty at first and then forming a solid line. "Do you get scared?"

She nodded. "Yes, I do."

"If you have a night-light it keeps the monsters away," he told her, eyes wide again as he shared his secret.

She smiled. "I'll remember that. Do you want me to leave this light on too?"

He blinked and nodded.

"Good night, Nicky."

Ashlyn got up and crossed the room, glancing at the bed where Nicky lay, his big dark eyes staring at her as she pulled the door shut.

"Is he okay?" Nick asked as Ashlyn returned to the living room.

She sat down beside Tain and looked at Nick. "I know this won't be easy, but you need to reassure him that this isn't his fault."

"I told you to keep your bloody mouth shut," Nick snapped as he glared at his ex-wife, his lips curling into a snarl.

"They were supposed to stay together."

"Who the hell is the parent? He's eight years old. For Christ's sake, Connie."

"Here we go, always blaming me for everything. I deal with them day in and day out. At least I don't have to deal with your shit anymore."

"Listen, you two aren't helping. And if you keep this up, I'm personally going to call social services again and have them do a child removal and see that Nicky goes to a foster family that isn't going to heap abuse on him." Tain pointed at Connie Brennen. "As it is, you have a hell of a lot of explaining to do already. Your ex-husband can contest the custody arrangement and likely take your children away from you for good. Don't tempt me to testify on his behalf."

Nothing but the distant hum of cars could be heard for a few moments, and even then it wasn't much of a hum. Tain glanced at the clock, finally realizing how late it was.

"I don't think there's anything else tonight. Mrs. Brennen, it's likely best that you go home now," Tain said as he stood.

Connie glanced at her ex-husband, who kept his eyes directed at the coffee table and didn't extend an invitation for her to stay. After a moment she stood up, walked to the door and pulled it open without a word, stomping down the steps as the door slammed shut behind her.

Ashlyn took a card from her pocket. "If you need anything, Nick, call."

He looked up then, his eyes brimming with unshed tears as he took the card from her hand, nodded and looked away.

Craig knocked again. This time he heard soft footsteps in the hall, followed by the sound of a deadbolt being retracted. Then a voice, muffled at first before coming into focus.

"Let me, Sara."

The door opened as far as the latched chain would allow, and Craig held up his ID for scrutiny. The man, who Craig guessed to be about his own age, pushed the door shut and then opened it fully.

"Matt McPherson," the man said, offering his hand. Matt had a firm grip.

"Constable Craig Nolan."

He followed Matt down the hallway, into a bright, open kitchen and dining area. A woman sat at the table, her hands wrapped around a mug, a thick sweater pulled around her body. She looked up.

Her blue eyes were overshadowed by dark circles, her cheeks gaunt. Even though she was sitting down, Craig could see that her clothing hung limply on her frame, as if she'd lost a lot of weight recently, and not weight she'd needed to lose.

"Constable Craig Nolan. I believe we spoke earlier on the phone."

She nodded as Craig pulled out a chair and sat down across from her.

"I realize this must be very difficult for you, Mrs. McPherson. I'm not here to pressure you or to make things worse."

"I can't sleep. I can't eat. I can't . . ." She swallowed. For a moment he saw nothing but her auburn hair tumbling over her head, and then she looked up as she hastily brushed her tears away before offering a short, hollow laugh. "There's nothing you can do that would make this worse."

Craig wished that were true, but he knew it wasn't. It was amazing the comfort people could find in a lie.

Matt came to the table and sat down, a cup of coffee in his hands. "Oh, sorry, I didn't even think to ask. Can I get you a cup?"

"That's okay. Really." He paused.

The woman across the table from him looked up. "You want to know what happened?"

"To start, when did this happen? You said you haven't been eating or sleeping, so I gather it's been days."

"Try weeks," Matt said. "She wouldn't even tell me."

"Don't talk about me like I'm not here, Matthew."

"You aren't here, are you, Sara? It's like you're hiding behind this wall and you won't talk to anybody. Not your sister or your mother or our minister. Sure as hell not me."

There was silence at the table for a moment, and then Sara turned to Craig, something resembling a spark of anger flickering in her eyes. "And what do you have to say about that?"

Craig took a deep breath. "I can give you the number for victim's services. You can talk to someone who's been through what you've been through, if that makes it easier for you."

"So you think I should just bare my soul to the world too?"

"No. I think you should do whatever you need to do to start to heal from this."

"It happened Sunday, July eighth," Matt said.

*July 8? Shit.* Craig made a note.

Sara hit the table with her hand. "Do you want me to talk or not, Matt? I don't need you filling in the blanks."

Her voice was shrill, the rising note of hysteria not just creeping by but setting up camp. Craig cleared his throat. "Mrs. McPherson—"

"Sara."

"Sara, I'm going to need to speak to Matt too. I have to know everything both of you remember about that day, even the week before. If you want to talk to me one at a time, that's fine. Or we can all talk together."

She looked down at the table, covering her mouth with her hand, her elbow propped against the placemat.

After a moment Matt got up. "I'll be in the TV room when you need me."

Once they heard a door click shut from somewhere down the hall, Sara McPherson looked up at Craig.

"You must think I'm a pretty cold bitch."

"No, I don't." Craig returned her gaze for a moment until she looked away.

"He's trying to help, be supportive, and I'm pushing him away."

"Everyone deals with grief differently, Sara. It's not my job to tell you how to feel about this. My job is to try to catch the person who did this. I'll do whatever I can to help you and your husband—"

She held up her hand. "Save the spiel. We have more people offering their help than we need. I just want to do this and get it over with."

Craig nodded. "Then I need you to tell me what happened." He picked up his pen, staring across the table at her until she blinked. "Whenever you're ready."

The door creaked open, and Taylor scurried into the shadows, away from the thin stream of light.

"I brought you some food," a voice said. She could see the shadow of the man, stepping into the center of the room, kneeling down and placing a cup, like a princess's cup from a fairy tale, down. He set a bowl on the floor beside the cup.

Her stomach gurgled as the scent of fresh bread wafted through the air to her nose. She liked to bake bread with Grandma on the weekends, and she knew that smell.

The shadowy figure stood and stepped toward her. She pressed her back against the wall, pulling her knees towards her stomach and hugging them with her bare arms.

He stopped moving.

"I'm not going to hurt you. I've brought you here to take care of you."

She said nothing, rubbing her arms with her hands, trying to make the goose bumps go away.

"You're cold. And you must be tired. Here." He turned, moving into the shadows in the far corner. She heard a latch unclick and a door creak open.

Taylor jumped to her feet and ran toward the light. She was through the open door when she stopped, staring at the girl before her.

A girl with long black hair and dark eyes was wearing a long white gown, kneeling on the floor eating bread and drinking from another fancy princess cup.

Taylor felt arms around her, pulling her back into the room.

"No no no no no no no. You aren't ready yet. You have to stay here. Now be good and maybe you'll get a pretty gown too."

Taylor felt herself being propelled into the darkness, and then she bounced against something soft. She heard a creak, like when she jumped on her bed at home. Then a little light came on, right above her, shining down directly on the spot where she sat blinking.

She turned around. Backing away from the small circle of light, she could see she'd been sitting on a small bed in the corner of the room. There was a window ledge behind her and the cup and bowl had been moved there from the center of the floor.

Then the light went out, just as the door clanged shut, and she was alone in the darkness again.

# SUNDAY

Ashlyn wondered why she'd never noticed her desk was so smooth and cool before. The metal always seemed cold and foreboding, but after a night like the one she'd had it felt wonderful to put her head down against it. She closed her eyes, thinking how nice it would be to just drift off for a few minutes.

She jumped in her chair and jerked her head up as something slammed against the desk beside her, the sound of the thud echoing in her ear.

"Cruel, heartless bastard," she said.

"You should thank me. Daly's here, and he wants to see us now."

Ashlyn groaned. She forced herself to her feet and followed Tain down the hall.

"Have a seat," Daly said as they entered, passing out drinks and food. "Sorry, Tain. I don't really know what you like for breakfast."

"Anything he doesn't have to cook," Ashlyn said.

Tain unwrapped the breakfast sandwich. "Sir, I'd like to file a sexual harassment complaint."

"You wish."

Daly glared at them. "I know you're both tired, but don't make me regret partnering you two on this. What have you got?"

"Not much for our efforts, I'm afraid," Tain responded. "Distraught parents, a domestic incident waiting to happen with the Brennens and absolutely nothing useful."

"What about the autopsy? Anything helpful there?"

They had endured the entire process as Burke, the coroner, worked. The one bit of good news was that he had found nothing that indicated abuse prior to Isabella's abduction, which eased some of Ashlyn's concerns about the family.

"No."

"No?" Daly arched an eyebrow as he watched Ashlyn reach for her drink.

"She wasn't sexually assaulted. Other than the marks, there were no traces of anything out of the ordinary on her body. No pollen, no dirt, leaves. Nothing that might pinpoint where she was being held. Isabella was wearing the same clothes she went missing in, hadn't lost weight noticeably, and her stomach contained remnants of bread and water. Not even something we can readily trace."

"How did she die?"

Ashlyn and Tain exchanged a glance.

"Don't keep me in suspense."

Tain cleared his throat. "Well, sir, it's at least interesting. She drowned."

"She drowned?"

"As best as Burke can tell, in a bathtub," Ashlyn said. "It wasn't salt water, and it wasn't chlorinated pool water. Just regular, generic tap water. But her clothes were dry."

"He's sure? With the time between death and discovery and the heat of the fire . . . ?"

Ashlyn shook her head. "Absolutely no damp patches anywhere. No wrinkles or stiff fabric, like you get when someone stays in wet clothing."

Daly rubbed his forehead.

"Time of death is within a few hours of her body being found. That's why Carl thought she was still alive. Rigor hadn't set in," Ashlyn said.

"I think we might want to consider having a profile done. Without sexual assault to consider, we're really stretched to find a motive for these abductions," Tain said.

"Julie Darrens wasn't sexually assaulted either, was she?" Ashlyn asked.

"No, but she could have been an object. He could have been building his confidence. The fact that he's killed a second time in the same way without escalating—"

"As far as we know," Daly said.

"I agree with Tain on this. How are we supposed to catch this guy without a clue about why he's doing it? Pulling the names of registered sex offenders won't even help us much." Ashlyn nodded at the food still sitting on the desk. "Aren't you eating?"

"It's not for me," Daly said. "So you agree with the idea of doing a psychological profile?"

"I'm willing to try anything to give us a lead. Right now, we're assuming the same guy abducted two girls," Ashlyn said. "They're dead. Odds are he's got Taylor Brennen. I want to make sure we get her home safe and sound instead of scraping her into a body bag."

Daly sighed. "We all want that, Ashlyn. I'll see what we can do then. What's next?"

"We're going to review all the statements from last night," Ashlyn said.

Daly moved a few files and picked up a slip of paper, passing it to Tain. "Sims went through all the video we had and managed to get a plate number for the car that Nicky Brennen got out of. Registered to Alex Wilson. His address is there."

"Did he do a background check?"

Daly shook his head. "I told him you'd handle it."

"Then we'll have a chat with Alex Wilson," Tain said.

"We also need to go over Isabella's case step by step, review all the witness statements."

"Don't forget you need to keep on top of the arson investigation, Ashlyn."

"I know, Steve."

His eyes narrowed. "Ashlyn . . ."

"That's more like it, sir. I can't have you being too nice to me." She stood up and tossed her wrappers into a bin. "Anything else?"

Daly covered his face with his hands. "I knew I shouldn't have signed your transfer papers."

He jerked on the box again and yanked it forcibly from the car, then drew a few rapid breaths, pushing his hair out of his face, letting the heat in his cheeks dissolve.

*Just calm down, look again.*

Under the seats, on the seats, behind the seats, in the standard compartment, in the special compartment. He crawled in as far as he could and stretched out with his hands until he felt the body of the car curling upward. There was nowhere left to check.

He clenched his fists and swore as he sat up sharply, cracking his head against the ceiling. *Goddammit.*

Then he whimpered. *Bless me, Father. I repent,* he repeated, over and over again, drawing deep breaths, rocking back and forth until he felt the tension in his body slip away.

*They aren't here. I lost them. I lost the packet. Where could it be?*

He thought of every place he'd been, between the fair grounds, the abandoned building and the place he called home.

There was nowhere else it could be.

He closed his eyes. *I'll have to order more.*

Craig walked into Daly's office and collapsed into a chair. "You're here early," Craig said.

"And you never left. I thought you were ready to pack it in when I was leaving last night." He nodded at the bag on his desk. "I brought you some food."

Craig reached for the bag. "I thought it might be a good idea to work one of these rapes while it was still fresh."

Daly nodded. "Did you come up with anything useful?"

"Well, I . . ."

The door flung open behind Craig, and he forced himself not to turn around. The shock turning fast to annoyance on Daly's face was enough to ensure him that Daly would deal with whoever had just stepped out of line, although he was pretty sure he knew who it was.

"What the hell do you think you're doing, Craig? Interviewing a rape victim without even bothering to call me?"

The sandwich went from tasting like moderately edible fast food to spongy paste in his mouth. That woman had a shrill voice, and her tone shifted easily between nagging and lecturing.

"You interviewed a rape victim last night? After I left?" Daly's annoyance was temporarily overshadowed with confusion.

"Another rape was reported last night. I went to take a statement."

"Without calling me," Lori said.

Craig didn't need to move a muscle to have a clear mental image of Lori standing behind him, hands on her hips, glowering at him.

When he finally did glance up, the only thing he hadn't factored in was the fiery red cheeks and flared nostrils. He turned to look at Daly, although his words were for Lori.

"It didn't seem important to you to stay and work on a fresh rape case, so why would I think you'd be interested in a report that came in about one from early July?"

"Are you just going to let him—"

"Ahem," Daly said as Lori sat down in a chair, uninvited. She stood up again. Craig noticed some of the color in her cheeks had dissipated.

"Until you hold the rank of staff sergeant or inspector or whatever it is you've set your sights on, you don't walk through that door without my permission." Daly pointed a finger at her. "Second, Craig has a point. You left last night of your own free will. I watched you. Craig's job is to follow any leads in the case until it's solved or shelved, not to second guess what you do and do not find pertinent.

"My officers don't prove themselves to me by having a head full of attitude and an axe to grind with everyone they work with. Have I made myself clear?"

"Quite."

"You're dismissed, Constable Price."

Craig reached for his orange juice as the door slammed shut, the closest picture on the wall shifting sideways. Daly's mouth hung open, and Craig held up his hands. "Like you said, she's tough."

Daly snorted. "I didn't realize she was impossible."

"Your reprimand might have done some good. Maybe she'll start to behave."

"Do you really believe that?"

Craig shook his head. "Not for a second."

Lori was waiting at Craig's desk, one hand propped against the cold metal surface, fingers drumming the table incessantly, the other hand on her hip. As soon as she spotted him her eyes narrowed and she straightened up.

"Don't you ever do that to me again," she said as she folded her arms across her chest.

"Do what?" Craig lifted the cup to his lips, moving around her and sitting in his chair.

"You went running to Daddy Daly and tattled on me."

"God, what am I, five? That might be your style, Lori, but it isn't mine."

Craig wasn't sure how to interpret the silence that followed, but he wasn't taking any chances. He didn't look up until she sat down across from him, all the fire out of her eyes.

"So what's next?" she asked.

"We need to go over all the old cases and review everything."

Lori groaned. "Wasn't there anything you learned last night that was helpful?"

He shook his head. "This guy is consistent. She was in the TV room, ironing. Her husband had just been called to work. One minute she was watching *Cold Squad*; the next minute she was being forced down the hall with a loose blindfold over her eyes and a knife to her throat. He followed the exact same procedure he had on all the other occasions. Gagged her, tightened the blindfold, tied her hands and raped her. Same as before."

"*Cold Squad*?"

"It's still in syndication."

"When did this rape happen?" Lori asked.

"July eighth."

She leaned back in her chair, tapping her pen against her nose. "This just doesn't make any sense."

"Does it ever?"

Her eyes narrowed, her mouth twisting. "What I mean is, there's no escalation. We have virtually the same report each time. Karen Chalmers, June fourteenth. Exact same, except she was already in her bedroom undressing when he turned up. Stephanie Bonnis, July twenty-fifth. Only thing different there was that she was unpacking groceries in her kitchen, and the perp made her leave her three-month-old son in his car seat screaming while he raped her. She begged him not to kill her or hurt her son and he hit her on the head."

"But he still didn't say anything. He just hit her. That's very controlled. He wasn't rattled by a crying baby. That rape happened at what, ten PM, after she got back from an emergency run to the grocery store, she said. Not something planned or part of her regular schedule."

Lori propped her elbows against her desk, resting her chin on her hands. "So even the noise, late at night, didn't seem to worry him."

"Funny that she'd just come in from the side door. The front door had a dead bolt on it and chain lock, and she didn't see him."

"He must have been inside."

Craig leaned back in his chair. "If he waited in the house he must have been pretty sure she was coming home and that her husband wouldn't be returning with her."

"Or this guy really is just a cocky sonofabitch who's gotten lucky so far."

"What dates do we have again?"

Lori picked up her notebook. "June fourteenth, July twenty-fifth and August eighteenth. And now July eighth."

"So it seemed like the third attack was closer to the second, until we got that call yesterday. The dates aren't getting closer together."

"Unless we've got women who haven't reported yet. Knowing how reluctant rape victims are to come forward, it's possible."

"We need to do a nationwide search, see if there are any other open rape cases that fit the pattern," Craig suggested. "It's not like this guy has just popped up out of the blue. He's meticulous, organized, confident. There's essentially no escalation in his attacks, which is unusual. He must have raped before."

"I agree." She turned her eyes toward the report in her hands, twisting her chair slightly to her left as though the conversation was over.

Craig looked up. Daly was watching them from across the room. His gaze was blank, but Craig sensed he wasn't too happy about Lori. For once he wished Daly would indulge him and give him a different partner.

Tain waited until Ashlyn hung up the phone. "Alex Wilson is on his way in."

She leaned back in her chair, covered her face with her hands and groaned. "You're kidding."

"Why?"

"Carl Parks just called to say that we could come over and take his statement."

Tain arched an eyebrow. "Without prompting?"

She raised her hands and shrugged her shoulders. "Don't look a gift horse in the mouth, Tain. I don't really want to keep him waiting, with what he's dealing with at home."

"You go talk to Mr. Parks. I'll talk to Alex Wilson."

"You're sure?" Ashlyn didn't wait for an answer. She stood and pulled on her jacket.

"Try not to look so happy to get away from me."

"It's not you. It's the station. I think the fresh air will do me good."

"Any chance of you finding out if the building is clear for us to enter?"

Ashlyn had started walking toward the door. She turned, continuing to walk backward as she pointed at him. "I'll try to stop by the station or call Quinlan about that on my way back. Call me on my cell if anything comes up."

"Hey, get me lunch when you're out."

"You don't have time to get over to Hooters?"

"Very funny, Ashlyn," he called after her.

The CD player clicked, and Ashlyn felt the smile spread across her face when she heard "Fare Thee Well Love" start. There was something about the music that went beyond the typical fluff the radios churned out and rehashed every few hours. It wasn't that she didn't like popular music. It was just that sometimes she wanted to listen to something that did more than drown out the silence. There was emotion in this music. She connected with it.

Not that emotion was something she lacked these days, and when the line about the lonely girl came on she wondered what she was doing listening to songs about loss as she drove through the city, on her way to Port Coquitlam, mountain shadow giving way to farmland. She hit the CD changer. "Til I Am Myself Again" came on.

When she arrived at the Parks' home it was clear it would be a long time before Carl Parks would be himself again. Ashlyn fought to keep her jaw from dropping, tried in vain to keep the shock from registering in her eyes.

The previous day he'd been covered in soot but otherwise strong, capable, in command except for the moment when he'd lost it, when he'd heard the girl was dead. Now, he had dark circles around his eyes that had nothing to do with residue from fighting a fire, no flush of exertion in his cheeks, the strong, confident bearing gone. Despite being elevated on the threshold of the house above her, he seemed a few inches shorter, a few inches thinner, pale. He clearly hadn't slept.

"I, uh, I can come back if this isn't a good time."

He half shrugged. "It's fine."

She followed him into the living room, sitting on the couch across from him. He looked around the room, at the ceiling, the corners and the points between the bookshelves. Finally, he looked at her, his mouth slightly open, his eyes pinched. "What do you need?"

"You told us that you found Isabella's body on the fourth floor, in a room in the back right corner. Is that correct?"

He nodded.

"You said she was lying on a table under the window."

Carl nodded again.

"Do you remember what kind of table it was?"

"What kind?" He blinked.

"A dining table, a child's play table, a school desk. Color, length, anything?"

He stared at her blankly for another moment, then shook his head. "What's this got to do with anything?"

"Carl, I know this isn't a good time," Ashlyn said, "but this is very important to the family out there that has to plan a funeral now for their daughter."

His shoulders sagged. "She's pregnant, you know. She can't even take some of the medications, in case . . . in case . . ."

He held his face in his hands for a moment, his elbows propped precariously on his knees, his legs quivering visibly. In the loose, white dress shirt and khaki pants he looked like a solid gust of wind could blow him right out of the lower mainland and over the Rocky Mountains.

Then the trembling stopped, and he looked up. "It was a gray folding table."

"Like the kind you buy at Costco?"

He blinked, rubbed his hand across the stubble on his chin. "Yeah, I suppose."

"Was there a blanket on it? Anything at all?"

Carl paused with his hand over his mouth, his elbows still digging into his kneecaps. "No. But there was something funny on the wall."

"Funny, how? What was it?"

He shook his head, holding up one open hand. "I don't know. Funny, odd. I barely saw it, with all the smoke, and it looked like it was some sort of graffiti, drawn in black charcoal. It seemed familiar, but I'm not sure what it was. I just wasn't paying that much attention, you know?"

She nodded. "It's okay. You're doing great." Ashlyn waited a moment before continuing. "Last night you said there was thick, black smoke pouring out the window when you went into the room, that you almost didn't see Isabella."

"That's right."

"Do you remember if the window had been opened or if it was broken?"

"Like I said yesterday, I'm sure our guys didn't break it."

"I just mean generally. Had it been left open, or was it broken?"

"You think she tried, she might have tried to get out?"

Ashlyn shook her head, forcing herself not to look away as he stared directly at her. All that grief and shock, the wild eyes . . . She hadn't even seen that much raw emotion at the Bertini house the night before. "No. She . . . she didn't die there, Carl. Isabella was already gone when he put her on that table."

"What's wrong with this world, that there are all these sick bastards out there, running around hurting people?" Carl slammed his fist down on the coffee table.

Ashlyn felt herself wince at the sound of the blow, although she'd seen it coming. "I wish I had answers for you."

"I don't want your fucking answers. I want to kill—"

Carl froze. He'd looked like he was about to jump up, knock the coffee table over, smash everything in the room he could get his hands on until those words came out of his mouth. The fury in his eyes gave way to a look of fear. The hard line of his mouth had dissolved, and his eyes had the glassy look of being filled with tears.

She didn't know what to say to him. So much grief, so much understandable anger, nothing that would make it all better.

Ashlyn flipped her notebook shut. "If you think of anything else, you call me." She fished a card from her pocket and stood. Carl's interlocking fingers were behind his head now, his body rocking back and forth. To him, she was already gone.

She walked into the hallway. There was a telephone stand by the entrance, and she set her card down and then took a second look.

Another police officer's card was sitting on the edge, partially tucked under the phone. Not surprising, considering the fact that Mrs. Parks had been raped. But Ashlyn had eventually been able to ask around and put a name to the constable who'd taken Carl from the scene the day before, and it wasn't Lori Price's card she was looking at now.

Ashlyn sucked in a breath and stepped outside, pulling the door shut behind her.

Tain took a sip of his water and glanced at the clock.

Alex Wilson had been waiting on the other side of the one-way window for almost thirty minutes. He hadn't broken out in a cold sweat as the minutes ticked by, and he hadn't started pacing the limited floor space in the small room.

He hadn't done a bloody thing except just sit there.

It was a new one on Tain. People slept. People paced. People drummed their fingers against the table and scrutinized every inch of the bland room. Some used cell phones they'd had hidden in their pockets. Others doodled. The odd pervert who had clearly never seen a cop drama on television took the time to jerk off, but nobody just sat and stared straight ahead blankly without protesting at their time being wasted in a police station.

Tain entered the room in a hurry, sprinted to the table, dropped notepaper and his water down and hastily turned back to shut the door.

"Sorry to keep you waiting." He was halfway down in the chair before he glanced across the table, deliberately wrinkled his brow and then looked straight into the eyes of Alex Wilson. "The officer who brought you in didn't offer you something to drink? Can I get you a Coke, a bottled water, anything?"

Alex Wilson shook his head, pushing his thick black frames up on his nose.

Tain figured ten-to-one odds Wilson was some techno-geek.

"I'm sorry we had to ask you to come down here on the weekend. Did the officer who brought you in explain what this is about?"

His stringy blond hair bobbed as he nodded, though Alex's eyes had an unusual way of staying fixed in one position, the rest of his head shifting without affecting his gaze at all. Tain glanced at the clock.

Thirty-five minutes and this guy hadn't said one word. Tain reached for the tape recorder. He cued the tape and recorded the session information.

"Could you state your name for the record please?"

Little lines formed around Alex's mouth, and his eyes widened just a tiny bit.

"It isn't a problem for us to record this, is it? It just makes the paperwork easier." Tain offered him a relaxed smile, like a schoolkid caught trying to skimp on his homework assignments.

Alex's gaze flickered from Tain's face to the tape recorder and then he opened his mouth. "Alex Wilson," he squeaked.

"Could you say that again, a little louder? These old things are garbage."

Alex repeated his name and ran a hand across his forehead.

Tain found the abrupt change in Wilson's demeanor interesting, but he wasn't sure what to make of it.

"Would you mind telling me, in your own words, what happened yesterday?"

"Wha-whaddya mean, what happened?"

"You were at the park near the fair . . ." Tain prompted.

Alex nodded.

"I need you to answer verbally, for the tape."

"Ah, ahem, yes."

"And you found a child."

The dull, blue eyes popped wide open then, and he coughed.

"Mr. Wilson, can you tell me how you found Nicholas Brennen?"

"Wh-who?"

"The boy you found at the fairgrounds, the one you drove here, to this police station, in your car." Tain stared across the table at the man, trying to look more indifferent about this interview than he felt. "You do remember bringing a boy to this police station yesterday, don't you?"

His cheeks turned so red Tain was sure he'd get sunburned from prolonged exposure. Alex coughed. "Yeah."

"Can you tell me what you were doing when you found him?"

Tain hadn't thought Alex's cheeks could get any darker, but somehow he managed to pull it off. "I, uh, I was on the walking path, at the park. The one with the hedges."

"Okay."

"He was wandering by himself. Crying."

Tain swallowed. "Sobbing, calling out or just with tears running down his face?"

Alex opened his mouth to answer, and then his eyebrows merged into one thick line across his forehead, underscoring the wrinkles on his brow. "I th-think just tears running down his face."

*You think?* Tain couldn't believe this guy. "What happened next?"

"Well, I asked him if I should take him to the police."

"You asked him if you should bring him to the police?"

Alex shrugged, pushing his glasses up with his middle finger.

"So, let me get this straight. You were on the walking path at the park, the one with the hedges. You saw a young boy walking alone, with tears rolling down his cheeks and you went up to him and asked if you should take him to the police? Not, 'Did you lose your dog?' or 'Are you lost?' but 'Should I take you to the police?'"

Alex swallowed and then nodded.

"Why did you think he needed to go to the police, Mr. Wilson?"

"I . . . I don't know. I was just trying to be helpful."

Tain unscrewed the cap on his water bottle slowly and took a sip. This guy was textbook weird. It was too bad Ashlyn wasn't there. Tain thought it could be interesting to see how Alex Wilson responded to a woman.

Especially a woman like Ashlyn, who knew how to handle herself.

"All right, Mr. Wilson. What happened then?"

"I took his hand and we walked back to the fairgrounds, to my car, while I dialed 911."

"You dialed 911?"

"Well, I dialed the operator and asked them to put me through to the police. . . ." Alex Wilson shrugged.

"What did the person on the phone tell you to do?"

"I . . . I don't know. I just said who I was and I'd found a boy alone in the park and that I was coming to the police station."

"Why did you do that?"

"Wha . . . whaddya mean, why?" Alex ran the back of his hand across his forehead.

"You've been at the fairgrounds before, right?"

Alex nodded.

"And you live to the south." It wasn't a question. Tain knew the answer.

"New Westminster, yeah."

"And yet you drove Nicholas Brennen all the way here, even though you found him not far from the border of Coquitlam, Burnaby and New Westminster, and you yourself live in New Westminster. See, to me, I'd think you'd know where your local police stations are. And even if you didn't, why not ask where the closest police station was when you were on the phone? Instead you drove him to the other side of the city."

There was absolute silence as Tain waited to see what Alex Wilson would say, if he said anything at all. Finally, the man shrugged.

"For the tape, Mr. Wilson."

"I don't know what you're asking. I . . . I phoned the police. I drove him to a police station. That's all."

"Well, Mr. Wilson, you have to consider it from my point of view. You don't live in this area. You didn't find the boy in this area. But for some reason you came to this police station with him. You came a long way out of your way."

Alex's mouth hung open for a minute, and he pushed the glasses up again, shrugging. "I . . . I didn't think. I just drove here."

"Did Nicholas Brennen say anything?"

Alex shook his head.

"The tape," Tain said.

"No."

"Nothing at all?"

"I asked if I should take him to the police. He nodded. I took his hand, brought him to my car and . . . and . . . and I drove him here. He didn't say nothin'."

"And, sorry, I've forgotten. Why did you think he needed to go to the police?"

Alex's face turned redder than a vine-ripened tomato. "I . . . I don't know."

"What was Nicholas wearing when you found him?"

"A white shirt, blue jeans, white sneakers an—" Alex stopped.

Tain waited, then tried to prompt him. "And?"

"That's it." The squeak was back in Alex's voice.

"Could I get your cell phone number again, just for the record, please?"

After a false start, Alex corrected himself and finally rattled it off. "I don't see why this is so important. The boy was lost. I brought him here. It's not against the law."

"You don't understand why we're interested in Nicky Brennen?"

His blond head shook, and then his finger reached for the glasses again.

Tain pulled out the newspaper he'd had folded underneath

his notepad, the one with the headline about Taylor Brennen missing and Isabella Bertini's body being recovered. He tossed it down in front of Alex Wilson. His red cheeks blanched.

"Do you understand now, Mr. Wilson?"

"You're beginning to look like a permanent fixture around here."

Ashlyn mustered enough energy to smile back at Adrian Vaughan, who was clearly recognizable in his jeans and T-shirt today, unlike the night before when he'd been wearing his turnout gear at the fire scene.

"I thought you were on nights," she said.

"Yeah, I'm actually just messing around with cars. My cousin, Aaron, he's got a bit of a classic he brings by sometimes. Lots of good shop tools around that we can use for free." He flashed her a smile. "Fringe benefits."

"You like old cars?"

"Some. Mostly, I just like working on them. Aaron and I have been making modifications to his old Corvette for years."

She nodded. He'd turned toward her, giving her his full attention, not looking like he was in a hurry to go anywhere. She stifled a yawn. "I'm still on the clock."

"Since yesterday?"

Ashlyn nodded. "Still smelling like I've been caught inside a chimney, too. Is Chief Quinlan in?"

"Should be in his office. Maybe we'll see you later."

"I hope not, if you know what I mean." Ashlyn walked away.

Paul Quinlan looked up at the figure leaning against his doorway. Her typically bright eyes and vibrant smile were overshadowed by dark circles and pale skin. Her mouth was drawn in an unusually hard line. "I hate to say this Ashlyn, but you look like how I feel."

"That bad, huh?" She sank into a chair.

"Pretty hard night," Quinlan said. "Rough call."

"We really need to get into that building."

"I doubt you'll find much there." Quinlan tossed his pen

down on the desk, turning around in his chair to face her fully.

"You're probably right."

"But you still want to take a look?"

"You know we have to."

"Technically, the building's a complete write off. I can take you in, but just you."

"Constable Tain needs to come with us."

"So this isn't about the arsons anymore, is it?"

"I'm still investigating the arson cases," Ashlyn said. "I'm not giving up on that."

"But the girl takes priority."

"Right now, the girl is our best lead to solving the arsons."

His eyebrows shot up. "Why? Because that other girl was found at the scene of one of the earlier fires?"

"It's a link we can't ignore, Paul." Ashlyn rubbed her eyes. "It's also a link we can't have everyone knowing about."

He nodded. "I understand that."

"Not even your men, Paul."

"Don't you want me to ask them to keep their eyes open on future calls? I saw the paper this morning. If there's a link we're going to have another fire on our hands soon."

"You can't say anything to anyone." Ashlyn sighed. "Every firefighter you have who's been on these calls is going to have it figured out. But right now, we don't want the press catching wind of this. The last thing we need is distraught parents showing up at fire scenes thinking their child is inside."

"Good point." Quinlan stood. "Let's go."

"I'll just call Tain and have him meet us there."

"Constable Tain," a voice called.

Tain stopped midstride, turning to see the smartly dressed officer—the one who'd escorted Mrs. Brennen away the day before when Tain had stopped her from assaulting her son—approaching him in the hallway.

"Constable Sims, right?"

The man nodded. He was one of those people who instantly pissed Tain off on some levels, with a uniform that seemed perfectly in place, like it was designed for him. Sims wasn't a big man, but he was fit, with short, dark hair, no glasses to conceal his blue eyes, and a dimple that seemed eager to show itself without the man even properly smiling. Hawkins was the poster boy for the leaders and established career officers. Sims was the quintessential pin-up boy for the recruits.

"Sergeant Daly asked me to run a background check on Mrs. Brennen yesterday. I thought I should update you."

Tain glanced at his watch. "Can you drive me to meet my partner?"

"Sure. I did the check. As you probably already know, there wasn't anything on file with social services. No reports of abuse, no reason for intervention with the family at all. Parents divorced three years ago."

Sims was right. Social services had told him that yesterday. Tain followed Sims to a car and waited until they were both inside to ask, "Is that all?"

"Mom has a record. Nothing new since her kids were born, but there was a time she was pretty active in the system."

Tain relayed the address he needed to be dropped off at. "Let me guess."

"Solicitation." Sims started the car. "And assault."

Tain thought of the way Connie Brennen's hand had struck him the day before, like someone accustomed to using her fists to make a point. "Who filed the charges?"

"Her alleged pimp. A guy with the street name John-John."

Tain snorted. "That's original."

"I did a search. I wasn't sure if you were familiar with him." Sims paused again. Tain let the silence be his answer.

"He's been in and out of the system forever. Street fights, money hustling, a series of break-and-enter charges, an armed robbery conviction that didn't stick on appeal. He did a two-year stretch for breaking the jaw of one of his working girls, and he was the main suspect in the abduction of a five-year-old child of another woman who worked for him."

"But not charged?"

"No. The child turned up suddenly when the cops started putting the heat on. Then the mother disappeared with her kid. The mother was the one who'd filed the initial report when the kid went missing, so without her and without a missing child to look for . . ." Sims switched lanes.

Tain frowned. Without a missing child the case dissolved, as though there'd never been a crime. If this got out prematurely, it could keep them from taking control of the abduction cases. He'd have to check it out quietly. "Did you find anything on why the investigating officers thought he did it?"

"Rumors she was holding out on him, taking some straight dope jobs on the side and not cutting him in."

Tain frowned. Why would John-John be interested in Connie Brennen's daughter now?

"The lead investigator was Corporal Frank Hay. He transferred to Vancouver Island a few years ago. His partner during the time of the case was Tim Winters."

"Corporal Tim Winters?"

"Yeah." Sims paused. "Didn't you work with him?"

"Yes," Tain said sharply. Sims looked like a puppy dog waiting to be patted on the head, eager to earn approval. On the one hand, if Daly was going to assign someone to collect data, at least Sims wasn't useless. But there could be such a thing as being too eager to please.

"Well, I'm sure he'll be able to tell you more, but there might just be a reason why John-John would be interested in Taylor Brennen now."

Tain glared at Sims, waiting for him to continue.

The dimple disappeared. "Well, I know this street girl named Cocoa. . . ." He glanced at Tain. "She told me that the word back then was that Connie got herself pregnant as her get-off-the-street card and that Nick Brennen was just the idiot who fell for her act. The only guy Connie was consistently, um, with when she was working was John-John."

"And Cocoa knows this how?"

"When I said 'girl,' I meant in name only."

"I see. So she's been a player for a long time."

"Mostly dealing these days." Sims glanced at him again. "I'm sure you know how it is. You need people willing to talk. . . ." Sims shrugged.

Tain turned to look out the window. "Yeah. Good work."

"Thank you, sir."

"Tain will do."

"Right."

Sims stopped the car, and Tain unclipped his seat belt.

"Now, there's something else you need to do."

Sims nodded. "Will it get me her phone number?"

Tain glanced up through the windshield. "Constable Hart isn't a door prize." He felt the fingers on his right hand tightening into a fist and consciously reached for the door handle, hoping Sims wouldn't see and that his own face didn't look as taut as it felt. He filled Sims in on what he needed and got out of the car.

The room remained as dark as it had been when she'd arrived, though she had a sense of light outside the black space she was trapped in. She couldn't put her finger on it exactly, but it was like waking up at home and having the room be entirely dark, but knowing that was only because the thick, denim curtains were drawn shut.

It was the way her mom liked the house after what she called a bender, after she'd come home laughing and stumbling down the halls late at night, so late she thought Taylor and Nicky were already fast asleep. The next morning Mom would always be the same, someone to tiptoe around. It took only a few backhands to know the late nights should never be followed by early mornings.

Even the afternoons usually consisted of Mom sitting in a dark room with the blinds down, moaning over a cup of coffee, which Taylor thought was disgusting. The fact that her sick mother could drink it seemed unbelievable. Whenever Taylor felt sick she didn't even want chocolate or sweet 'n' sour candies. Just the smell of coffee when she felt fine was enough to make her tummy do somersaults.

There was no real recognizable smell she could detect now, other than pee. Her desperate search for a bathroom had led her only to a bucket in the far corner, and when she couldn't cross her legs any longer she gave in and used it.

There was another faint odor she could barely detect. She guessed it was dust, if dust had a smell. Something about the lack of freshness, the absence of soap or cleaners . . . It reminded her of the smell in Grandfather's storage shed, the one where he kept the lawn mower.

Taylor heard the sound of shuffling feet coming toward her and hugged her legs to her body. Shafts of light shone in on the floor, falling short of the bed she huddled on, and the light behind the figure silhouetted him, making him look like only a dark form between her and the world outside the concrete walls she was surrounded by.

The door closed behind him, and for a moment, all she could hear was the sharp intake and release of breath, not unlike the mechanical sounds of a ventilator, like the one she'd seen Great Gran hooked up to before she'd died or like the sound of Darth Vader sucking air through his mask.

Then the dark figure shuffled toward her. She hugged her legs tighter and squeezed her eyes shut.

"What's that?" Lori asked as Craig returned to his desk, papers in hand.

"A list of all known sex offenders in the area, parolees and their modus operandi."

She scurried over to Craig's desk. "How did you get your hands on that? I've been stonewalled for half the damn day trying to get outstanding rape case reports."

"It's Sunday. You won't get anywhere. I called for this yesterday."

She straightened up. "Well, maybe there's something in there that can help."

"Bit like looking for a needle in a haystack," Craig said. "Must be dozens of perps here, and we haven't even got a clue what we're looking for."

"Sure we do. We're looking for some sick schmuck who gets his rocks off by forcing women to bend over."

"I thought rapists usually had a type they preferred. Brunette, blonde, redhead. Some defining characteristic they use to choose victims."

"Well, what have we got? Karen Chalmers was our first victim, at least, from what's been reported. She had black hair. Sara McPherson . . ." Lori looked up at Craig.

He leafed through a stack of folders, extracted a photo and passed it to her.

"Redhead," Lori said. "Hmm. Next is Stephanie Bonnis. She's blond."

"And Cindy Parks is blond."

"No brunettes, though. Guess I'm safe."

"Not enough information to base a pattern on," Craig said.

"What about locations?"

Craig shook his head, passing her the map. "I've marked all the spots. They're randomly configured, as far as I can tell."

"Yeah, I agree. Scattered in Coquitlam and Port Coquitlam. Karen Chalmers lives in Port Moody. I thought rapists were supposed to hunt in their own territory, stay in their comfort zone."

"There's only one thing about this guy I can say with absolute certainty," Craig said.

Lori arched an eyebrow. "Besides the fact that he's a sick sonofabitch?"

"Goes without saying. I'm just talking in terms of a profile. Nothing seems to fit any of the standard textbook talk about rapists. He's experienced. That's the only thing I'd bank on."

"There must be something that connects them."

"You and I both know it could be as simple as means and opportunity, but we're going to have to look through everything to see if we can figure out how he's picking his victims."

Lori sighed. "Just let me call home and cancel my plans for the next five years first, will you?"

"Under normal circumstances I wouldn't dream of letting anyone in," Paul Quinlan said as he passed Ashlyn and Tain helmets and boots. "If you need to bring a camera or anything, get it now. No telling if there'll be a next time.

"And at the first sign of trouble, we're done. No arguments, no bullshit. Either of you gives me any grief, I'll make sure you push paper for the rest of the year."

"Understood, Paul."

Tain let Ashlyn follow Paul, lingering back so that he didn't feel rushed. He let his eyes take in every detail of the charring, the pools of water gathered on the floor in a few places, the drip drip of a leak from a weak spot in a ceiling keeping time with his steps.

"You okay?"

He looked up to see Ashlyn, half a flight above him, looking down over the railing. "Have you been in a burned-out building before?"

"How d'you think I've been working these arson cases? Playing rummy at the station?"

There was no doubt in his mind most of the firefighters would be happy for her to hang out there, but he didn't say that. "It's a bit creepy."

"First time I went home and checked every smoke detector in my place. It's amazing how destructive fire is. A few days ago this was a serviceable building. In a matter of weeks it will be just a pile of rubble at the dump."

They reached the landing to the fourth floor. "Good thing the room you want is this way." Quinlan pointed to the far side of the hall. "That hallway doesn't look safe."

"How can he tell?" Tain whispered to Ashlyn.

"Experience," was the brusque reply from the man ahead of her.

Ashlyn looked over her shoulder at Tain, rolled her eyes

and gave him a quick grin, which he took as her way of telling him to keep his mouth shut so he wouldn't look stupid.

The next thing he knew Ashlyn was holding his outstretched hand, telling him not to let go.

"If it's bad enough for me to fall through, don't you think you should get out while you still can?" He snuck a glance down. It didn't look far to the floor below him.

Quinlan grabbed his other hand. "The fire didn't do this."

"I don't weigh that much."

"You weigh enough," Ashlyn said. Tain felt his arm slip as he slid back, more of his body falling through the hole. Her grip tightened. Her face was taut, cheeks flushed.

"It isn't far. Let go. Worst thing that happens is I twist my ankle."

Quinlan grunted. "Or you go right through those floor boards. See there and there." He nodded. "The floor is thicker there than it is there."

Tain watched Ashlyn look at the floor and then Quinlan. Then they started shifting their weight to one side.

"On three," Quinlan said. "One, two, three. Pull."

Tain felt his body jerk forward, until his waist was over the remaining floor. He started pulling his legs up behind him.

Quinlan stood up. "Back to the stairs, now."

"But—"

"Someone was using parts of this floor for firewood, or God knows what, before this building caught fire. There's no way to tell if it's safe, and I'm not taking any chances with the lives of two RCMP officers. I need you to catch an arsonist."

"Lucky for us we're of use to you," Ashlyn responded dryly.

"Or unlucky, as the case may be," Tain muttered. They followed Quinlan back down the stairs.

"It was a long shot to think we'd get something useful from the room anyway, Tain."

He blew his breath out. "I don't like to think of facing her parents with even one thing left that could've been done."

"You're no good to that girl's parents dead," Quinlan told him as they walked outside. "They need you in one piece to catch the person who killed their daughter."

They stopped at Quinlan's vehicle, passed back the equipment he'd lent them and walked to their car.

"What a waste." Tain took the keys from Ashlyn.

"Oh, I don't know. I do like to lift weights regularly, and it's been a while."

"I could tell."

She shook her head. "You're filthy. You need to go home and change."

"We should go to bed."

She extended her hand. "Give me the keys."

"Why?"

"Because you're in no shape to drive if you think I'd go for a proposition like that," she said as she snatched them from him.

"I meant—"

"Ashlyn," Quinlan called. They turned to see him yank open the door to his vehicle and toss his cell on the passenger seat. "There's another arson. It sounds like it fits the profile, and they found an angel on the door."

Tain glanced at her. "Angel?"

"We're not exactly letting that out. Don't need the press labeling these the angel arsons."

He grabbed the keys back, sprinting toward the driver's side.

"We'll follow you," Ashlyn called to Paul as she opened the car door.

Craig entered Daly's office and sat down.

"Where's your partner?" Daly asked.

Craig shook his head. "Beats me. She disappeared about forty minutes ago."

"She didn't tell you where she was—"

Lori rushed in then and muttered an apology. When Daly nodded she sat down beside Craig. He saw her brush a stray strand of hair behind her ear.

"What do you have so far?"

"Not much, sir," Lori said.

Daly arched an eyebrow. "What about known offenders in the area, unsolved rapes that might give us a history on this guy, a pattern to connect the victims?"

Craig responded. "We're working our way through the known offenders, but so far, none of them have the profile for it, unless they've taken a big jump forward since their last attacks. As you know, we have no DNA, no witnesses have come forward, and so far, we can't find a link between the victims."

"At this point, the only thing they seem to have had in common, besides being women, is being at home alone at the time of the rape," Lori said.

"Except for Stephanie Bonnis, if you count the baby."

"Then we'll pick this up in the morning and see what else we can do to work it," Daly said. "No arguments, Craig. You never even went home last night."

"There are still a few things I can check on," Lori said. "I want—"

"I want both of you in here, bright-eyed and bushy-tailed tomorrow morning, ready to go on this. I mean it. Go home and get a solid eight hours of sleep. We'll pick this up in the morning."

Lori keyed her password into her cell phone and listened to the new message. "Hi, honey, it's Vish. Look, I know you promised you'd get away tonight and we were planning to go down to the marina and have dinner, but this time it's my work getting in the way. There's a four-alarm fire, and we've been called in. I don't know when I'll get home, so don't wait up. Just think about three weeks sailing up to Queen Charlotte Island, maybe even going as far as Juneau. I'm really sorry, hon. I'll make it up to you."

Lori sighed as she switched the phone off and tossed it onto the seat beside her as she drove. Not like she could complain. Every night this week it had been her coming home to reheat dinner.

She smiled as she thought back to earlier in the day, the brief time she'd been able to sneak away from Craig and the case and have a few moments of pleasure, but the memory faded quickly.

"For fuck's sake, it's not getting any greener!" she yelled at the car in front of her, slamming her fist against the horn. It earned her the response of a raised finger.

For once she wanted to make it home when it was still considered the dinner hour.

She tapped her thumb against the steering wheel and thought about sneaking back into the office, looking through the files. Daly would be gone, and Craig had done more than enough brown-nosing for one career.

Ahead of her tires squealed and there was a thud, followed by the sound of a car alarm going off. Horns honked in stereo, and she craned her neck, trying to see what had happened in the intersection ahead.

Then the distinctive deep honk of emergency vehicles blared out above the sirens, and she glanced in her rear-view mirror, seeing the lights get closer.

*Dammit.* She inched her car as far off the road as she could to let them pass, reaching for the radio.

*Off early for nothing.* She sighed, wondering what she did when she wasn't working anyway.

Craig was halfway to his old apartment when he realized what he was doing. He swore and turned the car around.

When he'd returned to Coquitlam after his temporary transfer he'd found himself climbing the walls, unable to get used to being half a dozen floors up, surrounded by concrete and air.

Not to mention facing the colorless rooms and faint scent of second-hand BC bud coming from some other tenant's apartment that was giving him headaches.

Finally, he'd pulled open a real estate magazine and started making calls. Which was when his dad had turned up and interrogated him, until he admitted he wanted to get his own place.

His dad had insisted that he take the rental property. After all, as Dad had said, it was meant for Craig.

Craig had argued without saying what he really thought. It wasn't meant for him—it was meant for an idea. That someday Steve and Alison Daly would have children, and this would be one of the things they'd pass on to their kids.

The plan hadn't been to find out that Steve already had a child. One who was only sixteen years younger than Steve was, a product of a youthful indiscretion and a constant reminder to Steve's wife that another woman had given him what she couldn't.

In the end Craig had lost. Daly only got the upper hand on the job, but when Alison got involved there was no way to keep arguing without sounding like an ungrateful child.

The house was at the end of a quiet street, and he had room to park three vehicles in front, as well as a garage in the back, though he only needed one spot for his seasoned Rodeo.

A thick line of trees provided a buffer zone between the edge of his property and a walking path that curved back toward the main road. Off the living room there was one thing Craig was still finding it hard to get used to having: patio doors opened up to a deck and a fenced yard.

Already stores were displaying signs advertising special deals on summer merchandise. It might not be a bad time to look at patio furniture.

He could get a dog, like Tain's dog, Chinook. That was a nice dog. Craig had always wanted a dog.

Thinking about Tain for even a split second was enough for a torrent of memories to surface in his mind. Ashlyn. The girls. The tension. It had been a bad case from day one.

He'd thought he was over it, able to stop blaming himself. That he'd been able to put the past behind him and that he could move on without the constant compulsion to nail his hands to the cross again and again but just thinking about it had made him think about heading to the bar.

Craig resisted, went to his house and unlocked the front door. The mail waiting on the other side of the door was nothing more than bills demanding payment and flyers aimed at prying whatever cash was left from his salary out of his wallet. He tossed the stack of papers on the kitchen counter and opened the fridge.

After a cursory glance he straightened up, sighed and ran his fingers over his hair as he let the door fall shut. *Back to your old habits already. And you'd better cut your hair before Dad says something.*

He turned to the counter and pulled out the phone book, looking for the name of the good Greek restaurant he'd found that delivered.

Tain coughed. "How can you stand working these fires? This air is toxic."

"Bit like kissing a smoker."

"You mean licking an ashtray."

Ashlyn wrinkled her nose at him. "Spare me the details, Tain."

"I don't know how they can stand it."

"Doubt it bothers the smokers at all."

He glared at her. "I meant the firefighters."

"That's what they have a breathing apparatus for. And that's why they try to keep civilians back."

They watched as a firefighter climbed a ladder to the building and tried to take out a window. As the pane gave way, smoke shot out, and then the firefighter disappeared inside the building.

"Give me a good old-fashioned criminal with a gun or a machete any day," Tain said.

Ashlyn tried to suppress her desire to laugh and failed. Finally she managed to sputter out one word: "Wimp."

"Call it heightened self-preservation. You have to be wired wrong to want to run into a building that's engulfed in flames."

"And it's perfectly normal to chase wanted criminals down dark alleys, knowing they have a weapon and aren't afraid to use it?"

He shrugged. "It's still better odds. So what do you do

when you get called to these? Besides provide the entertainment."

She felt her eyebrow arch as she folded her arms and glared at him. Even under the streaks of soot on his face she could tell his cheeks paled.

"Well, let's just put it this way, Ashlyn. The boys seem to like having you around."

She almost smiled as she rolled her eyes. "Jealous?"

"Why? You sleeping with one of them?"

Her retort caught in her throat, and she coughed. "Even if I was, it would be none of your business." Her gaze fell on a group of men standing by the pumper truck. They quickly averted their eyes when they saw her looking at them.

"There isn't much I can do while they're fighting the fire, obviously. They actually have teams that come in after the fire is out and do a complete evaluation, check for accelerants, survey the area for evidence. The insurance companies swarm over the area too, hoping they can find ways to mitigate their liability. I get a stack of reports to go through, look for witnesses, and once it's confirmed as an arson, I sift through the evidence and hopefully come up with a lead."

"If the bulk of your work happens after the fact, why do you come to the scene?"

"You really don't get it, do you?"

"What? You want to distract these upstanding fellows from their work?"

Ashlyn fought the urge to smack him. "No. A high percentage of arsonists are firefighters."

"I always thought that was a myth."

"Why?"

"Isn't it like saying that a high percentage of criminals are police officers?" Tain shrugged. "Okay, we both know that some police officers are crooked. We both know it firsthand. It just seemed like a simplistic way of excusing the fact that there's a low closure rate for arson cases."

"That's because arsonists are exceptionally difficult to profile. I mean, there's your standard insurance fraud. That's usually easy enough to prove, or at least certify in your mind, even if you don't have the evidence for a solid case. Particularly if the person torches the place themselves. They have a better chance of getting away with it if they hire a professional to do the job, but then, if they hire someone, they risk leaving a trail. It's never foolproof.

"These cases, though, you have to try to figure out what's motivating this guy, why he chooses these buildings. There might not even be a reason. It could be just as simple as spotting an empty building and having the stuff he needs on hand."

Tain frowned. "So the strategy here is to have you spend as much time with the fire department as possible, see if you can work your way in."

She shook her head. "No. I'm supposed to keep my eyes open for anyone suspicious. The main reason for being here is to observe."

"How many fires are there that seem connected?"

"This makes six. The first one was June fourteenth. Then July eighth, and Robinson was still working the cases when they found Julie Darrens's body on July twenty-fifth. I started working these cases the next day. I was supposed to partner with Robinson, and then when they found that girl, he dealt with her and the officers from Burnaby, and then he died. Now the case is all mine."

"So you haven't been at it for long."

"Long enough to feel like I'm spinning my wheels."

"Do you think this fire connects to the one from yesterday?"

Ashlyn shrugged and shook her head. "I don't know. Unless there are a number of other fires we haven't picked up on, this guy has never done two back to back. But Quinlan said there's an angel."

"It could be the media coverage. Maybe this guy realizes he's struck a nerve and he hasn't held Taylor as long as he did Julie and Isabella."

She felt her face lengthen. "I hope you're wrong."

They stood, watching the flames engulf the structure before them, the ground shaking as something exploded on the far side of the building, and a thick column of smoke shot out a window.

"Do you ever think about it, about finding that girl?"

Ashlyn blinked and coughed, turning her head away from Tain. She felt his hand on her shoulder, the gentle squeeze before he pulled his arm back.

"I'm sorry." His face portrayed a rare, sober expression, no hint of amusement in his eyes.

"It's okay."

"I think about her all the time now, with these girls going missing."

They stood in silence watching the fire burst through the roof, hearing orders called out to retreat from one end of the building, until the ringing of Tain's cell phone cut into their thoughts.

Craig lifted the receiver. "Hello?"

"Wonders never cease. You actually did as you were told."

"Or so you think. I could be using call forwarding and actually be talking on my cell phone, still stuck in the station." Craig smiled at the silence as his dad hesitated. "I'm not. But I could be."

"Craig Nolan . . ."

"Why do you always pull out my full name when you're annoyed? Is that in a parenting manual somewhere?"

"Actually, I just know you don't like it."

Craig rubbed his forehead. "Would it be incredibly rude of me to ask what you want?"

"Yes, it would."

"You don't have to check up on me, you know."

"I'm not," Daly said. "It's just that Alison is still bugging me to pin you down for a date to have dinner."

"Tell her when the tyrant I work for gives me a day off I'd be happy to come over."

"Actually, she wants to come to your place."

"Wow, that's presumptuous. Invite yourself over and expect me to cook?"

"Be serious. I would bet a week's pay right now that there

aren't more than five things in your fridge and that half your cupboards are empty."

Craig didn't deny that. Daly continued. "Alison just wants to have a little house-warming dinner for you. She's promised to cook, clean and deal with the guest list."

Guests? Craig rubbed his forehead. "Fine, whatever. How does Tuesday sound?"

"Good. I'll let her know. You and Lori seemed to be getting along a bit better today."

Craig sighed. "I thought you wanted me to take the evening off, Daly." It was his way of dropping a hint. Revert to the work labels.

"Right, fine. I'll see you in the morning."

Craig hung up the phone and leaned against the counter, staring out the window.

*Grass. Damn. I need to get a lawn mower too.*

He started rifling through half-empty drawers, looking for a pen and paper to make a list.

Tain held up his ID and gestured to Ashlyn. "Tain and Hart. What the hell happened?" he asked the officer.

"A complete fuck-up. Everybody's pointing the finger at everyone else."

Several officers were trying to deal with a group of people standing outside Southside Recreation and Fitness Center. Even from across the parking lot the sharp edge of the voices resonated clearly, although Tain couldn't quite make out what was being said.

"Just give us the big picture," Tain told the officer.

"The girl came here with a church group at six PM. Some sort of youth activity night or something. There are fifteen kids with the group and six adult volunteers."

"That's a pretty good ratio," Ashlyn said. "Licensed day cares don't offer that much supervision."

"Yeah, but day cares have legal guidelines governing them. Youth groups with volunteer supervisors don't. The last female supervisor went through the shower area, promised she'd wait at the door. She watched the other girls go to the pool, but they were clustered together in a group. The volunteer, Joanne Anderson, said she tried to do a quick count of the girls and counted nine. She thought all the kids were there. Wasn't until one of the other volunteers asked where Lindsay was that they called the kids together, did a recount, came up a child short and started looking for her."

"And they were still missing Lindsay." Ashlyn glanced at Tain.

"Joanne and one of the other volunteers, Gabby Fry, went back into the change room, checked everywhere and then went through to the front desk. The staff at the desk said they hadn't seen the girl."

"Who called it in?" Ashlyn asked.

"The manager."

"How long did it take for officers to get on scene?" Tain asked.

"My partner and I were the first to respond. We were here in less than three minutes. We went in, took a preliminary statement and called for backup. There are two main entrances, one to the pool and gym facilities, one by the skating rink. There are also six fire escapes. There was no way we could contain the building on our own."

"And you aren't holding back any good news here?"

The constable, whose ID read Ogilvy, shook his head. "Sorry. We didn't see anything suspicious, and we realized pretty quick that whoever grabbed the girl likely went out a faulty fire exit in the back, past the change rooms. The door alarm wouldn't have triggered."

Tain looked at Ashlyn. "Are you thinking what I'm thinking?"

She nodded. "Where's the manager? I'll get a membership list. You," she patted Tain on the arm, "can wow the rowdy crowd with your powers of diplomatic persuasion."

"Or knock a few heads together." Tain turned to Ogilvy. "Okay. Take me to this church group first."

Ashlyn tried to extract the anger from her voice and failed. "I can have all of your staff taken down to the station and

questioned one by one. Of course, I'll need the complete
list. We'll call in everybody, whether they were working today or not."

"I think I should call a lawyer."

The manager was a surprisingly small man, considering
he worked at a fitness center. Ashlyn figured he must spend
more time pushing paper than lifting weights.

"Go ahead," she responded.

He stared at her without moving.

She nodded at the phone. "While you're at it, make sure
you call your insurance company."

His whole face wrinkled up like a shriveled prune.

"To prepare for the lawsuit you're about to have slapped
on you."

He gaped at her. "I, uh, what is it you need?"

"A membership list. Any security footage you have. Not
just by the change rooms. We want every tape from everywhere you have a camera running, for the last week. And
we'll need a complete list of all your employees, including
any on-call staff or anyone who's been let go or quit in the
past six months. Plus we want a copy of all your maintenance
records."

"Wha . . . ah . . . what do you need them for?"

"In all probability, whoever grabbed this girl took her out
a fire exit with a broken door. They were either extremely
lucky, or they knew the door was broken. I'm betting that
they knew. Which means they've been here before."

"Oh, okay, right." He blinked. "Do I have to give you this
information?"

"If you prefer, I can call the media and go outside and
make a statement about the fact that Southside Recreation
and Fitness Center doesn't want to cooperate with a police
investigation into the disappearance of an eleven-year-old
girl who went missing from its facility."

"Is that, um, really ethical? Isn't this like extortion?"

Ashlyn leaned her arms on his desk, staring down at him.
"I don't give a shit if you think I'm twisting your arm. I
haven't slept in almost forty hours, and Lindsay Eckert is the

second child who's gone missing this weekend. Yesterday I was examining the dead body of another girl who'd been murdered. You think I'm going to be worried if I'm not asking for what we need politely? You go outside and tell that to the Eckerts. You go tell them you don't want to give us this information because you didn't like my tone of voice."

He stared up at her, his thin lips quivering for a moment. "Fine. I'll get you everything you need. We'll cooperate in every way."

She smiled and sat down. "Thank you, Mr. Radcliff. Thank you very much."

The woman continued pointing at the recreation center staff as she spoke, tears streaming down her face, her scraggly hair only partially dry, a towel wrapped around her waist. Joanne Anderson hadn't taken time to change into her clothes when she realized Lindsay was missing. "I asked them to call staff down and have someone stand at every door. They refused."

Tain hoped she'd turn off the waterworks. It wasn't that he had a problem seeing a woman cry, but Joanne was borderline hysterical. It had taken every ounce of patience Tain had to get her to calm down enough to make the one coherent statement.

And he hadn't even gotten to the family.

"I heard her ask. She begged the manager to do something. It took him forever to call 911," Gabby Fry said.

Gabby Fry was dressed. Flaming red hair with a face full of freckles, she seemed to feel the need to explain that they had to get the kids out of the pool and clear the change rooms as quickly as possible. She'd changed back into her clothes when the kids in the church group did, she explained. Joanne Anderson had remained at the entrance, apparently wailing at the staff for their shortcomings the entire time until Tain asked to question her.

"I need you both to stop and think. Think back to when you first came in. Was there anyone you noticed watching you? Anyone who seemed a little unusual, out of place?"

"You mean like they were more interested in the kids?" Gabby Fry pushed her hair back from her face.

"Exactly. Did you see anyone?"

Gabby shook her head.

"Ms. Anderson?"

She collapsed onto the bench behind her. "How could we miss it? There was some monster here, and we didn't even see them."

Tain counted to ten and mustered all the patience he could. "Ms. Anderson, these people don't have horns and green skin." He knelt in front of her. Gabby sat down beside Joanne and put an arm around her shoulders. "They don't have a scarlet letter on their forehead."

"They should! How can we let these people out of our prisons without giving any warning to the public? She's just an innocent little girl."

Tain sighed. Joanne's body shook with sobs as she buried her face on her friend's shoulder. It almost looked comical, the taller, dark-haired woman leaning against the wiry red-head with the freckled face and cool composure.

"I'm going to need to talk to all the children who were here with your group."

Gabby blinked. "Uh, okay. You'll want to talk to Luke Driscoll. He's the tall one with the blond hair and glasses. Luke's in charge."

The girl tossed her hair over her shoulders, eyes wide. "You should do something about him. He's such a perv. He stands too close, you know what I mean? And he likes to look over our shoulders."

"Yeah, and he told us we should wear these shirts too," the other girl chimed in.

"Uh, aren't they your work shirts?" Ashlyn asked.

"Yeah, but I mean, look at them. It's like there may as well be a sign on here saying look at my boobs."

Ashlyn put her hand over her mouth, her elbow resting against the table in front of her. She pretended to be invested in rubbing her cheek.

"Seriously, he's creepy. You should do something."

"Ladies, have you talked to your parents about this?"

The teenagers recoiled. She doubted they could have looked more shocked if she'd just sprouted horns.

"Right. I'm not saying there's nothing to it, but my priority is to find a missing girl. *Comprende?* Did either of you see anything out of the ordinary?"

The girls looked at each other. The one who had been leading the charge against Mr. Radcliff ran her fingers through her silky blonde hair. "No. Nothing odd, nothing unusual."

"What about this church group? Did they just show up?"

"They come every month. Regular booking," the brunette said.

"Did anyone ask about them?"

Both girls shook their heads.

"And who would have known they were coming?"

"Well, anyone who works the front desk would know. It was in the book." The blonde, whose name was Stacey, leaned back against her chair, arms folded over her offensive work shirt, fingers tapping against her own arm. "Or anyone who comes here regularly on a Sunday night, I guess."

"Can you think of some regulars who come in on Sunday nights?"

The girls glanced at each other again, and the brunette, the follower, shrugged.

"Shouldn't you, you know, have a warrant or something?" the blonde said. All serious, like she'd just had her first original thought.

Ashlyn tried to keep her mouth from curling into a frown as she counted to ten in her head. These girls were driving her mad. Under any other circumstances it would have been comical to see Tain handle them. As it was, she could barely stomach their self-centered bull. "I only need a warrant if I suspect someone is hiding evidence from me. Do you have some information about this crime in your head that I should get a subpoena for?"

The girls giggled, the brunette, Chloe, blushing. "I just don't want to get in trouble with my boss."

"I assure you, it won't be a problem." Ashlyn slid a pad of notepaper across the table with a pen. "Just write down the names of anyone you can think of who's usually here on Sunday nights. And anyone who worked recently that knew the church group would be here."

Tain introduced himself and extended his hand.

The blond man with the quick smile returned his firm grip. "Luke Driscoll." The smile vanished as soon as he said his name, like it was an automatic reaction that had slipped out instinctively when he introduced himself, and that he'd suddenly remembered why the RCMP officer was there.

"I understand you're in charge of the church group."

"That's right. We come here once a month, sometimes more in the summer. Just a way to give the kids a change of scenery, a break from the monotony of church services."

"And which church is that?"

"St. Francis's."

"Anglican?"

"Catholic."

"So that would make you . . . ?"

That quick smile returned, without a hint of annoyance. "A volunteer. Not a priest."

"Okay." Tain made a note as he glanced down at the left hand. No ring. "Do you remember seeing anyone unusual, anyone watching the kids when you came in?"

The smile faded as Luke shook his head. "Everyone was in a great mood. We were chatting. We got in quickly. I guess I wasn't paying much attention to who else was around."

"Your group comes here once a month?"

"Yes, that's right."

"How do you decide when you're coming?"

"Third Sunday of the month. We always come the third Sunday of the month."

"And who would know about that?"

"Everyone who goes to our church." He frowned and then shrugged. "Anyone who visited and actually read the church bulletin could know. It's on our monthly calendar."

"What about your volunteers? You have the same group every time?"

"More or less. Sometimes there's a married couple, but they're on holidays."

Tain wrote down their names anyway, as well as the names of the other volunteers. "Can you think back to when you were here last month? Did you notice anyone then? Anyone on any of your previous swim nights who paid attention to your group?"

Luke's face was blank as he stared at Tain, then shook his head. "Really, we've never had any problems. Not that I've been aware of. And I do ask our volunteers to let me know about anything. You can't be too careful these days, you know?"

He looked over Tain's shoulder, and Tain turned to see what had caught Luke's attention.

"You're a real mess, Ashlyn."

She had soot smudged across her nose and on her cheek. Her dark eyes lacked their usual spark, and she'd clipped her hair, which was a beautiful shade of brown with highlights, back hastily. Pieces were falling forward, wisps framing her face.

"You're not much better, Tain."

He looked down at his ash-covered clothes. "No, I suppose not."

Ashlyn looked from him to Luke Driscoll but didn't introduce herself.

"Mr. Driscoll is the volunteer who organizes the church swim nights. They come here once a month, on the third Sunday of the month, but they've never had any problems."

"Constable Hart," she said, then looked at Tain. "I didn't get much out of the staff."

"What about a membership list?"

"Only after I threatened the manager."

"You what?"

She held up her hand. "Don't worry. I told him I was following your orders."

"Ashlyn . . ."

"Relax. Mr. Radcliff's staff couldn't wait to start filing complaints about his perverted ways. He's not going to say anything to attract more attention to himself. And I got everything we need. A membership list, a staff list, security tapes for the past two weeks and copies of the maintenance logs. No chance for these guys to doctor the records or conveniently misplace anything. What's next?"

Tain almost smiled. "Are you differing to my leadership?"

"Hell, no," Ashlyn said, and her cheeks reddened. She glanced at Luke Driscoll. "Sorry."

He smiled and shook his head. "Don't worry about me. Can I ask you something?"

"Sure."

"Have you two been in a fire?"

Ashlyn looked at Tain. "In a manner of speaking, yes."

Luke's face wrinkled with unasked questions, but Tain spoke this time. "We need to talk to all the children in your group."

For the first time since Tain had started talking to Luke Driscoll, he sensed some tension in the young man. Luke's shoulders stiffened and his eyes narrowed when Tain told him what they needed. "Don't we need to have their parents present?"

"This isn't an interrogation," Ashlyn said. "You or your volunteers can be present. We just need to ask the kids if they saw anything."

"But you've already asked the volunteers with our group."

"Sometimes kids see things they don't tell the adults about."

Luke stared at her for a moment, and Tain noticed she gave him one of her more innocent smiles before he nodded slowly. "All right. I'll come with you."

"Finally," Lori muttered, turning into the driveway.

She pressed a button and watched the garage door pull up, shake, then stop no more than a foot off the ground.

Lori pressed the button again. She heard a groan from the garage, and the door shuddered as it descended back to the pavement.

"Damn thing." She pressed the button again. Nothing.

She left the car in the driveway and went in the front door. A passing glance at the answering machine was all it took to know there weren't any messages to deal with. Lori went straight into the kitchen, made a plate of crackers and cheese and cold cuts, poured a glass of wine and went down the hall to the master bathroom.

A quick rinse of the tub was all that was needed before she started the water running. A relaxing evening, a soak in the tub and maybe some sleep before Vish got home would do her good. She reached around her waist and unbuttoned her skirt, kicking it into the corner. She started unbuttoning her blouse as she walked through the doorway to the bedroom, then rummaged through a pile of books on the nightstand, looking for the book on sailing that Vish had been nagging her to read.

It wasn't on his side of the bed, so she walked around to her side, figuring he must have put it on her nightstand as a hint. Sure enough, there it was, propped precariously on the corner. Vish's solution to all their problems, problems he thought were so small. They'd sail off into the sunset and it would be like the past four months never happened. Yeah, Vish was a dreamer. She picked it up and started walking back to the bathroom door, wriggling one arm out of her blouse and then the other, letting the shirt fall to the floor.

The minute they climbed onto the bus the chatter stopped, and then a girl called from the back, "When are we going home?"

"Soon. These police officers need to talk to you first, though." Luke stepped back, gesturing at Tain and Ashlyn.

"What we need . . ." Tain started.

"Are you really a police officer?"

"You don't look like a police officer."

"What's all over your clothes?"

"You stink."

"Can I see your badge?"

Tain glanced at Ashlyn, who was twisting her mouth the way she did when she was trying not to laugh. And obviously too busy trying to conceal her amusement to bail him out.

"Uh, you know, that's a good question. Just because somebody says they're a police officer, it doesn't mean they are." Tain pulled out his ID and passed it to the closest child. Child? What did you call kids ten and eleven years old, anyway? To him, they were all kids. "It's always good to check when somebody you don't know wants to talk to you."

"Okay." The kid passed on the ID. "So you really are a cop. Why do you stink?"

"Do any of you watch the news?" Tain asked.

There was a murmur of assent.

"Did you see that fire on TV?"

"That building that burned down yesterday?" a freckle-faced boy three rows back said. "Yeah, I saw that."

"That's where we were before we came here."

"Uh, buddy, the fire was yesterday."

Tain glanced up at the kid who'd spoken. A preteen punk in the making, slouched back in the last seat, Gameboy in his hand.

"That's right. It was. We went back today to look for evidence in the building. You can't really do that when it's on fire."

The rest of the kids laughed, and the insolent one looked up, giving Tain half a second of his undivided attention before he scowled and turned back to his game.

"Satisfied?" Tain asked as his ID was passed back to him. A young girl near the front put up her hand.

"Are you her boss?"

"No."

"Then why don't you let her talk?"

Ashlyn glanced at Tain and then the girl, a skinny child with a serious face and long, brown braids. "Constable Tain is just anxious to ask if any of you saw anything that might be helpful. It really is very important."

A few children exchanged glances, but there was silence on the bus, except for the beeps coming from the Gameboy.

"None of you saw anybody hanging around? Anyone who looked suspicious?"

More glances, a few murmurs whispered between friends, but nothing.

"What about on previous swim nights?" Tain asked. "Any of you remember seeing anyone a bit unusual, someone who seemed to be really interested in your group or in Lindsay?"

Still no response. Luke gestured for Tain to move aside, and he stepped forward. "Don't be afraid to tell them anything. If you know something, it's important you tell the police. Even if it turns out to be nothing, you won't be in trouble. It's just . . . it might help us find Lindsay."

"Did you see that?" Ashlyn whispered to Tain.

"What?"

"The murmurs, the red faces? Those boys saw something."

Luke had finished, and there was silence.

"Look," Tain said, "we can take care of this now, you can go home and we won't be bothering you again. Or we can drive back to the church, get your parents, take you down to the station and each of you can wait while we ask your friends one by one if anyone saw anything. We've got all night."

A loud bleep was followed by a curse, and the boy at the back let his hand fall against his leg. "Geez, man. It's not like it can help you."

"We don't know that," Ashlyn said. "Right now anything, even something that might seem small and insignificant, could be very important."

"It was a guy. He's always hanging around the change rooms when we're in there."

"What does he look like?" Tain flipped open his notepad.

"Wait a second," Luke said. "How do you know about this, Marvin? When did you see him?"

"He's a peeper. He comes into the change room and hides behind the lockers in the far corner."

"Wha . . ." Luke started to ask. Ashlyn cut him off.

"You mean the boys' change room, right?"

Marvin nodded. The other boys, who'd turned around to watch him, slid down in their seats, nodding as well.

"See, I told you it wouldn't help," Marvin said, shrugging his left shoulder.

"Describe him for us," Tain said.

"It's not like I got a good look. I wasn't trying to give him a free show."

The rest of the kids snickered and jeered until Luke told them to settle down.

"Whatever you tell us can help," Ashlyn said. "We're going to check him out. Even if he doesn't have Lindsay, he shouldn't be spying on you."

Lindsay groaned as she opened her eyes, but all she could see was darkness. As her senses returned, she realized the humming wasn't coming from inside her head but from outside, muffled through whatever she was stuck in.

She realized she was no longer being carried in someone's arms, but that the gentle rocking was from a moving vehicle. For one quick second the experience was no different than waking up late at night after a sleep in the back of her parents' van when they were on their way home from camping. But she couldn't see the blur of streetlights and headlights zipping past the windows, and as she tried to lift her hands to her face to push off whatever was blocking her view, she realized they were tied together and that the rope that bound them must be tied to something else because she couldn't move them very far at all.

She tried to wriggle her feet around, but her knee bumped up against something. Solid, not spongy. Lindsay nudged it again. A tire.

*I'm in a trunk. What am I doing in a trunk?*

Lindsay squeezed her eyes shut, trying to think, though she wasn't sure why she did that. Nothing could distract her anyway, other than the sudden squeal and the bump as she felt her body jerk before the car started moving at a steady pace again.

She remembered slapping Marvin's hand when he tried to pinch her bum, the way they'd lined up to go into the pool, Marvin pinching the clasp on her necklace and making it come undone so that it fell down her shirt and she had to fish it out of her bra, Joanne telling her not to dawdle, a bit of shoving as they walked down the hall, trying to put the necklace back on, Marvin twirling it around, hanging it over her ear, pinching her shoulder, squeezing the skin at the back of her neck, brushing her hair behind her ear, Joanne hassling her to come on.

All the other girls were almost ready when she got into the change room, and she had to hustle. She'd just pulled her swimsuit on, pulled out her ponytail and reached up to redo her hair when she realized the necklace was missing. It wasn't around her neck or her ear.

She'd grabbed her shirt and bra, but the necklace wasn't there. It wasn't clipped to her jacket either, and it hadn't fallen into her pants or shoes.

Lindsay had crouched down, looking around under the bench. There was no sign of her chain.

"Come on, Lindsay," Joanne had called from the other side of the partition, the one separating the showers from the change room.

"Just a minute," she'd called back, knowing she would be in serious trouble if she lost her necklace. It had been a special gift from her grandmother. She'd been bugging her mom to take her to get the clasp fixed because it seemed to always come undone if someone bumped it. Every time they came to the pool it was the same old story, with Marvin fiddling with the clasp. And every week in church, same thing.

Last time she'd gone to get a gift engraved for a baptism she'd asked about fixing the clasp. They couldn't do it that day, and she hadn't wanted to part with the necklace when she had a special church event coming up. She'd decided to wait to have it repaired. Big mistake.

She'd stepped out into the hallway, guessing it must have come off again and she hadn't noticed. Lindsay had turned right, working her way back toward the entrance. . . .

The car jerked again, and her head bumped against something hard and cold. Then the humming stopped, and she lay still, heart pounding in her ears as she wondered what was going to happen next.

Ashlyn and Tain walked down the hall toward the change rooms. It looked like any generic hallway in a rec center: concrete walls, white paint with stripes, nothing that stood out.

"They were horsing around here, as they walked down the hall," Ashlyn said.

"And the girls went in here." Tain turned and went into the ladies' change room. Ashlyn followed. "According to Joanne, their group would have been here."

Ashlyn flipped back a few pages in her notebook. "Yes, that looks right. All the other girls were ready, except Lindsay. They went around here, to shower and go out to the pool. Joanne stood at the door." Her voice trailed off to silence for a moment before she returned from the shower area. "And everything checks out. She had a clear line of sight to exactly the point where everyone was waiting, and she should have been able to hear Lindsay from where she was. There's nothing obviously wrong with the statements so far, at least, not that I can see."

"Me neither. So we have an honest church group that's been telling us the truth."

Ashlyn rubbed her forehead. "Or we really should go to bed and come back to this when we're thinking straight."

"Tempting."

An officer stuck his head in the doorway. "I think we've found something," he said. "Out back, not too far from the fire escape that's broken."

Tain nodded. "Keep it where you found it. We'll be right there."

"So, either someone came in and grabbed Lindsay . . ." Ashlyn's mouth twisted while she tapped her pen against her notebook.

"And nobody saw them, and they managed to get Lindsay without her making a sound." Tain shook his head. "Not buying that as the most likely scenario."

"Or Lindsay went back out into the hall for some reason."

Ashlyn walked back out into the hallway, Tain at her heels. She looked around on the floor and then up at the ceiling. "There. Security footage. We should check that tape first."

"Good thinking. But why would she come back into the hallway?"

"Sneak a kiss with a boy? The charming Marvin, perhaps."

Tain nodded. "Not sure about the charming bit, but a boy could explain it. The video should prove it one way or the other."

"Let's assume Lindsay came to the hallway herself. Whatever she was doing or planning to do, someone grabbed her. They took her here." Ashlyn walked down the hall, past the door to the men's change room, past the vending machines, into a little used corridor. "And went out there."

"The broken fire door. Walk right through and nobody even notices it was used." It was propped open now, an officer standing there. He pointed at some officers about thirty feet away. One was the officer who'd spoken to Tain and Ashlyn only a few minutes before.

"If they really did find something the theory holds water," Ashlyn said.

"What have you got?" Tain asked as soon as he and Ashlyn had covered the distance.

The other officer held up an evidence bag with a necklace in it. "Could have belonged to the girl."

Tain took the bag and held it up. "What do you think?"

"That's some sort of religious symbol," Ashlyn said.

"Sacred Heart," the other officer supplied with a shrug. "That's what it's called. The Sacred Heart."

"That's Catholic, right?" Ashlyn asked, looking at Tain.

"Catholic girl, Catholic group. We'll need to check with the kids, see if it's hers. Where did you find it?"

They pointed out the exact place on the ground, between a tree and a parking spot in a secluded area in the back of the complex, well away from passersby.

"If our guy parked back here he knows this place." Tain looked at Ashlyn.

She nodded. "Fits with him knowing about the broken fire door."

"Good work," Tain said to the uniformed officers.

"We still have a few patrols combing the area, just in case," the shorter, chubbier of the two officers said. His radio crackled, and the message came through loud and clear. Lindsay Eckert's parents were waiting for them.

"Tell them we're on our way." Tain watched Ashlyn's face fall and felt his own shoulders sag as they turned back toward the building. It felt like he'd already dealt with enough distraught parents for one lifetime.

"Mr. and Mrs. Eckert. My name is Ashlyn Hart. This is Tain." Ashlyn paused when she saw the Eckerts looking at their soot-covered clothes. "We were at an arson scene when we were called here."

The Eckerts nodded as though that made perfect sense to them. As though they were seasoned veterans, used to having the police get pulled off one case to come deal with their family tragedy. Ashlyn sat down across from them, and Tain sat beside her. "We want to assure you that we're doing everything possible to find Lindsay," he said, hoping his words didn't sound as hollow as they felt to him. The Eckerts appeared to be already well past denial.

"And what is that, exactly?" Mrs. Eckert asked. Her face was blank, emotionless as she looked at Tain.

"We're canvassing the area. Constable Hart and I have already spoken to all the witnesses, and we've got membership lists for the recreation center, the security footage from the cameras, and we'll follow up with every single person who was in this building today. This is a very public place. Someone will have seen something that can help us."

Mrs. Eckert's expression didn't change. "In other words, you've got nothing."

Tain glanced at Ashlyn. She reached into her pocket and extracted the bag.

"Do you recognize this?" she asked, holding it up.

The blank mask on Mrs. Eckert's face cracked as she gasped and a tear rolled down her pale cheek. "That's Lindsay's necklace. Her grandmother bought it for her. Sterling silver. She wore it everywhere."

Mrs. Eckert reached for the bag, and Ashlyn pulled her hand back.

"I'm sorry. Right now, this is evidence. We'll make sure you get it back when—" She looked at Tain. "Well, when we close the case."

"And when will that be? There have been other children. Just yesterday, another girl, and now our Lindsay . . ."

"Mr. Eckert, I'm not going to lie to you and tell you this will be easy." Tain sighed. "The only thing I can tell you is that we're going to do everything we possibly can to find your daughter."

He stood up and Ashlyn did as well. Tain handed Mr. Eckert a card. "Day or night, you call me if there's anything I can do."

For a moment, Ashlyn and Tain both leaned against the wall of the recreation center outside the manager's office.

Then Ashlyn pushed herself off the wall and started walking back down the hallway toward the change rooms.

"What is it?" Tain asked.

"What if our guy was waiting for an opportunity? Wouldn't this be a good place to watch from?"

She stepped beside the vending machine. "I can see about two-thirds of the hallway from here, and if I move just a bit, I can see the entrance to the ladies' change room."

"It would be concealed, easier for him to stay unnoticed."

"Now that we have the necklace identified as our victim's, it gives this theory about her coming into the hallway a lot of strength."

"Maybe we should have asked her parents if she had a boyfriend."

"There'll be time for looking through her diary and such later." Ashlyn rubbed her temples. "Did you see her parents? If Lindsay was the type who might have snuck off to be with a boy, I doubt she told them anything."

"She's a bit like you, then."

"Excuse me?"

"I bet you never told your parents anything you were up to."

When she'd first met Tain their fights had been real and continual. She'd taken him for a sexist jerk, and he was happy to let her think of him as such. Time and experience had proven he wasn't like that, but he was still arrogant, opinionated, and he'd defy authority on a moment's notice if he believed he was right.

Others knew him to be aloof. In the early days Ashlyn would have maintained he didn't know a damn thing about women, yet he had her pegged. She suppressed the grin that was rising, and then her face fell. "Shit. What now?" she murmured.

Tain turned as Sergeant Daly approached. It looked like all the blood had drained from Daly's face.

"You've worked the scene, talked to the witnesses?"

They both nodded.

"Informed the parents?"

"Yes, sir," Tain said.

"What else do you need to do?"

"We need these vending machines and the walls here, as well as the fire door, dusted for prints. The forensic identification section ne—"

"I'll deal with the FIS. I want you both to go home."

"But Steve—"

"But nothing, Ashlyn. When was the last time either of you slept?" He paused. Their inability to answer spoke for itself. "You're no good to anyone if you're exhausted."

"We've already got the security tapes, membership lists, staff list and maintenance logs for the recreation center. We talked to all the kids who were here with Lindsay, as well as the chaperones. We also found this," Ashlyn pulled the evidence bag from her pocket again. "The officers located it out in the back parking area, in a reasonably secluded spot between a parking stall and some trees. We think our guy grabbed her, took her out the broken fire door and to his vehicle."

Daly frowned. "It sounds like this guy was familiar with this facility."

"We hope so," Tain said. "It might give us our first solid lead."

"Okay, go. I don't want to see either of you until nine tomorrow morning." Daly looked them over. "And try to dress up a bit. We're having a sit-down with Burnaby. The officers working the Darrens and Bertini cases are coming to review all the material from our two girls and compare it with the two from their district."

Ashlyn groaned. "That should be fun."

Daly glared at Ashlyn. "They weren't too happy we went ahead and informed the family about Isabella Bertini without contacting them. I know," he said as Tain threw his hands in the air, looking as though he was about to protest. "You didn't do anything wrong."

"But we can't look a gift horse in the mouth either, right?" Tain scowled.

"At the end of the day, there'll be some hard questions about our inability to stop someone from preying on young girls in this area. This guy started off on Burnaby's patch. Now he's on ours. We're not going to let him go any further, but we're also not going to let people point fingers at us. If more headway had been made on the disappearance of Julie and Isabella before, we might not even have two more missing girls to look for now."

Tain shook his head. "They'll be quick to remind you that you only assigned one officer from the Tri-Cities to work the case with them, despite the apparent connection between jurisdictions."

"You let me worry about that, Tain. Until two days ago, this was still a Burnaby case. Now it's ours. We can't cut it in two like Solomon's baby and each take half. We have to look at the whole thing together and find out how this guy is working. And fast. And that's why I want you both to go home, have a shower and go to bed."

"Let's go, Tain. Before he offers to come tuck us in."

"Ashlyn." Daly practically growled her name.

She smiled back. "Don't worry. We'll be ready tomorrow."

"Nine AM. Don't be late."


Lori's planned glass of wine had turned into a full bottle retrieved from the kitchen and ready to be discarded into the recycling bin. The water had long since lost its warmth. She pulled the plug and started the shower, felt the tension in her muscles ease with the pulse of the spray against her back.

After she finished she walked into the bedroom and pulled a towel over her arms.

The bedroom was filled with shadows, from the dresser and wardrobe, the floor lamps in the corners. The curtains were thick enough to shield those inside from view but not so dense that they masked the external light completely. She couldn't see clearly outside, but she could hear the patter of raindrops against the roof.

It must be later than she'd realized. Lori turned to toss the towel back through the doorway, onto the closet floor, and felt the movement before she saw it. For a second it seemed as though her heart had stopped beating, and then it kicked into overdrive. A black form had sprung forward and grabbed her hard by the forearms. Now she was being twisted around, but not before she'd glimpsed the unconcealed portion of the face, the hard, angry line of the mouth, the way the eyes bulged.

Whatever strength she thought she possessed until that moment was proven useless within a matter of seconds. Her body was contorted, her torso twisted away from the intruder, her legs still facing the direction of the closet. She kicked at him and heard a groan. He let go of her arms, and then she felt the sharp pain of impact against the side of her head.

"Bitch," the voice hissed. This time, he grabbed her by the hips and forced her down against the bed. She tried to reach up behind her to claw at his skin. The click of a blade being popped open echoed in her ears, and she put her arms down as the blindfold was pushed over her head.

# MONDAY

"You're late."

"Some of us were working last night."

Craig felt his eyes widen. "Why? Isn't that what you have subordinates for?"

Daly sank into his chair, collapsing against the structure. "I can't expect them to work forty-eight hours without sleep."

The skin between Craig's brows puckered, and then he nodded. "The child abductions. I thought that Burnaby—"

"The last two kids went missing here in Coquitlam. We can't tell those parents that just because this guy started on the other side of city lines that we're going to let them handle it."

"No, of course not. Two kids in one weekend. Whoever's working that case has their hands full."

"Speaking of having your hands full, what about your cases?"

"Nationwide reports of unsolved rapes are starting to come in, as well as anything that looks similar to our guy's method."

"Right. Lori told me she'd made a call asking for that material yesterday. I told you she's sharp."

Craig glanced away, at the bookshelf behind Daly. He could feel his jaw clench.

"Your face always twists like that when you're angry."

"What difference does it make? All that matters is that we solve this."

"But it still pisses you off that she wants to take your credit."

"You're the one who told me I needed to work on being a team player. It doesn't seem to me like I'm the one who has a problem with that in this partnership. The pull down is always stronger. Don't you think you should give me a partner who's going to make me work with them?"

"Like I don't have enough problems already. Talk about mission impossible."

"I'm not that bad."

Daly leaned back, rubbing his forehead, eyes closed. "Name one partner you've had that you'd like to work with again."

"Ashlyn."

The bit of color exhaustion hadn't claimed already started to ebb. "Have you two kept in touch?"

Craig opened his mouth to speak and then drew a deep breath. "No."

"So what makes you think she'd like to work with you again?"

Craig shrugged. "I didn't say she would. The question was which partner would I like to work with again, and I'd like to work with her."

Daly glanced down at his desk for a moment, his face unreadable, even to Craig's experienced eye. "I imagine that case must bring up a lot of painful memories for all of you."

"It wasn't all bad." Craig forced himself not to look away, to block out the memories.

"Good Lord, that's like the equivalent of you saying you had a good time."

Craig frowned. "Getting back to Lori, though, she's late."

Daly glanced at the clock on the wall. "And I have a meeting to get ready for. Surely you didn't come in here to tattle on her?"

"No, that wasn't the point." Craig sighed, lifted his tall frame up from the chair, pushing his tousled hair back from his face. "But I'm not happy to be working with someone who knocks off early, shows up late and wants to take all the credit when they do decide to come to work."

"Noted. I want a progress report by noon."

"You mean you'll be out of your meeting by then?"

Daly closed his eyes and rubbed his temples as he leaned back in his chair. "If I'm still in one piece, yes."

"Okay. Noon it is. Are you buying?"

"Breakfast wasn't enough? And you need a haircut, Craig," Daly called after him.

Craig smiled as he walked away.

Ashlyn and Tain sat down across from their counterparts from Burnaby. She noticed they barely glanced at Tain, but she felt eyes lingering on her as she sat down and tried hard not to scrutinize them back.

Of course, they would have already met Tain. She glanced up with a polite, fleeting smile and turned her attention to the end of the table.

"Tain, have you met Sergeant Quinlan?" Sergeant Daly asked.

"Yes, sir."

"Good. Then I think I just need to introduce Constable Hart. Ash—"

"Constable Ashlyn Hart?" Sergeant Quinlan asked her, a warm smile spreading across his face. Fit, short brown hair, she guessed about twenty years older than she was, but nothing about him that really stood out, other than that he was the mirror image of the fire chief.

"That's right, sir."

"I've heard good things about you."

Ashlyn quickly averted her glance from Daly's face. "You must be Chief Quinlan's brother."

"That's right. He's been very impressed with your work on the arson investigation."

Ashlyn forced herself to avoid looking at Tain. "Thank you, sir."

"And this is Constable Urquhart and Constable Mullins," Sergeant Quinlan said. Both constables nodded at her.

The woman, Mullins, had short dirty-blond hair and dark eyes. She frowned. "Have you been reassigned from the arson investigations?" she asked Ashlyn.

Urquhart, who looked every bit the average guy with absolutely nothing unique about his features, from his regulation-length brown hair to his average height and brown eyes, said nothing.

Ashlyn looked at Daly, who cleared his throat. "That's part of what we'd like to address here. Ashlyn was already on the scene of the arson fire on Saturday when Isabella's body was recovered. It may seem tenuous as this point, but both Julie Darrens and Isabella Bertini were recovered from the scene of arson fires that have been linked. One of the things we want to look at is a connection between the arsons and the abductions."

Mullins's eyes narrowed. "I thought there were now six arsons that were linked."

Ashlyn nodded. "That's right."

"But we've only recovered two children, and two more are missing. The numbers don't exactly add up."

"Let's not be so quick to jump to negative conclusions." Sergeant Quinlan held up his hand. "It's definitely worth checking to see if there's a connection."

Mullins arched an eyebrow and stared down at the table, her grip on her pen tightening as her jaw clenched.

Ashlyn pretended to scratch her neck and took the opportunity to pull her shirt up slightly. She could feel Quinlan's eyes lingering on her and was fighting the urge to squirm in her chair.

This was going to be a long meeting. She reached for a glass of water.

Craig tossed another folder on the negative file and rubbed his eyes with his thumb and forefinger. A quick visual survey convinced him he hadn't yet covered a tenth of the reports he had to wade through.

A glance at his watch told him it was already half past ten. He didn't know what was worse, being stuck with a partner you had little use for, or relying on her to help do the leg work only to have them fall short.

He started reviewing the files with a different system.

Anyone with a connection to the lower mainland or something in their MO that correlated to the current crimes was flagged. Everyone else was tossed aside.

It wasn't the type of methodical background he normally went for. He remembered going over files with Ashlyn, watching her work a hunch, seeing her take the initiative on a case.

There'd been other partners he'd respected. Other partners he'd crossed the lines with, he reminded himself. Ashlyn had always been different. Maybe it was because she knew more about him than any of the other women ever had, and they'd still been able to work together, to even forge a bit of trust.

He'd meant to call her. Every time he picked up the phone . . . He sighed as he flipped open another file.

There was no sense beating himself up about it now. Not with a ton of work and a deadline.

And a deadbeat partner, he thought as he looked at the empty desk across from him.

"Constable Nolan?"

Craig spun in his chair. "Yes. What can I do for you?"

"I'm Constable Sims. I was supposed to look into some information for Constable Tain. Have you seen him?"

Craig opened his mouth to speak and then realized he didn't have a clue what to say. "Ah, sorry. No."

Sims glanced at his watch. "He must still be in his meeting with Sergeant Daly. If you see him, could you tell him I was looking for him?"

"Sure."

Craig stared at the straight back as it moved away. Could there be another Tain working for the RCMP? Something in Craig's gut told him he already knew the answer, leaving him to wonder what the hell Tain was doing meeting with Daly.

And why his dad had failed to mention that Tain was working in the Tri-Cities.

"This is what we do know. Julie Darrens was abducted on June fourteenth. That's the date of the first arson we have in this particular set. Isabella Bertini was abducted July eighth. That was the date of the second arson we've definitely linked. Julie Darrens's body was found at the fire on July twenty-fifth. I have another fire on July eighteenth, which doesn't seem to tie in at this point. Isabella's body was found at a fire on August eighteenth, and we were at the scene of the sixth fire yesterday when we got the call about Lindsay Eckert. I wouldn't exactly call that a thin link."

The dark eyes narrowed and Zoe Mullins turned her glare away from Ashlyn to the end of the table.

"But how does this help us with the case? As far as I can tell, we have no more leads now than we did a week ago, and yet we've recovered another body and have two more children missing."

"We do have evidence to review from last night," Ashlyn said. "There's a security tape from the hallway and we've reconstructed the abduction. A necklace Lindsay was wearing was recovered, which gives us a clear route to work with, something we don't have for Taylor Brennen. We're confident that whoever took Lindsay was familiar with Southside Recreation and Fitness Center. They used a fire door with a broken alarm, which meant nobody would notice when it was opened. Our guy waited in a secondary corridor that clientele had no reason for using. He parked in a secluded area around the back, near some trees. He didn't just get lucky. He knew what he was doing."

"We're still waiting on fingerprint results from where we believe the perp was hiding," Tain added. "It's the best lead we have so far."

"Do any of the members have records?"

"That's next on the list. Tain and Ashlyn are going to have their hands full reviewing the material we have so far," Daly said. "We'll let you know if there are any leads that come up as a result of the information we have."

Zoe's eyes narrowed again. "You mean none of this material has been reviewed? It's been about fifteen hours since Lindsay Eckert went missing, and with every second the trail is getting colder. What has your staff been doing?"

"Constable Mullins, Constable Hart and Constable Tain have been operating on my orders. Neither had slept since Friday. I ordered them to get eight hours, and I closed the scene personally. As much as I agree that the first hours are critical, we have to be pragmatic with this investigation. We now have four girls who've been abducted. Two were abducted this weekend, and the body of a third was recovered this weekend as well. Constable Hart is also still working the arson investigation, and there have been two fires this weekend. My officers simply cannot work five cases in a row without rest and be expected to perform their duties. To be blunt, until this weekend, this was your case. Your unit has had it for over a month, and has worked two abductions and one body recovery during that time. These two have dealt with more in the past forty-eight hours than you have in the past forty-eight days."

Ashlyn saw Zoe bite her lip and turn her head sharply, directing her gaze at her notepad.

"Sergeant Daly is right," Quinlan added. "We can't expect everyone to work until they drop. We have to pace ourselves and make sure we're sharp, focused. Tired officers make sloppy mistakes. This isn't a sprint. It's a marathon."

"Not that we expect to work banker's hours while this case is going," Tain said. "We're prepared to put in whatever time is necessary to get results. I've faced three sets of grieving parents this weekend. As far as I'm concerned, I'm going to do everything I can to make sure there isn't another set of parents added to that list anytime soon."

There was silence at the table. Daly lifted his glass to his lips and took a drink of water. Then he looked up with a polite smile. "Any other questions?"

"What can my team do to help?" Quinlan folded his hands as he leaned forward and turned to look at Daly.

"We need to go through everything there is about these girls," Ashlyn said automatically. "Teachers, school friends, instructors, camp counselors, the names of their dentists and hairdressers. Everything. If our guy is picking specific girls, he has to know them from somewhere. We need to see if there's a link between Julie, Isabella, Taylor and Lindsay."

Quinlan smiled at her. "Absolutely." He turned to his constables with a more intimidating gaze. "Constable Urquhart and Constable Mullins will find out everything, no matter how insignificant it may seem. Start with Julie and Isabella, and then we'll see how far Ashlyn and Tain have gotten. Since they've got a lot of material to go through, we'll work on Taylor and Lindsay if your team hasn't gotten there already," he finished, looking at Daly.

Daly glanced at Tain and Ashlyn, who exchanged a quick look and then nodded. "Right. Everybody knows what we're doing. This isn't about saving face. It's about getting this guy before he hurts anybody else. I suggest we meet back here tomorrow at ten AM. Review everything we have and see if there's anything promising that turns up."

Quinlan and Daly stood and shook hands, and Urquhart and Mullins turned and bolted out the door as quickly as they could as Quinlan walked down to their end of the table.

"It was a pleasure to meet you." He extended his hand, offering Ashlyn a warm smile. The expression cooled a degree or two when he shook Tain's hand.

Once Quinlan and Daly had left the room, Ashlyn glanced at Tain. "I was sure you'd be begging Zoe for her phone number."

"Don't be jealous, Ashlyn. All the women start batting their eyelashes when they see my charming face."

"If I'd known I wouldn't have agreed to work this with you. I don't want to get in the way of true love."

"You know, if I said that I could be up on harassment charges."

Ashlyn smiled at him as they walked down the hall. "You have said stuff like that and worse. And yet you're still blessing us with your presence."

"Until Quinlan hears how I talk to you. He'll have me out on my ass faster than I can say abuse of authority. How do you deal with guys like that?"

She shrugged. "I think I've just tuned it out."

"You were getting a little hot under the collar."

"Is that why you moved closer to me?"

"Like I need an excuse?"

She gave him a light smack on the arm. "Stop it, Tain. We're friends. Old friends, even, by comparison to everyone else around here. And I love the fact that I can relax with you and don't have to go through all that pretense and bullshit, finding my feet with someone I don't know. But you don't need to lay it on so thick."

"I thought that was part of my charm."

"Nothing if not persistent?"

"Squeaky wheels and all that."

Her nose wrinkled as she sat down at her desk, resting her chin against her hand.

"What?"

"I was just wondering what you do with your dog when you have to work for a few days straight."

"Chinook has a great day care. They operate a kennel too, and I know the owner. She's the breeder I got him from. I have a special deal with them, so when I'm working Chinook stays with her."

"I see."

He glanced up at her. She didn't even try to hold back the smile or the twinkle in her eyes.

"Look, she recently got some new purebreds. She's trying to persuade me to do some breeding."

"Is that what you're calling it?"

"Strictly a business proposition."

"How romantic." Ashlyn grabbed the list of Southside Recreation and Fitness Center employees from the top of the pile.

"That was so funny I forgot to laugh," Tain said. He picked up his phone and dialed. "Corporal Winters, please."

"Is that all you have?" Daly asked as he skimmed the notes while he ate.

Craig nodded. "I haven't been able to go through all the reports in detail. So far, I've identified five cases nationally that could fit with our rapist as part of a pattern of escalation, but even those are a bit of a stretch."

"With those rapes leading up to the current ones?"

"It doesn't seem possible that this guy is new. I think he's been at it for a while."

"What about local parolees?"

"Three who are long shots."

"Nobody who's really jumping out at you, who you favor?"

Craig shook his head. "Not yet. But like I said, I haven't read through everything in detail yet."

Daly watched Craig while he took a drink of milk, then asked, "What do you want me to do about this?"

Craig speared a potato with his fork and then glanced up. "What would you do if it was anyone else?"

"Is that really a fair question?"

"It should be."

"I can take Lori off this, no problem. But that leaves you on it alone."

"I'm not sure I see any difference between that and my current status."

Daly reached for the salt. "One way or the other, Lori's got some questions to answer. You don't have to worry about her coming through unscathed."

"But?"

Daly returned Craig's stare. "But you have to stop working alone. If anything, you've gotten worse since you came back to Coquitlam."

"Once you've had a decent partner, it's hard going back to dealing with imbeciles."

"Craig—"

"I know, I know. I have to give people a chance."

"You do, you know. You can't always assume you know best or that other people won't carry their weight." Daly sighed. "So you were right this time. That doesn't mean that next time you won't get paired off with someone better."

Craig looked him straight in the eyes. "I heard something interesting today."

"Oh?"

"You never told me Tain had transferred to Coquitlam."

Daly flinched. "Where'd you hear that?"

"Constable Sims was looking for him."

"Why?"

"I didn't interrogate the guy."

Daly pushed his tray aside. "I wasn't sure how you'd feel about Tain working in the same department as you again."

Craig's cell phone rang. After a few short words he hung up.

"As though this case wasn't bad enough already—"

"Another rape?" Daly asked as he stood up.

"And if it's the same guy, he's officially graduated." Craig let out a deep breath. "This woman's been murdered."

Tain turned away from Ashlyn as he responded to the person on the phone and lowered his voice. "Thanks for getting back to me, Tim."

"You know, when you worked out here in the sticks, you never had to lower your voice. Don't tell me people actually like you now."

"Can't you just turn up the volume on your hearing aid?"

"Know what the best thing about having those things stuck in your ears is, Tain?"

"Enlighten me."

"It's the closest thing to having a mute button for the wife."

Tain laughed. "That's something to strive for then."

"What can I do for you?" There was a quick pause before Tim continued. "Don't deny it. You're lousy at keeping in touch. And you're at work, so there's no way this is a social chat."

"You worked a case some years back," Tain began.

"I worked a lot of cases some years back. You'll have to do better than that."

"John-John."

"John-John? Is he still plying his trade? Filthy slime, that one. What do you want to know?"

"Well, clearly you remember him."

"Oh, I remember that guy. We were looking to put him down for the abduction of a little girl, the kid of one of his working girls. When we got close, the kid suddenly turned up on her doorstep and then the mother skipped town with her. No complaining victim, no remaining witnesses."

"Prosecutor wasn't prepared to take it further?"

"No way. Dropped it. I was always looking for a way to get back at John-John, but he may as well have been playing for the Canucks."

"Why? Always on the road?"

"No, 'cause he skated on everything."

"Shame that bump on the head didn't do something about your sense of humor, Tim."

"Yeah, well, my short-term memory has never come back, you know. One minute I'm following up a lead, and the next I'm being signed up for hypnotherapy."

"Geez. So you could never identify the punks who clobbered you?" Tim had been attacked while working a case. Tain had been reassigned to work it.

One of those cases that became a lingering nightmare, the kind you could never purge from memory, no matter how much you drank or prayed or cried.

"What difference does it make?" Tim said. "You guys— you, Craig, Ashlyn—you got them. Speaking of which, how's Craig doing?"

"I haven't seen him."

"Really?"

"You never even met him, did you?"

"No, but his name lives on around here."

Tain almost smiled. "I'll bet it does."

"What are you looking at John-John for, anyway?"

"You know the missing kids cases that have been in the news?" Tain glanced at Ashlyn, who was staring at her notes just a little too intently. He turned as far as the phone cord would let him. "Well, he might connect to one of them, but I need to keep it quiet. For now."

Tim Winters, Tim Winters . . . Ashlyn's eyes widened as it clicked into place for her. She wondered why Tain would be phoning him.

Ashlyn continued checking the employee list against the fitness center's work schedule. It was all pretty routine, with essentially the same people working the desk in the days prior to the church group's monthly booking, except for one name that had been scratched off and replaced with a standby person because one of the staff had phoned in sick three days earlier.

Doug Fisher. Where did she know that name from? She glanced up at Tain, who had partially twisted away from her in his chair, making it hard for her to hear his end of the conversation. Eavesdropping hadn't been something she'd considered until she saw him taking notes, adding to the book he'd started on the abductions.

What could Tim Winters have to do with this case? She stared at Tain for a moment, thinking he wasn't so different than when she had first met him, after all. He could still be a completely closed book. There were times he made Craig look downright sociable by comparison. She turned back to the lists in front of her, trying not to strain to hear what Tain was saying. If he was holding out on her she was going to kick his ass.

Everything about the room spoke of understated taste. The solid wood bedroom set contrasted with the golden walls. The drapes hung on a pewter rod, but between the gaps in the furniture there was no fancy artwork, no expensive paintings or wall coverings. Just one large picture frame hung above the bed, hosting a collage of images that were presumably memorable moments from the life that had been violently taken only hours before.

"We're ready whenever you are," a man on the coroner's staff said.

Craig glanced at him and nodded. "Give us a few minutes. We'll call you."

The few remaining people left without comment.

"Nitara Sandhu," Craig said quietly. "Twenty-three years old. Recently married."

"He left his stuff behind." Daly nodded at the bed.

"Not that it will do us much good. Looks like a generic blindfold and gag. Handkerchiefs like these could likely be purchased in hundreds of places."

"Generic rope too." Daly glanced at Craig. "So why kill her?"

"The only thing that's different that I can see is that she's East Indian."

"You thinking there's an ethnic angle? Why rape her at all then? Why not just pick another white victim?"

Craig shook his head. "A lot of the Chinese and East Indian families have multiple generations living together. This couple lived on their own in a good neighborhood, much the same as all our other victims."

"What are you thinking? That it was a statement that they didn't belong?"

"Not really. I'm not sure ethnicity had anything to do with it. This guy, he's got no type. Not blondes, brunettes or redheads. Some of these women have been short, some tall. The only thing that they all had in common was that they were home alone, with the exception of the baby, when they were raped."

"You still have to consider the ethnic angle as a possibility," Daly said.

Craig sighed. "I know. I'm not going to dismiss it automatically."

"But your gut tells you this is an escalation."

"Yes, but something still seems odd. He's been very deliberate, very controlled before. This time, he left things behind. It doesn't seem likely that they'll help us connect to him right now, but this is the beginning of an evidence trail that might help us convict him."

"I could see something being left behind if you've been interrupted, if you panicked."

"But he killed her. Not one of the other victims mentioned him choking them during the rape, so she was likely strangled afterward. You take time to kill someone because you've been interrupted but leave evidence at the scene? That doesn't make any sense."

The choking sobs from across the room had finally stopped sometime during the passing hours of darkness. Taylor thought they were well past sunrise now, but she was losing the certainty of conviction she'd had even a day before.

It had startled her when he'd brought in the other girl. She knew better than to try anything again, so she'd sat pressed up against the wall on the far side of the bed, listening to the scraping metal as another cot was added and the shuffling feet were matched by a long, steady *shhhhhh*, as though a heavy-bristled broom was being dragged across the floor.

The stream of light had shone on her for a moment when he'd moved aside, and she'd seen the pale face, the wide eyes, the hard rope gagging the girl's mouth.

Bedsprings creaked as the girl was pushed down on the mattress. Taylor saw the gag removed, and then the shuffling feet retreated, taking the light with them as the door clanked shut.

Then the girl had started to cry.

And the crying had escalated into screams, until at last the door had opened again, not with a plate of bread and a chalice—he'd taught Taylor that word earlier—of water in hand, but a rod and a rope of some kind. Taylor couldn't be sure because she could only see the outline in the dark, until she heard the crack of the whip and the responding cry of the figure on the other bed.

The girl had learned. When the shuffling feet retreated again, she must have pressed herself hard against the bed the way Taylor did whenever her mom gave her a licking and told her to shut her mouth but good or she'd tan her hide again.

"How much of a window do we need?"

"At least an hour, maybe more."

Ashlyn read the label on the video. "This one was activated at five PM. May as well sit back and scan the whole thing."

They watched the images blur by on the screen until the time stamp put the tape at about ten minutes before the church group was due to arrive.

"Ten to six. If our guy was waiting for them, he should be coming down the hall anytime."

They viewed the tape at regular speed. At six past six they could see Luke Driscoll entering the lower right corner of the screen. Within seconds, the rest of the church group was moving into view.

Ashlyn glanced at Tain. "Should we rewind it and watch it again?"

Tain grabbed the remote and rewound the tape without comment. Again, they watched as absolutely nobody went down the hall.

"Not one customer, not a staff person. Nobody."

"We may as well watch what happens now. If our theory is wrong, this is as good a time as any to find out." Ashlyn frowned.

Tain had a pretty good idea how she felt. Four girls, two dead, and here they were, grasping at straws. . . . "I'm just hoping there's something on here that's useful, Ashlyn. Otherwise we won't have a working theory or a lead."

They watched the group of heads moving up the screen, toward the change rooms.

"This angle is good for identifying them coming in, but it's hard to see the kids in the back."

"There she is."

"Where?"

"The one our friend Marvin seems so interested in."

"Looks like Luke is coaxing Marvin to get a move on," Tain said.

"Hello. What was that?"

Tain rewound the tape back thirty seconds, and they watched again.

"Is that a uniform of some kind?" Ashlyn asked.

"Hard to tell. That's the thing with this angle. It's great

for getting the faces of those coming down to the change rooms. But this guy is moving across the hall, keeping his head down, and Marvin's a pretty tall kid."

"Can you rewind it again?"

He did, and they watched it again.

"There, pause it," Ashlyn said.

Tain pressed pause and the image froze on the screen.

"Look at how Lindsay leans forward," Ashlyn said. "Like he bumped her."

"I can't see where this guy goes."

"He looks like he's moving right into the wall on the opposite side of the hall from the change rooms. What was there?"

"Nothing. It looks like it might be a dead space for the tape."

"Not important to monitor because you don't expect people to be creeping up and down the hallway against the far wall."

Tain pressed play, and they watched. "Look. Luke just took a slight step forward and glanced over his shoulder, like somebody moved behind him."

They continued watching until the hall was empty. Ashlyn leaned forward and tapped the screen.

"Look at that. Something shiny on the floor. It wasn't there before."

The tape played for another five minutes or so, and then the women's change room door opened. Lindsay's head emerged, and she glanced over at the door to the men's change room. Then she moved farther into the hallway.

Her eyes were glued to the floor as she let the door fall shut behind her and started walking slowly back toward the entrance.

"Look. She's picking it up."

Tain rewound the tape a few seconds. "Hell. Look at that, when her ponytail falls over her shoulder."

"What am I missing?"

"She's not wearing her necklace, the one her parents identified."

"The one that was found outside." Ashlyn swallowed. "That must be the chain there, what she's picking up."

"He's got the back of his head to the camera now, so we can't identify him."

"So she kneels down to pick up her necklace, and as she stands he grabs her and moves back toward the blind spot along the far wall. God, look how quick that was." Ashlyn shook her head. "This guy was ready. He knew she was coming into that hall."

Tain off shut the tape. "The good news is the theory fits."

"He was definitely waiting for her."

"But how did he know she was coming back into the hall?"

Ashlyn reached for her bottled water. "He bumped her. Remember how she leaned forward? Maybe it was deliberate. Maybe he undid the clasp on her chain."

"I don't know, Ashlyn. Not an easy thing to do without someone noticing. And what would make him so certain that she would go looking for it?"

"He'd be sure if he knew her. It was something important to her."

They sat in silence for a moment, Ashlyn drinking her water, Tain rubbing his eyes.

"We still have to watch the rest of the security footage."

"We will, but right now it's time for us to go to church." Tain stood up and popped the tape out of the machine. "This guy didn't just bump Lindsay. He bumped into Luke Driscoll. Maybe the devoted youth leader can give us a description."

Ashlyn laughed. "You're such a cynic."

"Me, Ashlyn? You're the self-proclaimed atheist."

"Agnostic, Tain. And I'm not talking about faith in higher powers. I'm talking about faith in people."

"In our line of work? Why the hell should I have faith in anybody?"

"You just shouldn't be so quick to suspect the worst in everyone."

"I don't. I happen to think it's highly unlikely you'd go on a killing spree."

She gave him a wry smile. "Gee, thanks for the vote of confidence."

"Of course, it could happen by accident if I let you drive," he said as he snatched the car keys off her desk.

"It could happen on purpose if you keep talking," she muttered, following him out the door.


"Preliminary indications are that she died around midnight, one AM. Ligature marks are obvious, and there's petechial hemorrhaging to support strangulation as the cause of death. Once she's on the table you'll know more. That's all I've gotten from Burke so far."

"Any idea what he used?" Craig asked.

The FIS officer held up an evidence bag with a few neckties in it. "Looks like he double wrapped them together, twisted them a bit to make it like one thick cord and pulled for all he was worth."

"Not that she stood much of a chance. She looks like she was barely five feet tall, and her hands were bound. Any idea if he brought this with him?"

"No such luck. They belonged to the husband."

Craig glanced at Daly as the FIS officer walked away.

"So it was an impulse, not planned," Daly said. "Not like the blindfold and gag and rope that he brings with him."

"And if he'd planned to kill her from the beginning, why not just use the rope? He didn't need to wrap it around her hands half a dozen times."

"Something happened. Something set this guy off."

They watched as the body of Nitara Sandhu was carried past them. A sudden cry came from the room across the hall, and a man lunged forward, falling to the floor as officers tried to hold him back from intercepting the body.

Raw grief. Craig swallowed. Every time he looked into the eyes of one of the living victims it felt like he'd been stabbed in the heart. Now, seeing this man collapse in a heap, crying . . .

"I've got to talk to Inspector Hawkins. We're going to

have the press all over us now." Daly put a hand on Craig's shoulder. "You call me if you need anything."

Craig swallowed and nodded. They could still hear Mr. Sandhu crying as officers moved him back into the other room. "I think we might need victim's services down here."

Daly glanced at the other doorway, his shoulders drooping slightly as he sighed. He nodded at Craig. "I'll call them for you."

*Come on. Somebody having an affair, sneaking out on their folks, anything. No neighborhood is this clean.*

Craig rubbed his forehead. It would be nice if there were places filled with people who were inherently good. Some *Leave It to Beaver* land where the residents did all the normal family things and nobody ever got in serious trouble.

He double checked his notes. There wasn't one house on this street he hadn't been to, and he didn't have a single clue or lead. No, nobody had heard anything. Around midnight? You must be joking. Everyone was asleep.

Craig walked down the road that intersected with the Sandhus' street. At the next intersection, he turned left and began working his way along the homes that shared a lane with the road the Sandhu house was on.

Nothing, nothing, nothing. He knocked on the door to the fourth house.

The woman who answered seemed to be descending back into the earth at a measurable rate per hour, the door handle just barely within her reach. She offered an automatic smile as she blinked up at him and reached for the glasses dangling from the chain around her neck.

Craig smiled back and sighed. The lenses on her frames were almost as thick as the panes of glass in the door.

"I'm sorry to disturb you. My name is Constable Nolan," he said, holding his ID about three inches from her wizened face. "I was wondering if I could ask you some questions."

"You know, don't you?" she said, peering up at him with wide eyes.

"I know?"

"I'm pregnant. We should run away."

"Gran. Alec, geez. What the hell are you doing, letting Gran answer the door to strangers?"

A lanky teenager rushed down the narrow hall, ducking at the last second to avoid a head-on collision with the chandelier.

"Don't let him take me," the woman cried, grasping Craig's arms with her clawlike fingers. "He wants me to himself."

Craig opened his mouth to speak but realized he didn't know what to say. The boy lunged forward, pried Craig loose from her grip and led her away.

"Come on, Gran. Alec," he called.

Another boy, half a head shorter, stepped into the hall and took the woman's hand. "Let's get a snack," he said, disappearing with the woman, who was now prattling on about whether or not they should take the kids and leave the farm.

"Sorry." The elder teen shrugged. "Alzheimer's."

Craig nodded and held up his ID. The boy's eyes narrowed as he studied it, and then his lopsided grin returned. "I'm planning to go to the Depot. Right after graduation." The smile faltered for a split second. "My dad says I have to have a degree before I chase after some thankless job that'll suck the life out of me."

"It's not a bad idea to have a degree anyway. Most of us do now."

"So what's this about? You're plainclothes, so you can't be here about the backyard parties at the end of the street."

Craig felt his eyebrows pinch together. "Well, I'm not, but tell me about them anyway."

The teen shrugged and moved onto the step, pointing down to the end of the block, the end of the street Craig hadn't been to yet.

"See that house there? The one with the satellite dishes on the edge of the roof, right on the corner? Well, they're always getting complaints, making the cops come by late at night to make them shut the music off because they have these parties in their yard that get pretty loud. My dad told us to stay away from them because they got busted for dealing pot."

Craig made a note. "Did they have a party last night?"

The teen nodded. "Yeah."

"Any idea what time they were in the yard?"

"Midnight, I guess. My mom works the three to eleven shift at the hospital, and she usually gets home around eleven thirty. She'd been here long enough to make herself a snack and go yell at Alec for not cleaning his room. I was on my way to bed, and the music came on. Always the same *boom-boom-boom*, making the dogs bark and the windows rattle."

"So they had it on for a while?"

He shrugged. "I put my headphones on."

"I didn't get your name."

"Ryan Lewis."

"Did you see or hear anything else last night?"

Ryan's mouth twisted as he shook his head. "Why? What happened?"

"A woman on the next street was murdered."

His ruddy cheeks blanched. Then the boy seemed to get even taller. "I wish I could help."

"Maybe you can. Here's my card. If you hear anything, let me know. I don't want you to go around snooping," Craig said, trying to mimic the stern tone Daly always used on him for lectures. "But maybe you could ask your mom if she saw or heard anything last night when she came home from work. Even the tiniest thing that doesn't seem important to her could give us a lead."

Ryan nodded, his mouth set in a firm line. "I won't overstep. But I will ask my mom."

"Thanks," Craig said, starting down the steps. He was halfway down the front walk before he turned around. "And ask if she saw anyone unusual around in the past week or so. You never know."

The teen nodded, his curly brown hair flopping with the motion, making Craig smile as he walked away. He pictured a slightly older Ryan Lewis in the red serge with his long hair getting measured by a frowning Steve Daly before Daly launched into a lecture about regulated appearance code.

"What the hell is going on out there, Daly? We've got some sadistic rapist terrorizing the women of this city, and now he's graduated to murder. What's being done to put a stop to this?"

Daly looked up from his desk. He was beginning to feel like all he did was sit at work, offering hollow answers about cases they couldn't make headway on. "Open cases nationwide are being reviewed, and we're looking at local known offenders who might fit the particulars."

"That's management speak bullshit and you know it. What's being done right now?" Inspector Hawkins slammed his hand down on Daly's desk for effect.

As though he needed to drive the point in. Daly waited until Hawkins's red cheeks deflated a bit and he sank into a chair. Then Daly answered.

"Craig is out canvassing the area, trying to find witnesses. He's been through the crime scene and will review all the evidence. He's on top of this."

Hawkins stopped rubbing his chin and stared at Daly as his cheeks went white and then flushed.

"Your little prodigal is working his ass off, is that it? What's Lori doing, making coffee?"

Daly felt his neck burn. "I haven't got a clue what she's doing—"

"Don't you think it's your responsibility to supervise her too? You have to stop pandering to that kid of yours and be a real team leader, Daly."

"You have a son who's an RCMP officer in this district too, Dennis."

"This isn't about me, is it?"

Daly clenched his hands into fists and leaned forward. "I don't know what Lori is doing because she never bothered to show up for work this morning. And she didn't think it might be important to phone in sick or make up some excuse and let us know what the hell is going on."

The color drained from Hawkins's face a second time. Finally, he sprang up from the chair and turned on his heel.

"I'm sorry," he said as he paced the room, arms folded across his chest, with his head down. "I'm just worried. We're going to take a beating over this."

"Look, I know we are. I don't know what more I can do. These rapes are right across the Tri-Cities. We've increased the overtime and circulated every bit of information possible to all officers. At this point, with no profile, with no geographic area to concentrate on . . ." Daly shrugged. "We're up shit creek."

Hawkins stopped pacing. "And what are you going to do about Lori?"

A sharp knock at the door prevented Daly from answering. The door sprang open, and Daly's assistant stuck her head in, glanced at Hawkins but didn't retreat. She extended her hand to pass him a note.

"There's been another rape," she said. "And I think you might want to handle this personally, sir."

Daly felt his heart flailing against his chest as he stood up to take the message. He glanced at the address. "Alderside Road in Port Moody. Doesn't mean anything to me," Daly said as Hawkins snatched the paper from his hand.

He looked up at Daly, his mouth hanging open.

"Get your coat. And call Craig. Hey!" He rushed into the hallway, Daly able to hear him yelling instructions at his assistant. "And tell them to make sure not a damn, bloody person sets foot in this house before we say it's okay." Hawkins barged back into the office, Daly still frozen at his desk, his phone in hand but the number not yet dialed. "What are you waiting for?" Hawkins demanded.

"I . . ." Daly thought better of what he wanted to say, mindful that Hawkins would only tolerate so much candor, even at the best of times, which this clearly wasn't.

He dialed Craig's number and watched Hawkins turn abruptly, rubbing his eyes, his lips moving silently.

Daly felt as though the floor had come out from underneath him. Hawkins looked like he was resorting to prayer.

He swallowed. Here he'd been thinking things couldn't get much worse.

It looked like he was wrong.

Tain tugged on the door. "Churches keeping their doors locked during the afternoon."

"Late afternoon," Ashlyn corrected. "When all those rotten kids are out of school and on the loose. This is the time of day I'd lock up if I lived in this neighborhood. Let's try for a side door."

They followed a narrow walkway around the building.

"This looks promising." Tain nodded at a side entrance with double glass doors. He walked up the steps and pulled on the door on the right, which didn't budge. Then he tried the door on the left.

"Seek and ye shall find," he said, walking inside.

"Maybe next time you'll think of 'knock and the door shall be opened to you,'" an older man said as he stepped into the foyer. He was dressed in black, with the only relief being his clerical collar. "I'm Father Benjamin."

"Tain," he said, holding up his ID. "My partner, Ashlyn Hart."

Only the faintest shadow flickered across his face. "You're here about Lindsay."

"We were hoping to ask Luke Driscoll some questions," Ashlyn said.

The priest's overgrown eyebrows merged into one thick line. "Luke is a respected member of this church, well-liked by all the families. He is very devoted to the youth program, and we're lucky to have him."

Ashlyn and Tain glanced at each other. Unsolicited defense? Tain noticed Ashlyn's eyebrow arch just a touch, and he coughed to conceal the smirk he felt tugging at his mouth.

"It must be reassuring to have such good people helping with the youth in your church. We just need to ask him about someone he may have seen at the rec center last night," Ashlyn said.

The eyebrows disconnected and after a slight pause, Father Benjamin nodded. "You're fortunate. Normally, Luke's at work, but he took a personal day today. He's quite upset about the incident."

The incident? Tain let Ashlyn take the lead, following Father Benjamin along a corridor, up a few steps, through an unmarked door, past a baptismal tank and into the sanctuary. He could see past Ashlyn to the bent head resting against a pew in the second row.

Father Benjamin cleared his throat and stepped aside. Tain nodded his thanks and followed Ashlyn to the first pew, where they sat down, twisting around to wait for Luke to look up.

"There's no news, then?" The voice came, loud and clear despite the fact that the blond head was still lowered against the pew.

"We're following some leads," Ashlyn said, her voice a bit quieter, more hushed than Tain was used to. "That's why we're here."

Luke lifted his head, the tousled hair giving way to the wrinkled brow, the red-rimmed eyes and the tear-streaked cheeks showing a bit of stubble. He stared unblinking at them but said nothing.

"We've been reviewing the security tape from the rec center," Tain told him. "Can you think back to when you were leading the group down the hall, toward the change room?"

"It's, uh, ahem, pretty much all I can think about," Luke choked out, his eyes welling up at first and then his cheeks going red as he cleared his throat. He'd regained enough composure to speak, but his fingers were digging into the wooden bench in front of him.

Tain wondered what had happened to the quick smile and calm composure from the night before. "There was someone who walked around from behind the group and came along the far side of the hallway. Someone you needed to move for, to let them pass."

Luke turned to stare at Ashlyn for a moment and then blinked. "I, uh, I just remember counting the kids, waiting for the dawdlers to catch up. I was only worried about keeping all the kids together."

"So you don't remember anyone moving behind you?" she asked.

"I, uh, I don't know. Why? What does it matter?" Luke's gaze drifted down to his hands and then below, to the back of the pew he was gripping, as though maintaining eye contact was requiring an enormous amount of energy and he didn't have the strength for the task.

Tain saw Ashlyn's quick glance, and he felt the corners of his mouth twisting a bit. "We have reason to think the person who took Lindsay was in the hallway when your group came in."

Luke's head jerked up, and the remaining tinge of color dissipated from his face. "So this guy was right there, right there, and I didn't even notice? What the hell is wrong with me?"

He slumped forward, and his shoulders started to shake.

After a moment, Ashlyn glanced at Tain and then slid off the pew, drifting away down the aisle, studying the architecture.

Tain finally put a hand on Luke's arm. "This isn't your fault."

"Tell that to the parents. They want me replaced as the primary youth worker."

The unsolicited defense and the desperation on Luke's face were starting to make sense.

"We figure this guy, he planned this." Tain pulled out a card and tucked it under the few exposed fingers. "If you do think of anything else, call us."

He stood up and walked toward Ashlyn, who had craned her neck to study one of the stained-glass panels.

"Noah's ark and the expulsion from Eden I get, but what is that?"

"You're asking me?" He shrugged.

"The sacrifice of Isaac," the scratchy voice said from behind them.

They glanced back and moved apart to give Father Benjamin some room between them. He nodded at the representation above the doors to the foyer. "Abraham is commanded by God to sacrifice his only son. Just before Abraham killed the boy with the knife, he heard God tell him his son was spared. He found a ram in the bushes and sacrificed it instead."

"What's the boy, Isaac, lying on?" Ashlyn asked.

"Wood. Abraham was commanded to give his son as a burnt offering to God."

Tain saw Ashlyn glance at him as Father Benjamin led them out into the entry area and opened the main doors for them to leave.

A burnt offering to God. He could picture Isabella in her purple shirt and green pants, placed upon a bed of sticks and straw and some shadowed figure offering a prayer, lighting a match and dropping it into the kindling, setting her funeral pyre ablaze.

Craig felt his stomach twist when he saw the sea of police-related vehicles. He double checked the address. It was the right house. Once he'd parked he got out of the vehicle and reached for his ID.

He flashed his badge and ducked under the crime-scene tape. As he moved toward the front of the group he noticed a few sympathetic glances being sent his way, but most of the people waiting averted their eyes as soon as he was in their line of sight. A gap opened, and he could see his bosses.

Hawkins was treading a footpath to China, and Daly was as white as a glacier. He glanced up, and his eyes met Craig's. Craig swallowed. Whatever was going on here, it was bad. Then Hawkins spun on his heel, saw Craig and almost ran down the front walk to him.

"This needs to be handled by the book. I don't want any shoddy work on this one. I expect you to supervise every minute of the evidence recovery." Hawkins grabbed his shoulder and almost pushed him up the walkway.

"Absolutely," Craig said, trying to keep the confusion he felt from showing on his face. He fought the urge to free himself from Hawkins's grasp. "We'll do everything—"

"You'll do more," Hawkins snapped. "You haven't been able to catch this guy, and he's started killing people. I'm personally supervising this case now, and I expect results."

Craig glanced up and saw the pinch in Daly's cheeks.

"So we have another murder here?" Craig asked.

Hawkins let go of him. "No, we don't. We have a police officer, your partner, who's been raped."

He strode up the remaining part of the walk, unaware or indifferent to Craig and Daly remaining like statues where he'd left them.

Shit. Craig moved forward automatically as Hawkins turned his glare back in their direction, a sudden image of Ashlyn's face flashing through his mind, making his throat constrict and his breath catch.

He knew how he'd feel if it had been Ashlyn. He could only guess that was something like how Hawkins felt about having one of his officers raped.

Hawkins opened the door. Craig glanced at Daly, took a deep breath and followed him inside.

The traffic situation Tain and Ashlyn found themselves in was more comparable to trying to navigate an oversized yacht through a crowded marina than driving on a road. It definitely was not a flowing stream of vehicles. Nobody seemed particularly motivated to get anywhere fast; big gaps were left unfilled, tempting drivers from other lanes to pull in. One person had pulled halfway off the road and put his hazards on, his hand gestures emphasizing the importance of the conversation he'd stopped and blocked traffic for.

Ashlyn heard Tain swear under his breath when they passed that particular motorist and turned toward the window so he wouldn't see her smile.

A year earlier, she hadn't even known his name. When she had met him, she'd developed an instant dislike for him. It was amusing to think back to their early working relationship, him keeping everyone, especially her and Craig, at arm's length.

It had been her first real experience in plainclothes work,

her first opportunity to prove herself capable of handling the challenges of multiple investigations.

Her first chance to test her gut and follow her instincts.

It had been a hell of a case. At the time, she'd felt like she'd gone through it keeping her head clear, remaining somewhat objective. It was only after they wrapped things up that the enormity of it all hit her, and it had almost been a knockout blow. Solving the case had only been the beginning. An internal investigation of their RCMP detachment had followed, along with disciplinary action for some, like Tain, and others had been fired.

The consequences Tain faced had been the toughest thing for her to take. She knew she deserved the same treatment, but he'd shielded her.

He'd even protected Craig.

And without either of them ever saying a word, the one thing she was sure of was that every single one of them had wanted to pull the trigger. . . .

For a while she hadn't been sure whether she could cut this job. The guys, normally stoic, had reeled from the fallout of that case.

Ashlyn squeezed her eyes shut. Even now, after all this time, she didn't want to think about it. Couldn't. She hadn't realized how glad she'd been that she wasn't dealing with the child abductions until she was looking at Isabella Bertini's body. Working with Tain was a blessing and a curse. He was a reminder, but she could joke with him in a way that allowed her to suppress her feelings. No need to worry that he was always second guessing her competency, that she'd be able to keep her emotions in check and do the work.

Even when she doubted herself.

She'd walked away counting the chance to work with Tain as one of the good things about that case. There had been other good things too.

Something she'd thought about the other day, when she'd seen the card in Carl Parks's house, feeling like her heart had just bounced up to the top of her throat. A lot of memories had come flooding back in that moment. Possibilities that had never been explored. But she'd bottled it up and refused to stagger under the force of the recall.

"Are you going to get that?" Tain's voice cut through her thoughts.

"What?"

"Your cell phone. Are you going to answer it?"

Ashlyn blinked, then grabbed her phone, not taking time to look at the caller ID.

"Constable Hart."

"Ashlyn, this is Alison. Alison Daly."

Ashlyn's brow had barely begun to wrinkle when she recognized the caller. Even the split-second hesitation didn't go unnoticed.

"Did I call at a bad time?"

"No, no. I was just . . . I just wasn't expecting it to be you. What can I do for you?"

"I was wondering if you might be free tomorrow night."

"Um," Ashlyn tried to scan her memory for reminders of any pressing engagements and glanced at Tain, who gave her a quizzical glance. "I think I'm free. Providing something doesn't come up at work. I'm working on this case right now. . . ."

The laugh from the other end of the line interrupted her explanation. "Ashlyn, after all these years, you think I don't know a cop's life is never really their own?"

Ashlyn's cheeks burned, despite the fact that Alison couldn't see her. "Sorry. I guess I'm just used to explaining myself."

"That's okay. I understand. I'm planning a little dinner, nothing fancy, for six thirty. Do you have a pen and paper handy? I'll give you the address."

"Is this at a restaurant?" Ashlyn asked, retrieving her notebook as she balanced the phone between her cheek and her shoulder.

The cell cut out, and when the line cleared Ashlyn repeated her question.

"No."

"Oh." Ashlyn swallowed. She hoped this wasn't a setup.

"It's nothing formal. We're having a little house-warming party for . . ."

Ashlyn frowned as the phone crackled in her ear. "Alison?" she asked into the static. Damn pockets. She'd had enough of dead zones when she lived in the mountains.

That thought brought back memories too, but she didn't have time to indulge. The phone cleared, and Alison's voice came back through.

Ashlyn confirmed the address and cut the call.

"Dinner plans, huh?"

"Shit. The cell cut out right when she was telling me who this little get-together's for."

"Does it matter?"

Ashlyn glared at him. "What would you think if you were the single person invited by a married friend to some stranger's house for a dinner party?"

"That I don't have to cook."

She wrinkled her nose at him. "Very funny."

"Why do women obsess about stuff like that? So you got invited to dinner. So some single guy is probably going to be following you around panting all night. It's not like you said you'd marry him."

"Following me around panting?"

"Oh, you know how it is. Single guy meets a cute girl and mutual friends have thrust them together . . ." Tain shrugged.

"Cute?"

He glanced at her. "What's wrong with that?"

"Beautiful, stunning, vivacious, pretty. All the words in the dictionary and you come out with cute." She shook her head as she looked out the window. "Makes me feel like I'm twelve."

"Hey, it could have been worse. These days, you have to be careful what you say to anyone if you're a single man. Heck, forget single. Guys are better off keeping their mouths shut, their eyes averted and not even referring to women cops as, well, women."

She groaned. "You know I'm not going to get bent out of shape over being called—"

"Cute?"

Ashlyn smiled and shrugged. "Yeah, not even that will get you into any real trouble."

"At least, not a formal complaint that will go in my file."

"I won't hold it against you."

Tain's face sobered. "So what's next?"

"I'd like to talk to FIS and to Daly."

"Any thoughts you'd like to share?"

"Well, I want to know if we got any prints from the recreation center. After all, that could be a big lead if we get a hit."

"You think that's likely?"

She shrugged. "I don't know. I mean, I think this guy had planned this. He was organized. He came prepared."

"You think he wore gloves."

Ashlyn nodded. "Likely. But if he didn't, then I bet money he's in the system somewhere, or should be."

"That's something that's been bothering me. He's so efficient. No evidence trail, no tip-offs to the media to taunt us in our investigation, no witnesses."

"It makes me think we should be looking at every open child abduction, see if there is anything that might connect to this case and give us a clue."

Tain shook his head. "God, you know what happens when you start looking at past cases."

The face of Michael Dunahee plastered on bulletin boards and milk cartons from one coast of Canada to the other flashed across her mind. The image struck her as being a close likeness to a much younger Craig.

She'd always wondered why Craig didn't change his name.

"Imagine all those years, never knowing," Ashlyn murmured.

"Sometimes I wonder if the parents, the ones we dealt with last year, would have preferred to not know the truth."

A sea of faces flashed through Ashlyn's mind, mothers crying, their husbands' reactions ranging from anguish to rage. "They might say that now, but until they knew, they wanted answers."

"Then they still had hope."

Ashlyn swallowed. It always got to her when Tain spoke softly. She was used to an assertive tough-guy front, the hard-ass reputation he'd earned for himself. Although he was far more relaxed and open with her than anyone else when he showed weakness, it cut deep. "There's still hope for Taylor Brennen and Lindsay Eckert. The one thing we know is that he doesn't kill them right away. But this guy, he's either really good or really lucky."

"And you're betting on good." Tain parked the car and switched off the ignition. "Me too. I wish we could find some way to tie these girls together so we could figure out his pattern."

"Burnaby's looking into that, right? For now, we can follow up with FIS."

"What does that have to do with Daly?"

"Maybe nothing," Ashlyn said evasively. "Let's see what FIS says first."

It was a scene that had become familiar to Craig in the past few months. Too familiar. A grief-stricken couple, the woman huddled on the couch, usually, like she was trying to keep people at a distance, like she had some kind of flu virus that a warm blanket, a cup of hot tea, a bit of time and lethargy could mend.

He just wasn't used to knowing the person masking the pain. Craig swallowed, thinking for a moment about Ashlyn, how she'd seemed to know exactly how he felt when they worked together, how everything in him had screamed to run away from that understanding, that feeling of having your soul ripped open and exposed. Every time he'd wanted to reach out to her he'd been held back by the realization that she could see into him, the feeling that there was nowhere inside himself that he could hide, and that honesty and openness had scared him. At times he'd felt as though his chest was constricting with such force that he couldn't breathe.

He glanced at Lori's wooden form on the couch, her eyes

vacuously aimed at some arbitrary point on the wall, not meeting the gaze of anyone who'd walked into the room.

Vishal Dhaval was a different story altogether. He'd jumped to his feet, his body bristling with energy, and then stopped cold as he set eyes on Inspector Hawkins. Hawkins stared back at him, and for a moment the whole room seemed to be holding its breath. Then Hawkins moved to the far wall, and Craig stepped into the center of the room, Daly beside him.

"Craig Nolan," he said.

Vishal blinked at him for a second and then shook his hand, muttering a quick introduction. "Call me Vish."

"And this is Sergeant Steve Daly." Craig paused as they nodded at each other. "Every member of our evidence recovery team is outside your door, waiting for the word, and I will personally ensure that they don't miss anything."

Craig crouched down, watching Lori as she stared just to the right of him, still not making eye contact, her head resting against her hand, her elbow on the arm of the couch, her whole body wrapped in a wool blanket with her long legs tucked underneath her.

The mug of tea in her other hand apparently had been forgotten.

The cup started to shake, and Craig reached out tentatively, gently taking the porcelain into his hands and steadying it. Her fingers slipped away.

"We're going to get him."

Lori turned to face Craig then, the despondent look giving way to a sullen stare. Her gaze jumped up to a spot behind Craig and slightly above him, and her eyes widened before she turned away.

He stood and shifted his body at an angle as he reached to set the mug down on the small table beside the couch so he could see what Lori had looked at.

Hawkins's cheeks turned a shade darker, and he cleared his throat, looking down at his toes.

Anyone who couldn't handle this shouldn't be in the

house. They'd only make things worse. Craig wished he could say it, but Hawkins outranked everyone present.

"Perhaps you could take Mr. Dhaval to another room and take his statement, and Inspector Hawkins can instruct the FIS people waiting outside," Craig said to Daly.

"I'll take Lori's statement," Hawkins said.

Craig felt his neck tense. "Respectfully, sir, I've taken all the statements on the previous cases, and I know what we're looking for. Frankly, so does Lori. It would be best if we can go over this and keep this as uncomplicated as possible."

"Yes, I agree," Vish said, gesturing for the other men to leave. Craig noticed Lori's boyfriend's face pinched when he looked at Hawkins, who paused for a second before complying.

"He's just being protective," Lori muttered once the room was empty.

"How long have you and Vish been together?" Craig asked as he pulled up a small chair, sitting across from her.

"Oh, not Vish. I meant, you know." She waved her hand. "Hawkins."

She was still staring off, at some spot on the floor now.

"If something happened to me, Daly would be a mess," he told her.

Lori looked him straight in the eyes then. "You're shit to work with as a partner, Craig. You've got Daly's stamp of approval on everything, and you're so fucking competent you make it hard for anyone else to look like they're pulling their weight."

She leaned forward, still staring right at him. "But now, now that it's me, you know . . ." She glanced away and blinked, lip quivering. She took a breath and looked him in the eyes again. "I'm glad you're on this."

Craig wasn't. He hoped the truth didn't show on his face, though he felt pretty certain that Lori knew he couldn't stand her. She leaned back against the couch and gave him a wry smile.

"I guess I'm in charge of this interview, aren't I?"

The hand that had been supporting her head earlier rubbed her forehead. Craig first noticed the shaking of her shoulders, and then the hand fell down over her eyes, her other hand clamped across her mouth as she started to cry.

When Tain and Ashlyn arrived at the lab, Greg Galloway was leaning back in his chair, stretching and making no attempt to stifle a yawn.

"Between this case and the rape cases, you guys are seeing me into a new apartment," Greg said. "The overtime has almost doubled my salary."

"Good to see someone's happy about all the crime," Tain muttered.

"Doing your best to spread happiness across the earth, eh, Tain?"

"I reserve one week of the year for promoting joy. December eighteenth to the twenty-fifth, annually."

Greg grinned. "I'm surprised you don't have a standing rental for a Grinch costume. Don't let his dour demeanor taint you, Ashlyn." He winked at her.

"He's not that bad," Ashlyn said, feeling her back straighten and her shoulders stiffen. "Where is everybody?"

"Another rape case. Second one today."

"Jesus." Ashlyn glanced at Tain, then Greg. "Any leads on that?"

"If there aren't, there'd better be soon. This rapist graduated to murder, and you know what that means."

"SSBB," Tain said.

"Big time."

Ashlyn's brow wrinkled as she looked at Greg, who didn't offer an explanation. She glared at Tain.

"Shit storm beyond belief." Tain turned to Greg. "What have you got from the recreation center?"

Greg leaned forward so his chair was level and pulled out a file. "Prints galore. You'd think half the people in Coquitlam had cozied up to that pop machine at one time or another. I had the prints run, and you got no hits. Your guy could be there—" he shrugged—"or not.

"We didn't get any tire treads from the back parking lot. As you already know, there was no security footage back there. I know that Daly had the officers ask everyone detained in the recreation center, and nobody remembered seeing a vehicle parked around back either.

"However, there are two red-light cameras within close proximity to the Southside Recreation and Fitness Center. I have already made a call and asked Traffic to pull all records of tickets within a two-hour time frame, an hour on each side of the abduction."

"Good thinking," Tain said.

"What about—"

"Patience, Ashlyn, I'm getting there. We did recover prints from the fire door, inside and out. Fewer prints than we got off the pop machine, and we ran them against each other. There were four sets of prints that were on both the fire door and the pop machine, but—"

"None of them are in the system. Still—" Ashlyn glanced at Tain—"it's better than nothing."

"And that's just about all I've got for you. We checked the floor thoroughly. There was no evidence of any kind of chemical or a substance that might have been used to incapacitate Lindsay, no blood to suggest she'd been injured . . ." He looked at them. "But then, you have a tape, right? I'm just boring you with the details."

"Still, this is more than we have for Taylor Brennen," Tain said, turning to leave.

Ashlyn put up her hand to stop him.

From the corner of her eye Ashlyn could see Tain frown, but she ignored him. "Before we go, I have a question."

Craig wasn't sure how much time had passed, exactly. When you're waiting time always seems to drag. Eventually Lori's shoulders stopped shaking. "Are you sure you're up to this?"

She took a deep breath and nodded. "It was just like all the . . . all the others."

"What did you do when you got home?"

"I, uh, made a plate of food, poured some wine, ran a bath

and grabbed a book from the bedroom." She rubbed the side of her face absently. "Sailing . . . Vish wants to take a holiday . . . sailing. Uh, you know. Up the Inside Passage."

"Sounds nice."

"So, I had a bath." She stared off for a moment, as though she'd forgotten what she was talking about. Then she snapped back. "Read. Ate."

"What did you do next?"

There was a long silence, but no change of expression on her face. Just the vacant stare. This time when she spoke the words came fluidly. "I went into the bedroom. I felt him before I saw him, you know? The room was dark, so it must have been around ten by then. I'd just tossed the towel on the floor when there was this movement. . . ."

After a moment of silence Craig quietly asked, "What happened then?"

"He was trying to twist me around. I kicked him. It must have hurt because he hit me."

"Is that when he . . . ?" Craig glanced at the bandage on her head.

She reached up and touched it automatically, then nodded. "He, uh, he called me a bitch."

"He spoke?"

Lori stared at Craig for a moment. "Shit, yeah, he did. I reached back and tried to claw him as he was pushing me down. . . ." Her face twisted, her gaze now focused somewhere off in space.

"It's okay, Lori. It's not your fault."

"Doesn't make me feel much better, though."

"Was there anything else that was . . ." Craig searched for the least offensive word. "Different? He spoke, he hit you. Anything else?"

She shook her head. "I tried to fight, but then I heard a knife click open, right beside my head. I heard that blade pop up, and I went numb . . . I just knew. Everything seemed so quiet, like the world had just stopped, you know, but then I heard the pitter-patter of the rain."

"Do you have any idea how he got in?"

"I never heard anything, but I ran the shower after my bath. I don't remember hearing him leave. He, uh, when he was done, he took the blindfold and gag off and told me if I said anything, he'd carve me up like a Christmas turkey. It seemed like forever, you know, lying there, and then I guess I just zoned out, waiting for him to either kill me or go. The next thing I remember is waking up this morning."

"Your hands were still bound?"

She wrung her hands for a moment. "Sonofabitch really tied them good."

Craig nodded at the rope burns on her wrists. "You did that trying to get free?"

"Yeah, for all the good it did me. It wasn't until Vish came home and found me that I got untied, and even then he finally had to cut through the rope." She swallowed. "Sorry. Tampering with evidence and such."

"It's okay. We've seen this rope five times before. I doubt he'd leave anything on it now."

Her eyes narrowed. "Five?" She sat up a little straighter. "What do you mean, five?"

"You weren't the only woman he attacked yesterday, Lori."

"He's graduated to multiple assaults?"

It was Craig's turn to avoid her penetrating stare, and she leaned forward and twisted his face until he had to look at her.

"What is it? What could be worse?"

He knew he couldn't keep the lie out of his eyes, and he watched as the unspoken truth hit home, her hand dropping from his face.

Tain tossed a folder on his desk. "Would you sit down or go for a jog or something? I'm getting tired just watching you."

Ashlyn spun around. "I thought you were reading those files."

"I am. My awareness of your pacing is preventing me from concentrating."

She hopped up on his desk on the far side of the stack of case folders he was going through, her legs swinging, but she kept her feet from banging off the drawers. "Good thing animosity doesn't hinder your work, eh?"

Tain glanced up at her. "You know, I didn't really enjoy having everyone hate me."

"And now?" She waited until his brow wrinkled and grinned. "I'm just kidding, Tain."

"So what's with Greg, anyway?"

Ashlyn felt her lip curl, despite Tain's teasing tone. "Could he be any more obvious?"

"Guys look at you like that all the time, Ashlyn."

She froze, then glanced at him as the way he'd said that started to tweak thought processes in the back of her brain, hinting at things she hadn't ever considered and wasn't sure she wanted to think about.

Tain had always struck her as being handsome, once she'd been able to get past his shitty disposition. Of course, she knew now that he'd been assigned to push their former supervisor to the edge and to find a leak in the department that was hindering their progress on the investigation.

And he was tall, athletic, with dark hair and a warm smile when he finally let his guard down. She'd seen him take things to heart, knew he felt deeply and was a compassionate person underneath the indifferent exterior.

But she'd been more than a little distracted with her partner at the time, as much as she tried to suppress it. Craig's memory still had a pretty good grip on her, along with all the 'what ifs.'

Tain had turned his gaze back to the file, but she knew he wasn't reading a word.

"What are you so antsy about, anyway?" he asked, finally appearing to give up on the pretense of reading.

"Just an idea."

"I'm listening."

She shot him a quick glance, then looked away. "I was hoping to talk to Daly."

He was studying her face. That much she was sure of. It wasn't just because she knew him, had worked with him before, seen the layers of his personality and understood how his mind worked, that she was certain she was under scrutiny. It was the way she felt her cheeks burn and her breath stick in her throat, like her body was having an allergic reaction to his stare.

Her face cooled, and she snuck a glance at Tain. He'd turned back to the folder, his eyes moving across the pages with the appearance of actually processing the material, his jaw set in a hard line, his skin a tinge darker than before.

Damn him. He knew she could counter the banter but hardly stand the silence. "What, no lecture?"

Tain didn't look up this time. "I can't make you talk if you don't want to."

She leaned forward, gripping the edge of the desk with her hands. "I never took you for a quitter."

"When it comes to women I prefer pragmatist."

"Is that why you're single?"

He did look up then, and what she thought she read loud and clear in his eyes made her regret her words.

"If you want to tell me about your idea, you will. I'm not going to play games with you. It's always nice to think your partner won't keep you in the dark. Something I'd think you'd know a bit about after working with Craig." He shrugged.

"You're a fine one to talk about that, Tain."

"Every time I say something, that case gets thrown back in my face. You know—"

"I'm not talking about that. I'm talking about Tim Winters."

His cheeks paled. "What's Tim got to do with this?"

"That's what I'd like to know."

They sat staring at each other, Tain titing back in his chair looking up at her, Ashlyn perched on his desk. When he didn't speak, she slid off his desk, leaning against it but breaking away from the relentless gaze she'd been matching.

Her hand bunched into a fist, and she tapped the files beside her absently. "I know you called Tim and talked to him about this case. And I haven't bugged you about it. All I have is an idea, something I want to try, and Daly might veto it automatically. It isn't like I know something and I'm holding it back from you."

"Look, your idea, if it's risky enough that you think Daly won't hear you out, don't you think it makes sense to have me back you up?"

"Is that your way of evading the issue?"

She watched his jaw jut out, a sight she'd grown accustomed to whenever he was thinking about something, usually something he was conflicted over. His lips settled into a slight frown.

"If I tell you, will you feel obligated to share with Burnaby?"

"Tain, we have two girls who've been murdered and two more missing. I can't believe that the Tain I know—" she leaned forward and poked him on the chest—"the Tain who has a heart of gold he tries hard to keep people from seeing, would put this investigation and the lives of a couple of girls second to a pissing contest."

"It's not about territory and credit." He grabbed her arm, holding it firmly so she couldn't pull back, and stared her right in the eyes. "Let me ask you something. Do you think these cases are linked?"

She felt her forehead wrinkle, her face flushed with her awareness of his proximity and his relentless gaze. "How can you even ask that?" She tried to pull back, but he wasn't letting go. "Of course I believe they're connected."

"So what would happen if the original investigating team got wind of a potential lead, something that would blow that theory apart? Something that could absolutely prove the cases weren't linked?"

Ashlyn swallowed, her arm going limp as she stopped pulling against him. "It would be an excuse. It wouldn't be their fault that more girls went missing. Just random, a fluke that so many abductions happened . . ." She felt her eyes narrow as she stared back at him. "How can you even think these cases aren't connected?"

"I don't. But this tip, the reason I called Tim—" he glanced away, his jaw twisting again before he drew a deep breath and met her gaze—"it could prove one of the cases isn't connected."

"And you think if we prove that, it will blow the whole investigation apart."

"Even if they continue to look at the other three cases together, that would give Burnaby two and us one."

"So they would take the investigation back, even though both of their girls were found on our patch."

"Tell me something honestly, Ashlyn," he said, his grip loosening as he moved his hand down to grasp hers instead of holding her arm. "Do you think that Mullins and Urquhart are the best investigators for this case?"

She drew a deep breath of her own. "No. You know I don't."

"Then you know why I haven't said anything." He released her hand.

Ashlyn lifted her limp appendage to her forehead, rubbing the skin as the tingling sensation in her hand subsided. Tain had turned back to the file, and she noticed he was even redder than before, though she wasn't sure at what point that had happened in their exchange.

She thought back to the obstinate, insubordinate officer she'd first met less than a year earlier, sentenced to find the leak in the department after getting into hot water at his old detachment and finding his name on his supervisor's shit list, for reasons not that different than the ones he was using to justify his actions now.

He tossed the folder down on a pile and reached for another one. She set her hand over his.

"You don't have to protect me, Tain. I'll back you up."

"How can you promise that without knowing what this is about?"

"I don't need to know the details. I trust you."

She stood up and walked away before he had a chance to respond.

Lori stood, but her shoulders sagged. "You know the MO as well as I do. He doesn't leave evidence."

"And you know there's always a chance. We have to try."

"There's no 'we' in this. I have to do this. You don't have to do anything."

Craig put his hand on her arm lightly. "We may not always get along, and we might not always see eye to eye about how to approach every aspect of a case. But we have never disagreed about asking our victims to go through the exam."

Her shoulders sagged even further, and she moved back, out of his grasp. Vish entered the room then and put an arm around her. Craig noticed she didn't draw closer to him for support.

"Craig's right," Vish said. "You aren't going to tell me that someone who catches these monsters for a living is going to let the guy who attacked her go free."

He shepherded her out the door then, not giving her another chance to protest.

Craig resisted the urge to step outside after them and draw a breath of fresh air, to get out of the cloud of tension that had been building in the house since his arrival. Instead, he turned and went down the hall until he found Daly.

Inside what he assumed was the master bedroom, Hawkins was barking orders and double checking everything everyone was doing. FIS officers gritted their teeth and Craig suspected they were biting back comments running through their minds.

"Damn it, I said to put it there." Hawkins spun on his heel, and Craig was pretty certain he missed the searing glare the officer shot him.

Daly glanced at Craig, barely raising an eyebrow. "How is she?"

Craig shook his head. "One minute she's pulling it together and the next she's falling to pieces. Not that I expect more from her than anyone else—"

"But?"

"She was reluctant to do the rape kit. Her boyfriend had to drag her out of here."

"I doubt it's something many women want to do. Just because she's a cop, it doesn't make her invincible."

Despite their hushed words, Hawkins's head snapped up then, and he marched toward them.

"Where's Lori?"

"She's gone to the hospital."

Hawkins's whole face wrinkled. "What for?"

"The rape kit."

Hawkins put his hand over his mouth and slowly pulled it down to his chin. "Is that really necessary?"

From the corner of his eye Craig saw Daly lower his gaze. He felt his shoulders stiffen. "You know it is, sir."

"I know no such thing," Hawkins snapped. "One of the officers who's had to comfort and support several women who've been raped is now caught up in this nightmare as a victim. We already know this guy doesn't leave DNA, so what the hell is the point of putting her through more trauma?"

"If this rape victim had another name, we wouldn't even be having this conversation, and you know it."

Hawkins's cheeks puffed out, flaming red, and his nostrils flared slightly. "Are you suggesting that—"

Daly interrupted him. "Dennis, I think we're all a little upset. Lori's one of ours. But Craig is right. If this victim were anyone else, we'd all try to persuade her to go to the hospital. This guy has raped several women, and now he's killed one of them. If there's even the smallest chance that we can find some evidence, we have to take it."

The cheeks deflated and cooled visibly. Hawkins turned on his heel and walked away.

"Forget Lori being able to handle this. Is *he* going to be able to cope?" Craig asked Daly as they retreated down the hall.

Daly shook his head. "I don't know. I really don't know."

The man lit the candles and gestured for Taylor to come. She hesitated for less than a second this time, and through the flicker of light she could just make out his smile.

"Well done, my child."

His face turned toward the other bed, and he reached out his hand.

"Come. Join us."

Taylor dared to sneak a glance in the direction of the bed, willing the girl to do as she was told. *Please, please, please. Just listen this time.* She held her breath.

At last, the springs squeaked and the girl crawled across the floor, sitting farther back than Taylor did.

"That is better," he said, only his unsmiling mouth really visible in the dim, orange glow. "We don't have much time. I have to prepare you."

*"For what?" Taylor had asked him on her first day. He had struck her face hard.*

*"Thou shalt not speak unless permitted. These are The Rules. You must obey The Rules to show God you are ready to go home."*

The new girl didn't ask and spared herself the smack, though Taylor consoled herself with the fact that the girl had already been lashed twice.

"Now, I expect you to echo what I say. Do you understand?"

Taylor nodded. From the corner of her eye she could see the other girl looking at her, trying to figure out what to do. Taylor kept nodding until the new girl's head bobbed up and down.

"I am the way, the truth and the life."

*"You are the way, the truth and the life."*

"No one comes to the Father except by me."

*"No one comes to the Father except by you."*

"I am the Lamb of God."

*"You are the Lamb of God."*

"Appointed to go before the last days of fire."

*"App..poinned to go before the last days of fire."*

"To cleanse the wayward of their sins."

*"To cleanse the wayward of their sins."*

"To teach the true word and prepare the chosen."

*"To teach the true word and prepare the chosen."*

"To make those whom God sees fit ready for His service."

*"To make those whom God sees fit . . ."*

"You interviewed Vish?" Craig asked Daly.

"Yes. He said he was called out to a fire last night and had left a message for Lori on her cell. He didn't get home until almost ten AM. He found her in the bedroom. Naked, lying on her stomach across the bed, her hands bound. She had rope burn from trying to get free."

Craig swallowed.

"What is it?"

"He found her at ten, and we got this call late this afternoon."

"You aren't thinking—"

"It makes no sense. Lori knows how important it is for us to get to the scene right away. Delays can cause contamination to the scene. There's some physical evidence that can deteriorate and be unusable."

"It's not like you can expect her to be thinking rationally about this, Craig."

"I know that, but it rained last night. Not much, but enough to soak the earth. We could have gotten a footprint. As it is, we may have lost our best chance at a solid lead because this call came in hours after it should have. I have a lot of people looking for answers, not just Lori."

"We've got to do the best we can with what we have and try to find a way to crack this case open."

"We need a profile. We need somebody who understands the way people think who can help us get inside the guy's mind and figure him out. So far, he's attacked blondes, brunettes, redheads. Some of these women are tall like Lori, and others are short. They're scattered across the city. I can't find any physical characteristic or geographic rationale that's giving me a clue about how he's picking his targets or where he's going to strike next, and without much physical evidence, we're stuck."

Daly rubbed his forehead and then nodded. "I agree. We have to do whatever it takes, especially since this guy has graduated to murder. So far, that's the only case where anything has been different, and I want to know why."

"Actually, it isn't. There was something different with Lori," Craig said slowly, flipping his notebook open to the right page. "Lori had turned, so she was partially facing him when he moved to grab her. He tried to twist her around. She kicked him, and he called her a bitch."

"He spoke?"

"Yes, and he struck her on the head."

Daly was silent for a moment. "You think she rattled him?"

"I . . . I'm not sure. It's odd that he spoke. Four other women and not one has heard a word from him, but after the rape, he took Lori's gag and blindfold off and told her he'd cut her to pieces if she tried anything."

"What time was he here?"

"Around ten PM, as best as I can figure, based on Lori's statement. Could have been a bit earlier because it got dark earlier last night with the rain, or a bit later."

"But Nitara Sandhu was killed around midnight, so it sounds likely that he was here first and then went there."

"We should have a team go back over there and check for any dirt, anything that might link this house to that one."

"It's worth a shot," Daly said. "And we can come up with the possible routes for him to have used and see if we can identify a suspicious vehicle. It stands to reason that he was upset if he spoke to her. It's a huge change in his MO."

"Not even a screaming baby prompted him to curse before."

Daly shook his head. "You know, Craig, she'd probably hate me for saying it, but good for her. Maybe we can voice ID him when we get him."

"At this point, I'm prepared to take anything we can use. It's certainly the best lead we've got."

"Says a hell of a lot about this case, doesn't it?"

"Huh. You don't have to tell me that."

Daly sank into his chair as though under the weight of a five hundred-pound barbell that he simply didn't have the strength to carry any longer. His cheeks sagged, and his eyes looked lifeless. "Tell me you have some good news."

"Greg matched four distinct sets of prints that are on both the pop machine at the recreation center and the fire door," Tain replied.

Ashlyn hadn't waited for an invitation to sit down and Tain finally sat beside her.

"That's something," Daly mumbled.

"Unfortunately, none of them were in the system," Ashlyn said.

Daly seemed to be forcing his head to rotate so he could look at her directly. "Since when did you become the voice of gloom?"

"I'm just relaying the facts."

His brow wrinkled, and he gave her a look that said, *Oh, please. Don't play innocent with me.* "I know that tone of voice, Ashlyn. God, this better be good."

"It could be."

Daly's shoulders drooped even farther, and he sighed. "I'm listening."

Ashlyn glanced at Tain, pushing her hair back behind her left ear. "I want to try to get prints from the scene where Isabella's body was found."

Daly frowned. "You tried. And failed."

"We did," Tain said, trying to keep his eyes from narrowing. "And, as I recall, Paul Quinlan told us it was our one shot and that if he ordered us out, it was the end of the discussion. After what happened, I can't see him agreeing to take us back in."

"Neither can I," Daly said, his gaze shifting to Ashlyn's face. "I appreciate that you want to do anything you can to make some headway. Having a crime scene, even a secondary crime scene, to work with could help, but I can't risk your lives and the safety of other officers by letting you go into a building that's been condemned. You're damn lucky as it is that Tain wasn't seriously injured before."

"I know that. I'm not suggesting we go inside the building."

"Then how do you propose we look for evidence? Telekinetically?" Daly's eyes had widened as he glared at her.

Ashlyn stared back. "Are you going to listen to what I have to say, or just provide dismissive jokes?"

Daly held his hands up and sighed.

"Firefighters access buildings all the time through secondary means," she started. "They use ladder trucks to get to windows, rappel from rooftops, climb fire escapes. What I was going to propose is that we use a hydro truck, or something with a bucket, to lift one person up there who can dust the window, photograph the area, see about reaching the table for prints. At the very least, a visual survey would provide us with more information than we have already."

"How so?"

"For starters, we don't know if that window was deliberately opened or if it was broken. We know Isabella was already dead, so she didn't break it trying to escape. But if the window was deliberately opened, we could have prints, and it could be that her abductor wanted to make sure that room burned."

"But why not just put her in the room where he started the fire?"

"I don't know, Daly. The other thing is that when Tain fell through the floor in the hallway, Paul said it looked like part of the floorboards had been removed. He theorized for firewood because that happens in some vacant buildings frequented by homeless people. But this building didn't have that kind of reputation."

"So, you're wondering if our arsonist removed the wood from the hallway. I don't see how you could know for certain without going back to where Tain fell through, and there's no way I'm letting you do that."

"I'm not proposing that. Paul figured we weakened the boards there when we walked across, and that's why Tain went through. There's no telling if there are other areas like that, ready to give way." She shook her head. "No, what I actually want to do is check under the table to see if there's kindling there."

Daly's mouth opened slightly. "You mean, you think maybe he was going to start the fire under her?"

"The preliminary report puts the fire starting on the second or third floor, in the room at the back on the right side."

"Why is it so vague?" Tain asked.

"They've only been able to take a look at the ground floor.

Typically, people who start fires start them on the ground floor, and because of what happened when we went in, Paul wouldn't approve going any higher in the building. But the one thing they know from the charring and debris is that the fire definitely started in one of the two rooms directly below where Isabella's body was left."

Daly's face wrinkled. "So, you want to do a visual survey, hope for some prints. This sounds like a hell of an undertaking without the chance of getting us much."

"Look, I know there are no guarantees. We could send somebody up there and get nothing. But this isn't just one case, and we owe it to these families to explore every possible avenue of investigation. If we did get prints up there, we could check them against the prints found at the recreation center. It could give us conclusive proof that these cases are linked, a piece of physical evidence that would help us convict this guy once we get him."

Tain nodded. "She has a point, sir. Right now, unless we catch this guy in the act or get a living witness who can ID him, we haven't got much to tie him to these cases."

"I know." Daly sat still, his eyes turned down toward his desk, his sober expression not hinting at any of his thoughts about Ashlyn's proposal.

When the silence hadn't been broken after another moment, Tain cleared his throat. "I'll do it."

Tain kept his gaze straight ahead, on Daly, so Ashlyn couldn't make eye contact with him. She knew he'd always had excellent peripheral vision, which usually came in handy, but he seemed to be ignoring her.

"So, you support this idea then?"

Tain nodded.

"If you're going to sign off on this, I'll be the one to go up," Ashlyn said, pointing a finger at her chest. "I suggested this. I'll take the risks."

Tain still didn't look at her. "Just because it was your idea, it doesn't mean you own it."

"I'm as capable as you are."

"I know that," Tain retorted. "I—"

"You know, right now I'm glad I didn't have more children." After a moment of silence, Daly continued, "I'll make some calls and see what we can do. It's late. Have you two even eaten dinner?" Daly glanced from Ashlyn to Tain. "Didn't think so. Go home. Get some sleep. You've got the meeting with Burnaby tomorrow, and you need to go through the open abduction cases before then. That's your priority now. Not the evidence recovery from the building, not who should climb the ladder, but being ready for that meeting. Understood?"

Ashlyn nodded.

"Then I don't want to see either of you until tomorrow. Go home."

Craig blinked as the light went on.

"Can't get much done in the dark, can you?"

Hawkins was still displaying that nervous energy so different from his usual demeanor, pacing, reaching out to fiddle with things and then pulling his hand back, like he'd just remembered he was in a crime scene.

"I'm just going over the checklists, making sure we've covered absolutely everything."

Hawkins nodded, moving to the window, looking outside. "They're getting restless, you know. Wondering why you haven't cut them loose."

"Respectfully, I didn't think that was my call."

"Right." Hawkins spun on his heel, scratching his head, his gaze darting across the floor and around the room, looking at everything but Craig. "You've done a good job on this. I shouldn't have charged in. Do we have everything?"

"As far as I can tell. I'm going to do one more walkthrough with the lists, but from what I've seen already, if Vish's nephew wet the bed when he was having a nap three years ago, we'll have the hard evidence to back it up."

Hawkins nodded. "Good."

"Maybe you should go ahead, tell them to pack up."

"You're sure?"

"I think they need to hear it from you on this one, sir. Besides, every RCMP officer is trained in evidence recovery. I can handle anything that might turn up, and if I see something big that's been overlooked, I'll just call them back. Vish and Lori are staying with family, so there's no rush."

"You're going to be here for a while then?"

"As long as it takes for me to be certain there isn't something obvious staring me in the face that I've overlooked."

Hawkins walked out of the room without another word. Within minutes, Craig could hear a number of doors closing, followed by the sound of motors starting.

He walked to the window. Hawkins was standing on the sidewalk as the rest of the officers drove away. Hawkins turned, looked back at the house, then trudged back to his own car.

What a nightmare. Craig's eyes took in things about the room he hadn't really noticed before, the symmetry of the wall hanging, the way the display of flowers and figurines on the cabinet seemed to suggest they'd been stolen from a feng shui coffee-table book. His gaze stopped on a framed photo and he moved toward it, then picked it up.

Vish and Lori, posed, smiling, looking like the picture-perfect couple, Lori in a flattering dress unlike anything Craig had seen her in at work, Vish in a suit.

What did Vish do? He realized that, in all the tension of the investigation and, because he hadn't interviewed Vish himself, he wasn't sure if that had been relayed or if he'd just forgotten. Not that it really mattered. Once they'd ruled out Dan Chalmers when his wife was raped, it didn't seem as important to know about the husbands. Especially not once Stephanie Bonnis had been raped in the exact same way.

Those first few weeks, looking as hard at the family of the victim as anyone else . . . Craig walked to the kitchen on autopilot. He couldn't blame them if they hated the police.

Each partner's alibi had been checked by uniformed officers who were assisting in the investigation. None of them had ever given any cause for doubt.

There it was, the ever-important list of contact numbers.

His finger traced the list until it came to Vish's work. The Coquitlam Fire Department.

Craig flipped his notebook open and wrote that down. He could feel the pins and needles sensations in his arms, prickling their way up to his shoulders and his neck, but he shrugged them off and moved to the bedroom to review everything one last time.

# TUESDAY

"What do you want first? Red-light camera reports or the open abduction cases?"

Ashlyn didn't answer, but kept fiddling with her pen as she rocked up and down in her chair, which produced a cry for WD-40 every time she rapidly shifted position. Tain leaned across their desks and snatched the pen from her hands.

"You heard what Sergeant Daly said yesterday. If you spent half the night worrying about getting into that crime scene that's unfortunate, but not my problem. Right now I need your head in the game. We have to get through this."

Her mouth twisted as her eyes narrowed. "I know. What did you start on yesterday? The abduction cases?"

He nodded as he sank down into his chair. "I'm halfway through, and I've only found two that are even remotely comparable. It isn't looking good."

"Do you want me to start on the red-light cameras, or would you prefer to get through these first for sure? After all, Burnaby expects this. They don't know about Greg Galloway's due diligence."

"You go ahead with the camera records. If it starts to look like I might not make it through the pile, you can always put those aside." He glanced at his watch. "It's eight AM now. We have until ten, right?"

"As far as we know."

He pulled the file and opened it, still having the feeling that she was watching him. When he couldn't shake it after a moment, he looked up.

"What?"

"Can I have my pen back?"

"Only if you promise to use it properly."

She stood and reached over to the second pile tottering on his desk, pulling the folders toward her.

He tossed the pen back and turned his eyes to the file.

"Do you want an examination table and a blanket?" Craig frowned at Bill Burke, the coroner, who responded with a simple smile. "You look worse than some of my regular clients."

"You get repeat business down here, do you?"

"Ah, the wit is intact. Though that's the kind of comment I expect from guys like Tain, who has been giving me repeat business lately."

"Perp couldn't kill him properly the first time?" Craig asked, thinking back to a moment and time when it had taken all his willpower to hold back from wrapping his hands around Tain's throat and throttling him.

"He's on the child abduction cases."

The words impacted like a physical blow. He'd just been so glad it wasn't him. "Oh, I didn't know. What have you got for me?"

"Well, this isn't news. It was clear she'd been strangled at the scene, and we didn't need to cut her open to prove that. I did check her fingernails and teeth for any indication that she fought back and got a piece of this guy."

The look on the coroner's face told Craig the answer. "Nothing?"

"Not a thing. She gripped the ties instead of her killer. All the threads we did get matched them perfectly." He slid a file off the counter. "But we got something off the ties."

Craig frowned. "Shouldn't FIS be handling them?"

Dr. Burke shook his head. "Not right away. They came to me to establish conclusively that they matched the ligature marks around her neck, which they do. But we did find a bit of blood on the ties. See this?" He passed Craig an evidence photo. "The streaking runs across the cluster of ties, which indicates it should match someone who handled them this way, so not from some accident that her husband had or anything else. Whoever bled on them definitely had them wound together in the way they were when your victim was killed."

"Well, that's something. Anything physical connecting this guy to the scene will help."

"Unfortunately, I can't promise you DNA."

Craig felt like he'd shrunk half a foot. "Why not?"

"It's a really small sample, not much for the lab to work with. I've sent the material over already, and I phoned personally and stressed how important this is." He scowled.

"Let me guess. You were yelled at about the fact that of course they know it's important after spending half the night at another crime scene."

"Something like that. If I thought it would do any good, I would file a complaint."

"I wouldn't. One of our officers was raped before he killed Mrs. Sandhu."

The scowl vanished. "I wish I had something more for you."

"Me too." Craig took the file copy and walked out the door.

A quick glance at the table was all Ashlyn needed to persuade herself that she should keep her eyes down.

Sergeant Quinlan had gone all-out, with Tim Hortons coffee, donuts and assorted cookies. It looked more like a social club event than a status meeting on an active police investigation into abductions and murders.

She wasn't quick enough to avoid catching a glimpse of the sour look that emerged when Daly walked in.

Tain moved around her, putting himself between her and Quinlan's end of the table. Within seconds Daly sat down on the other side of her and got straight to business.

"How far did you get with your background checks?"

Zoe Mullins responded with what could only be described as a seething tone. "Julie Darrens was nine. She played the flute and took lessons from a teacher in Burnaby. She sang in a youth choir and was about to start grade four at Holy Cross Elementary. From all appearances she comes from a stable family, three older siblings, no hint at discord, and she was a Girl Guide. Nothing out of the ordinary at all."

"Isabella Bertini was ten. She also lived in Burnaby, was a Girl Guide, and was about to go into grade five at the Burnaby Fine Arts School. She loved to draw."

"Same Girl Guide troop?" Tain asked.

"No such luck," Eric Urquhart inserted, appearing indifferent to Zoe's glare. "Different packs."

"There's no connection between the Girl Guide groups." Zoe cast a slit-eyed look at her partner.

"Still, there's always the possibility they could have been on some sort of weekend camping thing together, a rally that had a number of local packs involved," Ashlyn said.

"Ashlyn's right. You need to check that out," Quinlan told Zoe, who clenched her teeth as she looked down at her notes.

As though this case wasn't bad enough already. . . . Ashlyn felt Tain tense beside her. That sixth sense kicking in, knowing him as well as she did, she didn't need to look at him to know what he was thinking.

Zoe spoke deliberately, carefully. "Not to dismiss that suggestion, but Taylor Brennen wasn't a Girl Guide, and she was never in Brownies. So far as we can tell, Taylor's life was spent shuffling between her mom's, her dad's and her Grandma's house. The only other thing she did regularly was look after her younger brother. Nobody indicated she participated in any activities, and she attended Sacred Heart Elementary."

There was silence at the table for a moment. Ashlyn resisted the urge to scratch the place on the back of her neck that always itched when she felt uncomfortable.

"We have three girls, living in three different regions. Different schools. Two were Guides but in different packs. Beyond their gender, that seems to be the only thing any of them have in common," Tain surmised. "Any chance we could be looking for a school photographer or a substitute bus driver or someone that might have seen all of these girls?"

"It's possible," Eric said, nodding. "We can check that out."

"Of course, it is August. If this guy saw these girls during the school year, why start snatching them now?" Zoe said.

"We're grasping at straws to come up with a lead in this case," Daly said. "It's definitely worth checking potential school links. After all, we do have someone who seems to be comfortable moving from one region to another. There's no geographic link or focal area he prefers. Substitute support staff for schools seems our best bet, and we should still follow up on the Girl Guide angle. It's always possible that someone who had exposure to a number of girls through a Guide activity saw Taylor and just took advantage of the situation."

"That's right. We know the perp planned to grab Lindsay—" Ashlyn began.

"How do we know that?" Zoe said again, glaring at Ashlyn from the other side of the table.

"Video shows him moving behind her, making slight physical contact. Then the video shows her returning to the hallway to retrieve a necklace. We're guessing somehow he unlatched the clasp to lure her back out there. He grabbed her and took off. The necklace was found outside in the back parking area, though the video clearly shows it on the floor in the hallway. Her parents confirmed it belonged to her."

"It's too big of a coincidence," Tain said. "The technical guys called over this morning and said they'd blown up the images. Nothing tangible about our guy that we can work with, but still, we know he targeted Lindsay."

"Isabella and Julie were both taken in close proximity to their homes, Lindsay from a place she frequented on a regular basis with her church." Ashlyn glanced at Eric, sensing she had his interest, though it was clear she had nothing but Zoe's scorn. "Taylor was taken from the fairgrounds. Not her home, not her neighborhood, not a place she could normally be expected to be at."

"Are you suggesting that she might have been taken by someone else?" Eric asked.

Ashlyn shook her head, slowly at first, then more emphatically. "There's no reason to believe that," she said, hoping her cheeks didn't betray the truth when she thought about what Tain had said to her less than twenty-four hours earlier. "All I'm saying is that Julie, Isabella and Lindsay seem to have been definitely targeted. Taylor's abduction could have been more of an impulse."

"In which case, it would be more critical to find a link between the other three," Daly said. "It is possible Taylor's abduction was a crime of opportunity."

"And it's also possible it was someone else," Zoe said. "After all, this guy is taking his time, with more than two weeks between the first two abductions. Then more than a month goes by and he grabs two girls on the same weekend? That's a big jump."

"I think," Tain said, "it's most important that we examine all potential connections right now and keep an open mind. We don't have enough evidence to be sure of anything. We don't even have a specific abduction site for Taylor Brennen. We'd be foolish to rule anything out conclusively based on her not fitting the tenuous connection we've found so far."

"If Taylor Brennen wasn't abducted by the same person, this investigation should switch back to Burnaby and we should assume the lead on the case again," Zoe said, her eyes narrowing.

"That would be premature," Quinlan said. "Right now, Coquitlam is handling this case with our assistance. Surely you've not forgotten that the arson investigation seems to be linked to the abductions? All the arsons have been in Coquitlam. Are you prepared to take the lead on that investigation as well?"

Zoe's cheeks burned and for a moment, she glared at Ashlyn as though Ashlyn was personally responsible for every hardship she'd ever endured in life. Ashlyn turned her gaze back to the file.

"Right, so the next logical step is looking at Lindsay Eckert and seeing if anything about her connects to Isabella and

Julie, as well as pulling substitute support worker and teacher lists for the schools involved, and records of who did school photography or anything else that could tie in."

"Even the choir Julie was in," Ashlyn added. "Sometimes they use rented school buses to travel if they have an engagement, or they might have had a group photo."

"If you don't mind me asking, what exactly will you be doing while we're collecting all this information?" Zoe said.

"We have a fire scene to attempt an evidence recovery from. The concrete barriers that blocked fire trucks from accessing that side of the building have to be moved first," Daly said. "At this point, it's too soon to tell, but we're hoping that there might be some clues at the scene where Isabella's body was left that can help us with the investigation."

Ashlyn felt like her heart had jumped into her throat. Tain's eyes crinkled at the corners as he glanced at her, and she drew a deep breath.

She knew it was a long shot, but she had to test her hunch about that room. A hunch that had been building since they'd questioned Luke Driscoll at his church.

"From yesterday?" The doctor glowered at Craig for a moment and then went to the records desk. "What was the name?"

"Lori Price."

He pulled a file from the cabinet and flipped it open. "You'll need to speak to Dr. Zaid about this."

"Is he here?"

"I'll try paging her."

So much for a nice bedside manner. Craig was relieved that the doctor had turned his deepening scowl in another direction for a moment.

He hung up the phone and glanced at the clock on the wall, stared at Craig for a moment and then turned back to look at the clock again.

"She's . . ."

"Sorry, Mark." Craig heard the voice from behind him.

She came into his peripheral view as she leaned against the counter beside him. "What do you need?"

Mark, who hadn't introduced himself to Craig and had remained nameless until then, nodded at Craig and passed Dr. Zaid the file, leaving without a word.

She glanced at the file before looking over at Craig, who held up his ID automatically.

"Zafina Zaid," she said. "What can I do for you?"

"I need to know the results from the rape kit you did on Ms. Price."

"Follow me." She led him down the hall toward a small office, her long legs moving at a brisk pace but somehow maintaining an elegant, feminine gait. She glanced at him as her eyebrows rose over her black eyes. "Generally, the investigating officers are here during these exams."

"I know." He sat down across from her.

"No excuses. I can almost respect that." Zafina flipped the file open. "Not that I need to look. Fortunately, we don't do so many of these that we lose track."

She recounted the details succinctly and precisely, without even a hint of a blush in her olive cheeks. The doctor didn't glance at Craig until she was finished detailing the proof of trauma. "You don't look surprised."

"I'm not. The same guy has raped five other women that we know of."

"Ah." She tossed her silky, dark hair over her shoulder. "The bend-over bondage rapist."

Craig winced. "I don't think he's been dubbed that in the media."

"He's being called that by people like us, who have to see the results of his handiwork. No doubt the press is calling him something civil, like the Silent Stalker. Scary, but not enough for anyone to really break a sweat over."

"Tell that to my supervisor," Craig muttered.

"You're going to maintain that your department is doing everything it can when you weren't even here for the rape exam?" Her black eyes were enormous as she stared at him.

"You sound like a reporter, not a doctor," Craig said, standing.

She stood as well, her height enabling her to look him in the eye with ease. "We get reporters here, you know. Asking questions. Wanting to know who the investigating officers are."

"And in the future you can refer them to the media liaison person at the RCMP." He turned to open the door, stopping when he felt her hand on his arm.

"Look, I'm just warning you that there are some people who feel this case isn't being given priority. Until yesterday, I'd only heard whisperings within my professional community. Now I'm on every reporter's hit list for an interview. Don't tempt me to give them my candid opinion."

"Ms. . . . Dr. Zaid, I'm not here to tell you what or what not to say to the press. You do what you can live with, within the boundaries of your ethical guidelines in your profession. All I care about is finding the guy who's doing this and putting him away. Being hounded by reporters comes with the territory when you work in a hospital with rape victims and attempted homicides, and if you don't like it I suggest you find another line of work."

She followed him down the hall, undeterred. "So you're telling me that your department is doing everything it can. I doubt it. You want to know what I see? An overworked young officer trying to catch a rapist without a partner who's going to get hung out to dry if he doesn't catch this guy soon. Maybe if I said something, your superiors would at least give you some help, shoulder the blame."

Craig took a few more steps and then realized that she wasn't following him anymore. He spun on his heel and walked back to where she stood.

"I did have a partner. Constable Lori Price. Now maybe you can get off your high horse and try to appreciate why I wasn't here for her exam, and no, I don't have a new partner. We weren't exactly expecting this."

He pushed her stricken look from his mind as he spun around and walked away, the incident almost overriding the one thing that was different about Lori's case than the others.

There was semen present.

Tain tried to keep the anger out of his voice. "You are the most stubborn, infuriating person I've ever had to deal with."

"Oh, come on." Ashlyn twisted her face to give him a look of profound exasperation. "You've dealt with yourself plenty over the years."

"Why is it that you think being reasonable about something makes you seem weak? You don't have anything to prove here." He choked back what he wanted to add. That she didn't have anything to prove to him.

"Why is it that when a woman holds firm, she's stubborn and unreasonable, but when a man does it, he's principled?"

"This isn't about you being a woman."

"Really? Then why the hell do you have a problem with me going up there?"

"I . . . Damn it, Ashlyn, I don't have a problem with you going up there. But I said I'd do it. Why are you trying to stop me?"

"You said you'd do it to support my proposal to Daly."

"No, Ashlyn, I didn't. I said it because I believe it's our best chance for fresh leads in this case."

He watched her uncross her arms and reach around to scratch her neck, a mannerism he was used to seeing from her.

"I'm lighter than you are. If one of us has to go—"

"Hey, wait a second. I thought you wanted prints from the table and the window? Now you're talking about going into the room?"

She glanced away from him, toward the place on the grass where the truck was being moved into position, as close to the back right corner of the burned-out building as it could get.

He reached for her arm and held it gently but firmly until she looked up at him. Her face betrayed a mix of defiance, apology and frustration.

Tain shook his head. "I can't let you go up there."

"What if there's evidence, Tain? What if there's something in that room that could help lead us to the killer?" All the other emotions that had flickered across her face had dissipated into one sincere appeal, to his determination to solve this case.

"Christ, Ashlyn, you don't pull your punches, do you? Did you ever stop to think of what Daly would do to me if something happened to you up there, and he found out I knew you were prepared to take a risk like this?"

"Daly knows that, at the end of the day, I'm a police officer. I face risks on the job. Just like Craig."

Craig. Tain swallowed, feeling his breath stick in his throat. "This isn't about you being a cop. It's about acceptable risks. If you're go—"

"It looks like we're ready," Daly said. Then his gaze went to Tain's hand, still on Ashlyn's arm. "Is there a problem here?"

"No," Ashlyn said. She stepped back as soon as Tain loosened his hold.

Daly frowned. "Good. Then it's time for you to get up there."

She turned and walked toward the truck. Tain started to go after her, but Daly put his hand up to stop him.

Daly looked him straight in the eyes. "When you were assigned to work with her, I told you I didn't want any problems."

"I know that, but—"

"Why do I get the impression personal feelings are clouding your professional judgment?"

"I disagree. You're jumping to conclusions without all the facts."

"Really? Then enlighten me, Tain. Why don't you want Ashlyn going up there?"

Tain looked at Ashlyn as she put the required safety gear on. She'd be furious. And Daly trusted her. But Tain knew he couldn't forgive himself if anything happened to Ashlyn.

He looked at Daly and took a deep breath. "She's prepared to go into that room if she thinks there's evidence."

A voice called, telling Daly they were waiting for them. Tain held his gaze, unblinking.

Then Daly turned on his heel and marched toward the truck, pausing midstride as he saw the lift already being raised toward the window.

"No issues with heights?" Adrian Vaughan asked her.

Ashlyn shook her head. "It isn't like this is even that far up. I imagine twenty or thirty floors might be enough to make you catch your breath."

"When you're dealing with a fire you've got a lot of things triggering the adrenaline. I never really notice the difference."

"Really? I'd think it would be foremost in your mind."

"You think more about the kind of fire, potential explosives, people who are caught inside. And those are the background thoughts. You have to keep your training front and center, or you'll make mistakes that could cost you your life."

"I know what you mean," she murmured.

The radio crackled. "Ashlyn Hart, I expect you to follow your instructions to the letter. That means absolutely no unnecessary risks. Do I make myself clear?"

"Is your sergeant always so touchy?" Adrian asked.

She sighed. "If Tain were going up, Daly wouldn't care."

Adrian's eyes widened, and she put up her hand.

"It's not like that. I'm a friend of the family." She knew the part-truth was the easiest way out of the situation, not that she owed Adrian an explanation. Ashlyn picked up the radio. "Absolutely, Sergeant."

"I'm serious, Ashlyn."

"So am I. I'm only going to do what's necessary to help us solve this case."

"Ashlyn . . ."

"Look, Daly, I'll radio you every step of the way."

She passed the radio to Adrian as they jerked to a stop. He called in adjustments to line them up with the window in question.

The next few minutes were the worst part of the lift experience for Ashlyn. The jerking to a stop, jerking into motion, jerking to a stop again made her stomach flip because she couldn't prepare for the sensation. When the lift operator dropped them a little too much too quickly, she felt her throat fill and clenched the railing, white knuckled.

Once they were in position, Adrian offered her a sympathetic smile. "That's as bad as it gets."

"Thank goodness for that." She removed the camera and took a wide shot of the window, followed by a closeup of the pane of glass, still very much intact.

The window had been propped open on the far side with a piece of wood. Ashlyn photographed it as well and then peered between the ledge and the bottom edge of the window, moving from side to side in the basket and zooming in on the markings on the wall.

No wonder Carl didn't have a clue what it was. It looked like nonsense.

She started with the fingerprint powder next, covering the window ledge first and dusting it for prints. Then she dusted the bottom of the window.

"Are you going to do this to everything you can reach?"

Ashlyn nodded. "Actually, it would help if you could hold the window up so I can dust the wood."

He took the gloves she passed him and pulled them on before pushing the window up from the outside of the pane of glass, instead of the frame. Adrian raised it just enough for her to remove the piece of lumber. "It's staying up, actually."

"How is it going up there?" Daly's voice crackled over the radio.

Ashlyn and Adrian exchanged a smile, and she reached for the radio. "Fine. The window hadn't been broken. It was propped open."

When she was finished with the wood, she leaned in through the window and started dusting the table. It was just like Carl remembered. She was beginning to understand why it could be so difficult to find usable evidence at an arson scene, with soot and pools of water intermixing to ruin potential remnants of DNA or fingerprints that might have helped their case.

*The legs. If I can just get to the legs . . .*

That was when she saw the bundle on the floor. Ashlyn pulled herself back into the bucket and removed her gloves.

"What is it?"

"I'm not sure." She secured the camera strap around her wrist and wriggled back into the opening as far as she could.

Once she'd replaced the camera and put on a new pair of gloves, she grabbed the kit. "I'm going in there."

"Wait a second. I was told—"

"To take me up here and navigate this bucket into the correct position."

He glared at her. "You're going to get me into shit with your boss."

"Why is it that everyone seems to forget we're investigating a murder here? The murder of a child?"

"What good are you to her or those other kids if you fall through those floorboards and get yourself killed?"

She pulled herself up on the ledge. "That's a chance I'm willing to take."

"Is she doing what I think she's doing?"

Daly raised the radio without relinquishing the binoculars. Beside him, he could feel Tain stiffen, craning his neck to see what was happening.

"Ashlyn Hart, if you don't get back into that basket right now, I'll write you up for disobeying a direct order."

He could see the firefighter turn to look down, shrugging as he held the window. Then the man turned around and reached for something, still holding the window with one hand.

"All you can do is yell at her. I can't put this window down or she'll be stuck in there."

"What the hell is so important that she's gone in for?"

"Something on the floor. By the table."

"What is it?"

"I don't know. We couldn't tell. Jesus—"

The radio cut out, and Tain grabbed the binoculars out of Daly's hand.

"Can you see anything?"

Tain's shoulders sagged. "He's clipped himself to the basket and is halfway in the window."

Daly's hand covered his face. "What the hell have I done?"

"It's not your fault."

"Small consolation if something happens to her."

Tain lowered the binoculars. "Why do you think I told you? You think she's going to tell me the next time she plans to do something foolish?"

"If I'd listened to you, at least we could be certain there'd be a next time."

"That was the whole point, Sergeant."

Daly watched Tain walk over to the truck and lean against it as though he was stretching for a race, his head down.

Ashlyn had gently nudged the table aside, lowering her feet to the floor cautiously, hands still on the ledge.

The floor seemed solid and stable, though she had a fleeting recollection of the crack that had broken the silence when Tain went through the boards in the hallway.

She started with the table legs, completing the two closest to the window first and then moving to the third, the one nearest the bundle on the floor.

Just as she'd finished taking the prints from that leg, she felt the board under her left foot sag. Zipping her pouch hastily, she took a step to the side, toward the bundle, and heard the snap as her body jerked downward.

"Ashlyn, give me your hand," Adrian called. She knew it was pointless: She was too far from the window now, her body twisted away from him.

"Okay, give me your foot. Can you get your other foot out?"

Her left leg tingled, but there was no searing pain, no sign of blood. She put her hands as close to the hole as she dared and started to pull her leg up.

That was when things got tricky. She heard the tear before she felt it, presumably a nail slicing the skin.

Ashlyn lowered her leg again until she felt her pants pull free and moved her leg away from the nail. Then she lifted it slowly.

She managed to wriggle her foot through the opening, marveling at how something that found a way in could suddenly be too big to get out, when she heard the long creak as the floor beneath her groaned. Realizing she didn't have much time, she reached for the bundle and just managed to grasp it with her fingers as the boards sagged again. She fell a few inches and then she felt her body being pulled back toward the window.

"Stay as still as you can," Adrian told her. She could feel his arm tightly wrapped around her ankles, the bite of pain in the injured leg and guessed he was trying to wriggle back through the window without letting it fall on her.

Ashlyn could see through the floor now, to the room below. "Oh my God."

"What's wrong?" he asked frantically. "Are you . . ."

"Oh, nothing. I mean, I'm okay."

"I'm going to lift you up now. Try to keep your body steady, keep it from snapping down."

She tensed muscles she barely remembered she had. He jerked her up quickly, her legs not even impacting the ledge until her knees were back beyond the edge of the bucket.

"Give me that," Adrian grumbled, releasing her legs after she assured him she was secure. She reached back and passed him the fabric bag.

He grabbed the wood and stuck it back under the window ledge. "Now, let's get you back in here and get down. You're done."

"Not before you give me the camera."

Adrian glared at her. "You tempted fate once. Isn't that enough?"

"Look, you can hold me, right? I won't move forward an inch. Just give me the damn camera."

"What the hell is going on up there?" Daly's voice cut in over the radio again. They both ignored it.

"Fine," Adrian said, bending for the camera and passing it to her. "But I take it back."

"Take what back?"

"I wouldn't want you working with my squad. You'd get somebody killed."

The worst thing about the drive to the emergency room had been the silence.

Daly had dealt with the evidence, since he had to return to the station to check up on another case. That left Tain setting Ashlyn gingerly on the front seat, treating her like some delicate doll he thought would break if he didn't wrap her up properly before transporting her.

The pain that hadn't felt so bad when she was being cut open had become steadily worse. Adrian had wrapped her leg while they were being lowered, but the blood was spotting through already.

Once they'd reached the hospital, Tain had stuck a police identification tag in the window and left the car near the ambulance bay before picking her up and carrying her inside.

She tried for an appreciative but apologetic smile. "I can manage with just a bit of help, you know."

"Clearly, you can't."

"What does that mean?" she demanded.

"The Ashlyn I know would have taken my head off for treating her like a damsel in distress."

"The Tain I knew from a year ago would never—"

"Constable Hart?"

She pushed herself up on her good leg.

"I'm Dr. Zaid. There's no need." She held up a hand as Tain stood, about to pick Ashlyn up again. The doctor disappeared into the hallway and returned with a wheelchair. "Seems to be my week for police officers. Now, what have you done to yourself?" she asked as she wheeled Ashlyn away.

Daly glanced at the call display and groaned. He hadn't left the arson scene yet, and he knew he was running late.

"I haven't forgotten," he said instead of a greeting.

"Good. I've already started dinner."

"Okay. I won't be much longer."

He hung up the phone as Paul Quinlan marched over.

"What the hell was she thinking?"

Daly tossed his hands in the air helplessly. "You've never had a problem holding a man back when he knew someone was inside?"

Some of the fire left Paul's face. "You're going to give her a pass?"

"I've got an officer who was just raped by the perp she's been trying to catch, two girls who have been abducted and two more who have already turned up murdered and a serial arsonist running around, playing with matches."

Adrian Vaughan came into view as he walked around Daly to stand by Paul. "You knew she was going to cross the line. That's why you radioed up there."

"I didn't know anything until Tain told me. If I'd listened to him right away, I could have grounded her."

"Look, this fire department has had enough to deal with. The arsons, two of those missing kids turning up at fire scenes, and now one of our own has to bury his wife because she was raped and murdered."

Daly blinked. "Mr. Sandhu is on your squad?"

"Rav was transferred temporarily to fill in for someone on sick leave." There was silence for a moment, and then the remaining tension in Paul's shoulders dissipated. "Look, I know you're under pressure. I won't file a formal complaint, as long as everyone here agrees to let it go."

Daly glanced at Adrian, who stared back at him for a moment and then nodded. "You kick her ass," he told Daly, pointing at him. "She might be willing to take risks, but I wasn't prepared to let her die for it, not when I'm backing her up."

"Noted. Don't worry. I'll deal with her later."

"You'd better." Adrian walked away, giving Daly a chance to thank Paul for his leniency.

"It doesn't excuse what she did, but it sounds like—"

A voice cut through from behind them. "Boss! We've got another fire. A biggie."

"Suspected arson?"

"Not this time. Hotel fire. Occupants inside."

"Let's move." Paul Quinlan turned and started giving orders, Daly and Ashlyn's recklessness apparently forgotten.

Daly watched as, within seconds, the truck was pulling away, sirens blaring.

Tain had driven Ashlyn from the hospital to the station. She'd had a chance to shower and change before driving to the address Alison Daly had given her for the dinner party.

It didn't take long to get to the house, which was in the south part of Port Moody, on a relatively quiet street with lots of trees. As she sat in her car, listening to nothing but the sound of wind rustling leaves and the far-off calls of kids in a nearby park, she realized she'd been on autopilot, avoiding all the thoughts she kept suppressing.

She got out of the car and started limping to the sidewalk when she saw the Rodeo pull up. Even then, it didn't fully register, and when she realized whose vehicle it was she felt her cheeks burn.

He smiled as he got out of his vehicle. Craig looked exactly as she remembered him. Mentally she was kicking herself. She should have known right away who Steve and Alison would want her to have dinner with. Maybe she'd just been in denial.

All she knew was she was glad she had her hand on her car because her knees almost gave out.

"It's been a while," he said.

She nodded and limped forward.

Craig looked down at her leg. "What happened?"

She shrugged and offered a sheepish smile. "All in the line of duty."

The front door opened. "No crutches?" Daly asked.

Her eyes narrowed. "Try not to sound so disappointed."

"I might not complain about an excuse to keep you at a

desk for a few days right now. You should still keep off that leg, give it a chance to heal."

Ashlyn blew out a deep breath. "I will. I'll rest it all night while I sleep."

Daly led them into the living room. "Ashlyn, you might think you're getting away with this now, but I will speak to you about this."

"You just can't accept the fact that I might get hurt on the job. We wouldn't even be having this conversation if it had been Tain or Craig."

"Craig and Tain obey orders."

"What planet are you on? You must be living in a parallel universe." Her cheeks were burning now, and she forced herself to stare at Daly so that she didn't have to see the look on Craig's face.

"Stop trying to deflect responsibility by bringing up my past transgressions, Ashlyn. What did she do, Dad?"

She glared at him. "Craig—"

"I thought we agreed there would be no talk about work," Alison said as she walked into the room. "This is a house-warming party for Craig, not an inquisition."

"This is your house?"

"Whose house did you think it was?" he asked.

She hadn't thought it was possible for her face to get any hotter, but she'd been wrong. "But there's furniture."

"Courtesy of my parents."

"Oh, is that why there isn't plastic on it?"

"I took it off when I got here," Alison said.

"I didn't even know you were working in the lower mainland until now, Ashlyn," Craig said. "Someone neglected to mention that."

"I should have called. First it was the arson investigation, and then I got partnered with Tain on these child abductions."

"Where are things at with the arson cases?" Daly asked her. "With everything else going on, I keep forgetting."

"I've gone over everything that Robinson had for the fires June fourteenth, July eighth and July twenty-fifth," Ashlyn said. She noticed Craig's eyes pinch together, the twist of his jaw that had always betrayed the fact that he was thinking about work when they were partnered. "To be honest, we've got as much from the two fires this past weekend as we do from the earlier ones, which isn't much."

Alison called from the kitchen, reminding them that there was to be no talk about work and asking for help. Ashlyn got up, hobbling out of the living room, leaving the conversation about the cases to continue without her.

Daly relayed the status of the investigations, right up to Ashlyn's trip to the hospital.

"Do you have a working theory on your case?" Craig asked.

"Well, right now, best we can figure is that the arsons and the abductions are connected somehow. Julie and Isabella were both found at arson scenes connected to the cases Ashlyn is working on. What is it?" Daly asked. His eyes narrowed as he looked at Craig's face.

Craig opened his mouth to answer.

"Okay, dinner is ready. And I've already warned you about talking about work twice. We're going to have a pleasant evening socializing without any mention of crime," Alison said. Her eyes met Daly's first, then Craig's. "Understood?"

After dinner the conversation eventually returned to work.

"I don't think I've ever heard you mention Tain," Alison said to Steve.

"That's surprising," Ashlyn said. "Tain has quite a reputation."

Craig said, "Actually, Dad never talks about work at home, unless I'm there."

"What? Total separation of the job and marriage?"

"You think I want to go home and talk about you guys?" Daly said. "That's precious time I'd never get back, and I can think of plenty of better things to waste it on if I'm just looking to fill hours. It's called having a life."

"Maybe you should teach that class at the Depot, Steve," Ashlyn said, lifting her glass. "How to Be a Police Officer and Still Be a Person 101."

"You two would have failed," Daly said.

They took their dessert to the living room.

"I hope you don't mind," Alison said. "This gives Ashlyn a chance to elevate her leg."

Craig shook his head. "You know me, I'm not fussy. Strawberry-rhubarb crumble. You made all my favorites."

"That was the idea," Alison said. "So, what do you think of your present?"

"It's funny, I was just thinking about patio furniture the other day."

"Ah." Daly stood up. "Then you haven't seen what else is out there. Come on, I'll show you the barbecue. Just your basic starter, but I suspect you'll get a lot of use out of it."

"You mean I'm supposed to cook?" Craig followed Daly outside. "Are you going to give her a reprimand?"

Daly sighed. "Don't start."

"Come on. You and I both know there've been times you've crossed the line when you thought it was necessary."

"She almost got herself killed today, Craig. You have to be prepared to carry a lot in this job, but I'm not prepared to shoulder unnecessary risks." Daly sank into one of the patio chairs, and Craig followed suit, noticing that the evening was unusually dark, despite the fact that it was early.

"I thought it was unfair to put Ashlyn with a partner she'd have to keep an eye on, but Hawkins insisted." Daly rubbed the side of his face. "Turns out Tain is the reliable one."

Craig looked past Daly, in through the patio doors to where Ashlyn sat on the smaller sofa, chatting casually with Daly's wife. "You're being a bit harsh, don't you think? Would we even be having this conversation if it had been Tain?"

"No, because you'd think he deserved what he got. Just because you and Ashlyn worked together before . . ." Daly leaned back, looking up at the sky, his thought left unfinished.

"Why didn't you tell me she was here?"

"You were having enough problems with Lori. Did you want me to throw it in your face? 'Oh, by the way, Craig, the one person you actually have gotten along with over the years is here, in the lower mainland, but she's working with Tain.' I didn't think it was the right time to mention it."

Daly stood and started walking back to the house. He glanced over his shoulder as he opened the patio door.

Craig got up and followed him inside without another word. Alison was in the living room by herself. He left his parents and found Ashlyn in the kitchen.

"I told Alison she didn't have to do that."

"She didn't. After all, she cooked."

Craig took the tea towel off the stove and intercepted the dish Ashlyn was about to set in the drainer.

"They can air dry, you know."

"And they could've been washed mechanically if I'd phoned the repairman." He watched her silently, her hair hanging just past her shoulders now, a few inches longer than it had been when he first met her, her eagle eyes surveying his yard in the meticulous way he'd seen her survey crime scene after crime scene. "What's it like, working with Tain again?"

The corners of her eyes crinkled, and she shrugged. "Not as bad as I thought it would be." She glanced up at him and smiled. "Really. He almost took my head off at a crime scene before he knew it was me."

"Ah, so he has retained his unique charm."

"Older and a slight bit wiser, but don't tell him I said that."

"Which makes you, what? Just a bit older?"

Her eyes pinched together as she glanced at him. "Steve told you."

"He'll get over it."

"You mean he didn't send you in here to lecture me?"

"Ashlyn, do you really think I need him to ask me to? If I thought it would do any good, I'd tear a strip off you myself."

"So you think I'm hopeless?" The murmur of voices from the other room sounded like they were getting closer.

"You know that's not what I meant."

He didn't avert his gaze when she looked up at him again, a shadow passing behind her eyes so quickly that he almost thought he'd imagined it, but when his parents walked in and she turned toward them it was a forced smile that emerged. One that didn't reach her eyes.

"How long do you need to go easy on that leg?" Daly asked her.

She shrugged. "A couple of days."

"That's good. Then you won't be able to go anywhere tomorrow. That will give you plenty of time to rest."

"Tain can drive. The doctor said it's actually good for me to get up a bit, keep the blood circulating."

"Tain can handle things without you, and you can do your hobbling at home. You're taking the day off."

She opened her mouth to protest, and he raised his hand. Craig knew the look on Daly's face, and a quick glance at Ashlyn told him that deep down, she knew better than to argue with Daly when he got like this.

Craig thanked them for the dinner, and Ashlyn didn't try to avoid leaving when his parents made their exit. Part of him wanted to ask her to wait, but one look at his parents told him it wasn't a good idea. Not tonight.

Once they were gone he drifted around the main floor, not really thinking about what he was doing. Within a few minutes, he'd settled down on the smaller sofa, staring vacuously at the fireplace, his thoughts drifting back to that case last fall.

If it hadn't been for the temporary transfer he hadn't wanted—and had tried hard to get out of—he wouldn't have met Tain and Ashlyn almost a year ago.

It wasn't that he hadn't wanted to keep in touch. He'd picked up the phone more times than he could recall and dialed Ashlyn's number, but every time, he'd felt at a loss to know what to say and replaced the handset before the call went through.

There'd been so much he could have said in the weeks after, but he'd been wound too tight, fighting too hard to stay in control, dealing with too much of his life being exposed and the wounds still being raw.

He glanced at the solitary glass on the coffee table, wished he had more than juice and water on hand, and stood up. Craig flicked the light off and took the glass to the kitchen, wondering how well Tain and Ashlyn worked together.

Wondering why it bothered him so much that she seemed happy.

Lori sat on the edge of the bed, overdressed compared to her usual sleeping attire, blankly gazing through the window to the darkness in the sky, listening to the whir of the electronic toothbrush, the sound of water running, silence, then the splash of fluid being spit against the sink.

The usual bathroom sounds were just the background blur as she sat there, not really knowing what she should think about, not really knowing what was next. It had all come out from under her in a heartbeat, that second when she turned to find someone moving toward her in the darkness, someone who would change everything for her.

Send her life spiraling out of control, turn her world upside down or pull the rug out from under her feet . . . How many ways were there to politely say that someone had made a choice and that the result was that she had to get an HIV test, go through STD screenings, that she had to make a statement about what it felt like to have someone force her down on her own bed.

Lori yelped and realized she'd dug her nails into the flesh of her palms. She knew she'd heard the footsteps approaching, somewhere in the layers of sound and sensation her brain was processing, but she still jumped when she felt his hand on her shoulder and pulled forward from his grasp instinctively.

"I . . . don't think I can sleep in here anymore," she said, standing suddenly, reaching for her housecoat to pull over her already-covered body.

"I thought the doctor said it was best for you to try to regain control of your life, to not let this person take away anything more than he already had."

*Anything more than he already had . . .* What is that, exactly?

Her sense of security, her self-confidence, her dignity? She fumbled with the cord on her housecoat, her hand shaking so violently she had to physically force herself to stop and draw a deep breath as hot tears stung her eyes.

"You've got it all figured out, haven't you? Doesn't bother you to sleep in the bed I was raped on."

He got up from the bed and followed her toward the hallway. "Lori, you're being ridiculous. Yesterday you said—"

"Yesterday I was wrong," she snapped. "Oh, I'm sorry. You expect me to have this all figured out in a matter of hours and just move on. Well this isn't like charting a course for a sailboat, Vish, so give me a goddamned fucking break if it takes me a while to get it together."

She stomped down the hall, and the whole house shuddered with the force she used to slam the door to the den behind her, her shoulders quivering as she slumped back against it, her body sliding down as she covered her mouth and choked back her sobs.

Ashlyn's shoulders lifted before she forced her torso down again, remembering that her leg injury meant she had to sleep on her back and forgo the usual tossing and turning she did on any given night.

"Damn," she muttered, her eyes staring up at the blackness, only a thin shimmer of moonlight glistening on the chimes above her bed.

Bear chimes that Craig had bought her. *To remind you*, his note had said.

As though she could forget.

The next day, he'd been gone.

It had been glossed over, with terms like "unexpected" and "sudden departure" and "serious case" being thrown about to mask what it really was for her: Craig had been ripped from her life. She hadn't known until then how much she'd relied on him when they worked together before.

She squeezed her eyes shut, but all she could see was the look on Craig's face the first night she'd met him. . . .

When she opened her eyes his image remained.

She brushed the tears aside, the ones that always came when she thought of that case. Maybe that was the real reason Craig seemed so damned important to her. He'd gotten her through it all. Then he'd been gone in the blink of an eye.

Her thoughts shifted to the girls they were looking for, the body of Isabella Bertini lying on the cement in front of her, and she shut her eyes again, this time, her mind ready to rest.

"Martha."

"No, what's your real name?"

"Shhh. I don't want to get lashed."

For a moment, Taylor thought that the girl was going to listen to her, but then she heard the quietest steps coming toward her and felt the bed sag as the girl sat down beside her.

"My name's Lindsay."

"He says to call you Delilah."

"That's not my real name, and I don't like it."

"It's God's chosen name for you."

"Then why didn't God tell me Himself?"

Taylor opened her mouth to answer, then closed it again.

"What's your real name?"

She mashed her lips together, saying nothing.

"Are you Taylor?"

"Ho-how do you know?"

"We said a prayer for you at Mass on Sunday morning."

"Oh." Taylor felt her heart sink. It didn't make any sense. Why did she feel so scared that this girl knew her real name?

"We have to try to find a way out of here."

"Why?"

"He's going to hurt us. Those other girls . . . they're dead."

"What girls?"

"Didn't you watch the news?"

Taylor shook her head.

"The day he took you, they found a girl. What do you remember about the day he took you?"

*Nicky, Nicky, Nicky . . .*

"I was looking for my brother at the fairgrounds."

"That's where he grabbed you from?"

She nodded.

"Then what?"

*I'd opened my eyes, but all I could see was black. I rolled around a bit, trying to sit up, but I could feel the car and hear the engine. My leg bumped something, another leg, and I wriggled over as close as I could, my nose touching hair, but there was rope in my mouth. Just like the rope in your mouth when he brought you here. Wanting to scream and the person there, in the darkness, didn't wake up or say anything. . . .*

"Do you remember how you got in here?"

Taylor hugged her legs to her body, her chin resting on her knee.

"I want to go home," Lindsay told her.

She heard the tremor in the words and knew what that felt like, wanting to cry but needing to be brave, biting your lip or putting your face into the pillow if it was really bad.

"Do . . . you really think he's going to hurt us?"

Lindsay leaned so close that Taylor could feel her hot breath on her cheek. "I think he's going to kill us."

# WEDNESDAY

"You've got to be kidding me," Tain murmured as he listened to the message on his voice mail, Daly telling him that Ashlyn wouldn't be coming in as per his orders. Tain smiled, for a moment forgetting how much this complicated his life as he imagined the look on Ashlyn's face when Daly told her she was taking a sick day.

With Ashlyn not in, John-John moved to the top of his list. Maybe he could rule that out without any complications and keep her from getting into more hot water. His smile faded as he thought about what Ashlyn would say if she knew he was trying to shield her, but it didn't stop him from grabbing his jacket, a few files and walking out to the car.

Knowing it would be early for John-John to make an appearance on the streets, Tain did a little recon in the area where John-John usually worked, then stopped at a local Tim Hortons.

So far, the open abduction cases hadn't turned up anything pertinent. Daly had intervened and passed those off to Sims. Shit. Sims had left a message saying to see him about that Wilson character. . . . Tain flipped to the page in his notepad, hoping he'd remember to track Sims down. Something about Wilson just didn't sit right.

The list of recreation center member names hadn't yielded much in the way of criminal interest, but there it was, near the bottom, too much of a coincidence not to take a hard look at.

Alex Wilson was a member at the Southside Recreation and Fitness Center where Lindsay Eckert was abducted. Alex

Wilson wasn't exactly a rare name, but it was worth checking it out to see if it was the same Alex Wilson. Tain reached for his cell phone and glanced at his watch when he got the voice mail and left a message.

He was sitting in his car now, sipping coffee. Something he'd acquired a taste for during the past year, as he put in longer hours and spent more time working alone. A solitary figure stepped out of a doorway onto the sidewalk, glancing in the opposite direction, oversized hands stuffed in the pockets of the leather coat, the bald head reflecting sunlight.

Tain didn't need the quick glance at the photo to tell him who that was. He opened the door and got out of the car.

"Yeah?" Ashlyn groaned, her hand covering her eyes as she spoke into the handset.

"You actually stayed at home and you're sleeping in? There might be hope for you yet."

"Very funny, Steve." She risked exposure to the light with a quick glance at the clock. Ashlyn groaned. "I didn't realize it was so late."

"With all the hours on this case—"

"Yeah, yeah, I likely needed it. What's up? You want me to come in, after all?"

Daly laughed. "Can't blame you for trying, can I?"

She smiled as she sat up, inspecting her lower leg and foot. The searing pain that had escalated after she'd sliced it had subsided with the assistance of painkillers, but it hadn't returned during the night.

"Honestly, I just called to check up on you."

"I know."

"I meant—"

"It's okay, Steve. You're just calling to make sure I'm okay. No pain, no swelling and—" she propped the phone between her shoulder and her head as she removed the last of the bandages—"the wound is clean. Doesn't look like it's infected. I'll be parading around in short skirts again in no time."

"You didn't bump your head when you were up there, did you?"

She smiled, trying to sound mildly offended as she said good-bye and hung up.

Craig sat down across from Daly. "It was either genuinely funny, or the job stress is getting to you."

"Maybe a bit of both. But this time, amusement was the greater part of the mix." Daly's smile faded as he studied Craig's face. "Why do I get the feeling that what you're going to say isn't going to be good for my blood pressure?"

"As though much I say or do ever is."

"Point taken."

"Look, it's just something that came up last night, about the dates of those arson cases Ashlyn's working. June fourteenth, July eighth, July twenty-fifth, August eighteenth and August nineteenth are all dates the arsons have happened on, the ones that were linked by MO when the case was still Robinson's, right?"

Daly nodded. "And June fourteenth was when Julie Darrens was abducted. Isabella Bertini was abducted July eighth. Julie's body was found at a fire July twenty-fifth, and as you likely know, the two most recent dates corresponded to finding Isabella Bertini's body and the abductions of Taylor Brennen and Lindsay Eckert."

"June fourteenth, July eighth, July twenty-fifth, August eighteenth, August nineteenth . . . Doesn't anything else about those dates sound familiar?"

Daly paused. "Those are the dates of your rape cases."

"Three big investigations happening simultaneously and the dates match for all of them. Doesn't that strike you as odd?"

"There was also an arson on July eighteenth. You don't have a rape reported for that date."

"Which is hardly conclusive, given the stats on rape reports."

"Those same statistics could mean there are a dozen more rapes that we don't even know about yet. We certainly know there aren't a dozen more fires we haven't heard about."

"You don't have a child abduction matching July eighteenth either."

Daly leaned back in his chair and groaned. "What are you thinking?"

"Just that it's odd. It's got me wondering . . ." Craig paused, then shrugged.

"I find it hard to fathom how a rapist could connect to child abductions and murders. At least, this rapist. None of these girls has been sexually assaulted, a fact we haven't released to the press."

Craig frowned. "I'm surprised Hawkins wouldn't want to reassure the public with that small piece of consolation."

"Hawkins has certainly had his own agenda with all of these cases, from the beginning," Daly muttered. Then he glared at Craig. "And you know better than to repeat that outside this office."

Craig put up his hands. "No need to worry about me. I'm just hoping he'll back off from the rape investigation a bit. This thing with Lori seems . . ." He shrugged again, unwilling to voice his thoughts, even to his dad.

Daly reached for the ringing phone and barely managed two words before he hung up and passed Craig the note he'd scrawled.

"Another rape."

"We know there wasn't an arson fire last night."

"Careful. I'm starting to believe in coincidences. And the Tooth Fairy and Santa Claus."

John-John spat on the sidewalk as Tain approached him. "Fucking cops. I can smell you lot a mile away. Whaddya want?"

"Connie Brennen," Tain said. "I can see from the sneer that you know who I'm talking about."

"So what if I do? She hasn't been down this way in ages. Not since she roped some sucker into marital bliss."

"You telling me you didn't have a bit of an axe to grind with her? No lingering grudges, scores to settle?"

"What the fuck? Why'd I waste my time goin' after her now?"

"You've gone after others before."

John-John stared at him, and Tain glared back, waiting to see what he'd do.

Finally, John-John shrugged and sank back against the stairway he was leaning against, his oversized ass pressed against the concrete and spilling over like waffle batter when too much is put on the grill. "This business, sometimes you have to have a firm hand. Spare the rod and all that. You gotta know how hard it is makin' a bitch behave."

"So you admit you like to keep your girls in line."

"I don't 'like' it. I do what I gotta do to make sure the bills get paid."

"Just a respectable businessman."

"That's right. Fucking tax-paying citizen."

"And Jenny Fowler? That whole little mess with her girl was just what? Protecting your investment?"

The snarl returned. "Hey, I was cleared of that. No way you're coming back on me about that now."

Tain held up his hand. "I actually want to talk to you about Taylor."

"Taylor who?"

"You're serious? You can know who Connie Brennen is—and that's her married name—but you're telling me you don't know the name of her kid? The one born less than nine months after Connie stopped working for you?"

John-John's mouth set in a hard line, but he didn't try to get up again. "That Taylor. What about her?"

"I heard some interesting rumors."

"Yeah? She following in her mama's footsteps? Bit young, but there are those who'll pay top dollar for that sort of thing."

"Doesn't make your gut twist to think of some perv having a go at your own kid?"

John-John's face paled and then flushed hot. "What the fuck are you saying? Taylor's my kid? No fucking way."

"Word was you were Connie's steady back then."

He snorted. "Connie fucked anyone who could scrape up enough cash, and that you oughtta know that. When she got herself knocked up it could have been half of the local trade who was responsible."

"Bit of a stretch on the suspect list, don't you think?"

"She did a lot of business. Real efficient."

Tain felt his lip curl. "So you're telling me that you don't think Taylor Brennen's really your kid?"

John-John shook his head. "I mean, not like I'm saying I couldn't perform the services, but it coulda been anyone, like I said. Connie spent more time out of her undies than in them." He glared at Tain. "What d'you care, anyway?"

"You don't know?"

John-John stood up, but he didn't draw himself to his full height. "Like I said, haven't seen Connie in years."

"You not heard about the guy going around snatching young girls?"

"Them ones found in burning buildings?" He shrugged. "Heard something about it."

"He snatched Taylor Brennen last weekend."

There was no widening of the eyes, no change in the color of John-John's face, nothing to give Tain a clue about what he was thinking. Tain pulled a card from his pocket.

"If you do think of anything, anyone with some special interests, anyone with a grudge against Connie—"

"What good would that do? Those other kids, their mothers working girls too?"

Tain shook his head. "Just being thorough. Always possible when kids go missing that someone else takes advantage of it, you know? Try to hide their crime behind the obvious suspect."

John-John nodded as he sauntered off down the street, and Tain started walking back to the car.

*Now, I guess we'll see whether he was being straight with me.*

Craig held his ID up, and the woman pulled the door open.

He stepped inside the townhouse and followed her as she led him down the hall to a cozy living room.

"Can I get you some coffee, tea?"

"No, thank you. I'd like to speak to Michelle, whenever she's ready."

The woman looked up from the kitchen, visible on the other side of the counter that bordered the living area. "I'm Michelle."

Craig felt his eyes pinch slightly as the woman turned, replacing the jug of milk inside the fridge, seemingly unaffected by his failure to identify her as the latest rape victim.

He'd seen a bit of everything from these women. Anger, emptiness, desperation . . . For a woman who'd been raped last night, she was really holding it together.

"You sure?" she asked again, pointing at her mug as she sat down across from him.

He shook his head as she crossed her legs, her hands folded on her lap. "Where do we begin?" she asked.

"You're Michelle Bohner, and you phoned the station this morning to report that you'd been raped."

She nodded. "That's right."

"Can you tell me what happened?"

"Well, I'd just come out of the shower when he grabbed me."

"Did you see him?"

She shook her head. "No. I just felt his hands around my arms." She took a sip of her drink. "He pushed me down the hall into my bedroom."

"I know this might not be easy, but can you tell me what happened then?"

"He tied me up and raped me."

Craig took as long as possible to draw a big question mark on his notepad before looking up. "Can you tell me how he tied you up?"

"He took the cord off my bathrobe and tied my arms to the headboard."

"Together or separated?"

"Together," she said, holding her wrists together and lifting them over her head. "Like this."

Craig made another note. "Did he gag your mouth or cover your eyes?"

"He . . ." She looked away for a moment before uncrossing

and recrossing her legs. "He covered my face with his hand and told me to shut my eyes or he'd kill me. I just did what I was told."

"Okay, Ms. Bohner—"

"Mrs."

"Sorry. You live here with your husband?"

"And ten-year-old daughter, Jolene."

"Where was she when this happened?"

"She and her dad are away, camping. They won't be back until the end of next week."

Craig glanced at the bookshelf, a family photo on display. "What does your husband do?"

"Semi-retired. He used to be a mechanic, fixing fire trucks and stuff like that. Still goes in occasionally on call."

"I see. So, what happened next?"

She shrugged. "He left."

"How did you get free?"

"I worked my hands out."

"Did you take another shower, wash the sheets on your bed?"

Her eyes narrowed. "Uh, is that a problem?"

"Michelle, we really need to bring in a team and have them look for evidence."

"Isn't my statement enough?"

"I'm afraid it's exceptionally difficult to bring charges in rape cases and even harder to get a conviction. If we could find some DNA or fingerprints, we'd have irrefutable evidence to present in court that would help us put this guy away."

She stared at him for a moment and then blinked. "I . . . I'm not sure."

"Mrs. Bohner, I'm not going to lie to you. Without having rape-kit results and data from evidence recovery here at the scene, it will be virtually impossible for us to get a conviction."

She stared at him and blinked again, the color starting to drain out of her face.

Ashlyn sat down on the couch, propped her foot up on a pillow and reached for the first folder. She wasn't one to copy files and bring them home en masse. Typically, if a case had taken over her life, she'd be at the station anyway.

But something had niggled at her over the past few days, and she'd packed a bag complete with most of the general information on the abductions and arsons. When Tain had taken her back to the station to change she'd remembered to bring the copied files with her, and she silently gave thanks to whatever sixth sense had kicked in to motivate her to collect the data in the first place.

She opened the file on Julie Darrens and reached for a calendar and a pad of notepaper, her eyes already skimming the particulars noted inside, writing down *June 14* across the top of the blank page and underlining it, flipping the calendar back two months and noting as well that Julie Darrens had gone missing on a Thursday.

After she'd gone through the reports, Ashlyn set the file for Lindsay Eckert down, tapping her pen against the notepad resting on her leg, her fingers tugging their way through her hair.

She pulled the calendar out from under one of the other files and started counting. Not weeks. Nothing triggering there. Days between abductions? No. The intervals were random, scattered. She had a fleeting glimpse, a memory of doing the same thing, months before, when the missing teenagers' cases had been gathering dust on the shelves, right around the same time that the drug case was limping along on life support.

She looked at the dates between when the two girls were found, but that didn't help. They only had two.

Ashlyn pulled out her arson summary, making a new list, circling July eighteen. Why wasn't there an abduction for July eighteen? Was it possible there was a body they'd missed? She thought about all the open, missing-kids files that had been pulled because of this, but she couldn't recall one being brought to her attention that had seemed to fit the pattern.

Although she hadn't had as much time as Tain to review all the files. . . .

She counted the days between Julie's abduction and when they'd found her body. Exactly forty full days had passed.

Then she counted the days between when Isabella was taken and when her body had been carried from the burning building.

Forty full days.

She rested her cheek against her hand. It was something Craig had taught her, about looking at every angle on a case, even if it doesn't make sense to you.

Forty days.

She got up without too much trouble, noticing it was even easier now to cross the room to her iMac. She turned it on, limping to the kitchen for a refill.

It had to mean something. Random abduction dates, scattered locations the girls went missing from. Only two things connected that she could see. Fire and forty days between when they went missing and when they were found.

Ashlyn sat down in front of her computer and clicked on the Safari icon, then typed in the keywords she wanted information about.

Sims nodded. "One and the same."

"You're positive?" Tain asked.

"I even phoned the manager of the recreation center and got a description. Thick black glasses, bleach-blond hair, blue eyes, bit of a spindly freak. The manager's words, not mine," Sims added quickly.

"So his purpose in being at the recreation center isn't to use the weights."

Sims stared at him for a moment, and Tain was convinced the man couldn't have looked more surprised if Tain had grown a second head. "Guess not. He used to work for a photographer's studio, taking school pictures and group photos and stuff. Six months ago he started working at Cargo Clearance."

"Interesting."

Sims didn't pause as long this time. "It gets better. He took school photos at Holy Cross Elementary and Sacred Heart Elementary last fall. I double checked. Wilson took the school photos of them that have been printed in all the papers."

"Please tell me he connects to Burnaby Fine Arts."

Sims's smile faded. "Sorry. At least, not that I've found so far, but I'll check prior years. Could be she was in another group or something."

"Do we know why he changed jobs?"

"No." Sims passed Tain a slip of paper. "The manager wasn't very keen to talk about it. I figured some face-to-face persuasion might be in order."

Tain folded the paper and put it in his pocket, then snapped his fingers. "She was a Girl Guide." Tain turned and walked away.

Ashlyn unlatched the chain lock and opened the door.

"How's the leg?" Adrian asked, handing her a bundle of roses. She stepped back, setting the bouquet on the kitchen counter.

"Almost good as new." She led the way into her living room and sat down.

"But you stayed home anyway? That's not exactly the impression I had of you."

Ashlyn felt her nose wrinkle, and her neck itched. "I was ordered to take a day off."

"Ah," he said, surveying the room, glancing out the patio doors. "So this is home?"

"For now. How did you find out where I lived?"

He sat down in a chair opposite from her, close to her computer. "I have my sources. Seriously, I just wanted to make sure you were okay."

"Shouldn't I be the one sending you an apology instead of you bringing me flowers?"

Adrian offered a sheepish grin. "Yeah, I suppose."

"You were pretty choked."

"And I had all night to think about what I might do if I was working on a case like this." The smile faded. "I remember Carl bringing out that body, that one girl. It must get to you."

She guessed he could understand, on some level, but this wasn't something she was going to talk to him about. "Can I get you something? Tea, juice? My coffee maker is the third appliance this week that's gone on strike, and I haven't had a chance to deal with any of them."

"I'll give you the number for Bob. He's the repairman we use at the hall."

"That would be great."

His eyes surveyed the room, the few scattered, framed photographs she'd managed to get up since moving in, the lingering boxes waiting to be unpacked, stacked against the far wall, the plants gasping for water. Adrian's gaze lingered on the computer. "What on earth are you looking at?"

"Something about forty-day calendar cycles used in ancient times. Apparently some are advocating for the return to a forty-day month."

"Like the people who pushed for a change in daylight savings time?"

"It's not quite the same. I suppose there's a group out there voicing an opinion for just about everything."

He scratched his head. "Shame more people don't lead productive lives instead of whining about when to move clocks forward and back. What are you reading about this for, anyway?"

She bit her lip and looked slightly to the left of him. "Just something that came up."

"With your case."

Ashlyn looked at him. "What makes you say that?"

He nodded at the coffee table. "Files, calendars, notepaper . . . You're working." He held up his hands. "Relax. I'm not here to give you grief."

"Good. I heard more than enough from Tain and Daly yesterday."

A shadow crossed his face, his eyes betraying some darker thoughts that had surfaced in his mind, but the look passed almost as quickly as it appeared. "So, the forty-day month thing? How does that tie in?"

"That's what I'm trying to figure out. It might not be the calendar. I'm looking for anything significant about forty-day time frames."

"You mean like it raining for forty days and forty nights?" he asked.

"What's that from?"

His eyes widened. "Never heard of Noah's Ark?"

She felt her cheeks flush. "Of course. It's on Mount Ararat or something, but every time people try to prove it's there, they get shot at or kidnapped or struck by lightning."

Adrian leaned back for a moment, looking at her without speaking. Finally, he gave her a small smile. "Is it the job?"

"Is what the job?"

"The skepticism? I didn't peg you for such a cynic."

"I don't know much about religion. Noah's Ark is—" She shrugged.

"Biblical."

"I think even I'd worked out that much. What else can you tell me?"

"Just that when God judged the world, He sent rain for forty days and forty nights. I vaguely recall something about other references to the number forty, but it's been a long time since I was in Sunday school." He shrugged, smiled and stood up to leave. "I'd say you should talk to my cousin, but I think you deal with enough nutcases in your job already."

"Your cousin a priest or something?"

Adrian laughed. "You equate priests with crazy people? You really are a skeptic. No, my cousin was pretty hardcore. Spent a fair bit of time with the born-again Christians before getting drawn into some fringe group."

"Born-again Christians aren't fringe?"

"Okay, before getting into an even more bizarre group than them. Satisfied?"

"So he knows a lot about biblical . . . stuff?"

Adrian shrugged. "Spends a few hours a week loitering around the station working on his car, telling me about the wickedness of the world and how we're all going to be baptized to be purified before God."

"Family dinners must be fun."

The smile was back. "Slightly better than a root canal."

"Yes, but the department has a dental plan. Eradicating religious programming isn't covered."

"Does that mean I couldn't persuade you to come over on Sunday?" Before she had a chance to respond he put up his hands. "Look, if you're interested you know where to find me."

He walked out of the room, and she listened as the door opened and shut behind him, then got up to lock the door.

Daly gripped the arms of his chair, venting his anger into his fingers as Lori jumped to her feet.

"You're just saying that because you never wanted me on this case," she said.

His words came out controlled, calculated, despite her purple shade. "Sit back down and be glad I'm willing to overlook that remark, all things considered."

Lori did as she was told, her back as rigid as ever, shoulders squared, but some of the color had faded from her face.

"You aren't ready to come back to work."

"I disagree."

Daly ignored her. "Even if you were ready, you would have to be reassigned."

"That's ridiculous! Nobody knows more about this case than I do."

"And nobody is more likely to let her emotions override her judgment."

"When have you ever seen me do that on the job?"

"This isn't about your track record, Lori, which I have to say isn't stellar. You and Craig have had problems since the beginning." He held up his hand to silence her. "Right now our priority is solving this case as quickly as we can and making sure that we can get a conviction. Your participation in the investigation now would compromise that. A good defense attorney—"

"Fucking lawyers."

"We have to be realistic here. Your participation in this case could jeopardize an arrest." Daly stood, moved around to the other side of the desk and perched on the edge of the desk near her. "Go home. Take care of yourself. Spend some time with your family, friends, people who care about you and can support you."

She looked up at him, her eyes blazing, her cheeks ghostly white. "Don't make me go over your head." She hissed the words.

He lifted his hand. "There's the door. I'm not going to be coerced or pressured into making a decision that I know is wrong."

Lori stared at him, her mouth drawn in a harsh line, her back stiffening even more. She stood. "This isn't over," she said. She yanked the door open, then slammed it behind her with enough force to rattle the windows.

"Wha . . . what do you want?"

Tain noted that Alex Wilson's shoulders tensed, that his hand had dropped and not opened the screen door once he recognized the person standing on the front step, and the quick glance back toward the room he'd come from, as though hoping whatever was in there was securely hidden from a nosey police officer's eyes.

"Do you mind if I come in for a minute?" Tain reached for the handle.

Alex hastened to open the door and stepped outside instead, blocking the handle from Tain's reach. "What's this about? I told you everything."

"Just some follow-up questions. You have a membership at the rec center, the one on Twenty-fourth Ave."

"So?"

"Go there often?"

Alex Wilson folded his long, thin arms across his chest. "What are you? The bulk-up patrol?"

"It was just a question."

They stared at each other for a moment before Alex shrugged his right shoulder. "Often enough."

"Sunday night?"

"What about it?"

"Were you there Sunday night?"

"What do you care if I was?"

"A girl went missing from Southside Recreation and Fitness Center on Sunday night."

"I didn't find her brother in the parking lot."

"Nobody said you did."

"Then what do you want?"

All the anger and suspicion Tain had expected in their first encounter that hadn't been there, that had been suppressed under some form of guilt and fear, was surfacing now. Alex Wilson seemed to feel more comfortable on his home turf.

"Well, you're a member of that fitness center, and we've been trying to eliminate people from our suspect list for abducting Lindsay Eckert."

"What's that got to do with me?"

"We recovered some fingerprints from the scene, but, you know, there's plenty of passing traffic and such in a place like that. I was wondering if we could take your prints for the purpose of eliminating you, so we don't waste time looking for someone we know couldn't have taken her."

Alex's mouth hung open, a thin slit of darkness against his pale skin.

"Would that be okay?" Tain asked.

"Oh, I uh, I thought . . . Do I need a lawyer?"

"You didn't grab Taylor or Lindsay or those other girls, did you?"

He shook his head.

"Then there's nothing for you to worry about, is there? Just come down to the station and give them this," Tain said, removing a letter from his pocket. "Then, hopefully, we won't have to bother you again."

Alex took the letter and disappeared inside his house, promising to stop by on his way to work.

Tain walked back to the car. There was something going on with that guy.

"Now, you girls stay right here and don't move."

At first, nothing seemed unusual about that order to Taylor. There had been a few times that he'd made them sit for hours on the cold floor, usually after repeating the Pledges, as he called them, over and over and over again until the only thing she could hear in her head was the same words ringing in her ears.

Delilah—Lindsay—had even done well at sitting still this time. Taylor guessed the sores made it hard, but she was really trying. She hadn't been lashed yet today.

The door opened again, and a girl—the same girl Taylor had seen once before—walked in, carrying a tray.

She had long black hair and enormous dark eyes. Her skin wasn't dark-dark, not like what Taylor's mom called black, but it wasn't white either.

The girl set the tray down in front of them and then sat down on the ground, passing out the fancy cups and plates.

"You are ready now," she said. Taylor thought she sounded smug, like a schoolteacher who thinks you've finally got something you should have figured out ages ago.

The girl passed out the plates, thin wisps of steam rising from the bread, which smelled so good Taylor's stomach actually gurgled. There were pats of butter on the side of the plates, with small, flat wooden spoons.

"You can spread your butter on like this," the girl said, demonstrating how to use the flat spoon with the butter.

Taylor glanced at Lindsay and then reached for her bread.

The first bite seemed to dissolve on her tongue. Within seconds, the warm bread was gone.

She glanced at the door, then at the face of the girl who she'd almost begun to believe she'd dreamed about.

"What's your name?" Lindsay whispered.

"Hannah."

"Not your new name. Your real name." Lindsay reached for her bread.

"Hannah is the only name I need now."

"Don't you want to get out of here, go home?"

The new girl, Hannah, stared at Lindsay, who stared back at her. Then Hannah smiled. "I am going home. He says I'm almost ready. Like the others who used to be here. When they were ready, he took them home too."

"Ready for what?" Taylor asked.

"Ready to be pure before God."

"He's not sending you home. He's a sick person. He's going to kill you."

Hannah yanked the bread from Lindsay's hand. "Liar! You're the liar. Lies are the devil's work. She's evil," Hannah yelled, grabbing what was left on the tray and running from the room.

Once Hannah had disappeared, the man came and stood in the doorway. He shook his head.

"I thought you were ready. You still have much to learn."

Taylor felt a twisting inside her chest, but instead of coming in with the whip again, the man stepped back and locked the door behind him.

Daly rubbed his forehead, which did nothing to ease the pinch of the skin as he watched Tain pace back and forth.

"Maybe I was wrong," Tain said.

"Do you really think so?"

"Oh, I don't know. I mean, the guy definitely gave off a guilty vibe when he was here before, but not like it was about the girls. It was something else. When I asked about those girls, he seemed genuinely surprised."

"Then what did he have to be edgy about?"

Tain shook his head. "My gut, something about boys. The way he became still whenever I mentioned Nicky, the way he was too quick to defend himself and insist he hadn't done anything wrong . . . the fact that he never explained what he was doing in the park to begin with."

"Didn't you or Ashlyn tell me that one of the kids from Lindsay's church group mentioned something about a guy watching them change?"

"Yeah, but it wasn't Alex Wilson."

"You're sure?"

"Positive. The peeper was a lot younger. Wilson may be a bit of a seventies leftover, but he's not in the late teens, early twenties age bracket."

"So we need to take a good, hard look at Wilson."

"Sims did a thorough check. He definitely ties to Julie Darrens and Taylor Brennen, but I don't have a link for Lindsay or Isabella yet."

Daly thought about what Tain had told him, about Wilson's background. "Odd that he'd pick up Taylor Brennen's brother, drive him to a police station, the next day Taylor's picture, a picture he took himself, is splashed all over the news and he never says a word about it."

"That's what I mean. This guy, there's something going on with him. He was really uncomfortable with me showing up at his house today."

Daly frowned. "What were you doing at his house?"

"I went to talk him in to giving us his fingerprints for elimination purposes."

"Seriously?"

"Seriously. He didn't exactly admit it, but he didn't deny being at the recreation center Sunday night. I told him we had to print everyone and eliminate people we knew weren't involved so that we could try to find the person who took Lindsay."

"And he bought that?"

"My guess is, he was so relieved that I didn't think he'd nabbed the girls, he was willing to help. Like he was hiding something else that he was afraid I'd come to see him about, and when he realized it was just those girls, he stopped worrying."

"What's Ashlyn's take on him?"

"Unfortunately, she hasn't had a chance to size him up yet."

Daly's eyes narrowed slightly. "Why not?"

"Carl Parks was ready to talk at the same time Alex came in for his interview. She knew Carl, so she dealt with him. Truth is, I'd like to see how Alex responds to Ashlyn."

"What's your gut telling you?"

"This guy's got no use for women. Not in an aggressive kind of way, but I think he's afraid of them."

"It's not a crime to be gay."

"And I couldn't care less. But I'd put my money on his preferences being age and gender specific."

"Little boys."

"I think Ashlyn should talk to Nicky again, too."

Daly glanced up and stopped fiddling with the sticky notes he'd been rearranging.

"Just to be on the safe side."

"What are you going to do now?" Daly asked.

"Find out why Alex Wilson stopped working for the photographer."

"And then?"

"See if Burnaby has come up with a link for Taylor and Lindsay."

"You know, Tain, you could be right about Alex Wilson, and it could still be him."

"What do you mean?"

"The girls weren't raped. Whatever these abductions and murders are about, it isn't sex. Could it have something to do with working out some issue he's got with women by killing girls?"

"When I get my psychology degree I'll get back to you."

"Very funny."

"Sergeant Daly, why don't we have a profiler in on this?"

Daly glanced at the door until he felt reasonably certain nobody was lingering in the hall outside his office or approaching. "Some people are concerned that if we bring a profiler in now, it will send a message to the public that we weren't doing all we could from the beginning and we're trying to correct our mistakes."

"That's ridiculous. This wasn't eve—"

"Sit down, Tain, and lower the volume. It wasn't our case. You know that. I know that. You only got put on when Julie's body was found on our territory. That's still less than a month you've been working it, and that was as a back-burner resource person until the past few days. But the public won't care. We're under a lot of pressure, with this case and with one of our own officers being a victim of a serial rapist who's graduated to murder."

"So, what you're telling me is, someone's playing politics because we could use a profiler, and Craig could use a profiler as well, but if they bring one in now it will seem like the department didn't give a damn until one of our own was raped."

There was silence for a moment, and then Tain stood.

"I'll go track down Alex Wilson's former employer." Tain looked out into the hallway in silence, not moving, and then leaned down over Daly's desk.

"I thought lending Craig to that investigation last year was supposed to have earned you a big chip to cash in. Are you telling me that you don't have a favor left to call in, or that you won't use it for this?"

He straightened up and walked out of the room before Daly had a chance to respond. Daly leaned back and rubbed his temples, his eyes closed.

When he opened his eyes, he groaned.

Craig shut the door and smiled as he sat down. "That bad, huh?"

"I just talked to Tain."

"Ah. That can be enough to suck the will to live out of any senior officer."

Daly smiled. "I find it surprising you don't have any animosity toward Tain."

"I'm not a senior officer."

"And you share a common tendency toward insubordination and independence." Daly sighed. "And that's not all."

Craig's smile faded. "We worked together on a difficult case. Whenever you're in a tough situation and don't know who to trust, once you've worked that out you get pretty tight. You know that."

Daly nodded. "But I think there was more to it."

Craig could feel his neck burn and stiffen simultaneously. "I never crossed the line. Not with—"

Daly held up his hand. "It's none of my business."

"Damn right it isn't."

Daly drew in a sharp breath, but didn't respond to that. "You here to fill me in?"

Craig waited until he was sure he could siphon all the

anger out of his voice. "We went over the scene thoroughly once we got consent."

"What do you mean, once you got consent?"

"Our victim wasn't too keen to have us search for evidence."

Daly stared at him. He knew that look on Craig's face, the one that hinted at a thousand things being deliberately left unsaid. "Out with it."

"My gut tells me she wasn't raped."

"You're serious?"

"Look, if she was, it was somebody she knows and it wasn't our guy. She didn't know any of the holdbacks about his MO. According to her, he didn't bind her the same way or gag her. He tied her arms to the headboard with the cord from her robe and told her to close her eyes."

"Anything to corroborate that?"

"Nobody found her. She allegedly worked herself free and then threw out her robe with the morning trash."

"And called you long after the garbage was picked up."

"I've seen a lot of women react afterwards, you know? I've seen anger, I've seen denial, and I've seen desperation. I'm not saying I've seen it all, but what I haven't seen is calm, cool, collected and 'do you want cream in your coffee?' Add that she eventually called a lawyer before agreeing to let us search her house, and she absolutely refused a rape kit, despite the fact that I told her it was almost a certainty we wouldn't get a conviction without it."

Daly raised his hand to stop him. "What are you going to do now?"

"The only thing I can do. I'm going to work hard on the other cases. If we do find any prints of interest that pop up in the system, I can check them out, but she'd vacuumed the floor, changed the sheets and washed the original ones."

"I'm having a briefing in here tomorrow morning to review the arson and abduction cases. Maybe you should sit in."

"Why? I thought you felt there wasn't anything solid to suggest a link."

"Still, I'd like you to hear everything. The dates are a bit of a coincidence." He reached for his glass of water and opened the top drawer of his desk, removing a bottle of Tylenol. "You really need a partner on this case."

"Speaking of which—"

"You saw her?" Daly swallowed the painkillers and took a sip of water.

Craig's mouth twisted as he nodded. "She's not doing well."

"She wants to come back to work."

Craig snorted. "She's not touching this case."

"Personally, I agree. But she threatened to go over my head. I'm not saying she'll have any better luck higher up the ladder." He gave an almost imperceptible shake of his head. "I'm just warning you that she's going to try."

"Constable Tain. Tain," the voice called, the sound of quick footfalls getting louder as the person approached.

Tain relaxed when he saw Sims.

"There's someone here to see you."

"Who?"

"His name is Iggy Klipper."

Iggy Klipper? Tain stopped walking. "Did he say what he wants?"

Sims nodded. "He said he saw that girl at the Cloverdale Fair the day she went missing."

Tain scratched his head. One good, promising lead he really wanted to chase down, maybe something constructive to tell Ashlyn in the morning. Five seconds later and he would have already been out the door.

He stuffed the paper with the address back into his pocket. "Where is he?" he asked, following Sims back down the hall.

Ashlyn sat down on her couch, gesturing to the chair across from her. "Thanks for coming over."

Luke Driscoll sat down, his usual easy smile in place. "No problem. What happened?"

"I went through some floorboards."

The smile added a questioning twist to it. "Is that all in a day's work for you?"

She shook her head. "Not exactly."

"So, what can I do for you?"

"What can you tell me about the number forty?"

"Are you serious? You called me up and asked me to come over to talk about the number forty?" The smile hadn't disappeared from Luke's face, but his eyes had narrowed a touch, like he was lingering somewhere between intrigued and baffled.

"It has some religious significance, doesn't it?"

"Sure. There are some who believe that it take forty days for a soul to be purified, that it's a predetermined period of devotion and preparation."

Ashlyn grabbed her notepad and started asking questions.

# THURSDAY

Ashlyn barely felt a twinge of pain as she walked to her desk, perhaps a little slower than usual, but under her own power. She set her files down, tucked her hair behind her ears and started skimming through her messages.

Nothing, nothing, nothing . . . Nicholas Brennen. Hmm. She glanced at her watch, convinced it was far too early to call. She set that message aside.

That's when she noticed the folded paper, tucked partway onto a tray. She knew the handwriting immediately, pulled it out and sat down.

*Ashlyn,*

*We've had a witness come forward with some potential leads about Taylor Brennen's abduction, and Alex Wilson is turning out to be a viable suspect. I've put all the notes in a file, which is in the top drawer of my desk.*

*There's also a report from the lab in there with the data on the contents of the bundle you recovered from the fire and the photos you took of the object on the wall and the room below. There was also a message from Carl Parks for you. I put it in that file.*

*I'll be in early—Daly's bringing breakfast. He said he's putting a display board in his office, and he wants us in there at 8 AM, ready to go through everything.*

*Knowing you, it's 5:30 as you read this, so you should have enough time to get ready.*

*Tain*

Ashlyn set the note back on her tray, glanced at her watch and smiled. She went to his desk and removed the files.

"What did you do, wait until it was officially past midnight and come to the office then?"

She spun around, the words, "Will you . . ." already out before their gazes met.

Craig offered a half shrug as an apology. "Sorry. Looks like you're ready for this, though."

He knew her well enough to guess at what was going through her mind, but she had no opportunity to ask. Tain and Daly walked in.

Tain shook Craig's hand, offered a curt nod but said nothing.

"Okay, take me through everything we've got," Daly said.

"June fourteenth." Ashlyn pointed to the date at the top. "Julie Darrens went missing. She went with her oldest sister to pick up a few things at the corner store. This wasn't a daily ritual, but it wasn't uncommon. Julie had a tendency to dawdle, and her sister was walking briskly, trying to coax her along. She turned back and found the bag Julie had been carrying was dropped on the sidewalk. Julie was gone." Ashlyn tapped the evidence photos, one of Julie from school, one of the scattered groceries on the pavement. "They were walking past a vacant lot on one side. Across the street was park land, a treed section with walking paths about ten feet off the road. Since it was June and the trees were covered in dense, green leaves—"

"No eyewitnesses," Daly said.

"Same day, a building here—" Tain moved beside Ashlyn and tapped the map—"was set on fire. Simple gasoline accelerant, but the thing that stood out was the fact that wood had been cut out of the floorboards, stacked meticulously, doused in gas and then set ablaze. A charred doll was found lying on top, like a funeral pyre, and an angel had been hung from the front door."

"Similar scenario on July eight," Ashlyn said. "Isabella Bertini went missing. She disappeared from her own backyard, where she'd been playing with her sister. As simple as a ball rolling into the trees behind their home, and she never came back. The ball was found a few feet from the Bertini family property."

"The Bertinis have since put in a fence," Tain added. "Same day, another fire here." He pointed to the next location. "Same accelerant, same thing with the angel on the door."

"July twenty-fifth, another arson. Only this time, we didn't have another girl go missing. Julie's body was found at the scene. The fire was in Coquitlam, the lead investigators on the abduction cases worked from Burnaby, coordinating with Robinson, who was still in charge of the arson investigation then." Ashlyn shrugged. "And maybe the scene could have been handled better. We don't have much to go on." She tacked a picture of Julie Darrens's body up beside the date.

"Before that, though, we had another arson, same pattern," Ashlyn continued. "This one happened July eighteenth. No abduction and no body." Tain circled the place on the map where that fire had occurred. "And you'll note, no pattern emerging with our fire locations either. They're all over the place, just like the abductions."

"Someone who feels comfortable moving around," Craig murmured. Just like his rapist.

"August eighteenth. Taylor Brennen goes missing from a fair. We have another arson." Ashlyn turned and looked at Tain, who marked that location on the map with a number 4. "We're still working leads about Taylor's abduction."

Tain nodded. "I took a statement yesterday from a man called Iggy Klipper. He claims he saw Taylor at the fairgrounds without her brother. He said that she was approached repeatedly by a clown and also by a vendor selling jewelry."

"Did he see her go with either of them?" Daly asked.

Tain shook his head. "He didn't think much of it at the time, and he went out of town that day, to do a small fair in Victoria. He got back, saw her picture in the paper—"

"And came in to alleviate his conscience," Daly said.

"At least it's something we can follow up on," Ashlyn said. "And the critical factor is that on that day, we didn't just have a girl go missing. Isabella Bertini's body was found at the scene of the fire."

She removed more photographs from the file and tacked them up beside that date. "Exhibit A. A photo of a marking drawn on the wall near where Isabella's body was found."

"The sacred heart, a religious symbol," Tain said. "Also the name of the school that Taylor Brennen attended."

"I thought you hadn't been able to identify the markings originally," Daly said.

"We didn't," Ashlyn answered. "Carl Parks remembered what it was and phoned. Tain checked it out, and sure enough—"

"Carl Parks?" asked Craig. "What did he have to do with this?"

"He pulled her body from the building," Ashlyn said. She pointed at the next date. "That leaves us at August nineteenth. Lindsay Eckert is abducted from a recreation center in south Coquitlam. This is caught on video. Our guy is prepared. Looks like he managed to undo her necklace to lure her into the hallway. He kept just out of sight of the security cameras and grabbed her from behind, using a fire door that had a broken alarm mechanism."

"This guy knew who he was going after, how to get her alone and how to remove her without attracting attention," Tain said. "Same day, another angel arson here." He drew a number 5 on that location.

"How did the guy know Lindsay would go into the hallway for the necklace?" asked Craig.

"It was very important to her. A sterling silver necklace bought for her by her grandmother. She evidently never took it off," Ashlyn answered.

"But how would he know that?"

Ashlyn shook her head. "We're open to suggestions. So far, there are only a few things that seem to connect the girls, and they're a stretch. A couple were Brownies and then

Girl Guides, different packs. We have Catholic schools and public schools, but none of the girls attended the same school. They had different hobbies and interests."

"One thing that does connect these two," Tain said, pointing at Julie and Taylor, "is Alex Wilson. Alex Wilson took the school photos of them that have been running in the newspapers."

"What else is special about him?" asked Craig. "That seems pretty weak for naming him as a suspect or a link."

"He's the guy who found Taylor's brother at the fairgrounds. Instead of taking him to police services there, he called 911 and drove him here," Ashlyn answered.

Craig whistled. "That is interesting. Anything else to go on with this guy? What does your gut tell you?"

"That he's got nothing to do with the girls," Tain said. "He came in and voluntarily provided his fingerprints so that we could eliminate him from our investigation into Lindsay Eckert's death."

"Mr. Wilson is also a member at the recreation center where she was abducted from," Ashlyn told Craig.

He frowned. "Mr. Wilson seems a bit more connected than any completely innocent person should be. What's your plan?"

Tain sat on the arm of a chair. "Well, I wasn't entirely honest about the reason we wanted his fingerprints. Wilson is guilty of something, but what, I don't know. He left his job as a photographer—"

"A job that had him traveling around from school to school, church group to church group, Brownie packs, whatever—" Ashlyn circled a large area on the map with her finger—"all over this part of the lower mainland. He's a guy who feels comfortable with all the areas the arsons and abductions have been in."

"But you don't like him for this?"

Ashlyn glanced at Tain, who turned to Craig. "Ashlyn hasn't met him yet. My gut tells me no. I think he prefers boys, which is why he was so freaked out by being alone with Nicky."

"I'm going to talk to Nicky," Ashlyn said. "And once we know why Mr. Wilson stopped working as a photographer, we'll decide whether to bring him in again. We have nothing at this time to connect him to Isabella Bertini, though."

"Still, three girls out of four."

"My guess is, three girls out of five," Ashlyn said.

Daly and Tain both snapped their heads to look in Ashlyn's direction.

"Hear me out," she said, holding up her hand.

She taped the June, July and August calendars to the wall, the pertinent abduction dates circled, as well as the dates bodies were found. "I've marked the abductions in blue, the body recoveries in black and the arsons in green. If you count the days between Julie's abduction and Julie's recovery, you get exactly forty full days. Same thing with Isabella." She tapped July 18. "I think he took another girl here."

"Why?" Daly asked. "Why wouldn't she be reported?"

"I can think of a few reasons. She could be a pseudo-street kid, one who's been brought up hard, parents don't care. Or she's been mistaken for a runner."

"Possible," Tain said as he glanced at Daly.

"The thing is, forty is a number with religious significance. I did some checking. Some people think it's the number of days required to prove devotion and dedication. There are all sorts of biblical references to forty."

"It rained for forty days and forty nights," Craig said, "and Moses prayed for forty days."

"Right. So, take that, plus the fact that he built funeral pyres under the room where Isabella's body was left, and in the building where Julie's body was found, and he's hanging angels on the doors outside as though they're some guardian or something, plus the sacred heart drawing near Isabella's body—"

Daly leaned forward, his face buried in his hands. "Okay. Fair enough. We have to look at the possibility this guy is some religious nut."

"No sexual trauma to the girls. My guess is this guy thinks

he's preserving their innocence. He takes them for forty days of testing."

"And then they pass the test, and he sends them to heaven," Craig said, feeling the distaste in his mouth as his jaw twisted. "Sick."

"But that still doesn't explain to me why you think another girl went missing July eighteenth," Daly said. "I can't send people around knocking on doors over the whole city doing a head count."

Ashlyn pulled out five photographs. "The contents of the bundle retrieved near the table Isabella's body was found on. Five metal crosses. The first one—" she taped it up beside Julie's information—"inscribed *Deborah, July twenty-five*. The second one engraved, *Ruth, August eighteen*. The remaining three are inscribed, *Hannah, August twenty-eight, Martha, September twenty-eight, Delilah*, no date. If these are to commemorate their deaths, our next victim has just under a week to live."

"And she was abducted July eighteenth," Daly said. "He's got three girls."

"And all we've got to work with is Alex Wilson, chasing up this clown and the jewelry vendor from the fairgrounds, and tracking who made those crosses," Tain said. "Hopefully, they were distinctive enough that someone will remember the order. But they could have been done anywhere this side of the Fraser River."

There was silence in the room. Ashlyn finally sat down, near Daly, removing her juice from the drink tray.

Craig surveyed the particulars and glanced at Daly, who shrugged. Craig stood.

"June fourteenth. Karen Chalmers is raped." He made an *X* on the map, marking the location. "July eighth, Sara McPherson. July twenty-fifth, Stephanie Bonnis. No rape reported yet for July eighteenth, and we've got no abduction report for that date, just an arson." He held up his hand as he glanced at Ashlyn. "Not that I doubt your theory for a second. That girl is out there, just like my rape victim is still working through denial.

"Cindy Parks is raped August eighteenth. August nineteenth, Lori Price is raped. She fights him. He leaves, rapes Nitara Sandhu and kills her."

Craig marked the locations on the map, all as varied as the abduction reports and arsons. "I've been trying to figure out what linked these women. Obviously, there was no geographic connection. He wasn't favoring blondes, brunettes or redheads. He crossed ethnic lines. The only thing that appeared to be common to all of them was that they lived in detached houses, and he seemed to know when they would be home alone, as though he'd been watching them."

He set down the dry-erase marker and picked up a different color, starting at the top. Beside each case date except July eighteen, he wrote a number. "Any guesses?" Craig watched as they all looked over the information, first Tain and then Daly shaking their heads. "Ashlyn? If anyone figures it out, it should be you."

Her brow wrinkled. "Station numbers?"

Tain's eyes narrowed, and he pulled out a file, glanced at the list and then the numbers on the board. "How do they connect?"

"They were all girlfriends or wives of men who were on the fire departments called out to those arson fires."

Craig sat down, and Tain moved off the arm of the chair he was still perched on, slumping back into the seat. He rubbed his temples with both hands. "I haven't got a fucking clue how this all connects."

"You and me both," Ashlyn said. "Abduct girls to purify them for heaven, set fires for no apparent reason at all half the time, and then go rape women? It doesn't make any sense."

"Didn't you have another rape reported yesterday?" Tain asked.

Craig nodded. "But there's a lot about it that doesn't fit, and our victim wasn't cooperative with us doing an investigation of the scene. Evidence destroyed before she called it in. Plus, she was beyond calm. And the MO doesn't match the other cases."

Daly leaned back in his chair. "That case doesn't seem to fit. Regardless, there's as much reason to believe the rape cases are connected to the arsons as there is to believe the arsons connect to the abductions. The arsons seem to be the link. Okay. It looks like you three are working together now."

"What about Lori?" Craig asked.

"You can't be serious? You can't let her back on this," Ashlyn said, her eyes wide as she stared at Craig and then Daly. "Not since she's been raped."

"It might not be up to me," Daly replied. "If it is, she'll be on medical until fall."

"Don't you have some pull?" Ashlyn asked.

"I used up a lot of influence getting Tain on the abduction cases and keeping him there. Look, Lori's booked for holidays in September anyway. If Hawkins knows what he's doing, he'll keep her at home where she belongs."

"It's been bad enough with the abductions and arsons," Tain said, looking at Craig. "Please tell me you have something to go on."

"No prints in the system, so far DNA has only been recovered from Lori's rape kit, and we haven't got results back yet."

"But these women are all girlfriends or wives of firefighters?" Ashlyn asked. "I take it you mean live-in girlfriends."

Craig returned Ashlyn's gaze and nodded.

"Then what you need is to join the fire department and get yourself a girlfriend." They all looked at her. "Seriously. The only link you've got is the fire department. My job was supposed to be hanging out, being around, keeping my eye open for anyone showing signs of stress, who might be responsible for the arsons. If all your victims had a tie to the fire department, it's possible the rapist is a firefighter. Someone in there, someone who knows all of them, knows where they live."

"It would make sense," Tain said slowly. "Wouldn't firefighters know when a unit's been called out to a big fire too?"

"So they'd know when a particular guy would be on a call, leaving his wife or girlfriend at home alone. . . ." Daly nodded. "Ashlyn's right. You need to get inside the department, but I'm not so sure about needing a girlfriend."

"Think about it. Craig goes through all the motions a rookie would. You've got the house, so that's no problem. Maybe you can flush this guy out, make him tip his hand."

"What about the firefighters who've had contact with Craig and know he's a cop?" Tain asked.

"They're all on leave," Daly said. "I can make sure they don't come back. If we do this."

"Look, it's just my opinion, but Craig would fit right in. He just needs a girlfriend who would get noticed."

"You," Tain said quietly.

"Me?"

"You've been around those scenes. You know a lot of the guys, and I've seen the way they look at you. Trust me, you come in 'off the job' for a day with Craig on your arm, and he's joining the department. . . . Our guy won't miss that. Plus you know these cases. No sense bringing in someone new who would need to be brought up to speed. You and Craig have worked together before."

Craig glanced at Ashlyn first, then Daly. "What do you think?"

"I don't like the idea of putting Ashlyn in as bait."

"You could have a unit watching the house every hour she's at home alone. Silent motion detectors to alert them if anyone tries to enter. Our guy wouldn't know, but Ashlyn could have an earpiece to alert her, and the team watching the house would have instant notification if someone broke in," Tain said.

"There's no guarantee he'd even go after Ashlyn," Craig said. "It could be just as valuable from the perspective of her evaluating the scene. If she goes through all the motions with me, she can have more access to the other firefighters and everyone who connects to the department. That would give her a chance to see if anyone seems suspicious. Everyone I come in contact with, we do a check on, regardless."

"And if you put it out there that Ashlyn's on leave as disciplinary action for her stunt the other day, then she's got a perfect excuse for not being at work," Tain added.

Daly frowned. "I don't know. How will I explain it to Paul Quinlan?"

"Tell him it's out of your hands, ordered by the bosses." Craig glanced at Ashlyn. "It makes sense. You have the perfect excuse for pulling her off the case right now, from external appearances anyway. She'll still be actively on duty, but she already knows a lot of these guys, which gives her a head start. Our rapist has attacked another police officer, so he's not likely to be scared off. Every single person I cross paths with, right down to Paul Quinlan, gets their name run through the system."

"It sure as hell beats sending out a memo to all the firefighters asking them to not leave their wives at home alone," Tain said.

"Tain's right. We're working with some pretty thin leads, and if this guy holds to form, next week we'll have another arson, another rape and another body on our hands," Craig said.

"I'll do it, Daly. I want to."

Daly put up his hand. "Out. All of you. I need to think."

Two hours later Craig walked into his father's office without knocking and shut the door.

Daly stood, hands on the window sill, staring outside. He straightened and turned.

"Craig Nolan, I expect you to knock like any other officer in this building."

"I'm not any other officer. I'm your son."

Daly's face darkened. "Oh, this is rich. You're usually the one telling me not to treat you differently, not to do you any favors."

"And I don't want you to treat me any differently than you would anyone else. That's the goddamn point!"

Daly pointed a finger at him. "Watch your mouth."

Craig grabbed the back of a chair, squeezing the padding

with his fingers, letting the anger course through his arms, hoping some of it would evaporate instead of finding its way into a response. He looked up at his father. "There's only one thing for you to consider: if this was anyone else, would you try it?"

They stood staring at each other. Craig knew the answer to his question. They'd been grasping at straws for so long, on the arsons, the abductions and the rapes, and there was a good chance having a man inside the fire department could help them make headway on at least one of the cases, if not all of them. It was the right thing to do.

It wasn't the job holding Daly back, and Craig knew it. It had more to do with fear and regret for the mistakes Daly had made himself as a much younger man.

Mistakes Craig was a constant reminder of.

"I'm not a kid. This is my job. If it was anyone else—"

Daly raised a hand to stop him, then shrugged. "Go get Tain and Ashlyn," he said quietly.

When they returned to Daly's office Daly ignored Craig and walked up to Ashlyn, put his hand on her shoulder.

"Are you sure about this?"

Ashlyn nodded. "Positive."

"If anything happens to you—"

"SSBB," Tain said. "I'll park outside the house myself and monitor her when she's alone if I have to. Neither of us—" he pointed to Craig—"is going to let her get hurt."

Craig knew that look. Daly's logic was fighting against his feelings as he weighed the pros and cons. Finally, he reached for his phone.

"I still have to get this cleared. Meanwhile, you—" he pointed at Ashlyn—"go see Nicky Brennen."

Ashlyn knelt down by the car mat on the floor, where the boy was playing. "Hi, Nicky. Remember me?"

He glanced up and offered her a shy smile and a quick nod.

"What are you building?" She sat down on the carpet near him.

"It's a special garage for fixing the old cars."

"Do the old cars break down a lot?"

He shook his head. "Not really. In the old days they didn't make junk."

Ashlyn smiled. "Is that what your dad says?"

Nicky nodded. He'd been leaning forward, partially lying on the floor, but now he sat up and looked at her. "You're looking for my sister."

"That's right."

"But you haven't found her."

Ashlyn shook her head. "I'm afraid not. We've been looking everywhere we can think of." He nodded, his big eyes wide. "Could we talk about that day again?"

Nicky tapped two pieces from his building kit together. "Will it help you find Taylor?" he asked eventually, back to moving cars and toys.

"It might. It could be very helpful for us." He looked up from his toys and gave her a quick nod. "What do you remember about the man who found you at the park?"

Nicky shrugged.

"Did he say anything to you?"

"He called me a special little boy."

"Do you remember what he was wearing?"

"Jeans. And a T-shirt."

"The whole time you were with him?"

Nicky's tousled curls bobbed as he nodded.

"He didn't have a jacket?"

His blond locks shook this time.

"Did he say anything else?"

Nicky shook his head again. "Just called someone and said he'd found what he was looking for."

Ashlyn felt her eyes pinch. "I thought he called the police."

"He did. After."

"Oh. Okay." She tucked her hair back behind her ears. "Did he touch you?"

"He held my hand."

"Was that when he took you to his car?"

Nicky nodded.

"Anything else? Pat you on the head . . ." Ashlyn shrugged.

"No. But . . ." Nicky fiddled with the K'NEX now, clipping pieces together absently, but quietly.

"It's okay. You can tell me."

Nicky's nose wrinkled. "It's supposed to be a secret."

Ashlyn put her finger to her lips. "I won't tell. Promise. But it might help me find out what happened to Taylor."

Nicky pursed his lips for a second and then leaned towards her, whispering, "He took my picture."

She played dumb. "You mean he took a picture you had in your pocket?"

The blond curls shook again. "No. He had a camera."

"Oh. Did he just take one picture?"

More shaking.

"Can you tell me where you were when he took your picture?"

Hawkins tossed his hands up as if to say, *What do you want from me?* "Look, Daly, she's at a desk. It's the best I can do."

"Not for her, Dennis. She shouldn't be here. Have you seen her? She's lost weight already, and she's got dark circles under her eyes."

"So she looks like shit. What do you expect?"

"How about enough common sense from her bosses to keep her at home and make sure she gets counseling. It's not like she's a cashier at Safeway. She was on the case hunting this guy. I don't want her coming anywhere near it."

"You always underestimated her."

"No, Dennis. You overestimated what she was ready for. She's capable of being a fine officer, but she's not ready to work without a net. Lori needs supervision. Now more than ever."

"You've gone just about as far outside the boundaries of rank as I'm willing to let you, Daly. Okay, she made some mistakes, maybe could have handled things a bit better. But we both know Craig was prepared to cut her loose the first time she did something on her own initiative."

"I don't think you're being fair."

"Really? Craig hasn't got the best track record when it comes to partners." Dennis turned and gestured to the info boards set up in the office. "What's this about?"

"Progress on the arson, abduction and rape cases."

Hawkins turned a chalky white. "Are you trying to tell me they're linked?"

Daly stood up, running down the particulars, watching Dennis's face get longer with each new detail.

Craig groaned when he saw his desk and almost turned on his heel, but his annoyance propelled him forward. As though she knew he was approaching and what he was thinking, Lori spun around.

"You can't go through this." Craig took the file from her hands.

"Are you saying you won't tell me where things are at?"

"Lori, you know I can't talk to you about this investigation."

"You've got to be kidding me." She stood up and looked him in the eyes. "Every other . . . everyone else has the courtesy of being informed. You telling me I don't deserve that?"

"Don't twist my words. You know this isn't about what you deserve to know. And you know damn well you're going after more info here than we ever give the victims."

She blinked. "Craig, I really need to know if you're making any progress."

"Some." He pushed past her and gathered all the files and relevant information into a box. "And that's all I'm prepared to say."

"I'm back at work. Officially approved, you know."

"But you're not back on this case."

"Yeah, but you don't have to treat me like shit. Common courtesy to a fellow officer."

"Lori, this isn't about you being my colleague or my former partner on this case. Anyone comes waltzing through here and wants to know the latest, I'm going to tell them to read it in the *Sun*. You know that."

"You were always such a hard ass, you know? Worst fucking partner I ever had."

Craig shrugged, turned on his heel and walked away, thinking it cut both ways.

"So what kinds of cars do you see going by your house?"

Nicky showed her how PT Cruisers and Sunfires and other average cars would go by. "Then there's the school buses." He pulled one off his shelf and drove it past his house.

"What time does the school bus go by?"

"Early in the morning and then again in the afternoon."

"What about other vehicles? Are there any cars you see in the afternoon a lot?"

He shrugged. "Sometimes fire trucks go by, and I like to run to the window and wave in case it's Dad."

"That's nice," Ashlyn said, smiling. "Are these the cars you see here, at Dad's?"

He nodded.

She propped her chin up on her hand, resting her elbow on her knee. "Can you show me what cars you saw when you were still staying with your mom?"

It was a similar scene, but then he went to his shelf, fingering one car for a moment.

"What's special about that car?" she asked him.

"Well, it used to come by our house a lot. It's a Corvette. I always watched it go by," Nicky said, still fiddling with the car.

"Why don't you show me?"

He took it off the shelf and brought it to the mat, making it drive down the road very slowly.

Ashlyn mocked a puzzled expression. "Can't that car drive very fast?"

"Oh, it can. It's a fast car. But he never drove it fast. Always really, really slow while he looked out the window at the houses."

"I bet you didn't mind, because it's a nice car."

Nicky shook his head. "I liked watching it."

"When did it stop driving by your house?"

"After Taylor went away," he said quietly. "Before Dad said I could stay here all the time."

"You know what, Nicky? You've been such a big help. I brought you something." She handed him a bag, and he pulled out the model truck, his face lighting up like the sky above Washington on July Fourth.

He ran down the hall to show his dad, and she followed him. While Nick senior expressed proper enthusiasm and managed to persuade Nicky to go back to his room to play, Ashlyn felt Tain's eyes searching her face.

Their gazes met, and she had a pretty firm belief that he knew exactly what she was thinking. Now they had to tell Nick Brennen—on leave from the department, fighting his wife in court for permanent full custody of their children, waiting to hear if his daughter would be found alive or if she was never coming home—that his son had been exposed to a possible pedophile.

Nick showed them out, and she waited until they were halfway back to the car.

"What kind of car does Alex Wilson drive?" Ashlyn asked.

"Red Honda Civic hatchback."

"Not exactly a car that stands out around here."

"Nope. Why?"

She told Tain what she'd learned and relayed what Nicky had said about the Corvette. "The way we've seen it, all of these girls were known before they were taken. It could be this guy was watching her for a while, looking for an opportunity. Julie went missing in her neighborhood, Isabella from right behind her house. Taylor always seemed odd, disappearing from the fairgrounds."

"But not if he was watching for a while, saw his chance when she got separated from her brother and went for it."

"All that stuff about the second phone call, the photos . . . That's really sick."

Tain nodded, his mouth twisting with distaste. "I'll ask Daly if he can have Sims look into it."

"I can do it. What do you think I'm going to do all day? Clean house and cook Craig dinner?"

A smile flickered across Tain's lips. "More like tell him to cook his own damn dinner when he walks in the door." He put his hand on her arm, looking down on her. "You don't have to do this. I know I put you on the spot."

Ashlyn shook her head. "No, Tain, you put the job ahead of the people involved, which is what you've got to do. It's a great idea. That doesn't change because it means I'm going to be the one playing the part. I'm up for it."

"I know."

"Then you should never doubt that you did the right thing by putting this forward and suggesting me. Don't think of it like losing your partner. You can call me whenever, we can still hash over the case, and I'll do the paperwork."

He smiled as he stepped back, his hand falling away. "That almost makes up for hitting the streets on my own."

Daly looked at the box Craig was carrying. "What are you doing?"

"Taking all of this stuff home."

"You could make copies for Ashlyn to work from."

"It's not that. I found Lori snooping through my desk."

Craig shut the hatch to the back of his Rodeo, locked it and looked at Daly, who was resting a hand on the spare tire on the back of the old sport-utility vehicle.

"I told him she wasn't ready to come back."

"For all the good it did. What's the deal with this anyway? Lori have some kind of clout with Hawkins?"

Daly shrugged. "Your guess is as good as mine."

"But he signed off on the plan."

"On one condition. We have to bring Paul Quinlan in on it, keep him informed." Daly looked up and met his gaze, and he shrugged. "There's nothing I can do about it. They don't want the department to look like it's dropped the ball on any of the ongoing, pertinent investigations. Hawkins wants us to reassure Quinlan that we're taking the arsons seriously. Besides, we need someone to facilitate your new career on the department. Quinlan can do that."

"This means exposing our link about the rape cases."

"Which affects the fire department as well. They've got men on leave, one burying his wife, one hoping his daughter will be found alive. Hawkins felt that someone on the department needed to maintain confidence in us."

"Like we're not doing all we can . . ."

Daly's fingers drummed the tire, and then he let out a deep breath. "I could call in a few favors to bring in a profiler, but if I do, Hawkins could make it his mission to see you transferred out."

"Did he say that?"

"He's made it clear I'm not to step any further outside the boundaries."

"Look, Dad, we have a chance to maybe make some progress with this. I'm not trying to tell you how to do your job, but I'd hold back a card or two before exposing your hand. If we can work this thing to closure without a profiler, then you still have cards to play. And if we have to do an end-run around Hawkins, we'd better make sure we're covered so he comes through it looking like the mastermind behind the whole thing."

"Funny, I never thought of Dennis as one to play the political game on every big decision, particularly when he's been so uptight about making progress after Lori's rape."

"There's something odd there. If it was anyone else . . ." Craig shrugged.

Daly turned to walk away. "I know. Believe me, I know."

Daly had phoned Ashlyn to tell her he wanted to see her in his office when she returned to the station. When she arrived he updated her. "We've already had silent alarms set up around all the windows and doors. There was a rental available behind Craig's, one that bordered the alley. We've signed up for it and got a team moving in. They have all the monitoring equipment on site and a clear view of the yard from an upstairs bedroom."

"I seriously hope they won't sit up there with binoculars watching the patio doors."

"Funny. No, we're putting up a satellite dish, which is really a cover for a camera. The back entrance will be monitored visually from there, and the front entrance will be watched from a remote camera set up from Craig's house. I still want you keeping all the exterior lights on, Ashlyn. I'd prefer it if we find this guy without him coming after you."

"Me too."

She watched the shadow cross his face as he glanced at his desk for a moment, his fingers tapping the surface absently, like they often did when he was thinking hard about something. When he lifted his head to look at her, she felt her gut tighten.

"Daly—"

"Hear me out, Ashlyn. This isn't a simple assignment. And it's complicated by the fact that you personally know your partner."

"I don't see that as a complication. I see that as a bonus."

He looked at her for a moment, tried to bury his real concerns. "I just want to make sure you're comfortable with this."

"Daly, it's Craig. I'm perfectly fine with this."

"Maybe that's the problem."

She tossed her hands up. "What's that supposed to mean?"

"You know Craig, and you know Tain. Tain almost covered for you the other day. Your personal relationship with both of them could compromise their judgment. And yours."

"Personal relationship? We're colleagues. We work together. I've been partnered with Craig and with Tain. Partners have to get to know where each other's limits are and when to give them some latitude."

"Ashlyn—"

"Daly, I'm not going to do anything." She sat up straight as she looked him in the eyes, "I won't compromise Craig's safety or my own. I'm simply going to be the doting girlfriend by day and the investigator behind the scenes. I'll relay everything to Tain, and I'll make sure every person we come in contact with is screened. That's it."

"I'm still not sure about this."

"Daly, it's Craig. I'm in good hands. Seriously, you've got me working with someone I can trust. That's all I can ask for."

He sighed. "There's a van scheduled to meet you at your apartment in forty-five minutes. They'll move your stuff."

For the first time since this idea had come up she looked uncertain.

"You didn't think we'd go about this halfway, did you? This guy has to believe you and Craig live together, or he's going to work it out. Guys around the department know you're a cop, so when you're out with Craig . . ." He shrugged.

"I get the idea."

"Is there anything else you need?"

"Does Craig have Internet access?"

"I don't know. How crucial is it?"

"I can check some things from our system from remote access, and it will enable me to do online searches for related case information. I've been using it at home."

He reached for his phone. "Then I'll make sure you're hooked up."

When Ashlyn came downstairs from unpacking Craig asked, "Did you have enough room?"

"How many clothes do you think I have?"

He shrugged. "It looked like a lot."

She opened her mouth to offer a retort and then shook her head. "It wasn't all clothes, Craig. Pictures, books, stuff that I would actually have at home. You know, to make it look like I really live here."

"Have you reviewed all the security information?"

Ashlyn nodded as she sank into a chair. "Daly really went overboard."

"I drew the line at having audio feeds in the bedroom."

"How thoughtful of you."

Craig glanced at the coffee table for a moment and then got up. "Can I get you anything?"

"So we're still in phase one of our relationship, are we?"

"What's phase one?" he asked as he walked to the kitchen.

"The stage where you still offer to serve me before you start complaining about all the housework I haven't done all day."

"I thought I wouldn't start in about that until tomorrow. Last chance," he called.

"Cranberry tea."

"I meant a cold drink."

"Thought you said anything." Ashlyn got up and managed to straighten her face by the time she reached the kitchen door. "How do you feel about this? Really?"

She couldn't see his face because his back was to her. He filled the kettle, located a tea bag and a mug and waited for the kettle to boil. Then he unplugged the kettle and poured the water. He opened the drawer and removed a spoon, all without speaking or looking up.

"I think my dad's having a coronary."

"It's not like we haven't shared the same roof before."

"Not the same thing." He passed her the mug, and she backed out of the doorway, turning on her heel, careful to avoid eye contact.

After she sat down on the smaller couch she blew on her tea for a moment and tested it. Then she looked over at him. "Daly's not always impartial when it comes to giving me assignments."

Craig smiled. "I know the feeling."

There was a knock at the door, and they exchanged a glance.

"That better not be him coming over to check up on us," Ashlyn said. Craig got up and she listened as he went down the hall and then opened the door.

When Craig returned Tain was following him.

"Have you got your computer set up yet?" he asked her. She shook her head.

"Then you'd better get to it. Daly wants to make sure everything is working so we're ready to go tomorrow morning." He passed her a box. "He's got you an e-mail account and a messenger system that you can use to relay information directly to him. Daly says he wants you to keep the phone lines clear when you're home alone, so that the team monitoring you can call and check on any potential false alarms."

"God. He really is going overboard, isn't he?" she said as she looked at the laptop and folder in the box. When she got no sympathy from Tain she forced herself to her feet. "Upstairs or downstairs?"

"Phone jack or cable?"

Ashlyn turned to Tain. "Phone."

"The spare room upstairs has an empty desk and a phone jack," Craig said.

As soon as Ashlyn left the room, Tain sat down.

Craig frowned. "We haven't even started. What could possibly—"

"Someone was watching the movers at Ashlyn's place."

"Are they sure?"

"Somebody turned down the block and parked, started to get out of their vehicle, and then Ashlyn arrived. The driver didn't think anything of it until he realized the guy had gotten back into the car and was still sitting there. As soon as Ashlyn went into the building, this guy drove off."

"Tell me he got a license plate."

Tain shook his head. "When the guy pulled out, another moving van came down the street, going in the opposite direction. He double parked our guys in. They'd had some words before, and the driver was pretty choked about being held up, waiting to start loading. By the time the argument was over . . ." Tain shrugged.

"Shit." Craig's mouth twisted. Then he looked up at Tain. "You thinking what I'm thinking?"

The sound of footsteps coming down the stairs silenced both of them.

"Okay, there. Satisfied? It's all done, it works, ready to roll." Ashlyn glanced from Craig to Tain. "What's going on?"

"Just wondering if you'd be a good little kept woman and get me some dinner. I'm starving," Tain said. He gave her the most innocent smile he could manage.

Her hands went to her hips, and then she tossed them up. "As it so happens, I think there are leftovers." She turned on her heel and walked to the kitchen.

Craig shook his head. "When I was working with Lori I should have taken a page from your book."

"Lori Price?" Tain snorted. "That one would have you written up before you could say sex, never mind sexual harassment. How's she doing, anyway?"

"Not good."

Their eyes met for a second before Ashlyn returned to the room. Tain pushed the weight from his face and forced a grin.

"See, this is bringing out your hidden domestic talents."

"Just because I don't cater to you on a daily basis doesn't mean they're 'hidden.'"

"I'll just have to drop by more often. Wouldn't want you to get out of practice."

She glanced from Tain to Craig and then reached for her tea. "I'm going to bed. Don't forget to rinse that before you go," she said to Tain.

He waited until he heard her reach the second part of the stairs. "There's always a chance it could be nothing. Daly said we shouldn't jump to conclusions. He's got an extra team monitoring your place for a few days, and someone's watching her apartment. Just in case."

Ashlyn heard the door shut, then footsteps coming up the stairs. She sensed him stop at the doorway.

"That's my side of the bed."

She didn't look up from her book. "You sleep by the fireplace."

"Not while you're here, I don't. Move."

Ashlyn set *Cross* down on her lap. "Are you serious?"

"Stay where you are and you'll find out."

He disappeared into the walk-through closet, into the bathroom. For a moment she tried to go back to the book, but her mind was focused more on Craig's imminent return than anything else. She marked the page she was on.

The bathroom door opened, and Craig came back through the closet and into the bedroom. He pulled his shirt off and glared at her.

"I meant it, Ashlyn."

"Really, Craig."

After a moment under his relentless gaze she muttered, "Fine," and moved over.

"How did you know I usually sleep on the other side, anyway?"

Ashlyn lifted a copy of *A Good Day to Die*, which glistened in the firelight. He took it from her, setting it down on the nightstand. She turned on her side to face him.

"This guy doesn't break in when men are home. Being on this side or that side doesn't make me any safer, but you're willing to have a stupid argument just to put more distance between me and the door."

He was lying on his back and didn't turn to look at her, instead staring up at the ceiling, his right arm folded back, his hand tucked under his head.

"And I am capable of defending myself. Just last night, I slept all alone."

Craig turned to look at her, the somber expression reminding her of the Craig she'd first met a year before, the Craig who had carried the weight of the case, and a hell of a lot of guilt about his past, on his shoulders. "Are you seeing anybody?" he asked.

She felt her jaw drop and forced it back up as she tried to decide what she wanted to say to that.

"Seriously, Ashlyn."

"Are you?"

"That's not the point."

"Well, if you don't mind me asking, what is?"

"Is there any reason a man would be coming to your house to look for you?"

Even in the dim light she sensed a shadow passing behind his eyes. "What did Tain tell you?"

"It's possible someone was watching you when you were with the movers." He told her what Tain had said earlier and shifted his left arm under the pillow.

She blew out a long, slow breath. "Craig, there could have been a dozen reasons the guy left that have nothing to do with me."

"All the same—"

"Everyone is overreacting because of this case."

"Nobody wants to see you get hurt."

"Neither do I, but you're all beginning to sound like broken records. I'm not your little sister, and I don't need you rushing to my defense every time you see someone step on the playground you don't like the look of." She could see his face harden at her words, his shoulders taut. "Look, I didn't mean it quite the way it sounded. It's bad enough having Daly looking out for me, but I've had Tain playing the overprotective-partner thing to the hilt. I just want everyone to let me stand on my own two feet."

Ashlyn started to turn onto her back, but he reached for her shoulder and stopped her.

"It isn't you I don't trust. It's the guys out there."

His hand slid down onto her arm, and then he pulled it back to his side of the bed. For a moment they both lay face to face unmoving, and then Craig turned away and switched off the lamp.

She rolled over, gently rubbing her arm to try to alleviate the pins-and-needles sensation that bombarded her when he touched her, listening to his breaths, which hadn't deepened yet.

"No." The word came out of nowhere, unexpectedly breaking the silence.

"No what?" Ashlyn asked.

"The answer to your question. I'm not seeing anyone."

He rolled over all the way, his back to her, and her head snapped back against the pillow again, her eyes wide as she stared at the ceiling.

# FRIDAY

Neither of them mentioned the conversation in the morning. They began working their way through a list Quinlan had provided through Daly of things Craig needed to get to work at the fire department.

"What's next?" Ashlyn asked Craig.

"I have to go pick up some uniforms."

"That's it?"

He shook his head. "Fortunately, I was on a volunteer fire department during university, so I have enough training to get by, although Quinlan gave me some refresher videos. I have to watch those later. First, a full physical exam by the department doctor. And them I have to get a pager."

"What's the pager for?"

"That's what they use to bring in volunteers on call. And regular firefighters who might be needed for backup if there's a big fire, like one of the angel arsons."

"They page those guys in?" she asked.

Craig nodded. "Smaller departments still use radios. They have a tone that gets broadcast and then the call center relays the information."

"Hardly secure. Any journalist with a police scanner can pick it up and be at the scene before the department has even responded."

"Why do you think they're using pagers here? And not just journalists. Anyone with a scanner can know who's just been called out of their house in the middle of the night."

"Can you imagine? You live in some small town where everyone knows you. You get called out to a fire and come back hours later to find your stereo's gone because some thief with a scanner knows you live alone and that you'll be out for a few hours."

"If they used them here it could be harder to pin down a rape suspect."

A tingling sensation worked its way down Ashlyn's spine. "Anyone could know whose wife was home alone. . . . Scary."

"Maybe the departments will catch up to the twenty-first century before the rapists catch on and start relocating."

"Well, it doesn't have any bearing on this case. Whoever's doing this has to be connected to the department. There's rotation for who's on call and who isn't."

"Hopefully I can get that information from Quinlan to-morrow."

"You're starting rotation then?"

He nodded. "Two day shifts, followed by two night shifts. Four days on, four days off."

"So do you get paid by the fire department and the police department while you're doing this?"

Craig gave her a wry smile. "Be serious."

"There should be something in it for you. After all, you've got a girlfriend to support now."

"One with her own credit cards."

"Did I ever tell you about the course I took in check forging?"

"Ashlyn . . ."

She spent the next twenty minutes or so trying to occupy herself while Craig got his uniforms, inspecting every item the store sold, trying to feign interest in shopping while making mental notes of every guy who looked at her side-ways while the salesclerk fussed over Craig.

An approving whistle had her turning before she thought better of it.

The clerk was offering her admiration for how Craig filled out the uniform.

"Check him out," the salesgirl said, calling her over. "What do you think?"

For half a second she wondered what the male equivalent of *cute* was, but she knew what was expected. "He looks hot."

"See, I told you," the clerk said as she turned back to Craig.

Once Craig had gone back into the change room, the sales-girl snapped her fingers. "Boots. What size does he take?"

Ashlyn felt her face lengthen as she tried to remember every time she'd seen Craig put on shoes or boots, and then she shook her head. "I don't know.'

The clerk gave her a knowing grin, but stopped short of winking. "Come on. You must have some idea."

Tain felt his eyes narrow with annoyance and then widen as he realized who was sitting in his chair, flicking through his notes. He pulled an extra chair from the desk he was walking past and set it down next to his own work area.

The youth leaned back, rocking in Tain's good chair, a half grin on his face. "So this is where you hang out, huh?"

"It's where I work."

"And the babe you had with you the other night."

Tain frowned at him. "Constable Hart's desk is right there." He pointed to the one across from his. For some reason, looking at the two desks facing each other now reminded him of when his own desk had been pushed far against the wall, away from the team he worked with, back when Ashlyn and Craig had sat across from each other.

"You're so predictable."

"Excuse me?"

"Can't admit you think she's fine. Got to be all pc."

"What would you know about it?"

"Hell, you tried going to school anymore? I mean, sometimes you just don't like somebody because they're a jerk, you know? Now the school counselor wants to figure out if it's because they're white or orange or have a wimpy voice. Got to put bullshit labels on everything when it might just be that they're a jerk."

Tain suppressed a smile. "You're pretty sharp, Marvin."

"I've got life experience."

"Evidently. And if you can learn to watch your mouth, you could have a career in the police department."

"Nah. Maybe the fire department. But it's, you know, super hard to get in."

Tain nodded. "So I hear. What else would you want to do?"

Marvin shrugged. "Not sure."

"So what brings you by?"

He watched the boy's face harden. "She's not coming back, is she?"

Tain couldn't blink under Marvin's relentless stare, so he drew a breath and decided to play it straight. "It's not looking good. We're doing everything we can."

"But it's been days. I read that in most abduction cases, every day that goes by increases the odds the victim's been murdered."

"That's usually true. But this case is a bit different."

Marvin looked up from where his fingers were pulling at a loose drawer handle. "Are you putting me on?"

Tain shook his head. "I'd bet money she's still alive."

"Probably wishes she wasn't."

"What makes you say that?" Tain looked up, seeing the figure approaching, the questioning glance at the boy seated at Tain's desk.

"He's probably, you know . . . doing stuff to her. Stuff she wouldn't like." He shrugged.

"If Lindsay comes home, in time, with help, she can be okay. She's got a family that loves her and a lot of friends like you who care about her. And it sounds like she's a strong person."

Daly sat down on the corner of Tain's desk and extended his hand. "Sergeant Daly."

"Marvin Ferguson."

"You know, Marvin, there's something I'd like to show you. It might help you remember something important. You up for it?" Tain asked.

Marvin shrugged again. "Yeah. You got a pop machine around here?"

Tain reached into his pocket and flipped Marvin a two-dollar coin. "Just down the hall, there." He waited until Marvin was halfway across the room before he stood. "I'll show him the video of the lobby before Lindsay went missing, see if he remembers our guy."

Daly nodded. "Not a bad idea. Shouldn't we be showing it to all the kids?"

"We tried Luke Driscoll, and he didn't remember anything. Most of the parents are a bit freaked out, blew a gasket about us asking questions without them present."

"You'd think we'd get more cooperation from people who want to protect their children."

"They're scared. People do all sorts of crazy things when they're afraid, especially when kids are involved." He didn't think he really had to explain that to Daly.

For a second Daly's eyes took on a distant look. "What have you got planned after this?"

"I'm supposed to be tracking down the clown and jewelry vendor from the fairgrounds, but I'm going to take Marvin home after we're finished."

"What about those photos of Nicky Brennen?" Daly asked.

"Ashlyn's supposed to start looking into that later."

"Right. Let me know if you hear from her."

Tain nodded, rummaging through another file, retrieving photographs of red Honda Civics and silver Corvettes.

Ashlyn rubbed the bridge of her nose before tossing the magazine down on the coffee table in front of her.

This was the one place she was reasonably certain the rapist wouldn't be found, and the one place she'd spent the better part of her day. Once she'd established that every nurse and receptionist on site was female, she'd proceeded to flip through the magazines lying around, finding not much of particular interest and absolutely nothing that got her any further along on the case.

Of all the places to be stuck on a beautiful summer day . . .

She glanced out the door to the hallway and felt a prickling sensation in her shoulders as they tensed.

He looked like he must have been mopping the same bit of floor for five minutes until he saw her look up. Then he glanced away and shuffled off down the corridor.

She fished around in the purse she was carrying and removed a scrap piece of paper, jotting down a quick description of the man who'd been watching her.

Ashlyn glanced at the clock. She knew that patients were usually kept waiting anywhere from ten to thirty minutes in the exam rooms. Craig's physical was going to take at least an hour, depending on which tests the doctor felt were necessary, and he'd been gone for an hour now.

She got up and stepped into the hallway, turning in the direction she'd seen the cleaner going.

After a few moments, Tain knocked again.

This time, he heard someone lumbering down the hall toward the door. He wasn't surprised when it opened a crack a moment later, revealing the overgrown eyebrows that dominated the face of Father Benjamin.

"Do you have news for the family?"

"I'm afraid not, Father. But I was hoping to speak with them."

The already creased face added wrinkles as Father Benjamin frowned. "I'm not sure that would be wise. The Eckerts are still quite distressed."

"I understand that. This won't take long."

Father Benjamin seemed to have mastered the art of stopping just short of scowling, making Tain sense his disapproval without exactly pinpointing what it was about the face that gave it away. Somehow, the priest made Tain feel guilty, as though he was doing something he knew he shouldn't.

But he'd need more than a look of practiced condemnation used for hellfire lectures to put Tain off.

Lindsay's mother looked about to faint, clutching the top

of her blouse tightly, and Mr. Eckert started to stand until Tain motioned for him to sit back down.

"I don't have any news. I'm sorry," Tain said. There was silence for a moment before the high-pitched voice of Lynn Eckert cut in.

"Why are you here then? We know she isn't here. You should be out there, looking for my daughter."

She crumpled into a ball, her back shaking with the sobs.

"There, there, Lynn. Come on, come lie down." Father Benjamin cooed as he rubbed her back, coaxed her to her feet and led her from the room.

As far as Tain could tell, Ted Eckert seemed to find nothing unusual in the priest's behavior. He stared blankly out the window as though his wife wasn't coming apart at the seams, his daughter wasn't missing and his world wasn't spinning out of control.

"Mr. Eckert, I spoke to Lindsay's friend Marvin. He was very helpful, and I do have a few leads to follow." Tain drew a breath, waiting for some reaction from Lindsay's father. When there wasn't one, he went ahead. "Would you mind if I talked to Lindsay's brother and sister?"

Ted Eckert's head snapped around to stare at Tain then, his previously pale cheeks filling with red. "Why?"

"Mr. Eckert, it's possible the person who took Lindsay was watching her. I'd like to ask Danielle and Caleb if they saw anyone around."

After a moment, Ted Eckert nodded and walked down the hall, back toward the door. He climbed the stairs at a snail's pace, as though his feet were weighed down with cement blocks that made it hard for him to move his stocky frame upward at any respectable pace.

"Dan . . ." he tried, his voice getting stuck in his throat. He coughed and then tried again. "Kids."

Within seconds, two doors opened, one revealing an older version of Lindsay, the long, silky hair pulled back in a ponytail. The other door revealed a young boy about Nicky Brennen's age, with straight blond hair and rosy cheeks, which didn't really fit with the generally colorless tone of the rest of the family.

Mr. Eckert turned on his heel and started clunking back down the stairs.

Tain held up his ID and, for what felt like the hundredth time that day, cursed Ashlyn's absence.

"My name is Tain," he said.

"Huh. Lame." The girl rolled her eyes, her arms folded across her chest, her hip parked against the door frame.

"I need to ask you some questions," he said, trying to resist the urge to scowl at her.

"About my sister?" the boy asked.

"That's right." Tain looked down at him. "Did you see anybody around your house who seemed to be . . . to want to talk to her?"

"Like her friends?"

"He means, like strangers," the girl said, rolling her eyes at Tain again and taking her brother back into his room, sitting down with him on the edge of his bed. "People who shouldn't have been here."

Caleb's cheeks puffed out, and he shook his head. Tain looked at the girl, who shrugged and shook her head.

"What about any cars outside that aren't usually there?"

"Plenty of those now," Danielle said.

"But before. Any around like this?" He extracted an envelope of pictures from his pocket, pulling out the first one, passing it to Danielle.

"Seriously? These things are all over."

"So, no new ones hanging around your street, say, the week before Lindsay went missing?" He reached out and took the photo from her, sticking the picture of the red Civic back in the envelope. Tain passed her another photo. "What about that one?"

Her face lengthened, and then her nose wrinkled. "I think so."

"I've seen that car," Caleb said, looking up at Tain. His eyes looked as big as a puppy's, and he almost smiled.

"Really? Where have you seen a car like that?"

"Outside when I came home from school."

"School? That must have been quite a few weeks ago."

Danielle shook her head. "No, we all go to a year-round school. Not much since . . ." She shrugged. "You know. It's holidays next week anyway."

"You saw this car outside your house? When you last went to school?"

Caleb nodded.

"And you last went to school . . . ?"

"The Friday before Lindsay disappeared."

"Thanks. That's really helpful," Tain said, backing toward the door hesitantly.

"Go play," Danielle told her brother, crossing the room as he went to his table to color a picture.

She shut the door and looked up at Tain as she stepped into the hallway. "You cops, you haven't got a clue, do you?"

Danielle walked past him into her room and slammed the door.

Ashlyn had deliberately managed to spill half the water that hadn't already sloshed over the sides when she kicked it. "Oh, geesh, I'm so sorry! I'm so clumsy. Here." She grabbed the bucket. "Let me help."

"Tha-that's okay. I can do it," he said. He bent down, grabbed the handle of the bucket, his gaze instantly going to her legs, which were bare below the knee-length skirt she was wearing, the cut from a few days before barely noticeable. He fumbled with the bucket as he moved it a safe distance from her, and managed to force himself upright, but only glanced at her face quickly before he resumed mopping, his eyes focused in her general direction, about a foot off the floor.

"Gee, I'm really sorry. I'm uh, looking for a pay phone. My cell phone died." She did her best to offer a wide-eyed smile.

"We . . . uh . . . there—there's a phone down by—by the doors. Th-that way," he said moving toward the main hallway, out of the secondary hall he was standing in. "They, uh . . . there . . ."

"There you are. I wondered where you got to."

Her head spun around, and she plastered on an instant smile. "All finished?" she asked, moving forward and ignoring Craig's hand. She wrapped her arm around his waist instead, and glanced back at the man with the fish pin on his collar.

"Thanks." She gave him what she hoped was a flirtatious smile and then leaned against Craig. "Did you have fun?"

He looked down at her. "Did you?"

"Unless your doctor is a viable suspect, that's the only one in the building I caught looking at me."

Ashlyn felt his hand on the small of her back as he opened the door and ushered her into his vehicle. "You're supposed to be creating a suspect list, not chatting them up."

"I wasn't close enough to see his name tag. 'Unidentified cleaning person' wasn't going to be very helpful."

He frowned at her and shook his head as he shut the door.

Craig felt his chest tighten as he felt Ashlyn's head brush against his arm. She smelled of . . .

He realized he didn't have a clue, but whatever it was, it was nice. Not too heavy and demanding, but still appealing.

Was it just him, or was she finding this tough?

A clerk finally came over to offer assistance. Without even looking at Ashlyn, Craig felt the slight nudge against his arm as she turned, pretending to inspect the pagers on display, all the while scrutinizing employees while he explained his business.

"One of our managers handles that. It's a special account. I'll go get him."

"What's wrong?" Craig asked, watching Ashlyn rub her shoulder.

"I must have slept funny."

Craig's fingers were automatically starting to work on the knot that seemed to be causing her tension when someone said, "Can I help you?"

He turned to look at the man, apparently one of the managers, and explained he was there to get a pager issued by the fire department.

"Do you have your employment letter?"

Craig held up the piece of paper in his opposite hand.

"Everyone on the department comes to me. I want to make sure you've got the most reliable equipment possible. . . ."

He gestured for them to follow him behind the counter to a desk in the back. Craig felt Ashlyn tense again, but she didn't show it in her face, maintaining a steady smile.

She stood back, letting Craig take the far chair, then sat down and crossed her legs. Her skirt inched a bit higher. While Craig discussed the pager and how it worked with the manager, Ashlyn leaned back and managed to look bored with the whole process.

Craig noted the manager seemed to have grown about an inch taller, and his motions lacked the fluidity of ease, but he kept his eyes riveted to Craig's face, as though afraid to look at Ashlyn. As though afraid to betray his thoughts.

It wasn't until they got up to leave that the manager chanced a glance at her, his eyes not even taking in her warm smile, but moving straight down to her body, his skin glistening.

Craig made a point of shaking his hand, confirming his hunch. The manager was sweating, despite the air-conditioning.

Once they'd returned to his house and started unloading their purchases he said, "You know, I didn't think you had it in you."

"What? To be a first-class flirt?"

"Not exactly your style, but I have to hand it to you. You got yourself noticed."

"For all the good it did."

"What are you talking about? That guy at the telephone place, you made him break into a cold sweat."

"So you didn't see the other guy?"

Craig felt his forehead pinch. "Evidently not."

"When the employee went back to get the person to help us, he called someone else out. The guy we talked to, he was sent over to handle the account and told to present himself as the regular manager for it. The other manager was lurking in the hallway, watching the whole thing."

Craig glanced at her as he put the groceries away. "Is that why you wanted the outer chair?"

"That, and it kept my legs visible."

He looked at her. Ashlyn's lips had twisted into a sour look. "Feeling the need to take a shower?"

"Hey, I've encountered my share of creeps, and I usually don't try to encourage them. The thing is, a lot of times rapists go undetected because they don't appear unusual. The guy who was helping you with the pager could have been flustered by my presence, or he could have just been agitated by the fact that his boss was watching him handle this, like it was a test."

"What about the boss? Catch his gaze wandering from his employees?"

"He noticed me, for what it's worth. Whether or not he was interested . . . I can't really check these guys out, anyway, unless I can come up with a home address."

"So as far as the case goes, we're no further ahead." He poured a glass of juice and passed it to her.

Her eyes narrowed. "And beyond the case?" she asked.

"Just think of how good it's been for your ego."

She glared at him, took her juice and walked away.

The silver Corvette meandered down the road, seemingly oblivious to the honks of the vehicles behind it.

Finally, the driver pulled partially off the road, letting an agitated motorist pass, waving his middle finger and shouting curses at the same time.

He paid no attention to the stream of cars that whizzed by, intent on his task. He'd nudged his car in beside a small Sprint that was pulled right up against the curb, but he couldn't stay here.

Once the road was clear, he pulled back out and continued

moving along the block, looking for a place to stop. Nothing. It was wall to wall cars without any obvious spot he could take advantage of.

From the far end of the street he could see the girls, walking along, talking, tossing their hair over their shoulders, waving coyly at a group of boys who were trying to look more interested in skateboards than the smiling creatures in halter tops and shorts, indulging in Slurpees and giggling as they strolled toward the house he was just passing.

Damn! His hand struck the steering wheel, and then he prayed for forgiveness.

*If you were meant to watch her today, there'd be a space*, he told himself.

He watched in the rearview mirror as the girl and her friends walked up to the house and sat on the ledge of the porch, bare legs dangling, still sneaking glances at the boys on the corner between their whispers and giggles.

"That's not exactly light reading," Craig said as he crawled into bed beside her.

"No, it isn't."

"Anything jump out at you, something we might have missed?"

Ashlyn set the file down on the nightstand and lay down. "Nothing so far. I would agree with your assertion that this isn't someone new. Whoever's doing this, he's raped before."

"Just nowhere that we've been able to find a record from."

"That's the problem with these cases." She sat up, punched her pillow up and lay back down on her side, this time facing him. "Rape victims are understandably reluctant to report their attack, and in the meantime, the guy goes out and attacks other women. By the time a pattern emerges, there are multiple victims in his wake, especially if he's this good."

"The department needs to look at better ways to handle these cases so that women aren't afraid to come forward."

"It isn't just the department, Craig. It's society. Some people still have the attitude that it isn't the worst thing that can happen to a person, or that if a woman gets raped she must have asked for it, or she might have consented and then cried rape. We have women complicating the issue by using rape as a cover or a ploy for sympathy, and we have some segments of our population looking at women who've been raped as 'damaged goods.'"

"What's the solution then?"

She shrugged. "Society's attitude about sex needs to change. You have to go to the root source, and with politicians being caught paying for hookers or with their pants down in the office and then trying to lie their way out of it . . . well, we're just reinforcing the idea that most men don't respect women. It's more subtle than it used to be, but it's still there."

"It isn't just men who pay for sex."

"Not anymore, but the overwhelming majority paying for it are men."

"I suppose it sounds weak to say it's better to pay than take it by force."

"I think it's best if two consenting adults have a relationship based on some degree of respect, instead of negotiating a price per performance."

Craig smiled. "In an ideal world, Ashlyn, love would be based on giving instead of getting and we'd put the needs of others first, and not just the sexual needs."

"Women would be seen as valued partners instead of burdens."

He arched an eyebrow. "I thought you weren't bothered by all the harassment you got last year."

"I expect it. And that's part of the problem. I work in a field where women are still outnumbered. I'm young. What am I supposed to do, gain twenty pounds so guys won't bug me?"

They lay there, looking at each other. There was a hint of color in her cheeks that he wasn't used to seeing, her mouth drawn in a hard line for just the briefest moment. Then she lifted her hand to rub the shoulder that had been sore earlier.

"Still giving you trouble?"

"Maybe I pulled the muscle by lying on my arm last night."

"You don't usually sleep on that side?"

"I usually sleep on my stomach."

"Roll over."

She opened her mouth but then closed it and turned around.

He kneaded his fingers over her shoulders, massaging around the tense areas and then gradually working into the knots, feeling the stiffness in her ebb away.

# SATURDAY

Ashlyn's mouth twisted while she considered whether to start with the suspected pedophile or the rapes. She absently picked up dishes from the table, took them to the kitchen, rinsed them and then looked at the dishwasher.

*I should talk to Adrian about that repair guy*, she thought, turning to the fridge for the juice.

Neither option seemed likely to get her any closer to their abductor, but she had to start somewhere. She walked up the stairs, went into the spare room that was doubling as her office, and started her computer. Then she started doing searches of child porn sites.

The doorbell rang and she went downstairs to let Tain in.

"Hungry?" he asked, holding up a bag of muffins.

Her whole face wrinkled. "No, and you won't be either when you see what I'm looking at."

He followed her upstairs. "Jesus," Tain said when he sat down at the computer. "Is this all local?"

"Evidently there are regionalized groups for photo swapping."

"And God knows what else." Tain turned away from the desk to where she sat on an extra chair she'd brought upstairs. "There must be an easier way to try to track this?"

"If there is, I'm open to suggestions."

"I know someone who was working in the morality crimes division. Still is, I think. I'll ask him if he's got any tips."

"I thought they dealt with physical-abuse cases."

"That's one thing about broad, general definitions. You can be assigned anything."

"Did you make any progress yesterday?"

"Well, Marvin came to see me."

Ashlyn's eyes widened at that. "Oh?"

"Not much useful there. He didn't remember seeing any specific vehicles around, but he also admitted he'd never been to Lindsay's house and they go to a different school. And he remembered Lindsay being bumped, but they were too distracted to notice anything else, and they weren't paying attention to Luke at all."

She nodded, her mouth twisting wryly. "Not surprising."

"I also talked to the Eckert kids. They also remember seeing a silver Corvette, but couldn't be more specific. It was recent, before Lindsay disappeared."

"So we could be looking for someone who drives a silver Chevy Corvette. Any idea what year?"

"I'd guess the '78, which was their silver-anniversary edition. There are loads of them around."

"Something else for me to check on, then." She frowned as she looked at Tain. "What about that support staff list Eric and Zoe were supposed to go over?"

"I'm meeting with them later."

She smirked. "Lucky you."

"We could always move the meeting here."

"And keep me from all the domestic chores I've got? That's okay. You can handle them."

Tain's smile faded. "You learn anything useful?"

"On the rape cases?" She shrugged. "A list of names to check out."

"But nobody leaping to the front of the suspect list."

"Not yet. Craig's on day shift today and tomorrow, and then he's on nights. Hopefully, by then we can screen most of the people he comes in contact with and see if there are any flags."

He nodded.

She sighed as she leaned back, resting against her arms. "Tain, what about that other potential lead for Taylor's abduction? Have you chased it down?"

"Yeah. I don't think there's anything to it." He gave her an overview of the situation, and John-John's reaction.

"Make sure you tell Daly."

"Your concern is touching."

"I'm serious. Daly will back you up."

Tain nodded, got up and started walking out of the room. "I plan to talk to him later. You let me know if you need anything."

"Let me know if you learn anything," she told him as she followed him down the stairs.

"You'll be here all day?" He pulled his shoes on, reaching for the front door.

"Pretty much. I have to go back to the store and pick up some extra boots for Craig. They didn't have enough in his size and had to have them sent over from Maple Ridge."

He nodded and winked at her. "I'll give you a call after the meeting, let you know how much Rob Quinlan misses you."

She groaned and shut the door behind him.

Craig had his back to the group of firefighters, so he didn't see which one spoke. "Not bad, rookie. Maybe once you get a handle on polishing the truck up properly, we'll let you take it for a drive."

"I fail to see what cleaning a vehicle has to do with your ability to handle it on the road," Craig said.

The men sitting around watching him work all laughed. "Oh, that's right. From the person who's driving a '91 Isuzu Rodeo."

"That runs like a charm."

"Way we see it, anyone who spends hours polishing this baby isn't going to want to get it stuck under a low bridge or scrape the side of a semi that's hugging your lane."

Craig bit back his response to that and rinsed out the dirty water. "What's next?" he asked after he'd finished cleaning up.

They looked at each other and grinned.

"New boy's eager to show us his stuff," one said.

"I don't know. Maybe we should go easy on him. I'm not sure he's up to it," another said.

"Yeah, but they're coming 'round to take the calendar

photos tomorrow. What are they calling it this year? *Light My Fire?*"

There were snickers at that. "Yeah, and they say men are pigs. All these women wanting to see us with our shirts off."

"If having my picture taken is the worst you can throw at me, maybe I should be helping you boys get into shape. You don't want to look like you've been sitting around on your oversized backsides watching others work, do you?"

Jeers and whistles were the response, as well as a steely grin from the one in the front, who'd had the most to criticize about Craig's cleaning abilities so far.

He stood up and pointed at Craig. "Right, pretty boy. I'll see you in the gym."

Craig followed him upstairs, ignoring the comments from the men walking behind him.

Tain sprinted up the sidewalk and didn't even knock on the partially open door.

"All right, that's enough, break it up." He glared at Nick Brennen, "I said, break it up. Back off."

Nick turned and put his fist through the wall.

"You're going to pay for that." Connie Brennen screeched the words.

"Fuck, since I met you, all I've been doing is paying." Nick raised his hand, his breaths shallow and rapid as he glared past Tain, pointing behind him. "And if you think that piece of trash is going to take my kid away, you can go to hell."

Tain turned to see who'd walked in behind him.

"She's my kid," John-John said.

"I thought you told me there was no way you were Taylor's dad," Tain said.

John-John shrugged. "Some things came back to me after you left."

Tain exhaled. "You know, I don't think Mr. Brennen is an idiot, John-John. I think he knows Taylor wasn't the product of a virgin birth. You don't know anything until you've had a DNA comparison done. Meanwhile, Nick Brennen is her legal father. He's named on her birth certificate, he's raised her, and she shares the same last name. And as far as I'm concerned, he's the only person here who really gives a damn about her. Nick." He turned to face him. "Go home. Stay away from your ex and stay away from this piece of garbage. Don't do anything that's going to jeopardize you getting full custody of your kids."

"But what if he . . . what if she? I mean, what will happen?"

Tain put a hand on his shoulder and steered him toward the door.

"You're her legal father, even if you aren't her biological parent. The courts aren't going to take her away from you to give her to some drug-dealing pimp with a second set of rooms on East Hastings."

"But Connie—"

"Nick, right now, we just want to find Taylor and bring her home. It isn't helping you or her or me, for that matter, if this gets in the way. And Nicky is her brother. The courts aren't going to tear apart two children to put one with an incompetent parent."

"But sometimes, it's happened. I know good men who lose their kids, even when the mom is a useless sa—"

"I'll do a report for you for the court. I'll do whatever I can. Let's just hope we get to the point where you have to worry about that. Now, are you going to go home and be with your son so that I can get back to finding your daughter?"

Nick Brennen swallowed and nodded. Tain watched until he got into his car and drove away. His cell phone rang. Tain pulled it out and looked at the time and swore under his breath.

After making an exhaustive list of every site she'd searched Ashlyn tilted her neck from side to side, rubbing at the little kinks that had settled in, and tried something different.

She whistled and redid the search, localizing it to British Columbia, reducing the results by over a thousand.

"Well, that's a start . . ."

After a few hours of taking notes about the relationship between sex and fire she clicked on an archived new article and leaned back, her eyes popping open as she processed the details of the incident.

Then she ripped out a fresh page of paper, made a list of notes and wrote down the reporter's name.


New guy makes the meals, new guy does all the cleaning, new guy has to kick ass in bench pressing and an assortment of other physical tests. . . . Craig hated to admit it but he hadn't been at the gym enough lately. Some of those muscles burned.

After he'd finished showering and changed, he walked into the sleeping area with his duffle bag. "So? Do I pass or what?"

One of the guys pointed him to a locker. "All yours."

He pulled the door open and started unpacking a few things Quinlan had told him he'd need to keep at the hall.

And a few things Quinlan hadn't mentioned, like Ashlyn's picture.

They'd had to drive around to half a dozen different places and get cozy for the camera. He'd also found a picture of them from last fall, Ashlyn with shorter hair, which helped make it look like they'd been a couple for a long time. He pinned up a picture of Ashlyn alone and someone offered an appreciative whistle.

"Hey, haven't I seen her around?" somebody asked.

Another guy snapped his fingers. "Isn't she that cop? Working on those arsons?"

"Who cares? She can hang out around here anytime."

"What's this?" a new voice asked. "We letting anyone have a locker 'round here now?"

"Rotation C, meet the new boy."

"New boy got a name?"

"Craig Nolan." He turned to survey the next shift starting to filter in.

One of the men looked at him and then past him at the locker. He marched over, his eyes narrowing.

"What the hell are you doing with her picture? She's a cop, not a pinup girl."

Craig held up one of the photos of them together. "You got a problem with me having pictures of my girlfriend?"

One of the men from Craig's shift walked toward his locker, patting the new man Craig was speaking with on the shoulder.

"Adrian has a thing for the ladies."

Adrian scowled. "Shut up, Brett."

"Well, geez, you've been the self-appointed guardian of her virtue ever since she started working on the arson cases. You and that partner of hers."

"I wouldn't have to be if you weren't all a bunch of pigs."

"Face it, you didn't know she was seeing someone and you just wanted to get into her pants."

Adrian lunged at Brett, and Craig stepped in, holding him back.

"Back off," Craig told him.

Adrian held his hands up and backed away, his face red, eyes blazing. Once Craig was reasonably sure it was safe to turn around, he pointed a finger at Brett.

"Don't you ever talk about her like that in front of me again."

He slammed his locker door shut and walked away.

The street was proving as busy today as it had yesterday.

He finally managed to find a spot, right across from her house, and pulled over.

She was hanging around at the corner today, swinging around a lamppost as the boys tried to jump the curb with their skateboards.

She needed to be rescued.

He practically jumped out of his skin when he heard the *tap-tap-tap* on the passenger window and turned to see a woman in a uniform standing there, a ticket book in her hands.

His hands shook as he leaned across the seat and rolled down the window.

"You're being issued a parking ticket."

"Why? What's the problem?"

"This is a permit-only zone. Your vehicle isn't displaying the proper permit."

"But I'm in it, so I can move it, no problem. No big deal."

"Once the ticket is written, it has to be issued."

"You could see I was sitting in the car."

She glared at him, tapping her pen against the paper. "What I can see is you're parked in a restricted permit zone, watching a group of kids who live in this neighborhood. Next you'll be giving me some song and dance about being a PI, hired by one parent to check up on the kid because the other parent has custody or some crap like that, but frankly, I don't give a shit. My job is to make sure the people who park in these spots are the ones who've got a permit. You don't. End of story."

The woman ripped the ticket off and tossed it on the seat. "Now move on, before I feel the need to call you in."

His fingers slipped on the keys twice, and he rubbed his hands on his pants. Then he started the car and drove away.


"Sorry to . . ." Tain stopped as soon as he saw Daly's face. Daly offered a slight nod toward a chair and Tain sat down, waiting.

"Your list of substitute teachers. All the ones who worked with one child we left clear, two of the girls marked in yellow, three in blue. Same thing," Zoe continued, tossing another pile of papers an inch thick down in front of him, "with the bus drivers."

"And these are the school and group photographers." Eric slid a file across the table.

There was silence for a moment, and Tain could see Daly looking down, his face hard.

"Should I assume nobody connects to all four?" Tain asked.

"Why should they? Our guy isn't involved with all four girls."

"What are you talking about?"

"Taylor Brennen," Zoe snapped. "You thought you'd hold back on the fact that Nick Brennen isn't her real father, that there's someone out there with a pretty compelling motive for grabbing that girl."

"Just a second. For starters, we don't know that John-John is her father. From a legal standpoint, Nick Brennen is her dad. I talked to John-John myself. He seemed genuinely surprised that anyone was asserting that he was Taylor's dad."

"That's not the tune he's singing now, though, is it?"

Tain lifted a hand and then let it fall to the table. "Then why's he going over to Connie's place flipping out if he grabbed her?"

"The point is you withheld vital information to this investigation because you wanted to stay in control of it. Here you give us your bullshit about working as a team and not being after the credit when you're sitting on relevant information that affects how this case is handled."

"I'm not sitting on anything. If you want to talk about credit, fine, let's talk about who fucked this case up from day one and let it get out of hand, to the point where four girls have gone missing."

"Three."

"Four, at least."

Zoe's eyes narrowed. "What the hell does that mean? You think there are other parents out there not looking for their missing kids? You'd say anything right now to try to justify keeping this case and you know it."

"Okay, that's enough. Both of you, sit back down," Daly said. "This isn't helping anybody."

"I'm not happy about this." Rob Quinlan looked at Tain. "We're being kept in the dark."

"Look, this case has snowballed, and there are other investigations that are affected by it. I can't just throw open the files for anyone now," Daly said.

"Are you saying we're being officially shut out, after doing all this legwork?" Zoe spat the words.

"I'm saying that if you have a problem with how it's being handled, you have to go to Inspector Hawkins."

Tain noticed Rob's shoulders sag, just the tiniest bit. It was about time Hawkins did something useful.

"I appreciate everything your team has brought to the table. Right now, I can't disclose anything else about the status of the investigation," Daly said.

To Tain, Eric looked indifferent, Zoe's face was burning, her eyes bulging, and Rob Quinlan looked like he was choking on hot sauce. He stomped out of the room, Zoe waiting only a second before she got up and marched after him.

"Sorry about all of this," Tain said to Eric as he stood up.

"Don't worry about it. I wouldn't want to work with her either."

Once Eric had left, Daly walked to the door. Without looking at Tain, he paused only to say, "My office. Now."

When Ashlyn got to the store she asked for the salesgirl who'd helped Craig the day before.

The man leaned across the counter and winked at her. "Nothing she can do for you that I can't." He frowned, looking her up and down. "Unless . . ."

Ashlyn wondered when guys started being so fucking obvious, or if this case was really just making her hypersensitive. She tried to suppress her disgust. "I'm here to pick up some boots my boyfriend ordered. Craig Nolan."

"Oh, hi. We got those in." The salesgirl came out of the back room with a stack of boxes balanced precariously in her arms. She walked past the counter to a display area. The man's eyes followed her movements, focused on her backside and the swishing of the short skirt she was wearing.

"Fire, police or paramedic?"

"Excuse me?" Ashlyn stared at him.

"Your boyfriend. Which is he?"

She almost had to correct herself. "Fire."

"You look the type."

Ashlyn felt her eyes narrow, in spite of her best efforts to remain relaxed and nonjudgmental. "What kind of type is that?"

"Here we go," the salesgirl said, ignoring the conversation between Ashlyn and the salesman. "Now, I know Craig paid

for these yesterday, but I still have to get you to sign this."
She removed an invoice record, made out in the names of
Craig and Ashlyn Nolan, with Craig's address at the top.

"My last name isn't Nolan."

"So there's hope for me yet," the salesman said, winking at
her again. "Just sign his name for him."

Ashlyn did and grabbed the stack of boxes, pausing as she
turned and saw the salesman holding the front door open
for her. Despite the surprisingly cool breeze she stepped out
into, she felt her cheeks burn with the certainty that this guy
was mind-fucking her as she walked away.


"Where the hell have you been?" Vish demanded when she
walked into the house.

"At work," Lori responded, glaring at him.

"You should know you shouldn't be out wandering around
alone."

"I wasn't wandering around alone. I was just driving home
from work."

"Whatever. I thought you were staying here."

"Oh for Christ's sake, stop treating me like a baby! You're
acting as though walking out the front door will make me a
target for every pervert around."

"It doesn't take walking out the front door and you should
damn well know that. What the hell are you doing back at
work already, anyway?"

Lori stiffened and started to march past him. He moved
in front of her.

"I'm not having this conversation with you. You're being
completely unreasonable about this."

"Me? I'm trying to protect you, to make sure you're okay,
that you work through this properly. How can going back
to that job and dealing with psychopaths and freaks all day
help you?"

"See, I knew you wouldn't understand. Just get out of
my—"

She glared at him as he grabbed her arms, enraged, ignoring the pleading in his eyes.

"This isn't helping you."

"You're damn right about that! It isn't. All you're doing is making me stressed and agitated. I may as well have stayed at work."

"You can't be serious. You're going to use me as an excuse? You're going to try to convince yourself that I'm driving you away? Lori, look at yourself. You look like shit. You're tossing and turning half the night. You need help."

"So what, you're going to solve all my problems? By trying to persuade me to stay here all day and be a happy homemaker?"

"If that's what it takes for you to feel normal again, then yes."

"Normal? You want me to feel normal? How the fuck do you think I'm supposed to ever feel normal again? This guy comes in here and . . . and . . . and now you want me to leave my career because you don't think it's suitable and that's supposed to help me feel normal?"

She yanked herself out of his grip and turned around, grabbed her coat and keys, and slammed the front door behind her.

"Where were you?" Craig asked as soon as Ashlyn returned to the house.

"Forging your signature at a shoe store."

He gave her a wry smile and grabbed the boxes as she slipped off her sandals. "Very funny."

"Seriously. I had to sign some paper saying I picked these up."

"Don't want customers trying to get a second order free." Craig set them on the small table in the corner of the kitchen. "Thanks for doing that."

"And thanks for cooking," she said, surveying the array of pots simmering on the stove. "My trip to the store was a bit more interesting today." She leaned against the counter and grabbed a carrot from the tray of vegetables he was dicing. From previous experience she knew he was actually a good cook, but he seldom bothered when he was alone. Unless he had company, Craig tended to live on takeout.

"That girl give you more insight into male anatomy?"

She laughed. "Hardly. Her co-worker was there and he's a real womanizer. Ass man too."

Craig frowned at her. "Nice."

"No different than some of the guys we worked with last year."

"Probably not much different than any number of guys you walk past on a given day. Especially working those arson cases."

She chewed slowly as her eyes pinched together. "You know something that I don't?"

"You're quite popular."

"I don't think I want to know what that means."

"Where are you going?" he asked her as she started to walk into the hallway.

"Upstairs to change. These short skirts are driving me crazy."

"Maybe you can sue the department for harassment, making you wear those."

"I'm going after hazard pay for the high heels," she called back.

Craig lifted the cutting board and scraped the vegetables into the pan just as the doorbell rang. He started to run to answer it and then stopped, turned the burner down, and walked to the door.

For a moment they stood looking at each other. Craig tried half a dozen different lines in his head and couldn't think of what to say. She solved the problem for him.

"Can I come in?"

He opened the door wider and stepped back. "I'm just making dinner."

"Smells good."

Lori followed him down the hall into the kitchen, where the contents of the pan were sizzling.

"How did you find out where I live?"

"It wasn't hard."

Craig glanced at her. "Not exactly reassuring."

"I meant for someone in the department."

"Right. What brings you by?"

"No 'can I get you a drink?' or 'want to stay for dinner?' or 'how have you been?' formalities from you, huh?"

He flushed as he looked up, but she offered him a bitter smile.

"At least you're consistent. You don't baby me." She stiffened. "Sorry. I'm intruding."

Craig followed her gaze to the hallway, where Ashlyn had paused.

"No, not at all." Ashlyn walked into the kitchen. "Can I get you something to drink? Tea, juice, lemonade?"

Craig noticed the pinch of Lori's eyes, followed by the slightest widening, as though she'd just made a connection.

"You work for the department, don't you?"

"Um-hmm. Iced tea?"

"Sure."

Lori glanced at Craig, looking like a poker player who'd just picked up a winning hand.

"Why don't you two go into the living room while I finish dinner?" Ashlyn said. "I'll call you in a few minutes."

"Lori isn't staying," Craig said.

"You know, Craig, department policy and all that jazz. Could really hurt your career if the wrong people knew you're involved with another officer."

"It's none of your business," he told her.

"Really?"

"We aren't partnering now, so what I'm doing in my personal or professional life has nothing to do with you."

"I want back on the rape case."

"You're dreaming."

"I don't think so. And I think you can help me with that."

"Lori, go home. Honestly, you aren't even ready to be back on the job. I'd let someone take this rape case away from me before I'd be willing to work with you on it."

She smiled and set her glass down on the counter. "If

that's the way you want it, that's fine." Lori held up her hand as Ashlyn started to follow her into the hallway. "I can see myself out."

He inched the tape forward a millisecond at a time, paused it, studied the image for a moment, and then backed it up.

Perfect. The more sophisticated technology became, the easier it was for him to convert frames from tape to his computer, where he could save them as images. She'd make a nice one for his collection.

Once he'd transferred all the data, he printed the image off, studying her. An eye-catcher in her own right, vivacious, a real intelligence to her, despite the casual indifference.

Nice legs. And a real nice ass.

His smile faded as he heard footsteps coming down the hall, and he stuck the photo into his bag, glancing at the clock and cursing being held up again, on a Saturday as well. He wasn't even supposed to be working today, but with summer vacations and staff being sick, he was on mega-overtime at the moment.

And there was a fire tonight. Not as big as some, but big enough for a quickie.

She was on the wrong rotation, though. He stuffed the personal information in beside the photo and cleared his computer screen so that nobody could see what he'd really been doing.

"Anything else to go off?" Craig asked.

"A few things to chase down, but not much. You know, you'd think it would be easy to sit around a house all day and just track down info, but it's enough to drive me crazy. What about you?"

"Remember being a cadet at the Depot?"

Ashlyn offered a sardonic smile. "Does anyone ever forget?"

"Today was like a repeat."

"That much fun, huh?"

"I thought police officers were bad. These firefighters are

pretty competitive," Craig said, getting up to answer the door. "Did you see Tain?"

"Briefly. He was supposed to call back . . ."

Craig stepped back while Daly walked past him wordlessly. He followed Daly back to the living room.

"Did you know?" Daly demanded.

"About what?" Ashlyn asked, remaining curled up on the couch.

"About another possible motive for the abduction of Taylor Brennen."

"Is this why I didn't hear from Tain? You didn't suspend him, did you?"

"I came pretty damn close, Ashlyn. First you and now this. Since when do you cut me out of the loop?"

She opened her mouth and then looked at Craig before turning back to Daly.

"Look, Burnaby's bungled this from the beginning, and there was no reason to think that Taylor's abduction wasn't connected to the other girls. If we jumped to conclusions and let them take the case back, we wouldn't be where we are now. What about the connection to the fires? And the rapes? Taylor's case fits those patterns."

"We know that now, Ashlyn."

"Tain checked it out, quietly. We just didn't want anyone getting excited and getting ahead of what the facts merited."

Daly sank down on the sofa and leaned forward, looking at her. "So you're saying Tain told you and you agreed to keep quiet."

Craig watched her, caught the split-second hesitation.

"I'm saying that Tain did the right thing, and I supported his decision."

"That doesn't answer my question."

"I'm not hanging him out to dry to cover my own ass here."

"Ashlyn, this is the second time you've demonstrated to me that you can be reckless. Is this how you work on the job, or is this the influence of Tain?"

"It's on me, Daly."

"Then I'm pulling you out of here."

"What? I don't think that's a good idea," Craig said, moving around behind the smaller sofa to stand behind Ashlyn.

"Craig, you can stay in the department and we can get that list checked, but I'm not having an officer in an undercover role if I can't trust her."

"The guys at the department believe she's my girlfriend. Pulling Ashlyn out could jeopardize my position there.

"Dad, you know damn well if Burnaby had caught on to the possibility that Taylor's abduction wasn't linked, they would have snatched that case back. You'd be dealing with Coquitlam families you couldn't help." Craig sighed. "I know Tain, and I know he's capable of a lot of things, but not for the sake of his ego. He did this because he believed it was right."

"There was a time you weren't so quick to trust him."

"But I've always trusted Ashlyn, and so have you."

Daly stared back at Craig for a moment before he shifted his gaze down to Ashlyn.

"My question here is whether Ashlyn and Tain trust me. You both could have come to me and I would have supported you. I can protect you if I know what the hell you're doing."

"I . . . I'm sorry. There's been so much stress you've been under, and I'm not just saying that to try to brush this off. You know the hours Tain and I were putting in. Stuff came in, and we just had to roll with it and sort it out as best we could. There were times I was looking for you and you were caught up with Craig or Hawkins or at a rape scene. Tain wanted more information before he put it forward because we were still actively working with Burnaby, and then once he'd tracked it down, I was pulled off for this."

"When did he tell you?" Daly asked.

"Everything? This morning."

"But you knew about it before."

"I knew he was holding something back, and he told me enough for me to support his decision."

"Did Hawkins flip out?" Craig asked.

"Hawkins already cut the team from Burnaby out of it, so Tain's on his own, except for whatever help you can give him. But Hawkins did call to tell me he expected me in early tomorrow morning for a meeting."

Craig saw Ashlyn look up at him.

"When did he call?"

"Twenty, thirty minutes ago. Just as I was driving over."

This time, Craig's gaze met Ashlyn's before he moved around the sofa and sat down beside her.

"Then it might not have anything to do with Tain. Lori showed up here. And she thinks she can use my alleged relationship with Ashlyn to get back on the rape case."

Ashlyn had gone upstairs before Daly left. Craig found her already in her pajamas, in the spare bedroom. "Thinking of exchanging vehicles?"

"Very funny."

Craig picked up the photo, resting a hand on the back of the chair she was sitting on. "What's the significance?"

"Taylor Brennen's brother remembered seeing a car like that around their house before she went missing." She leaned back and looked up at him. "The kid's a car fanatic. He noticed it. Tain asked Lindsay Eckert's brother and sister. They remembered a similar car in the area."

"Hardly conclusive. There are a lot of '78 Corvettes around."

"Still, easier to track down than red Honda Civics."

"Isn't anything?"

She smiled. "We're grasping at straws, but you know how it is. We have to check out everything."

"Well, if you're thinking your abductor used this vehicle, you've got a little glitch to consider."

The smile vanished. "What's that?"

"No standard trunk. Storage is behind the seats. There are three compartments, one with the battery, one for general storage and one for the jack."

"You're telling me with a backend like that there's no room for a kid to be stashed?"

"Well, you could put stuff on top of the compartments and use one of those screens that pull up, the kind people have in station wagons to conceal anything that might be interesting to car thieves. I'm just not sure that it would be the most practical. Whoever grabbed these girls had to pull the seats forward, stuff them in there, and the slightest bump or wiggle could reveal their presence to anyone looking. It would be risky." He set the photo down. "But he could have scouted out the area in this car and had another vehicle he used when he grabbed them."

"I don't know. It seems to me he was opportunistic. He grabbed Isabella when she went into the woods for a ball. You couldn't know beforehand that was going to happen and plan to take your car with the trunk instead."

"Unless this guy is a fortune teller." Craig started walking down the hall to the bedroom. "Do you need the bathroom?"

"No, already done." She followed him. "If he is, then he knows we're coming after him. Wouldn't he change his methods or move?"

"I guess that depends on whether the future is fixed and unalterable and we're all just pawns on somebody's chess board, or whether we have freedom to make our own choices."

The light from the bathroom reduced to a trickle, and she climbed into bed. Within minutes he was lying beside her.

"We are not having this debate," she told him.

"You're no fun."

"Maybe the guru with the chess set made me an unhappy pawn."

"Thought we weren't having this discussion."

She grabbed the extra pillow between them and hit him over the head. "Not my fault. I'm just a puppet with somebody else pulling the strings."

Ashlyn started to turn over and felt the pillow land against the side of her face.

"I take it you don't believe in a higher power controlling your destiny."

She tossed the extra pillow on the floor. "If we're all just pieces in some cosmic game, then what's the point of what we do? It isn't anybody's fault that they're a rapist or a child murderer or an arsonist. It's that cosmic being that's responsible."

"So we should arrest God?"

When she turned to look at him, she was surprised to find his face only a few inches away. It was becoming so normal to touch him in public, she'd found her hand going to his arm or his waist automatically when they were together, but lying there, virtually nose to nose, his presence wasn't just another part of the routine.

"Have you never felt like blaming God for all the suffering you see?" She shrugged. "Even for the things you've had to deal with in your life?"

"So that I could avoid taking responsibility myself?"

"You know what I mean, Craig. Life isn't fair. Some people start with harder lives than others ever live to experience."

He was quiet for a moment. "I know. I don't have all the answers."

"Yet at quarter to eleven on a Saturday night, when you have to get up and go to work tomorrow, you want to debate about free choice?"

"I was curious to know if what I thought you believed was correct."

"Can I ask you something?" When he nodded she took the plunge. "Why don't you go by Daly?"

For a moment there was silence. "Nolan's my middle name," was all he said.

She felt as though a dozen butterflies had just fluttered into her chest as he rolled over, little more than a dark shadow beside her as she lay staring at his back. After what felt like hours, wondering if she'd hurt him, Ashlyn propped herself up and saw that he was already breathing deeply. She collapsed back against the pillow, staring wide-eyed at the ceiling for the third night in a row.

# SUNDAY

Ashlyn was sitting with Tain at the dining-room table, catching up on the meeting with Burnaby that she'd missed the day before. "You're kidding me."

"Nope." Tain grinned. "I've never seen a chick look so pissed."

"Not even one you were hitting on at the bar?" She smiled. "Is Daly getting you some help on this?"

"Sims is now my loyal servant."

"What did he do to piss off the powers that be?"

"Your guess is as good as mine, but I'm not complaining. He's thorough. Although he'll be disappointed when he finds out about you and Craig."

She groaned. "Is it something in the water these days, or what? Never mind," she said when she saw his eyes pinch together questioningly. She told him about the rear design of the '78 Corvette. "I checked. Craig was right."

"Damn him."

"Still, we should check them out. Even if someone was around the area, you never know if they saw something."

"True. It just feels like one step forward, three back on this."

"What else is still pending? It seems like every time we have a plan, something sidetracks us and we're chasing down new leads. What have we forgotten?"

"A big, fat circle around the name Doug Fisher, who did some on-call desk work at Southside Recreation and Fitness Center."

Ashlyn nodded. "He was the only staff person who wasn't

working a normal schedule during the week before Lindsay's abduction."

"Hardly conclusive."

"And I know his name from somewhere."

"Okay, I'll run that down. I also have a lead on our clown and jewelry vendor. They're at the Pacific National Exhibition today."

"You're going to the PNE? Lucky you."

"I won't be riding the rides, Ashlyn, or taking in a concert. Just going to track these two down. Imagine if we found witnesses to Taylor's abduction."

"I'd be wondering why they hadn't come forward."

"They could also be suspects."

"Hey, that would be a first on this case. Did you ever find out why Alex Wilson stopped working as a photographer?"

"I'm just one person, not Superman, you know."

"And your friend from morality crimes?"

"He'll call you, but it sounds like it's hours of tedious screening and a lot of luck."

"Wonderful."

"We also need to go through the runaway and missing-persons reports for July eighteenth."

"I'll add that to my list."

Tain leaned back in his chair, scratched his head. "So what else will you be doing?"

"There's a guy who has a contract to do repairs for the fire halls. I'm going to track him down and see about getting him to fix Craig's dishwasher."

Tain's eyebrows rose. "How . . . domestic of you."

"Actually, I thought anything mechanical was men's work."

He whistled. "Don't let Hawkins hear you discriminating against the better half of the department."

"I'm not discriminating against the better half."

"You're in a mood."

"Ever try sleeping with Craig?" She groaned as soon as she realized what she'd said. "Never mind."

After she gave him a rundown of the other things she

planned to cover, he left. She started a load of laundry, grabbed a glass of juice and returned to the computer, prepared to devote one more hour to scanning vile websites for photos of Nicky Brennen.

Hawkins let out a long, slow breath as he sank into the chair across from Daly. For a moment, Daly kept his eyes focused on the desk while he rubbed the stubble on his chin. Then he looked up.

He looked almost as bad as Lori. Daly felt his stomach plummet and twist.

"There's no easy way to put this. Lori knows that Ashlyn is staying at Craig's."

Daly nodded. "They told me last night."

"She's trying to use it as leverage to get back on the rape case."

"Then it's time for somebody to deal with her. Discipline her, suspend her, put her on forced medical. . . . Can't we require a psych evaluation to deem fitness?"

Hawkins's eyes drifted away from Daly's face to the bookshelves, retaining a glossy film, as though they weren't really focused on anything.

"It's not that simple," he finally said.

"Well, it should be. She could end up jeopardizing Craig's and Ashlyn's safety, as well as compromising this case. You can't expect me to stand by and let her self-destruct or take other people down with her."

"She's having trouble here, trouble at home . . . She needs something to put her back up against, you know."

"That's not my problem. She needs help. Before she hurts somebody else."

Hawkins sighed. "I know. I know." He stood up and walked to the door, pausing with his fingers on the handle. "I just wanted to give you warning, so you knew what was going on."

"What I want to know is what's being done about it."

"I'll handle it," Hawkins said.

The door closed behind him.

Daly leaned back, his hands covering his face. He had a bad feeling about this.

The three girls moved to their spots automatically, kneeling against the cold floor while he set out the bread and wine.

They moved through the recitations flawlessly, he observed. Even the defiant one responded promptly, did all she was asked.

He smiled approvingly before lifting the bread.

"This is my body, broken for you. Eat of my flesh and we shall be one."

He tore off a piece and passed it to the girl he called Hannah—whose real name was Maria—who also tore off a piece and passed it to Taylor, who he'd named Martha. She did the same, passing it to the girl he called Delilah.

Delilah tore a piece of bread away and glanced at the others, unsure, before passing the bread back to him.

He smiled at her.

"Eat my flesh."

When he put the bread in his mouth, they did the same.

Once he'd swallowed, he repeated the process with the wine.

"This is my blood."

He lifted the cup to his lips and drank from the chalice, wiped the edge with a napkin and passed it to Hannah. Slowly, it made its way from girl to girl until they had shared the contents.

"Let us pray." He folded his hands together and closed his eyes most of the way, observing through the tiniest slit that they had all closed their eyes as well, sitting obediently in silent contemplation.

He let his thoughts drift to the other one, the one still out there, lost, soon to become a harlot. God's voice was growing louder now, telling him it was almost time.

"These guys have been making you jump through hoops ever since you got here," Paul Quinlan said to Craig as he gestured for him to sit down.

"They're taking their best shot."

"Always do." Quinlan's smile faded. "Any progress?"

"Ashlyn's checking out everyone we've been in contact with since I joined. You've got a list of all the volunteers and firefighters for us?"

He nodded. "I hate to think of giving it to you, but there's too much at stake. And if I've got an arsonist on my hands, I want him caught. He's jeopardizing the lives of every man here." Quinlan passed him a file. "It looks like your employment information, but all the names are in there. Just don't let anyone else get their hands on it."

"Once Ashlyn's checked them, it will be destroyed."

"You can circumvent the chain of evidence?"

"We're checking everyone I come in contact with. If there's a name on there that looks promising, you're going to introduce me."

"Kind of an end run, isn't it?"

"I'm beyond caring. I just want this guy behind bars." Craig stood. "There was something else we were wondering about."

"What's that?"

"Security cameras. You keep taped footage on file?"

Quinlan nodded. "A few weeks' worth."

"Any chance of us getting a copy?"

"Sure. How do you want me to get it to you?"

"Courier it to Daly at the department. He'll make sure we get it."

"How does Ashlyn like pushing papers?"

Craig smiled. "Believe me, she's paying her penance for that stunt she pulled."

"Mrs. Nolan?"

"Uh, who's calling?"

"Craig Nolan was at our store a few days ago, getting a fire-department pager." He rattled off the name and location, and she felt her neck itch.

"Yes, I was there. What can I do for you?"

"The department is reissuing new pagers to some

people. It looks like there's a better one on the market now that we have available. Can you come by and pick it up today?"

"I don't have the other one. Craig's at . . ." She swallowed. "He's working."

"Oh, well, that's okay. If you want to pick this one up today, he can drop the other one off tomorrow or the next day."

She agreed to drop by and hung up the phone.

*Okay, I've gone through the missing persons files for July eighteen. As expected, nothing that fits our profile. Still no sign of any photos of Nicky Brennen being posted. Damn, what if they're for Wilson's private collection?* She tossed her jeans on the end of the bed and changed into a short dress.

When she got to the telephone outlet that doubled as the company's main district office, she pushed the sunglasses up on her head and leaned against the counter, explaining her business.

Within minutes the man who'd been watching her from the hallway when she'd been there before appeared, equipped with smiles and pleasantries, holding out a chair for her, double checking all their information.

"Mr. Nolan or you can drop off the other pager anytime. This one really will work much better. . . ."

Ashlyn tuned out the techno-babble, but she did take note of how his gaze seemed to continue to find its way back to her instead of the gadget he was holding. When he passed it to her, his fingers lingered on her skin for just a smidge longer than she liked.

She smiled and thanked him, keenly aware of his close proximity as he followed her back to the main counter.

"When did you say Mr. Nolan could drop the other pager off?"

*I didn't,* she thought. But she forced a smile.

"I'm sure he can bring it by tomorrow or the next day. He'll be working nights then."

Whatever trivial nonsense he said to that barely registered. She wrote down his name as soon as she got back to her car and underlined it twice.

Tain waded through the clusters of children and preteens filling the spaces between the rides, wondering how many actually came with adults. It was a sea of opportunity for some child snatcher.

*People think because it isn't Toronto or Los Angeles, nothing bad can happen*. He shook his head as he approached the row of vendors.

Tain found his first likely suspect, walked up behind him and tapped his shoulder.

The clown spun around. "You don't look like my usual customers."

"What about her? She look like one of your regulars?"

"Her?" The clown took the picture, his exaggerated mouth turning down into an enormous frown. "She looks familiar."

"Think back to last weekend, the fair in Coquitlam."

"Oh, her. Yes, I think I saw her. Tried to get her to sit down and get her face done, but she ran off." He passed the picture back.

"And you didn't think it might be relevant to tell us that, what with her going missing that day?"

The clown's face froze. "I didn't know."

"What's your name?"

"Who's asking?"

Tain held up his ID.

The clown's expression didn't change. "I don't see how I can help you."

"That's for me to decide, not you. I'm giving you a choice. You either answer my questions here or come down to the station."

The clown sighed, and the cheery, child-friendly voice vanished. A raspy one replaced it. "Look, I've got a sheet, all right? But for nothing like that."

"What for?"

"Petty theft. Name's Bert Klavic."

"That's your full name?"

"Robert, if you must know."

"You telling me you didn't come forward because of your record?"

"Everybody's anal these days about hiring criminals, especially for stuff like this. I've been clean for two years, you check yourself. But nobody wants a convict, even just a thief, around their kids."

"It's quite a career change."

"Not really. It's a good way to distract parents while they aren't paying attention to their wallets. Not that I do that. But you'd be amazed what they'll shell out to make their kids shut up."

Tain almost laughed as he shook his head. "Creative, I'll give you that."

"Anything else?"

"There was a jewelry vendor who might have talked to her."

"Him." The clown spun around and pointed down to the end of the row. "Now, he's one they should take a look at booting."

"Why?"

"Just watch him for a bit. Wait until a girl buys a necklace."

He started to move away, and Tain grabbed his arm. "Anyone else who might have seen her?"

The clown frowned, then shrugged. "She ran off in the direction of the merry-go-round. It was beside the park."

Tain let go, but he didn't leave.

"Sometimes, there was a religious nut there, trying to talk to people."

"Was he there that day?"

"Look, I'm not sure. But he got kicked out a few times for scaring some kids. Some load about saving them from their carnal desires or something."

"Merry-go-round guy, he working here?"

Bert shook his orange hair. "Sorry. Think he went to the fair in Aldergrove."

This time, when he turned to walk away Tain didn't stop him.

Craig glanced up and smiled. "What brings you here?"

She held up the pager. "Seems the one you've had for forty-eight hours isn't good enough."

"Happens sometimes," said one of the men leaning against a counter between chewing his mouthful of sandwich. "Wives are always bitching about that guy giving out the wrong pager."

Craig noticed Ashlyn's left eyebrow arch as he offered her his old pager.

"No, thanks. You get to take that in tomorrow."

"You're out anyway."

She smiled. "But I have other things to do."

"That reminds me." He went to his locker and removed a large folder. "My employment information. Can you take that home?"

She took it from him and looked at one of the other men by the counter. "You were on that one arson a week ago, weren't you?"

He nodded. "Nasty call that was. Heard you got suspended."

She shrugged. "When you've got missing kids, you've got to go the distance. Bosses don't seem to get that. We've got a dishwasher that doesn't work. Adrian told me there's a repairman you guys use who's pretty good."

"Bob." He flipped open a cupboard and grabbed a piece of paper, writing down the number. "He ends up fixing most things for the guys around here. Dishwashers, dryers, stoves. Does a bit of plumbing too, strictly on the side. Not much of a talker." The man passed her the paper. "But he gets the job done."

"Thanks."

"I'll walk you out," Craig said, putting his hand on her

back as he ushered her to the door. "What's the real deal with the pager?"

"Just what I said. Called me up and went over everything again. Wanted to know when you were working," she murmured.

"And the repair guy?"

"He connects to the department, doesn't he? Makes sense to get your dishwasher fixed and charge the RCMP at the same time."

"There's a complete staff list in the folder. I told Quinlan we'd destroy it once we checked everyone out."

"You know all those guys are still watching us from upstairs, right?" she asked as he opened her door.

He bent down and kissed her on the cheek. "The things I do for this job."

She smacked him with the folder, and he walked away.

Tain introduced himself and held up his ID.

The man didn't respond.

"We going to do this here or at the station?"

The shaven head lifted, the steely eyes unblinking as the tattooed arms flexed.

"Look, I've got all day. All I have to do is call the exhibit coordinator and mention I have to take you in for questioning in the disappearance of a young girl—"

"Fine. What the hell do you want?"

Tain held up the picture of Taylor. "Remember her, Lex?"

Lex scowled. "At the fair a couple weeks ago or something."

"But you didn't think it might be important to phone that in?"

"You damn cops, always stirring up shit for people doin' nothing wrong."

"I like your little setup here. Polish these glittering things up nice and shiny and then get the girls to come over, half of them wearing low-cut T-shirts, bending over your displays." He frowned, pretending to compare the setup to the other ones on the strip. "Is it just me, or is this table a bit shorter than the rest of them?"

The scowl became a snarl. "Look, she was alone. The clown tried to get her to sit down, but she took off. Bit young for me."

"Did you see where she went?"

"Over by the merry-go-round. Looked like she was going to go to the park, but that Jesus freak stopped and talked to her."

"Did you see what happened then?"

"No. Bunch of people came by. Never saw her again."

"What about the Bible thumper?"

"Gone."

"And you didn't think that might be important when you found out the girl was missing?"

"Hey, one day, every couple hours different security staff came around to clear him out of there. Going on about carnal sin or some such crap, freakin' kids out. One girl was bawling 'cuz he told her she was going to hell."

"What did he look like?"

"Like your average nutcase."

"Seriously."

"I don't know. Nothing about him stood out. Average. Not too old, short brown hair, not too tall but not a shrimp either. Not fat but not super-skinny."

"You're a real help, you know." Tain slapped one of his cards down on the table. "If you think of anything else." He walked away.

Lori walked in the door and was halfway into the living room when she saw the suitcases.

"What's going on?"

He didn't look up from his newspaper. "I don't think we've got much left to say to each other."

"Vish, really. I—"

He put the paper down and stood. "I'm serious, Lori. I think you should move out."

They stood in absolute silence, him staring at the wall behind her, her staring at him, trying to will him to shift his gaze and look her in the eyes.

"You never could accept my job. This is just your excuse to try to get me to be something I'm not. If you want some secretary or schoolteacher who'd punch a clock, why didn't you shack up with one of them to begin with?"

"That wasn't what I wanted," he said, his voice sounding strained, as though he was fighting to choke the words out. "But you've never been satisfied with this."

"What about our plans? Sailing up the coast, maybe Alaska? Can't we try—"

"You don't get it. I'm past trying. No matter what I do, it's wrong. I'm too supportive, too sympathetic, too demanding, too critical. Where'd you sleep last night, Lori? You think I just went to bed and didn't give you a second thought?"

She swallowed but didn't answer.

"You either agree to counseling, or you leave."

"So this is love, huh? A list of conditions, snap my fingers, get over it and move on?"

He shook his head. "You've always been so damned good at manipulating me. Not this time."

"Vish . . ."

"You're the one who walked out that door. You walked away from me. I called everywhere I could think of, left dozens of messages on your cell and at work, and you didn't even call back. You just waltz in here like everything is fine and it's okay to treat me like shit. Well, it isn't, Lori. It never was."

He walked away, and she heard a door shut, presumably his den door. She waited five minutes, then ten, and when he didn't come out, she picked up the bags and walked to the front door, not bothering to brush away the tears streaming down her face.

Tain double-checked his messages, then picked up the phone.

"Is Greg there?"

"Day off."

"Who's in charge, then?"

"Bobby, I guess."

"Get him for me." When that was met with silence, Tain added, "Please."

"What do you want, Tain?" a voice said after a moment. A voice that was chomping on something as it spoke.

"Why the hell don't I have the results from the fire scene back yet?"

"We're swamped. Short staffed, under budget, summer holidays." More chomping.

"I don't give a shit. This is a multiple child-abduction and murder case. Since when doesn't it get priority?"

"Since a rapist sunk his claws into one of our own."

"You're telling me that's still got you backlogged?"

"Look," the voice said after it swallowed, "best I can do is remind Greg you need this and hope we can get it all done for you by Tuesday."

"We've got a working timeline. We expect another arson on our hands in a few days. This could make the difference between saving a kid's life or carrying her body out of a burning building."

"Shit, well, cry to your bosses. I mean, I'm just following my own orders, and nobody's going to thank me if I pull an end run around my supervisor. You might get away with that, but we aren't all so lucky."

"Then I'll do what I have to do."

"And I'll warn Greg."

"Thanks," Tain muttered, slamming down the phone.

"Um um um."

He watched her walk up to the front door, fiddling with a collection of keys until she found the right one and disappeared inside.

Rob leaned back and smiled. *Thank God for security cameras*, he thought as his fingers traced the shape of her on the photo he'd printed out.

Yes, she'd make a fine addition.

"Now, I just need a fire to keep her man out, and I'll be set."

The house had proven perfect. They lived in a quiet neighborhood, lots of trees, plenty of concealed access to the front door or any of a number of ground-floor windows.

This was one he thought he might like to take his time with.

He looked up to see an elderly woman glaring at him, dawdling along with her fluffy dog in tow. Rob started the engine, folded up the map he'd had out as though he'd been lost and checking his directions, and drove away.

A glance in his rearview mirror told him the woman was still watching. He checked again one last time before he reached the end of the block, seeing the Rodeo pull in to the drive.

Rob swore again and drove away.

# MONDAY

Sunlight was streaming through the windows mercilessly when Ashlyn finally admitted that it must be morning. She opened her eyes.

The covers from Craig's side of the bed were tossed back. She glanced at the clock, almost regretting the hours she'd lost track of as she'd continued with her research the night before, coming to bed long after Craig had already fallen asleep.

Her stomach was grumbling, and then she realized she smelled food. She pushed her covers back and went downstairs.

"Smells good."

Craig glanced at her. "Don't you think you should get dressed?"

She looked down at the oversized dark green shirt that hung past her hips, the plaid pajama shorts protruding below. "I'm better covered than when I'm wearing those short skirts. Did you mean to leave the door open?"

That's when the screen door rattled, and she heard footsteps in the hall. Craig smirked, and she turned to find herself face-to-face with Tain.

"Are those your pajamas?" he asked.

"What's wrong with this?"

"It's completely messing with my fantasy life. You really wear that to bed?"

"No. I sleep naked," she said, grabbing the plates from the counter and walking into the dining room. She could imagine Craig turning his back to conceal his amusement, the look on Tain's face, but when they joined her at the table they'd both regained whatever composure they'd lost over her comment.

Tain whistled. "You know, Craig, you're really outdoing yourself. I almost feel guilty enough to take you out to dinner."

"As long as you don't want to cook for me." Craig passed the toast to Ashlyn. "The department is paying for all of this right now anyway."

"Yes, but it was still nice of you to cook," Ashlyn said.

"Well, it was clear you weren't going to. I was beginning to think you expected breakfast in bed."

"Some of us were working late."

"Some of us are working two jobs," he responded.

There was a moment of silence at the table until Tain spoke. "Find anything?" he asked Ashlyn.

She nodded. "I have your probable cause for a search warrant for Alex Wilson's place."

Tain's lip curled. "Sick bastard."

"Shame he doesn't fit for the peeper at the recreation center," she said as she went into the hall and retrieved the file she'd set out for him.

Tain snapped his fingers. "Actually, you know that kid who was working at the fitness center, the one who'd come in on call? Doug Fisher. I figured out where you knew his name from."

He pulled the file from the stack he'd brought with him and passed it to her as she walked back to her chair. She opened it, starting skimming and whistled.

"Are you thinking what I'm thinking?" she asked.

"I checked. He never worked a shift when the church group came in, not at the front desk. But he was a customer every Sunday night, theoretically working out in the weight room."

"You planning to pull his photo and see if Marvin can ID him?"

Tain nodded. "And I'm going to bring him in for a chat, regardless."

"Good thinking. Anything else?"

"A possible lead on the guy who took Taylor."

She stared at him. "And you were just going to casually mention that when? On your way out the door?"

"It's too soon to be certain. I've got one more potential witness I can talk to before I track this guy down."

"Will that be possible?"

"It seems he was kicked out of the fairgrounds repeatedly for scaring kids with his religious dogma. The security department is bound to have a record on him."

"I wouldn't be so sure," Craig said. "A lot of the security staff is hired in specifically for summer events. University and college students."

Tain shook his head. "There still has to be a supervisor I can track down. And I thought you guys had some leads."

"We have a few, but so far no hits on the police checks," Ashlyn told him.

"How old are these guys? Early- to mid-thirties?"

Ashlyn shook her head. "Younger. Twenties."

"Then you might not find anything in the system, even if they've been in trouble."

"Juvenile offenders who've managed to keep themselves clean for a couple of years," Craig said sourly. "When are we going to get rid of this ridiculous idea that a sixteen-year-old can't form intent?" He looked at Ashlyn. "Tain's right. You might need to look in the newspapers for any leads on local teenagers being sentenced as young offenders in the past five years or so."

She nodded. "I did. And I have a reporter to talk to. There's one case that I found particularly interesting. It happened in Cloverdale. Boy grabbed a girl, forced her into a barn, lit a lantern, pinned her down, and she resisted. The hay caught fire, but he didn't stop. The fire brought people to the scene pretty quick. The girl cried rape, there were signs of a struggle, and he finally admitted enough to get slapped with a minor charge. Sixteen, so he got his time in a juvenile facility and wasn't labeled a sex offender. He was also charged with arson."

"That does sound promising," Craig said. "But how are you going to find out who it was?"

"What I'm going to do today is compile a list of our most likely suspects, and then I'm going to beg, bribe or threaten this reporter until he tells me if our teen is on the list."

"You're assuming he knows," Tain said.

"He has to. Those kids go in and out of court and get seen, even if their names aren't printed. Think about the Taber shooter. Identity protected until he disappeared from a halfway house. Suddenly pictures taken of him years earlier are on the front page of newspapers from coast to coast."

Craig nodded. "She's right. This reporter, if he covered this case, he'll know."

Tain's cell phone rang, and he answered it. His face stiffened as he listened to what was said and then curtly replied before hanging up.

"Women's intuition strikes again."

Ashlyn frowned at him.

"A family just came forward. Their daughter has been missing since July eighteenth." He grabbed another piece of toast. "I'll talk to you later."

Craig also stood.

"Where do you think you're going?"

"To have a shower. I cooked; you clean."

Daly looked up at the sharp knock on his open door.

"What is it, Sims?"

"Sir, I thought I should bring this to you. DNA results from Nitara Sandhu's murder and Lori Price's rape." Sims set the files down on the desk but didn't move.

"What is it?"

"Lori was trying to sign for these when the lab sent them over."

Daly pursed his lips. Damn Hawkins. If he wouldn't deal with her . . . He looked up at Sims and nodded. "Thank you for telling me. And thanks for intercepting these."

"Do you want me to take them to Craig's house?"

"No, I'll handle it."

Sims nodded and left.

Daly sighed as he pulled open the first file and started reading. Within a moment, he'd gotten up, file still in hand, closed the door and sat down.

Once he was finished reading, he leaned back and whistled. Then he reached for a Tylenol.

"What the hell am I going to do about this?"

Sims met Tain in the hallway outside an interview room. "They're waiting for you. I got them some tea."

"Thanks." Tain paused midstep. "You want to sit in on this, or do you want to follow up on something else?"

He could see the conflict on Sims's face, half wanting to be on the front lines of the abduction case, half wanting to be on the street.

"Likely makes more sense for me to chase down leads. More efficient."

Tain suppressed the smile. "Remember our friend Alex Wilson? Check this out. Ashlyn found our probable cause for a warrant on his place." He passed Sims the file. "With everything happening, I never made it to his old employer. Go sweet talk him into telling you why Alex left his job and then get the warrants. We want to arrest him."

Sims nodded. "Should I . . . I mean . . ."

"Get everything ready, then come and find me. We'll go get him together." Tain started to walk away and then turned around. He passed Sims another file. "And if I'm really held up, pick up this guy. You can tell him we're questioning recreation center employees, just eliminating staff and people from our fingerprint hits."

"But?"

"We think he's the one who's been peeping at boys in the change room. He's got history."

Sims nodded again and walked away.

Tain opened the door to the room where Mr. and Mrs. Sanchez were waiting.

"I'm Constable Tain."

"You're the one who can help us?" Mrs. Sanchez looked up, dark eyes filled with tears, her black hair pinned back from her face.

"I'm going to try," he told her. "I understand your daughter went missing July eighteenth?"

She nodded. "Maria. I've brought a picture." She pulled it out of her bag and passed it to him.

Long dark hair, dark eyes, a sweet smile . . . Pretty girl. Tain looked at Mr. Sanchez. "Can you tell me why you didn't report this until now?"

His whole face fell. "God help us, we were illegal. We . . ." He shrugged as Mrs. Sanchez started to sob. "We're legal now. Now we can leave the church. We came straight here."

"You've been living in a church?"

Mr. Sanchez nodded. "Holy Redeemer."

"Catholic?"

Mr. Sanchez nodded again.

*Are all of these girls Catholic? Lindsay, yes. Isabella was. Julie went to Holy Cross and Taylor . . .*

"I need to know how long you've been there and the names of everyone who had contact with you at the church, at least for the month of July."

"You cannot think it is someone from the church. They have been wonderful to us," Mr. Sanchez said, gaping at him.

"Well, somebody took her, and if you haven't left the church building until now . . ."

The Sanchezs looked at each other and then started to tell their story, while Tain wrote everything down.

Ashlyn opened the door.

"I'm Bob."

"Ashlyn. Thanks for coming over." She glanced at her watch. "Wow, that was fast."

"No problem. I do a lot of business for the guys on the department. Kinda get viewed as a part of the team, you know?"

"Kitchen's this way." She glanced at her watch. Craig would be furious.

Bob started to work on the dishwasher as the phone rang.

"Hi. Oh, yeah?" she said, glancing over her shoulder. Bob didn't seem to be paying much attention to her, but she still moved farther down the hall.

Daly filled her in on the rape kits. "There weren't any DNA matches at Michelle Bohner's house because she'd done a pretty thorough cleanup."

"Oh? And what about a physical checkup? Do you think that's necessary?"

Daly hesitated. "Who's there?"

"Guess it doesn't hurt to check things out."

"Potential suspect?"

"Uh-huh."

"Where's Craig?"

"Out."

"Ashlyn—"

"Sorry, I think I missed what you said. The physical exam . . ."

"She declined to have one. So no DNA there either. But we did get prints, surprisingly enough not hers or her husband's, almost as though she'd cleaned the place from top to bottom just before the alleged rape occurred."

"So what turned up?"

"Prints for a guy named Bob Gliddon. He's in the system for an assault charge, and he did a stretch on a rape charge when he was nineteen. He's also done some contract work for the fire department."

"Yes, I know." She could feel her heart pummeling against her chest, and then she heard the door open and let out her breath. "He's here now."

"Ashlyn—"

"Did you want to speak to Craig?"

"You mean he's there? Good. Fill him in."

"I will."

She hung up. Craig glanced in the kitchen and then stepped toward her, his smile disappearing as soon as he was out of the repairman's sight.

"I thought I told you not to let anyone in while I was out."

"He was early." She glanced at her watch again. "And you were late."

Craig nodded at the phone. "Daly?"

"Seems our repairman's prints were all over the headboard of Michelle Bohner's bed."

"You think he's a viable suspect?"

"He did time for rape when he was nineteen. I think you should talk to her."

He nodded. "When he leaves. And you're coming with me."

"Craig, seriously."

"I'm on the verge of asking Tain to stay here tonight."

"Don't be ridiculous." She saw the look in his eyes and sighed. "Fine, fine, okay, whatever. I'll be upstairs getting paperwork done."

The man shook his head and snorted. "Look, I don't want any trouble with anyone. I just want to run my business and be left alone."

"I only have a few questions."

"It's never just a few questions. It's questions, followed by a subpoena, followed by court dates. I mean, that's what you're after here, right? Police don't come around asking about why some guy lost his job months earlier unless they're looking at charging him."

Sims sank into a chair and slid a photo under the man's nose.

"Oh, good God." He winced and pushed it back.

"Mr. Williams, I know that's not a pleasant thing to look at. And it isn't a pleasant thing to have happen. Now, there's a man who lives not too far from here whose daughter is missing. And that same man now has to hear that his son—" Sims tapped the photo—"has been victimized by a pervert like Alex Wilson. I think a bit of inconvenience to you and me isn't so much to ask so that this family sees some justice."

Williams blew his breath out and leaned back. "Yeah, he worked for me. Good worker too. Always early, always willing to stay late, willing to put in extra shifts on evenings and weekends in the fall for all the church groups and youth groups and choirs and such. Never stole anything, never talked back." He shook his head, gritting his teeth. "Should have known he was too good to be true."

"What happened?"

"We did a Scout troop one night. Most of the kids had gone, but one boy hadn't been picked up yet. The Scout leader said he was going to the bathroom and then he was going to phone the parents. Came back and found Alex coaxing the boy to pose for him. Alex denied it, but the Scout leader called me and threatened to talk to the police. I just live upstairs, so I was here in no time, and I took the camera. Told Alex not to sweat it, that the pictures would clear him."

"And they didn't. The boy didn't press charges?"

"Well, the Scout leader was negligent. You know how it is. He left the kid alone with a stranger. . . ." Williams shrugged.

"And it wouldn't look too good for your business if it came out that you'd been sending a pervert into schools to take photos of children, would it?"

Williams sighed. "No. And I haven't had a decent night's sleep over this since it happened. It isn't like I feel good about it."

"Just not bad enough to pick up the phone and maybe spare some other poor kid from being violated."

Williams turned away. "I've told you what I know. Now get lost, and let me get back to my business while I still have one."

Tain looked up to see Sims approaching.

"How did it go with the parents?" Sims asked.

Tain shook his head. "They were illegals, so they didn't report her missing. All this time, holed up in a Catholic church, insisting nobody's had access to their kids."

"Denial, huh?"

"Big time. How'd you make out?"

Sims filled him in and then showed him the warrant. "We're ready to roll on him whenever. I wasn't sure if you wanted to go after this other guy first or not."

Tain glanced at his watch. "I'll ask a couple of guys on patrol to track him down. If they can bring him in after a few hours, we should be able to handle both this afternoon."

"This is the life of detective work, huh? Nonstop, all hours, whatever the case needs?"

"My dog is filing to divorce me as his owner."

"Good thing you aren't married then, eh?"

"Yeah, well, you punch a clock. What's your excuse?" Tain didn't wait for an answer. He walked away to find the patrol cops he wanted to ask for a favor.

Michelle Bohner's face sagged when she recognized Craig.

"This isn't a good time."

"Is your husband home?"

"He's still away."

"Your daughter?"

"I told you before. Jolene's with him."

"Then why is this a bad time?"

She swallowed. "Look, it's just, I'm getting . . . Look, I'm expecting company."

"This won't take long, Mrs. Bohner," Ashlyn said. "But it is very important."

Michelle Bohner looked from her to Craig, and then her shoulders sagged. She turned on her heel, not bothering to open the screen door for them. "Fine."

Craig glanced at Ashlyn. He almost smiled when he saw the look in her eyes.

Once inside, it was his first real taste of being back on the scene with his old partner. Her eyes took in everything, but not in a really obvious, intrusive way. She just had the ability to scrutinize her surroundings and make mental notes for future reference, ones that often proved essential to piecing together her impressions of a crime. Ashlyn may have been inexperienced on the job when they first worked together, but she'd never been sloppy.

"I was wondering if you could provide a list of all the people who were in your house, say the week prior to your attack," Craig said, noting there was no offer of a beverage this time. Michelle Bohner had promptly sat down across from him, leaning forward with her hands clasped together, her backside on the edge of the cushion, as though she expected to jump up suddenly at any moment.

Ashlyn's cell phone rang, and she glanced at the display, then at Craig apologetically. She left the room for a moment, leaving Craig and Michelle to sit in silence. Craig almost wished Ashlyn would take the lead with this woman when she came back. Unlike Lori, Ashlyn didn't feel the need to prove herself by taking control.

"Look, Mrs. Bohner, I've already told you how difficult it can be to get a conviction in cases like this. You phoned the police. You made a statement. You consented to let us search your house for evidence. One of the things we need to do now is eliminate any prints that had a reason to be there so that we make sure we don't suspect people who had legitimate business in your home."

Her eyes stayed focused on a spot on the coffee table, an imaginary stain that she leaned forward and rubbed with the end of her sweater.

"Nobody should have been in my bedroom."

"Nobody at all?"

She shrugged, still avoiding his gaze. "Just the family. And I had cleaned the house earlier that day, so even then . . ." She shrugged again.

"So you didn't have a reason to have anyone upstairs? No leaky toilet or faulty electrical outlet or something that required you to call in a repairman?"

Her head snapped up then. "Why do you ask?"

"Mrs. Bohner, I'm just trying to think of any possible reason that someone might have been upstairs. Little things that might not seem important could make the difference between identifying a viable suspect or accusing the wrong person."

She sat with her mouth hanging open, the lower lip

trembling visibly, staring first at Craig and then at Ashlyn as she walked back into the room.

Craig glanced at Ashlyn, willing her to understand that he'd be okay if she wanted to jump in on this. He watched her mouth twist slightly, and then Ashlyn pulled a photo down from a shelf, one of the ones tucked in the back a bit.

"Is this your husband?" Ashlyn asked, holding the picture up as she moved over to the couch Craig was sitting on. Ashlyn sat down beside him and passed him the photo.

"Yes."

"Which department is he with?"

Michelle shook her head. "None, not now. Early retirement. Got cancer. All that ash and crap that firefighters breathe in, you know. He was cleaning that garbage out of the engines. Still fighting over the medical."

"I hear more and more firefighters are getting compensated for things like this."

"And they should," Michelle said. It was the only thing she'd said with conviction since they'd walked in.

Ashlyn leaned forward a bit. "Mrs. Bohner, we do have a possible suspect. Having that list Craig asked you for, it isn't to cause problems for your friends or family. It's just to make sure we're looking in the right direction. If the name we're looking at is on your list, then we'll know we haven't found the man who raped you. And if it isn't, then we'll bring him in for a chat at the station and hopefully press charges. That should help give you some closure. It isn't perfect, but it's the only thing we can offer you."

"And then I suppose you'd want me to explain why anyone was up there and prove what they were doing and that it was legitimate business."

Ashlyn glanced at Craig, and he looked back at her, shrugging slightly. Just then, the front door opened.

"Hey, babe, I managed to fit that job in early, so I stopped and got us some . . ."

The words stopped as soon as Bob walked into the living room and saw Craig and Ashlyn sitting across from Michelle.

"Make yourself right at home," Craig said. This time

when he glanced at Ashlyn, he watched her eyes widen and then narrow. She clenched her teeth and looked at Michelle.

"It would seem you have some explaining to do, Mrs. Bohner."

"You can't do this," Alex Wilson squawked.

"We can, and we are," Tain told him. "Look here. It says we have the right to seize all photographic equipment, films, photo albums, video tapes, DVDs, CDs that might be storing photos, your cell phone—"

"Oh, and you're under arrest," Sims said.

"On what charge?"

"We found your pictures on the Internet. Distributing child pornography. Not only something that even BC judges are known to frown on occasionally, but something that will earn you a special place in the hearts of your fellow inmates. They've got their own little scale of filth, and this will put you right at the bottom."

"Where you belong," Sims added.

"You babysit him, Sims. I'll watch these guys." Tain turned to find himself nose to nose with Greg.

"You can't call my guys and hassle them about your cases," Greg told him.

"The hell I can't. I'm still waiting on prints from the fire scene. The one where Ashlyn almost killed herself to get that evidence. Shit, Greg, we think he's going to kill another girl this week. That means in a matter of days we'll have another body on our hands and another fire."

"Hey, it's not like I'm trying to make your life difficult, Tain. It's just the way things are. We're swamped. Short staffed, operating under what should be our standard budget, overworked . . . What the hell do you want me to do about it?"

"Look, Greg, I go over your head on something like this, it isn't personal. The only thing I care about right now is solving this case before we've got another dead child to deal with."

"Then do me a favor and try not to shut down a porn

distribution network between then and now. Couldn't you have waited a few fucking days for this?"

They'd been walking through the house, surveying the search when they stepped into a back room, the mother load. Walls of videos, dated and labeled, photo albums, stages for posing kids on . . .

"Overworked and operating under budget," Greg said, shaking his head as he looked around. "Who the hell is going to catalog all of this?"

"Jesus," Tain said, feeling his stomach drop.

"Somehow, I doubt he'll be up for it," Greg muttered.


Daly groaned. "What?"

"They've been having an affair. She said it goes back to her husband's days with the fire department."

"Then why cry rape?"

"Seems the neighbor heard a lot of . . . noise," Ashlyn said as she passed Craig and Daly their drinks and sat down, her lip curling. "Michelle was afraid her husband would hear about it and start asking questions. Not even dumb enough to think about the fact that she's got the guy strolling in the front door in broad daylight."

"So she lies and says she's been raped. She wasted police resources and manpower . . . ." Daly shook his head. "What do you want to do about this?" he asked Craig.

Craig shrugged. "It's your call. She definitely deserves to be charged for filing a false report. Waste of man hours, money."

"So what's next for you two?"

"Well, we've eliminated the department repairman as a suspect."

"Good work, Craig. That's stellar progress," Daly said dryly.

"I get the bed all to myself tonight," Ashlyn added.

Daly looked like he'd stuck a wedge of lemon in his mouth.

"What Ashlyn means is that I'm on night shift, so this is the first real opportunity anyone would have to come after her."

Daly nodded, his mouth still twisted.

"I've got a list I'm working on," Ashlyn said. "So far, nothing's really jumping in the name check with the department."

"Well, I hope you can come up with something, and fast. Tain and Sims have gone to arrest Alex Wilson." Daly glanced at his watch. "Good work on that, Ashlyn. I have to go."

After Daly left, Ashlyn asked, "Is it just me, or does he seem unusually tense?"

"Probably just doesn't want to think about us sleeping together."

"Well, tonight he doesn't have to."

"No. Tonight he has even worse things to think about."

"So, Alex. It looks like we have a lot to talk about."

"I've got nothing to say."

"Well, not that it matters much. Your private video collection speaks volumes."

Tain sank down into the chair across from Alex Wilson and leaned back, arms folded across his chest. Sims was leaning against the wall, watching.

"You've got no right . . ."

"Oh, but we do, Alex. Remember the search warrant? Signed by a judge. We've got hard evidence, linking you to distribution of child porn via the Internet, as well as your own personal collection."

"Not to mention the reason you lost your job," Sims added.

Alex's head jerked up then, and when he saw their faces, his shoulders sagged.

"Williams won't talk."

"He already did," Tain told him.

"I knew I should have just walked away. I knew . . ." Alex's jaw clenched, and he looked back down at the table.

"Of all the people to be in the park that day, it just happened to be you. There you were, probably jerking off in the bushes while you watched the little boys at the playground, and out of nowhere this blond, curly-haired boy appears, all alone."

"Opportunity like that, you've got to jump on it," Sims said. "Couldn't let him walk away on his own."

"You never know what might have happened to him," Alex mumbled.

"You mean what might have happened that would have been worse than having you take advantage of him and make photos for perverts with his face on them?"

"Not the same as those girls," he responded, the thin voice barely above a whisper.

"Fuck, no. But bad enough that this little boy's dad is already worried about his missing daughter, and now he's got to hear about this."

"He gets his hands on you, he's liable to string you up by your balls," Sims said.

Alex turned white. "I . . . I should probably call a lawyer."

"That's your right. And believe me, with everything we've got on you, you won't be going anywhere." Tain leaned forward, resting his arms on the table. "You know, the first time I set eyes on you, I knew there was something odd about you. Never really liked you for taking the girls, but you smelled of fear." He leaned back. "I imagine that's how you'll be smelling for a lot of years to come. Boys inside are going to love you."

"That's sick, you know. You people are so full of yourselves, saying you're supposed to uphold the law, then taunting me about getting raped in jail."

"We uphold the law for law-abiding citizens. You cross the line, you're on my 'don't give a shit' list. Scum like you gets raped in jail, some might call that justice." Tain stood. "Come on, Alex. We'll send you down for processing and make sure you get your lousy phone call."

They'd barely started walking down the hall when the officers Tain had asked to pick up Doug Fisher came in with him, leading him toward an interview room.

"We'll be back in a few minutes," Sims told them. "Maybe you could get him a drink, get Mr. Fisher settled while he waits?"

Tain felt Alex's arms tense and he looked at Doug, who'd lost all color when he set eyes on Alex Wilson. Tain couldn't quite put his finger on why, but he felt his gut twist.

He walked a bit faster, nudging Alex forward and out of Doug's line of sight.

Ashlyn rubbed her forehead with both hands, her elbows propped against the desk.

"Is it that bad?" she heard Craig ask from the doorway.

"There's no way I'll get this reporter to take me seriously. I haven't got a guy with a record anywhere on this list, other than Bob."

"A record that we know about."

"Well, ones I don't know about aren't doing me much good, are they?"

"What about guys in the right age range for a juvenile record?"

"There are too many. I can't give him a list of three dozen suspects. It will look like I haven't got a legal leg to stand on, and I don't."

"Parts of this case have been a bit of a nightmare."

"Which parts?"

"Mainly, working with Lori."

"Couldn't have been too much fun to have to deal with her as a victim either."

"It was a hell of a lot easier than working with her, and I feel like a jerk for saying that."

She looked at him for a moment. "You're just being honest, and it's only me here. I know you well enough to know you aren't trying to be cruel."

He looked away from her and drew a deep breath. "Then you'll understand when I tell you I want you to carry this with you everywhere. I don't care if you're just going to the bathroom." He set the device, similar to a pager but with an activation panel on the side, down on the desk, still not looking at her. "You hit 911 and the guys monitoring you will be here instantly. And I want you to keep the bedroom door locked.

Once you've cleared that space, protect yourself. The idea isn't to get you hurt."

"We don't even know this guy will come after me," she said. "I'm sure I'll be fine."

He put his hand over hers and did look at her then, straight in the eyes. "All the same, I want you to promise me."

"You going to call and check up on me too?"

"Just promise me you'll do as I ask," he repeated quietly.

There'd been moments when she'd seen Craig be assertive, slam a door so hard it almost separated from its hinges, or be completely enraged, but it was the quiet in his voice, the fear in his eyes that was worse than anything she'd seen him dish out before. She could argue against his stubborn streak, but not this.

She nodded, taking the personal alarm and putting it in her pocket. "I'll be careful, Craig. I promise."

Tain frowned. "Did you see the way Alex and Doug looked at each other?"

"It makes sense that they would know each other, at least in passing. Alex was a regular at the fitness center where Doug worked."

"Yeah, but my gut tells me there's something more to it than that." Tain bit his lip. "I feel like I'm walking into this blind."

"I did a thorough check on him. Nothing in the system, other than that one charge."

"A slap on the wrist for a bungled break-and-enter charge when he got caught climbing in the window of an eight-year-old boy's room." Tain stared at Sims for a moment, the ideas starting to form. "Can you talk to Doug's parents?"

Sims shrugged. "If you think it's important."

"I do. And if they aren't willing to tell you what happened to Doug when he was a child, then mention the name Alex Wilson."

"What are you—"

"Just go, and quickly. I'm going to stall on this, keep it nice and light and boring and all about this guy's job until you get back."

Sims's eyes narrowed, but he didn't argue. "Okay, never mind. I'm gone."

Tain scratched his head as he watched Sims walk away. They were only scratching the surface with Doug Fisher, and he needed more than he had to nab him.

"You wanted to see me?"

Daly turned to look at Lori and nodded. "Please, have a seat."

She remained standing in the doorway, half in the hall, glancing around as though looking for an excuse not to enter. Daly remained standing, leaning against the window ledge.

"Have a seat, Lori."

She sighed, walked into the room and slumped into a chair. "Can we make this quick?"

"That depends on you."

"What's that supposed to mean?"

"I don't like being pressured."

She swallowed but stayed silent.

"You've been going over my head to try to get back on the rape case. I'm going to tell you for the last time, that's not going to happen."

A sly smile emerged as she straightened up slightly, crossing one leg over the other. "Oh, I don't think we'd be here if I wasn't getting somewhere on this. Sounds to me like there won't be much you can do to stop me."

"You might be thinking that. You might even think you've got an ace in the hole, guaranteed to get what you want. I wonder, Lori, is there anything that could come out that you wouldn't want people to know about?"

She stared at him, the color slowly ebbing from her cheeks. "Are you threatening me?"

Daly shook his head. "No. I'm not threatening you. I don't

work that way, Lori. I'm not someone who's ever felt the need to sleep my way up the ladder. This job has never been about my ego. It's my career, but it's got nothing to do with making a name for myself."

"I don't like your inference."

"And I don't like you. Since the start of this case you've been causing problems. As an officer, sure, you had potential. Personality-wise, you were difficult, bossy, stubborn, and you lied about the investigation to steal credit. I don't find any of that very commendable. And you were reporting on everyone. I don't like that either."

She shrugged. "When you're a woman in this department, you have to make friends to get ahead. It's always been the same old story."

"I think you're reading from an old playbook. I see women officers rising through the ranks on a regular basis. Ones who deserve to."

"So you're saying I don't? You think I should go back on patrol, or maybe push papers at a desk for the rest of my career because I'm damaged goods?"

"Don't put words in my mouth. I'm saying you shouldn't come back on this case. And you should get some counseling, take some time to deal with this."

She pointed a finger at him. "Technically, I wasn't injured on the job, so you can't make me go through therapy."

"No, but I can keep you off the rape case. For now, that's enough."

Lori stood up, arms folded across her chest. "You don't get it. As long as I don't get back on this case, it'll always be the horse that bucked me off. Nobody's going to trust me to back them up as a partner. And there'll be that fear, what if we put her on the street and she draws a rape? Will she be reliable? If you keep me off this case now, you're killing my career."

"If you'd done what we asked, taken the medical leave, gotten counseling, I wouldn't have an issue. But I'm not putting you back on this."

"We'll see about that. I have friends with more influence than you."

Daly moved behind his desk, picking up a file. "And I have some very interesting reading here. DNA results from your rape kit." He saw her eyes widen, her face tense, but he didn't stop. "The only question is whether or not I have to use this."

She gaped at him for a moment. "You wouldn't."

"It's up to you. Push this, and you'll see how far I'm prepared to go." He tossed the folder into his top drawer. "I've got several copies."

He put his hands down on the desk and leaned forward. "This isn't personal. I'm interested in protecting the lives of the officers working this case, and I intend to get an arrest that leads to a conviction. And I won't have you, or anyone else in this department, jeopardizing this investigation. Now get out. And this better be the last I hear about this."

She stomped out of the room, slamming the door behind her.


"Mrs. Fisher? I'm Constable Sims."

The older woman's face didn't flinch. "What's he done now?"

"I just wanted to talk to you about Doug."

Her eyebrows arched slightly at that, and then she pushed the screen door open with her meaty hands. Sims followed her inside.

"So he's not in trouble?"

Sims paused. "I'm actually wondering about what happened to him. When he was a child."

She wasn't a woman of obvious reactions, but Sims saw the way her whole body froze, even for just a few seconds. Whatever Tain suspected, Sims figured he was dead on.

"Why don't you ask him?" Mrs. Fisher said.

"I'm asking you."

"It's not for me to talk about. Doug wouldn't like it. And it's none of your business. We dealt with your people long ago and it's over."

"Is it really ever over, Mrs. Fisher? Or have you just tried to forget about it?"

She shrugged. "What's the difference?"

"One is like having an exterminator come through the house and get rid of the bugs. The other is when the bread crumbs are pushed under the counter and the bugs might be out of sight, but they're still there."

She picked up her knitting and went to work, slowly and methodically moving her oversized fingers as the metal ends of the needles clacked together.

Sims leaned forward. "Mrs. Fisher, please. It's very important."

She didn't look up, and she didn't respond.

After a few minutes, Sims took a deep breath. "Then tell me about Alex Wilson."

"Anyone else who seemed a little off?"

Tain was doing his best to keep his gaze on the face across from him, and off the clock on the wall. He'd started by doing a very meticulous run-through of Doug's employment history, how long he'd worked at Southside Recreation and Fitness Center, who'd trained him, etc., etc.

From there, Tain asked him questions about specific coworkers. The longer they talked, the more Doug's shoulders relaxed and the more willing he was to share tales about the people he worked with whom he didn't like, the ones who were having sex on weight benches or using the pool after hours.

Tain made notes, pretending it was all fascinating, asking questions to clarify things. When he finally did look up at the clock again, it was more than two hours since he'd sent Sims to the Fisher home.

"Can I get you anything? A hamburger, a sandwich?"

Doug shrugged and then nodded. "Okay, sure."

Tain wrote down what Doug wanted quickly and stood. "There'll be an officer outside the door, in case you need anything. I won't be long."

*Come on, Sims. Where are you?* He relayed clear instructions to the officer waiting outside the interview room, then headed for the cafeteria.

Craig sat down in the living room, across from Ashlyn. "Wasn't Tain supposed to look into that?" he asked.

Ashlyn nodded. "He just hasn't had time."

"Last year, all those girls . . . It was a tough case."

"But you could understand it," Ashlyn said quietly.

Craig stared at her.

"It's not . . . Look, what I mean is, as sick as it was, even I could understand it. This rapist, I can even understand that. Doesn't mean I like it or agree, but abducting girls, holding them for days and feeding them nothing but bread and water and then drowning them, placing their body in an abandoned building and setting it on fire? I don't get this at all."

"I suppose with the rapist, it all goes back to what we talked about, unhealthy attitudes toward sex and relationships. You know, you sounded like a bit of a feminist when you were talking about that."

Her nose wrinkled. "I don't exactly fall under that umbrella."

Craig tossed the file down on the coffee table. "So you don't believe in equal opportunities for men and women?"

"Advocate for it all you want, but nobody's working on a way for men to get pregnant that I've heard of."

He smiled. "What exactly do you think?"

She leaned back. "I believe each individual person should have the opportunity to do whatever they are physically, mentally and psychologically capable of. I'm not interested in advocating for women to have the chance to do anything they want. That's different from what they're capable of, for starters. One of my friends married a firefighter. She said the department got turned upside down over the issue of hiring women. It might surprise you to know this, but the wives of the firefighters had more of an issue with it than the men did."

"Worried about their husbands sharing sleeping quarters with women?"

"Nothing so ridiculous. It just boiled down to the fact that they didn't think that the average woman was capable of meeting the physical demands of the job. And when their husbands go into a burning building, they want the best person possible backing them up. They didn't care if it was a man or a woman, or if they were pink with purple polka dots. They just wanted their spouse to have the best chance possible of coming out alive."

Craig nodded. "I can appreciate that."

"You see, that's where some of these lobbying groups take things too far. There are a lot of women who aren't fit enough to be police officers. Not just physical fitness, either. It takes a lot to be able to handle your fear on the street. You feel like you have to work twice as hard as anyone else to prove yourself, and yet there's still this lingering doubt about whether you can really hold your own."

"Which is ridiculous," Craig said. "Men get beaten and even killed on the job as well. Bullets don't care if you're male, female, black, white or otherwise."

"The physical side isn't where I see women falling short. It's the mental toughness and the psychological fitness. Your old partner, Lori, she's heading for a big brick wall that's going to come crashing down on her, and she'll have no career left if she keeps at it."

"Which is actually sad, because she is very capable."

"But at this point in time, she's not up to the task. She's dangerous, not thinking rationally. I don't care what women think about me saying this. I wouldn't want her backing me up on the street right now."

Craig was silent for a moment. "So all these comments between you and Tain . . ." He shrugged.

Ashlyn laughed. "You know, it sounds terrible, but this case brings back memories. I think we just had to let off some steam to cope with it. Every time I think about one of these girls being grabbed, or when I was standing over Isabella's body . . . all I could think about was . . ." She shrugged. "You know."

Craig watched her draw a deep, shaky breath, but he didn't comment on it.

"So, you ready to share your views?" she asked.

"On this subject? Not a chance."

"You really are impossible, you know that?"

He stood up, paused by the end of the couch where she was sitting and placed his hand on her shoulder with just the lightest touch. "I'd choose you to back me up on any call, Ashlyn. You've always held your own on the street and in the office."

"Even if I am making predictable, sexist remarks to Tain?"

"Even then."

She put her hand on top of his. "Thanks, Craig. Do you want some dinner before you have to go?"

"That's okay. We eat together at the hall."

She got up as soon as he'd pulled his hand away. "I guess that means microwave entrees for me alone, then."

"If this goes on long enough, I could always teach you to cook."

"I'm capable, you know."

"Really? I'll withhold judgment until you present me with some evidence."

Tain was just about to open the door to the interrogation room when he saw Sims walking toward him. He passed Doug's lunch to the uniformed officer and sprinted down the hall.

"What did you find?"

"Hell of a hunch, Tain."

"So you got the information we need?" Sims passed him his notes, as well as an old file.

"I had to chase that down. It took longer than I thought it would." Sims glanced at his watch. "Shit, sorry."

Tain held up his hand as he glanced over the notes, whistling. "Forget about it. This is perfect. Ashlyn and I had a feeling."

"How do you want to handle this?"

Tain tore a scrap of paper off and wrote on it. "Have someone else go get him for an ID and then come join me."

Sims turned to leave, and Tain looked up to see Daly walking toward him.

"Good work with Wilson."

"Thanks. It looks like we'll have another arrest before the day is through."

He relayed what they'd learned and Daly nodded. "That's great, but I take it this means you're no closer to nailing our child abductor?"

Tain shook his head. "Ashlyn's on it, as much as she can be. We haven't had any hits so far, though."

Ashlyn stretched the phone cord as far as it would go and just managed to nudge the door to the refrigerator shut.

"Hi, yes, I'm still here."

She listened to the voice on the other end rattle off the info, the rushed words becoming a jumble.

"Sorry, can you say that again, a bit slower?"

"Look, I don't have time."

"Make time, or I'll come over there with a warrant and shut you down while I go through your records myself."

"What's your badge number?"

Ashlyn rattled it off. "And be sure to mention that you were failing to cooperate with an investigation into the abductions of five local girls, two of whom have been found murdered. Wait, never mind. I can mention that for you when the press starts camping on my doorstep."

The person on the other end of the phone repeated the information, and Ashlyn wrote it all down.

"Thank you very much," Ashlyn said. "This has been really helpful. I'd like to send a sketch artist down to work with you to make a drawing of this guy."

"Yeah, yeah, whatever," the voice muttered, and then the phone clicked.

Tain introduced Sims to Doug Fisher when they returned to the interrogation room. "Sorry we took so long."

"Whatever. I wouldn't mind getting out of here soon, though."

"Well, we just have a few more things we'd like to cover."

Doug shrugged again. "I've probably told you all there is to know about the people at the recreation center."

"But it must bother you, working there, having to serve people like Alex Wilson."

Doug blinked, his cheeks turning a pasty white. "Wh-why should it?"

"Oh, come on, Doug. You know," Sims said.

"Does it bother you when he sits and watches the kiddie pool?" Tain asked.

"Or do you set him up with special viewing privileges?"

"I . . ." Doug licked his lips, then reached for the soft drink. "I should maybe call a lawyer."

"What would you need a lawyer for, Doug? You didn't have anything to do with those girls, did you?"

"No. I swear I didn't."

"And we all know Alex doesn't swing that way," Sims said.

Doug crumpled down against the table. "You guys know."

"We aren't interested in playing games with you, Doug. It's better if you give us your side of the story, straight. Alex has been arrested, and we've got police going through his house right now. If you don't tell us what we need to know, the evidence will."

Doug pushed himself up. "He took some photos of me when I was a kid."

"Was that all he did?"

"I thought you knew."

Tain shrugged. "We know enough."

"Yeah, things eventually got out of hand. It started with me raking leaves and mowing the lawn at his house. Turned into me coming in for cookies and . . . and when my parents found out, they freaked."

"Didn't he go to jail?"

Doug shook his head. "Boiled down to my word against his, and the cop who caught it back then, this Hawkins guy, he was on a bigger case at the time, just wanted to clear this up. I didn't really remember, but my mom told me once, after my dad left. The police convinced them I'd be labeled and everyone would know."

"So your parents split over this?" Sims asked.

Doug nodded.

"And you never got any counseling or anything."

Tain waited until Doug shook his head.

"We've got police officers bringing someone down here. Are they going to tell us you're the one peeping at boys in the change room where you work?"

Doug finally looked up and met Tain's relentless stare. He nodded.

"Okay, what I want you to do is write a confession. But before you do, have you ever touched a boy? Ever?"

His head shook, not emphatically, but with the tiniest motion.

"Don't lie to me, Doug. I'm going to work something out for you, but this is a one-shot deal. You blow it, everyone really will know about your problems."

Doug's head shook again. "I swear. I-I've wanted to, okay? I . . . It's like I'm my own worst enemy, and I want to stop myself because it's sick, but I can't."

His whole body was shaking. Tain stood and slid a pad of paper across the table, along with a pen.

"Write your confession, Doug. I'm going to go talk to my boss."

Sims followed Tain back into the hallway.

Tain turned to the officer outside. "Keep a close eye on him."

Daly was at his desk, and Tain didn't even pause when he knocked but walked right in. Sims hesitated at the doorway.

"That boy came down, Marvin. He identified Doug Fisher," Daly said.

"We've got to make sure he gets help."

"What are you suggesting?"

"He needs therapy, not jail." Tain sat down.

"Tain, you never struck me as such a bleeding heart."

"I'm serious, Daly. He said an officer named Hawkins persuaded his parents to let it go without pressing charges, his parents split up, and he's been drifting ever since. Alex Wilson should have been jailed years ago, but because Hawkins was apparently on a more important case at the time, Wilson was left to prey on children in this community for more than a decade."

He watched the color drain from Daly's face.

"Look, all I'm going to say here is that I think Doug needs help. He needs counseling. So far, all he's done is look. Name one teenage boy who hasn't snuck a peek at a girl, given the chance? I'm not saying it's okay. I'm just saying, with what he's been through, we can try to understand."

Daly nodded. "There are some programs, places that deal with kids like this. I'll make some calls."

"And Hawkins?"

"Get a statement from Doug and from Mrs. Fisher, and bring them to me."

Tain nodded.

There she was. Like so many other Mondays before, friends nowhere to be found, hanging out all alone.

He didn't know what the deal was. Friends at swimming lessons, having extra long weekends with the part-time parent. . . . He didn't really care. All that mattered to him was that it was predictable.

Which made what he had planned possible.

He had to admit he didn't have the best vehicle for this either, but with the minor modifications, nobody ever suspected a car like this would be carrying a child he'd snatched off the street.

It was the perfect vehicle because it wasn't a van or an SUV. No darkened windows that hinted at what they might conceal. Just a classic car with an average guy behind the wheel, his crosses and crucifix tucked away beneath his shirt and jacket, nothing external to hint at any eccentricities.

Aaron knew there were some who thought he was insane.

He knew the guys on the department, where his cousin worked, thought he was a right-wing nutjob. They'd conspired to make sure he never got on the department, he was sure of it.

No matter how much Adrian swore it didn't work that way.

But it didn't matter. He'd thought helping others would give his life meaning.

Now he realized his purpose was to help others, just not in the way he'd thought.

Aaron glanced at his watch. It was almost time.

Time to save another girl.

Craig jumped in the back of the truck, wondering if the crash course he'd had really was going to be enough for him to handle himself in a real fire.

Quinlan jumped in beside him. "Usually, I wouldn't be here, but I thought you should know. This one fits the pattern."

"Shit. I don't have any way of getting a message to Ashlyn."

"I thought she was being watched."

"She is, but . . ."

"Look, I'm going to hold you back, make sure you don't get put in over your head here. And I'll radio out a call so your sergeant knows."

Craig nodded. "Thanks."

Ashlyn glanced through the peephole and then unbolted the door.

"Alex Wilson is behind bars."

She saw the gleam in Tain's eye, the hint that there was much more to tell.

"Come on, don't hold back now." He followed her inside and the phone rang. "Just a second. I'd better get that."

"Craig's personal secretary, huh?"

"Hardly. Most likely it's him, checking up on me."

Once she was finished on the phone, she hung up, exhaled and leaned against the hall wall. "It's another arson fire."

Tain frowned. "These guys watching you, are they checking license plates of vehicles around the area, just in case?"

Ashlyn blinked. "Uh, I haven't a clue. To be honest, they were so concerned about making this a complete safe house, I tuned out most of the techo-stuff after a while."

"Ashlyn, really."

"Do you have any idea what it's like, Tain, to know you put yourself at risk and have everyone harping on you twenty-four seven about how dangerous something is? Like you all think I'm completely fearless and the best thing for me would be if I was shaking in my boots, scared out of my mind?"

"That's not our point, and you know it."

"But it wears you down, you know what I mean?"

He sighed. "Still, I wouldn't mind talking to those guys. . . ."

His cell phone cut in then, and he answered it. After a moment he said, "Okay, I'll bring her with me," and hung up.

"Tain, seriously, I'm fine."

He shook his head. "It's not that, Ashlyn. Another girl's gone missing."

# TUESDAY

It was hours later, just before dawn, when Tain and Ashlyn arrived in Daly's office to brief him.

"Tell me we have a lead," Daly said.

Tain shook his head. "Nobody saw anything. She went outside to draw in her sketchbook. Her parents didn't notice anything until she was late for dinner."

"Of course not. Why should parents pay attention to their children?" Daly looked up at Ashlyn. "Sorry. So we have another girl missing, and we're no further ahead with this case?"

Ashlyn set a drawing down in front of him. "Composite sketch of a possible suspect."

He frowned. "If nobody saw anything, where'd you get this?"

"I tracked those crosses to a cash purchase made in New Westminster, and I sent the sketch artist over this afternoon to get a description."

Hawkins walked in then. "We have a description? Why the hell haven't we released it to the media?"

"It's tentative. What we need to do is see if the clown and the jewelry vendor from the fair can ID this as the guy who was seen with Taylor Brennen just before she disappeared."

Hawkins pointed a finger at her. "I don't give a shit about it being tentative. The public is outraged. We look like we're getting nowhere, and we need to reassure local residents that our streets are safe and we're making progress."

"For Chr—"

"Tain, shut up." Daly glared at him for a moment before looking at Hawkins. "It's too late now for the newspapers anyway, but I agree the picture shouldn't be released yet."

"And why the hell not?"

"We expect him to kill another girl."

"Which is a hell of a good reason to ask every citizen to be looking for him, if you ask me. Maybe the stress of this is clouding your judgment."

Daly's eyes narrowed. "If he wakes up in the morning and sees his picture on the news, what do you think he'll do? He was going to kill one of them already. Why not kill them all and take off?"

Hawkins swallowed. "This isn't my call, and it sure as hell isn't yours."

"Tain, Ashlyn, go home. Sleep. I'll have officers track down the ID on this guy. Tain, come back at noon. Ashlyn, don't come back at all, unless we call you in."

"If you get a lead on this guy, I want to be there."

Daly held up his hand. "One step at a time. And close the door."

As soon as they left, Daly looked up at Hawkins, his eyes burning.

"You are dangerously close to being written up, Daly. I'm warning you—"

"No, Dennis, I'm warning you." Daly pulled a file from the top drawer of his desk and handed it to Hawkins. "Right now, I'm not inclined to hang you out to dry on this. My officers are working from behind because they're cleaning up your old messes."

He watched Dennis's eyes scan the papers, the rows of wrinkles that emerged seeming to age him ten years in less than two minutes.

"Steve, I—"

"Right now, Dennis, I only care about one thing. Closing these cases without any more of my people getting hurt. Now, you either support my call on this, or you pull me off. But don't expect me to keep my mouth shut."

Dennis turned and yanked the door open, slamming it behind him as he left.

When Craig dragged himself up to the front step of his house, a shot of adrenaline surged through him. He reached for his gun instinctively and then cursed.

It was the one thing he couldn't risk taking to the fire department.

Craig set his bag down on the steps. The door was open, and he entered cautiously. Then he checked each room on the main floor, stopping at the safe long enough to reclaim a weapon.

There'd been no sound from the rooms above him while he'd been moving through the ground floor, but he cautiously started up the stairs, gun ready, moving slowly and making sure he avoided the creaky spots.

When he'd checked all the rooms, he felt as though something had reached inside his heart and squeezed it, pushing all the air out of his lungs in the same instant.

He walked back downstairs and heard movement from the doorway. Ashlyn looked at the door and then him.

"Geez, I thought somebody had broken in."

He closed his eyes and exhaled. Then he glared at her. "Where the hell have you been? And don't touch that door. Unless you left it open when you went out, someone did break in."

"I left you a note, Craig."

"Where?"

"On the fridge, on your memo board. There was another abduction last night." She wrinkled her nose as she walked past him, eyes sagging. "I don't have to ask what you were doing."

Craig picked up the phone, and after a moment he followed her into the kitchen.

"Did they have a good explanation?" she asked.

He shook his head, his mouth twisting into a wry smile. "Since you were out, they shut off the alarm monitoring."

"Can't wait to see how they explain that in their reports."

"Someone's going to come over, use the patio door to come in and dust the front door. We can leave it open so it's not as easy to see them check for prints and then they'll lock up on their way out."

"We going somewhere?"

"Bed. You look as tired as I feel."

She glanced at her watch. "For a few hours, but then I have to get back on this."

"I talked to my dad. He said he ordered you to come home and rest and that Sims can handle it from here."

Ashlyn sighed. "Fine. We got a composite sketch of our suspect."

"That's great."

She started to climb the stairs. "Unbelievable. I'd planned on making you breakfast this morning."

"Don't worry about it. You can make me lunch later."


Sims glanced at his watch. "You're early."

"Any other case, Daly wouldn't have dreamed of sending us home. We go at these like sprints."

"This one's more of a marathon."

"And I damn well hope we're in the home stretch. What have you got for me?" Tain asked.

"I tracked down your clown and the vendor from the fair. They both gave me a positive ID on our composite sketch. This is definitely the guy who was spreading his version of good news on the fairgrounds."

Tain skimmed through his messages. "Damn." He glanced up at Sims. "Not about that. There are two guys we have to track down who might be able to give us an ID on the suspect."

"The merry-go-round guy who's working out in Alder-grove."

Tain's eyes narrowed. "How did . . . ?"

"I asked Bert and Lex. Surprisingly helpful for guys with records. I've already been to Aldergrove."

"I don't like the sound of that."

"Hey, I tried. He couldn't tell me any more than the other

two did. Well, other than a bit more of the twisted doctrine this guy was spewing about being cleansed in the baptism of death and purged by fire."

"Cleansed in the . . ." Tain covered his face. "Shit. Right in front of our fucking eyes and we couldn't see it."

"See what?"

"The girls had drowned."

"He baptized them and held them down?" Sims asked, his jaw dropping. "Jesus."

"It's as good a guess as any. We'd better hope that security guy is in today. He's been on holidays, which is why I still don't have a message from him. He was supposed to be back on the job yesterday."

"Let's go, then."

"Just give me a second. I have to make a call."

Tain dialed and then tossed Sims a coin. "Can you get me a soda? I'm going to need the caffeine. Thanks." He heard a quiet voice on the other end of the line answer. "Craig, thank God you answered."

The voice on the other end of the line sounded groggy. "Why? What's up?"

"Nothing, it's just . . . Look, are the officers watching your place noting license plate numbers?"

"They're supposed to be. Well, I think photographing all cars and then getting the prints developed."

"I think you should get them on that right away."

Silence. "Okay. Why?"

"Just a feeling I had last night when I was talking to Ashlyn. There was this car. Did Ashlyn tell you?"

Craig groaned. "Be serious, Tain. Look, it's just as well you had her with you last night. Someone broke in here."

"You're on night shift again tonight, aren't you? What are you going to do?"

"Hope like hell you're ready to bring in your suspect so she's at work."

"Look, I've got to go. I've got my cell. Call me before you leave for the fire hall and we'll come up with a plan."

Tain hung up and swore beneath his breath. Then he grabbed the information he needed and went to meet Sims.

"There's nothing more I can do," Hawkins said.

"That isn't good enough. There must be something," Lori argued.

"Well, there isn't. You're going to have to deal with that."

"You said if I was ready to make a change we'd have a future."

"That was before."

"Before what? Before the rape?"

"That has nothing to do with it, Lori, and you know it."

"So this has all been for what? Stroking your ego?"

"That wasn't it."

"Really. Prove it."

"Lori, damn it, there's nothing more I can do. Nothing. Now just let it go."

"You don't get it. I've got nothing left to lose on this."

"Don't be ridiculous. How about Vish? What about your career?"

"If they don't put me back on the rape case, my career will be as good as dead and you know it."

"No, that's not true. Daly, he's right to make that call. You shouldn't even be back at work, and if it wasn't for your constant abuse—"

"You're accusing *me* of abuse? How's this going to look when it comes out? Just another sorry old bastard abusing his position for sexual favors."

He shook his head and laughed, a hollow staccato laugh. "Jesus. How could I be so fucking blind? And I thought I loved you. Prepared to piss it all away if you'd just snap your fingers—"

"I'm here knocking on your door and you tell me to leave. Don't you dare tell me you were ready to put it all on the line."

"You didn't leave Vish. He kicked you out. Don't give me that look. I know. He phoned me. He'd figured it all out.

Now here you are, putting the screws to me again, trying one last time to get your way, and if I don't do what you want, you'll expose me. For all the good that'll do your career. You think people won't want you backing them up on the street? Nobody will want to promote you for fear people will think you earned it on your back."

She slapped him hard across the face and pulled her hand back to slap him again, but he grabbed her wrist and held it until she squirmed, trying to wrench free.

"Once I'll let go. Do it again, and I'll go public myself and make sure you take your share of the blame." He could feel her tremble.

"You wouldn't dare."

"Lori, the only thing I can do is give you a heads up about an arrest. Maybe get you in on it. But I can't put you back on the case." He let go of her arm. "I'm sorry."

She backed away, her eyes wide and wild, as though it was her face that had been struck instead of his. Then she turned on her heel and walked away.


"Constable Ashlyn Hart," she said again, spelling out her badge number. "Oh, give me a break. I've talked to three people in that office, and nobody knows how to answer my question. I want to speak to a supervisor."

She sat at the desk, tapping the pen against the notepad in front of her, waiting while her call was transferred again.

Finally, a person answered. Ashlyn repeated her name and her request.

"I'm not sure I can give that information out. Our employees have rights."

"Look, I'm not interested in charging any of them. I won't even tell you if they admit they were grabbing a coffee at Starbucks instead of finishing their route. But I need to know the names of each person ticketing on that street for the past week and how to contact them."

"Maybe if you had a warrant."

Ashlyn clenched the pen. "If I get a warrant, I'll be coming into your office and going through your records personally, and not just for last week on that street. I'll be looking for the months of June, July and August for half a dozen other streets that relate to this case. Now, at this moment, I'm feeling generous. The last girl that was abducted was taken from this street and we believe she was being watched. That means one of your people might have seen a suspicious vehicle, someone hanging around. Their memories are fresh."

"Look, you know, I'd like to help you. I'm not just trying to be difficult."

"Fine. I'll be there in an hour. And I'll be calling all the affected employees off the streets until I'm done interviewing. I'm sure my supervisor can let the press know that you're helping us with our inquiries and therefore too busy to do much ticketing, likely for the next week anyway. I can be very thorough with my interviews if I have to be."

"Just a minute," the voice grumbled.

When Ashlyn had the information, she smiled. "Thank you. Have a wonderful day."

"Well, when are you planning on getting them developed?" Craig glanced up at the ceiling. He could hear Ashlyn moving around the small room as he listened to the voice on the phone. Then he responded. "Yes, I need them right away. No, don't worry about that. It's fine if you're a man down for the next two hours. I don't have to leave until four thirty. Right. Yes, it is very important."

Craig hung up his cell as Ashlyn came down the stairs. "Any luck?" he asked her.

"After I basically threatened to go over there and rip the supervisor's head off."

"Tain's been teaching you his version of diplomacy?"

"What's with people being so uncooperative?" Ashlyn sighed. "Maybe I bring out the worst in people."

Craig laughed. "Hardly. Hey, you have that list of all of our potential suspects, right?"

"You mean Quinlan's master list? Or the short list of names that fit the young offender theory?"

"That one. Three dozen or so, right?"

She nodded. "Sitting in the red file beside the computer. Why?"

"What have we got on their vehicles?"

Ashlyn shook her head. "Nothing. We were strictly looking for an existing record. The only one even connected to the department with a record is Bob, and we should have known we wouldn't find anything. The fire department screens its staff thoroughly."

"Yeah, but don't we have checks on all the peripheral guys? The ones from the store where they get their uniforms and the pager company?"

Ashlyn sighed. "Not really. I don't have their home addresses, so all I could do was a name check. In two cases, I didn't even get local listings under the names that I could positively match. No way to be certain about a record check without more information."

"And they have really common names too, don't they?"

"Not obscure ones, that's for sure."

"Listen, if you get time, and I stress the 'if' there, can you see if you can get some more information on them?"

"I'll try. I'm going to have the phone tied up for the next hour or so."

"No problem." Craig watched her go back upstairs and waited until he heard her pull out the chair before flipping his cell phone open again and making another call.

"Nothing unusual? Well, what about cars you ticketed along there? Yes, for the whole week." Ashlyn rubbed her forehead.

"Um, I ticketed a blue Taurus and a silver Neon and one of those PT Cruisers. That one was black."

"All just standard violations?"

"Parked in the handicapped spot with no sticker, no money in the meter."

"Anything else?"

"I'd make lots of money if I could ticket those skateboarders always hanging around on the corner, cutting out into traffic. One day, someone's going to smack into them and I'll feel sorry for the driver, you know? Those kids don't pay any attention to what they're doing."

"They hang out there all day?"

"Mostly in the afternoons and evenings. I was in that area in the morning last week, so I didn't have to deal with them."

"Thanks."

Ashlyn flipped her notebook open. Dog walkers, residents . . . no skateboarders. She picked up the phone and dialed.

He answered after one ring. "Tain."

"Ashlyn Hart."

"What's up? Everything okay?"

She ignored the note of concern in his voice. "Just wondering, in your canvassing last night, did anyone mention skateboarders to you?"

"No. Why?"

"I'm talking to all the meter maids who were ticketing in the area for the last week. One mentioned there's usually a group on the corner in the afternoons and evenings."

"You want me to swing by, ask some questions?"

"Aren't you tracking down a clown or something?"

"Sims did that. We're trying to find the security guy. He's our last shot at putting a name to this guy. Positive ID, though. Confirmed by three guys at the fair."

"Okay. I'll see if any of the other people ticketing on that street can help. Tain, if you get an ID on this guy, you call me."

"I will. Don't worry. You'll be with me on the arrest."

"Good. Use my cell phone. I've just finished charging it."

"Right. Bye."

"This is it," Sims said.

"Let's hope driving halfway across creation's been worth the trip."

They went inside and Sims started to explain to the receptionist why they were there.

"No offense, but we want to talk to whoever's in charge," Tain said, pulling out his ID.

Sims glanced at him. "It's a wonder Ashlyn puts up with you."

"She knows me. Spend an hour with us, and you'll hear her dish it right back."

"You're wrecking my image of her."

"You should see her in her pajamas."

Sims's cheeks went red. "And I asked you for her phone number. Geez . . ."

"We aren't involved, Sims. She's sleeping at Craig's."

Tain almost smiled when he saw the look on the young man's face. He wasn't sure which option Sims considered worse: himself or Craig, but Tain felt no pang of guilt, no need to explain.

The receptionist returned, the manager in tow.

"What can I do for you?" he asked.

Tain held up the ID still in his hand. "We need to talk to the main staff person who worked security at the fair in Coquitlam during the week of August twelfth to the eighteenth."

"We staffed that mostly with university and college students."

"I know. That's why I said the main staff person."

Tain and Sims followed the man, who'd identified himself only as Joe, into his office. "We understand there was a man removed repeatedly from the fairgrounds that week because he was frightening children with his religious propaganda."

"So? What does that have to do with us? Or you, for that matter?"

"We believe he may be a key witness in the child abduction case."

Joe sat down on his desk. "I see. Well, I don't think we can help you. I mean, I wish we could—"

"There was supposed to be a main supervisor overseeing things at the fairgrounds. Are you telling us that you had probationary workers on duty without supervision?"

"Some of those students have worked for us before, or work for us part-time year round. They were hardly all probationary staff."

"Then we need a list of their names, addresses and telephone numbers."

"Do I have to give that up without a warrant?"

"Do I have to tell the press your security company may have violated operating procedure and is reluctant to cooperate with the investigation into the abduction of a child from the fairgrounds you were paid to monitor?" Tain smiled. "Besides, I called. I was told there was a staff person who supervised the fairgrounds. Witnesses have an older man, not a student, present at a number of the removals. His name was . . ." Tain leafed through his notebook. "Fred Hibbert."

"Fred's on holidays."

"He was supposed to be back yesterday."

"A permanent holiday."

"You fired him?"

Joe glared at Tain and then cleared his throat. "Look, here's his address and telephone number. Does that get you off my back?"

"Only if he can help us. If he can't, I'll be back for that list. And I promise I won't be as charming if I have to make this trip twice."

Tain looked at Sims as he turned around, and the younger man automatically started walking out the door.

"Just wait," Joe said. He got up from the desk, went to a computer and hit a few buttons. Then he pulled a sheet of paper from the printer.

"That's everyone," he said.

Tain took the list. "Thank you."

"Ever heard about flies and honey, Tain?" Sims murmured as they left the building.

"We have the list. That's all that matters."

Ashlyn tried to siphon the frustration from her voice, thankful she was on the phone so she didn't have to suppress her scowl. "Look, I already talked to Marci. She said there are usually a bunch of skateboarders hanging around on the corner."

The meter maid answered. "Not every day. Mondays are

pretty quiet, from what I've seen when I'm in the park with my own kids. The girl you're looking for, Angie, she was always around. But not the rest of them."

Ashlyn stifled her groan. He must have been watching her longer. He had to know Monday was the perfect day. . . . "Can you think of anyone in the past few weeks that you saw hanging around, anyone unusual?"

"This time of year with a park across the street? Take your pick."

"It's really important. We think this guy would have been watching her for a while. Likely come along, park and sit in his car, pretending to look at a map or something, but really watching the girls."

"Well, there was this one guy. . . . He had binoculars. But he was watching the park."

"What did he look like?"

"Short, bald, fat guy. Drove a red mustang."

"Anyone else?"

"This guy I couldn't ticket because he'd pay to park, get out and piss on the bench."

"Lovely."

"There was one other guy. I ticketed him just a few days ago."

"What was his story?"

"Who knows? He'd parked in a no-parking zone, so I slapped him with a ticket."

"Remember what he looked like?"

She rattled off a quick, generic description, one that fit perfectly with their composite.

"Any chance you remember what he was driving?"

"Yeah, an old Corvette. Silver. I remember because it seemed weird, all these religious stickers and that metal fish and crap."

"Where? On the bumper?"

"No. Inside the car, on the driver's door."

"Weird." Ashlyn felt her heart pound against her chest.

"Tell me about it. Thought it was bizarre that some religious nut would have a car like that. Don't they usually drive something, you know, not vain and showy? You want his plate number?"

Ashlyn smiled. "That would be great."

"You think he did it?"

"He might know who did. We have to consider everything," Ashlyn lied.

She wrote down the number, then hung up the phone.

Taylor and Lindsay both sat on their beds, not moving more than their eyes as they watched Maria clean the room.

"He says he wants everything to be perfect. Today's my special day. I'm going home."

Taylor's eyes flickered in the direction of the new bed, the girl staring wide-eyed, her tear-streaked cheeks pale, her mouth and hands bound. She'd cried a lot when she was brought in, way more than even Lindsay had, and she'd tried to get out twice.

"Kicking and screaming won't help you," Lindsay had told her. Taylor thought it was odd. Lindsay, who'd been so sure that he was going to kill them. Lindsay would have been so glad to have another girl there willing to try to escape just days before.

Maria was prattling on about her "special day" and how wonderful it was going to be, and that if they were very good, they might have a special day when they were ready to go home as well.

Taylor thought of the whip he'd used on the new girl the night before, the screams that ripped the air and made Taylor cringe as the girl's body was cut over and over again.

She wanted to go home.

When Tain answered the phone he'd hoped it would be Ashlyn. Instead, he heard Craig ask, "Any luck?"

"Still working on it. Close, though."

"Ashlyn's made some progress."

"What did she say?"

"Something about a silver Corvette. She has a plate number."

"Then I can assume she's tracking it down and even if the security guy's a dead end, we'll have a name."

"Security guy gives you your warrant, though, doesn't he?"

"Fuck, exigent circumstances."

"You're planning for those, are you?"

Tain smiled. "If I need to. Geez, look what you made me say, Craig. Sims is plugging his ears."

"You should be more considerate. Not like he asked to work with you."

"Who does? But it's not my fault. I failed Sensitivity Training 101."

Tain could hear Craig laugh. "I'm off to the station. I had the guys take the photos in and told them to go over every vehicle tonight. In the morning I'll have a list to cross check against the names we've got."

"And in the meantime?"

"Look, I called Daly. He said that he'd give you two hours, and then he'd pull Ashlyn in, if not before."

"Why two hours?"

"He needs time to think up an excuse."

"She's going to be wondering why we even sent her over there."

"Ashlyn knows why, and we actually have all the information we're going to get. Daly should pull her out."

"Do me a favor? Don't tell her that when I'm around."

"No fixed address? For Christ's sake." Ashlyn half laughed, half groaned. "How the hell can you register a car in this province with no fixed address?"

She stared at the information, really not much more than a name, because the only address listed was one of those rental boxes in a Mailboxes, Etc. store in Port Coquitlam. This guy could be anywhere.

Aaron Vaughan. Aaron . . . an old, classic car . . . Ashlyn snapped her fingers and ran down the stairs, sticking her cell phone in her pocket as she ran out the door, making sure she locked it behind her.

As soon as she'd pulled out onto the street, she dialed Daly's number.

"It's time for you girls to get ready," he said. "Come with me."

Taylor glanced at Lindsay, who kept her eyes straight ahead as she walked to the door. Maria was smiling, her dark eyes sparkling. Beside her, Lindsay's eyes were overshadowed by dark circles, her cheeks drooping.

Ever since she'd been stuck there, Taylor had been thinking about writing stories. She was good with her words and good with her descriptions. Everyone said so. It was a strange thing for a girl her age, but in some ways, she had her mother to thank.

Her mother was always going on about what people looked like, how they failed to keep themselves up. The only time she'd ever seemed to pay attention to Taylor was when she was pointing out someone with waxy skin or a flawed complexion.

Taylor had worked hard to learn the words so that she knew what her mom was talking about. It earned her a fleeting moment of approval instead of a smack for being an idiot.

He led them into another room—just Maria, who still insisted on being called Hannah, Lindsay and her. The new girl, the one who didn't have a new name yet, was still tied to her bed.

The new room had a shower and a table with hairbrushes and clips, and three new dresses hanging in the closet.

"You girls need to shower. Make sure you use the soap. Then get ready with your new clothes. It's Hannah's special day today, and we're going to celebrate."

He shut the door behind him, Taylor hearing the faint click as he locked it, and the shuffle of his feet as he moved away.

The man who'd answered the door was wearing pants and a wifebeater, a few days of stubble on his chin, and he reeked of stale booze. "Yeah, what do you want?"

"Are you Fred Hibbert?"

"Who's asking?"

Tain held up his ID. "Constable Tain, Coquitlam RCMP. You used to work for the LM Security Company."

"Used to is right," he said, and snorted. "What do you want?"

"You were supervising at the fair in Coquitlam before you went on holidays, right?"

"I was supposed to be. That was the problem with that company. Short staffed, so they bounced me around all over the place. I complained and got sacked."

"But you were at the fairgrounds for part of the time?"

He nodded and shrugged. "Briefly. Why?"

"Do you remember this guy?" Sims asked, holding up the composite.

"Looks like that religious nutcase I dealt with a couple times. Man, he was a real piece of work. You want a complaint in writing about him, I'll give it to you, gladly."

"What we'd really like is his name," Tain said. "Tell me you wrote him up or something."

Hibbert's face fell. "Sorry. By the time I dealt with him, I was late for the other rotation I had to deal with. I let my main guy there write him up. I think his name was Avon or Adrian or something like that."

Tain held up the staff list. "Which of these guys should we talk to first? It's urgent."

Hibbert tapped the page. "I left him in charge."

"Thanks. And if you think of anything," Tain said, passing him his card.

"See? I can be nice," he told Sims as they got in the car.

Sims just shook his head. "I'll call these numbers and see if I can find Sean Becker."

"Geez, Craig, your girl can't get enough of you."

Craig turned to see Ashlyn walking through the parking lot toward the garage. He grabbed a rag to wipe his hands and tried to walk casually to meet her.

"What's going on?"

"Is Adrian Vaughan here?"

Craig nodded. "He's covering a shift for someone."

"I need to talk to him. It's important."

Her eyes were shadowed with concern, but she sizzled with a nervous energy that she often displayed when things got heated on a case. "I'll go get him."

Within a minute, he'd returned with Adrian.

"Oh, hell. You two want to talk to me because I asked you out?"

Ashlyn shook her head. "Nothing to do with that. It's about your cousin."

"Which one?"

"Remember you told me you have a cousin, bit of a right-wing religious zealot who comes over and works on cars, sometimes hangs out here?"

Adrian nodded. "Yeah, Aaron."

"I need to find him."

"Why?"

"Adrian—" Ashlyn glanced at Craig, who gave her just the slightest shake of his head. "It's just really important. We believe he can provide critical information about our child-abduction case."

"Aaron? I don't see how."

"Do you know where he's living? His driver's license has a mailbox in Port Coquitlam for him."

Adrian turned from her to Craig and then shrugged. "Sure. He moved into this religious compound, but then the group got run off. Don't really remember the whole deal. He just told me they'd all gone, and he was still there, keeping the place ready for when they came back."

Ashlyn wrote down the address, and then her cell phone rang.

"We found a name," Tain told her.

"Aaron Vaughan."

"Geez, I owe you a drink now, don't I?"

"I've got an address." She gave him the directions. "I can meet you there in ten minutes."

"We can pick you up."

"I'm at the fire hall."

"Okay, we'll meet you there, then. I'll call Daly and get backup. And you wait for us."

Craig glanced over his shoulder, then followed her to her car. She popped the trunk and pulled out her Kevlar.

"You think this guy is armed?"

"A religious nut who drives a Corvette? Who knows?"

Craig glanced at the men in the garage again, all watching him and Ashlyn, Adrian's face distorted with confusion.

"I have to go."

"Be careful."

She nodded. "You too."

Craig watched her drive away, then turned back to the garage, Adrian still watching him.

The men playing cards all laughed.

"God, I can't believe some of these broads. Dress me up in a Santa suit and suddenly I'm their idea of a sexual fantasy."

"Got to wonder how desperate they are, fantasizing about you."

"Father complex. Jolly fat man who brings presents."

Craig groaned inwardly. Hours of stories over dinner, first about the women who liked special pumpers, and now this.

"So, you guys get all these women throwing themselves at you just because you're firefighters?" he asked them.

"Your turn next, buddy. Oh, they'll steer clear when they see your girl around, but any night you want a taste of something else, you'll have your options."

"That's not my style."

"No? You aren't married."

"Maybe I should be," he murmured, more to himself than anyone else.

"We don't just get the chicks. Plenty of other nutjobs around here," Adrian said. "All the wannabes?"

Most of the men at the table groaned then.

"Don't even get me started on those guys."

"Living vicariously. Can't make the cut so they hang out, want to volunteer."

"What's wrong with that?" Craig asked.

"They didn't even make the volunteer cut," another man said.

"That one guy, you know, at the place where we get our pagers? He's, what, failed three times now?"

"I don't know why they keep letting him try."

"Probably want to keep him happy, you know, managing our account and all that."

"Which one is that?" Craig asked. "Greg?"

"No, the other one, Rob. He's the one who handles all the accounts."

"I had someone called Greg. He said he did it all."

The men laughed. Craig looked around, and nobody met his gaze.

"All right, enlighten me. What's the joke?"

"You must've taken Ashlyn with you."

"Why do you say that?"

"Rob loves to watch the ladies. He can't handle a customer with a pretty girl on his arm."

"Must be why he wants to be a firefighter," said one of the other men who'd just walked in. "So he can flex his pumper."

They all laughed, except Craig. He was thinking about how Ashlyn got called back to pick up a new pager.

Once they'd finished washing up and getting dressed, Taylor and Lindsay sat down. Maria, or Hannah, continued to buzz around the room, picking up their clothes, folding them, putting everything back the way they'd found it.

"Were you like that at home too?" Lindsay asked.

"Like what?"

"Fussy. Always cleaning up and looking after stuff."

Maria shrugged. "We have a big family. Everyone has to help."

The latch clicked, and the door opened. He stood there, dressed in black, except for his white collar. Once he'd looked them over, he smiled.

"It's time."

He took Maria's hand, leaving Taylor and Lindsay to follow them.

When they got back to the main room that they'd stayed in, a large door on one wall had been opened, revealing an oversized fish tank, as far as Taylor could tell. She'd never really seen anything like it.

Along the far wall, all the shutters had been pulled back, revealing windows and even one that was nothing more than a screen, the warm sunlight and gentle breeze filtering in through the sheer drapes.

"I am the way," he began.

"You are the way," they echoed.

"I show the path to God."

"You have shown us the path. . . ."

Taylor peeked at Lindsay as they recited the words, the words he'd spent hours teaching them, hour after painful hour of sitting with their knees pressed against the hard concrete, learning the pledges, learning how he wanted them to respond. . . .

Lindsay stared blankly ahead now, her lips moving automatically, the words coming without resistance. Taylor had seen the wounds on her back when she'd washed, still scabbed and looking angry and sore. Lindsay had even winced as she pulled the dress over her head.

"It is time," he said.

He reached for the bread and followed the ritual, and then they shared the wine.

Once they were finished, they sang a short hymn and then he stood up, extending his hand to Maria, the girl he called Hannah, who took it.

He led her to the tank and lifted her inside.

"I will baptize you and cleanse you of your sins."

He pushed her backwards, under the water. Taylor waited for him to let her up.

Maria started to squirm under the water.

"Pray for her, girls. Her spirit is willing, but the flesh is weak."

"He's going to kill her," Taylor whispered.

Lindsay lunged forward, grabbing at his hands. For a moment, he let go of Maria, who pulled herself up, clutching the side of the tank as she gasped for air.

"This is it?" Tain asked as he jumped out of his car.

Ashlyn nodded. She pulled her gun out of the holster. "Apparently, he was part of some religious sect that had set up camp here. The rest of them left, but he stayed on."

"Okay. We believe he has four girls. He's not afraid to kill them." Tain finished relaying the orders. "Sims, you lead your team around back. Ashlyn, you're with me."

Tain, Ashlyn and four other officers made it to the front door with little concern. All the windows on that side were boarded up, and there was no evidence of anyone. Once they got to the front entrance, it was another story.

The lobby was wide and two hallways ran toward the back of the building, a large, wide staircase climbing up. Tain gestured to two officers, sending them to check the main floor.

"Let's go up," he whispered to Ashlyn, nodding for the remaining officers to follow them.

"Shouldn't we wait for the all-clear?"

"I have a bad feeling about this."

She nodded. "Okay, let's go."

They started up the stairs, each taking a side, tilting their heads back to try to see if anyone was observing them from above.

Once they reached the second level, Tain quickly assessed that the access door was locked on their side. The main floor had been cleared, and he gestured to those men to try to open the second-floor door.

They continued upward, toward the top floor. Ashlyn reached for the door and turned the handle all the way. As she pulled it open, they heard a scream.

Tain and Ashlyn ran in the direction of an open doorway across a large, empty area from where they were. They could clearly see that nobody was in the main room, with most of the side doors closed. Ashlyn half turned, gesturing to the side doors, waiting until other officers went to check them.

They reached the door as another scream ripped through the stillness. Tain peered around the doorway.

"Oh, Christ," he said, rushing in.

Ashlyn was partway into the room before she could really see what was going on. A girl tied to a bed against a wall, crying silently because she was bound and gagged. Another girl was sitting on the floor, just staring. Her mouth was open with no sound coming out.

The man, dressed like a priest, had been dragging another girl across the room to a tank, her hair being pulled in one hand, a whip secure in the other. She screamed again, and he pushed her into the water, raising his hands with the whip as though he was going to strike her.

"Police! Stop. Don't move," Tain said.

At that moment, another girl lunged upward, out of the tank, giving the man the distraction he needed. He grabbed her, spinning around, pulling her in front of him.

"Get behind me, Satan."

"Let the girl go," Tain said.

"She is God's."

"Not yours."

"I am the way to God."

"Let her go, and you can explain it to us."

The other girl jumped up then, grabbing him around the neck, pulling her scrawny arms tight. Ashlyn could see the murkiness of the water, blood coming from the wounds on the second girl's back.

"Taylor, go over there," Ashlyn whispered to the girl on the floor. Taylor looked up at her and blinked.

"Go."

Sims rushed forward then and grabbed Taylor, pulling her back.

"Aaron, it's time for us to end this," Ashlyn said.

He turned and looked at her. "Harlot. Whore. You have not been saved from your wickedness."

"Well, if you let the girls go, maybe you can help me with that."

"You're beyond help. They have to die before sin takes

hold, or they will be separated from God forever." His eyes were bulging.

The girl trying to choke him, who was too weak to have any real effect, bit his cheek and he screamed, letting go of the other girl as he turned and punched the one behind him. She fell back. For a moment Aaron was clear, but he was turning. Ashlyn fired, but he twisted enough for the bullet to strike his shoulder.

His eyes blazed as he ran toward the window. The girl in the tank had slipped beneath the water, but Aaron was getting closer to the last girl, the one on the bed.

"Whoever gives one of these little ones a cup of cold water will not lose his reward. See? This is my blood, poured out for you," he said, holding a stained hand up for the girls to see, licking it. "He who loses his life shall find it."

"There's no way out of this." Tain grabbed the girl who'd fallen on the floor and pushed her behind him. Ashlyn could just see her still wriggling, trying to get back into the room as another officer pulled her from behind. Tain moved toward the tank slowly, and she nodded. He put his gun away and reached down to lift the body of the girl from the water.

"If I cast myself from this height, He will summon a thousand angels to carry my body to the earth."

Ashlyn still had her gun trained on him. "Aaron, let's talk about this. You need to—"

He jumped through the screen, screaming as his body fell from view.

"No. Christ," Ashlyn swore, rushing to the window. "Call an ambulance."

"You mean call a coroner," Sims said, stopping beside her. "Look at his neck."

"But the girls . . ." Ashlyn said, turned around. "Shit."

Tain was kneeling by the girl who'd been in the water, performing CPR.

Craig was finding it hard to wait, not knowing what was going on, when the alarm sounded.

Quinlan again jumped on the truck beside him. "It's a medical call, not a fire."

"That's still good news. Ashlyn identified the suspect. Hopefully they arrested him."

Quinlan nodded. "Good. I assume it wasn't one of my men?"

"Your guys are all clean, as far as the arsons and abductions go."

"What about the rapes?"

"We still aren't sure about that."

As they pulled in, Craig saw Adrian's face go white and then he looked at the vehicles already there, police cruisers, Tain's car, Ashlyn's. . . .

Quinlan put his hand on Craig's arm, which was the only thing that kept Craig from racing forward. He drew a shaky breath as Quinlan called out the orders, leaving Craig nothing to do with the scene.

The men Quinlan had ordered in disappeared into the building. Craig moved beside Adrian.

"You're a cop, aren't you?"

"That bad as a firefighter, huh?"

"No. Just . . . with everything happening and Quinlan shielding you. You're okay as a firefighter."

"Good. Because if you even think about telling anyone, I'll have to arrest you."

Adrian looked at him. "How many have you got working the arson case?"

Craig shook his head. "I'm working the rape case."

"You mean . . . Ashlyn, she's bait? Man, maybe it's just as well I thought you guys were an item. I don't think I could take a girl who puts herself at risk like that."

The first group of men were returning now, a girl on a board, followed by another girl on a board, and then two girls walking down with firefighters, being led toward the paramedics who'd arrived.

When the last group came down, Craig almost swore. Not dead, but not good either. He looked up from the ashen face to see Tain, Ashlyn with her arm around him, telling him something.

She looked up and their gazes met.

Then the forensics team arrived, and a group of them were sent around the building.

"Where's Aaron?" Adrian asked Ashlyn.

Her mouth opened, but no words came out. She shook her head. One of the other officers came forward and asked for Ashlyn's gun.

Adrian's eyes widened. "You shot him?"

"I didn't kill him."

"This is just a formality," the officer told her. "No deadly force. All accounts say it was completely justified, that maybe you should have popped him in the head."

Ashlyn turned back to Adrian and Craig, but before she could say anything Quinlan grabbed Adrian by the shoulder and pulled him away, out of earshot.

"What happened up there?" Craig asked.

"Baptism of death." Ashlyn turned around, her eyes resting on Tain, who was bent over the front of his car, his shoulders taut. "I've got to go talk to him. He really wanted this to end clean, you know?"

"If you didn't kill him—"

"He jumped out the window. Broke his neck and splattered like an egg. I don't figure him for our rapist, but we've got no way to know for sure now."

"Unless we catch someone else," Craig said.

"Well, you don't have to worry about me. I won't be home for hours."

# WEDNESDAY

"Craig. Wait up. There's a call for you."

He set his bag down and went back to get the phone.

"You just leaving?" Ashlyn's voice. Still heavy, with exhaustion he guessed.

"On my way home," he told her.

"I'm still at the station."

"Any idea when you'll be done?"

He heard her breathe out. "Not a clue. Likely won't be long, but I might have to sit through another round of questioning."

Exhaustion and guilt. "If you guys need anything, call. I got some sleep last night. How's Tain?"

"He'll be okay."

"Good."

Craig hung up and saw Quinlan walk over.

"Good thing you have the next four days off."

"You thinking more guys are putting it together?"

"Just maybe it'll give you a chance to get this guy."

"I hope so. Hey, you know the place we get our pagers from? What's the name of the guy who handles the account?"

"Rob Kearns. Why?"

Craig shrugged. "Just checking everyone connected."

Paul Quinlan stared at him for a moment. "Do they teach you how to lie, or does it just come naturally?"

Craig smiled. "Not natural enough if you know I'm doing it."

Dennis Hawkins sighed as he slumped down on the bench across from her, the little diner humming with the morning rush. It was an out-of-the-way place, the kind of truck-stop diner that he never took Lori for even knowing existed. "What is it this time?" he asked her.

"Can I order you something? The breakfast special?"

"I can't stay. What do you want?"

She wrapped her hands around her mug of coffee, staring down at the table for a moment before she looked up at him. "I'm sorry."

"That's a first."

"Really."

He swallowed, studying her face. He'd heard it all from her, believed everything, until he'd realized he'd never had a clue what she was really after from him. Dennis shrugged.

"Then I trust there won't be any problems."

He started to get up, but she reached across the table and put her hand on his.

"I went back to Vish. Promised him I'd quit or take a desk job. It's . . . it's what he wants, you know. And it's all I've got left, really."

He stared at her, willing her to say more, tip her hand if necessary, but not really sure what to say to that.

"I always loved him. I loved you too. You probably don't believe that I'm even capable of it," she said with a thin smile. "But it's true."

"Lori, I—"

"No, just let me say it. I had to look at my priorities and my future."

"You mean I no longer had anything to offer you."

"I mean you said you didn't want me anymore."

"It was never like that. Just not being threatened. I'm not going to abandon my wife and tear everything apart because you say you're going to go public."

"I'm not going to do that."

"So I have nothing to worry about?"

"No, not a thing."

"Then I hope things work out. I can see about a transfer you know."

She shook her head and waved her hand. "There's only one thing I want. Just one last call."

He looked at her face. Some of her color was back, and the black circles under her eyes were fading. Her energy was bubbling again. Not boiling like it usually did, but starting to simmer.

"I'll let you know."

This time when he stood, she didn't stop him. He turned and walked away.

"What on earth can they still be talking about?" Tain muttered.

Sims returned, passed him a bottled water and set one down in front of Ashlyn.

"Deciding whether or not to suspend me, I'd guess," she said.

"You?" Tain shook his head. "Christ, Ashlyn, if you hadn't done what you did, that girl would have been dead for sure."

"Any word on her condition?" Sims asked.

Ashlyn held up two empty hands. "Not so far."

"Seems almost unfair, bringing Taylor Brennen out of that and subjecting her to the circus she'll face in court now."

"What are you talking about?"

"John-John filed some sort of suit. I've been summoned as a witness," Tain told Ashlyn, picking up an envelope from his desk and waving it in the air. "If there's any justice at all for her, he won't be her dad, or she'll at least get to stay with Nick Brennen, where she belongs."

"You think he'd want her, if she wasn't his?" Sims asked.

"Taylor is Nicky's sister. That counts for something," Ashlyn murmured.

"I'd want to keep her," Tain said.

Ashlyn's nose wrinkled. "I'm having trouble picturing you with kids, Tain."

"If I can raise a dog, I can raise a kid."

She laughed. "Kids do more than go fetch."

"So does my dog."

"True. Your dog finds dead bodies in the woods."

"See? Raising him to follow the family career path."

"Yeah, but as I recall, your dog has a personality."

"Very funny."

"You know what I still don't understand?" Sims said. "How did they connect?"

"They were all Catholic," Tain responded. "I talked to the parents at the hospital. Seems our man made customized religious charms or pendants for all these girls over the past few months."

"What about Maria's family?" Ashlyn asked.

"They had him come to the church to take an order. That's how he saw her." Tain looked over as Daly and a group of senior officers entered the room. "Here we go."

Ashlyn stood, her eyes fixed on Daly's face. He gave her a tiny nod.

Once they'd dealt with the compliments from their superiors and a press conference, Daly intersected Ashlyn. "Come to my office."

She followed wordlessly, sinking down in her chair.

He went to his locked drawer, removed her gun and passed it to her.

"No suspension, huh?"

Daly shook his head.

"What did that cost you?"

"Nothing. On this case, under the circumstances? You didn't even use deadly force. Every single officer at the scene backed you up, and a girl made a statement."

Her eyes widened. "They've got one talking already?"

"Angie. Taylor hasn't said a word, and Maria hasn't stopped screaming. From what the doctors said, he almost killed her."

Ashlyn felt her lip curl. "He was spouting that religious garbage right to the end, you know?"

"Guess he never heard of 'Thou Shalt Not Kill.'"

"Well, if someone had to die today, I can live with it being him."

"Go home. Get some sleep. You'll feel better after a few days off."

"After we close the rape case."

Daly shook his head. "I'm pulling you out. It's too much right now."

"Right now, almost everything I own is at Craig's. I'm either sleeping there, or supervising a move."

He looked at her for a moment, face blank so she couldn't tell what he was thinking. "Craig doesn't have a shift tonight anyway, so you shouldn't be in any danger."

She stood up, reached for the door and then paused. "Any word on Lindsay?"

"Critical condition. Every hour she holds on increases her chances." Daly nodded toward the hallway. "You'd better go before Craig sends out a search party."

Craig listened to the message again, trying to place the name, and then it clicked.

He dialed the number and glanced at his watch, consoling himself with the idea that any average family would be up by now.

A voice yawned a greeting into the phone.

"May I speak to Ryan Lewis please?"

"Hang on." The phone clunked against a hard surface, and then a voice yelled for Ryan to come to the phone.

Another voice answered after a moment, the voice Craig vaguely remembered.

"This is Constable Craig Nolan. You called and left a message for me."

"Hey, yeah, sorry to call at home. I was away camping until yesterday, and that's when I heard something. You haven't . . . have you already caught the guy?"

Craig rubbed his forehead. "No, not yet."

"Well, this might not be anything."

"That's okay. Whatever you heard, I'll check it out."

"Okay, well."

Craig could hear him moving, sounds in the background getting quieter and louder simultaneously, as though he was moving away from a blender in the kitchen and toward a stereo. Then the music stopped, just as Craig placed the album as *The Rising*, which left him to wonder where his copy had gotten to.

"You know how I told you about the house on the corner?"

"I hope you didn't go over there, snooping around."

"No, no, nothing like that. But the people who live there, they have a nephew about my age, Tommy. He stays with them sometimes when his mom has to work. When I got back from camping he was there, so he came over and we got talking.

"He was telling me about this guy he saw in the alley the other night. Says this guy was there . . ." He paused. "You know."

"Enlighten me."

"You know. Jerking off. In the lane right behind that woman's house."

"Did he get a good look at him?"

Ryan rattled off a description, generic as it was.

"What night was this?"

"Sunday night."

"He see anything else, like a car?"

"That's the thing. There was a car parked down at the end of the alley, blocking it. Really pissed off Tommy's family because they couldn't get in. Tommy wrote down the make and model and license plate number and said they should call someone, have it ticketed or towed."

"Let me guess. They didn't want to, because of their strained relationship with the local authorities."

He could hear the smile in Ryan's voice. "Something like that."

Craig wrote down the information. "This is all great. Really helpful, Ryan."

"Enough to get me a tour of your precinct?"

"Enough to get you a tour."

"Cool. But that's not all."

"You have more?"

"Tommy's family was going on and on about how they'd seen that same car about a week earlier. He went back and asked when I was so interested."

"Are you telling me it was in the lane the night Nitara Sandhu was murdered?"

"According to them, it was. So what's that worth to you?"

"Name your price."

"Well, a shooting lesson at the range would be cool."

Craig was just coming back down the stairs when Ashlyn walked in the door.

He stopped short. "How did it go?"

She held up her gun. "Cleared. Where are you going?"

"I have a suspect."

"You do? Let's go."

"Ashlyn, you should stay, get some rest." He looked at her for a moment, then threw up his hands. "Fine. You know what? I'll call Daly, see what he wants to do."

Within ten minutes, he'd joined her in the living room.

"We're waiting?"

Craig nodded. "Daly's sending someone to the place where he works to see what he's up to. Should be able to bring him out without too much trouble."

"How'd you catch on to him?"

As soon as Craig filled her in, the phone rang again. Ashlyn reached to the end of the small couch and grabbed the phone before Craig could, ignoring his frown.

"You aren't going to believe this," Daly told her.

"Try me."

"It's his day off."

"Have we got a home address?" she asked, putting the question as much to Craig as to Daly.

Craig nodded. "But we might need a warrant."

Daly's voice was talking in her other ear. "I'll run the warrant through. I want you two here to pick it up. I've got a couple officers here who can go out with you."

"Feeling awfully generous, Daly."

"You put a lot of hard work in on these cases, and I

know you want to get this guy. Plus, I'll never hear the end of it."

"We're on our way."

As soon as Lori saw Craig and Ashlyn enter the building, she felt her stomach flip.

Ashlyn had been there all night on the other case. Now she was here with Craig? Lori stared at them as they walked down the hall, becoming smaller, her pen tapping against the files in front of her, and then she smacked her forehead. So that was why she was at Craig's. Working the rape case too.

She picked up the phone and dialed Dennis's cell.

"How come I haven't heard from you?"

"There's nothing to hear."

"Then why are Craig and Ashlyn marching into Daly's office along with a group of officers who look like they're about to storm a building?"

The silence was followed by a sigh. "I'll see what I can find out."

As soon as she put the phone down, Lori got up. If Hawkins was thinking about backing down, she still had a card or two she could play.

"What the hell was that about anyway?" Ashlyn asked after they'd left Daly's office.

Craig shook his head. "Hawkins has been unpredictable ever since Lori was raped. He threatened to take the case away from Daly."

"Is that why Daly's chewing on aspirin like candy?"

"Can't be easy babysitting us."

He tried to sound flippant, but fell short. The line of his mouth, the look in his eyes . . . Craig worried about his dad but always buried it deep.

When she didn't respond he asked, "You ready for this?"

Ashlyn put a full clip into her gun. "As ready as I'll ever be."

"Robert Kearns, this is the police." Craig called again. He banged on the door with his fist, harder this time.

Silence.

Within seconds the door was shaking on one hinge, and they were scouring the house. It took only a moment before the officers who'd gone into the basement called the all clear. He wasn't there.

Ashlyn looked out the kitchen window. "Garage," she called. She ran out the back door, through the yard, Craig following.

Kearns was standing near the back, his hands in the air. Ashlyn guessed the garage was about thirty-five feet long, an extended area at the back equipped with tools and saw-horses, lumber leaning against the walls. She could see the two officers they'd sent around standing in the lane, looking through the two-car door opening, guns drawn but holding back. Then she saw who they were deferring to.

"Shit."

Craig moved inside the garage nice and slow, approaching the suspect. "It's okay, Lori. We've got him. Isn't that right, Rob?"

Rob Kearns swallowed and nodded.

Lori stepped forward, her jaw clenched. "Say it," she hissed.

Craig glanced at Rob, turning his gun in Lori's direction.

"I need to hear him say it."

"Lori, this isn't going to make things any better." He kept moving slowly, to shield Rob Kearns.

"Say it," she screamed.

Ashlyn had stepped inside the garage, just by the door. Craig signaled her with his free hand to stay where she was.

Lori lifted the gun a bit higher, pointing it at Craig. "Call them off."

He glanced at the officers behind her, who moved around the side of the garage, into the yard.

"I want to hear him say it." Her voice was thick and low. "I want to know why."

"Lori, put the gun down. There'll be plenty of time to talk about what he did at the station."

She started to laugh. "You think I'm going to fall for that? Jesus, Craig, what do you take me for? A fool? There's no evidence. We've got nothing to tie him to any of this. If he doesn't confess, he'll walk."

He fought to keep his voice calm, to speak patiently and with confidence. "That's not true, Lori. How do you think I found him? An eyewitness places him at the scene of one of the rapes."

"You're lying."

"Lori, put the gun down." He stepped closer to her, completely shielding the rape suspect from his former partner.

As soon as Ashlyn heard the shot, she saw Rob jump aside. Craig fell. Ashlyn turned toward Lori, telling her to put the gun down.

Lori was turning her gun at the man who'd raped her.

Ashlyn squeezed the trigger and watched Lori stagger back, bulging eyes staring straight at Ashlyn for a moment as the gun clattered against the concrete and Lori fell.

One of the other officers, who'd moved around to the side of the garage, rushed forward, kicking the gun away from Lori. Ashlyn turned and saw the suspect on the ground beside Craig, a pool of blood oozing from his body. She'd been too slow to stop Lori from getting a second shot off, she realized as she knelt on the ground beside Craig.

"Call an ambulance," she yelled at the other officers outside.

It felt like forever, holding Craig's hand, telling him to hold on, until the paramedics arrived. They tried, unsuccessfully, to pry her away. Nothing they did seemed to stop the blood. She knew she was losing the battle to keep the panic out of her voice. "Jesus, can't you do something?"

"Ma'am, you need to stay here," a voice told her. She felt hands tugging on her and shrugged them off.

"I'm not leaving him. Craig—" She squeezed his hand. "Hold on. I'm right here. I—"

"Ma'am, really, you have to stay here."

This time she felt strong arms grip her from behind,

around the waist, pulling her back. She twisted and tried to resist, but she felt Craig's hand slipping from her grasp.

Tain had felt his chest tighten when he'd heard there were officers down. Craig and Ashlyn's arrest had gone horribly wrong, but nobody was saying more. "Couldn't they tell you who'd been shot?"

Daly's face was white. "Two officers down. That's all I know."

"They had a team, right?"

Daly nodded, and then he stopped cold.

When Tain reached the doorway, he felt like he'd taken a bucket of ice water in the face. There'd been the odd moment he'd seen Ashlyn wipe a tear away, but he'd never seen her like this.

Her beige shirt was soaked red, and the skin on her arms was shades darker than normal, the blood stains there already dry.

She looked up then and saw them, her face a pasty white.

"Ashlyn, what happened?"

"They won't tell me anything, Daly. They won't even tell me if he's alive."

Tain and Daly moved into the room, and Ashlyn put her arms around Daly's neck, her body shaking.

"I'll go see what they can tell me," Tain murmured. Nobody needed to ask. He'd seen the impact of unspoken truth hit home in Daly's eyes the minute he saw Ashlyn.

Craig had been shot.

Daly shook his head as he undid Ashlyn's grip on him. "I'll go. They might not tell you anything, either."

Tain watched Daly turn away, draw himself up and walk out of the room.

"Come on, sit down." Tain took Ashlyn by the arm and got her settled, removing his coat and putting it around her shoulders.

"Constable Ashlyn Hart?" a voice asked from the doorway.

She looked up, and Tain felt the pressure in her hand as she squeezed his arm.

The man held up his ID. "We need to ask you some questions."

"Go on." Tain nodded. "We'll wait here for you."

Ashlyn squeezed his hand and stood up again, her legs wobbling as she took a deep breath and then followed them out of the room.

As soon as they had left, Daly returned.

"They took her for questioning already. What the hell's up with that?"

Daly sank down into a chair, not the one Ashlyn had been sitting on, which was smeared with viscous red streaks. "They won't tell anyone anything. Straight, uncensored interviews, all their ducks in a row before we know more."

"Political posturing while our friend might be dying in there? This is bullshit."

Daly shook his head. "I can tell you this. The three people shot were the suspect, Craig and Lori Price."

Tain's elbows propped on his knees, his face in his hands. "What the hell was she doing there?"

Daly didn't answer.

The man was your quintessential pencil-pusher—balding, with thick black glasses and Coke-bottle lenses. He'd been doing most of the talking. The two nondescript women with him also made notes and glanced up to scrutinize Ashlyn's expression, she guessed to gauge her responses.

They asked her question after question about what happened next, the few minutes that had seemed to pass in slow motion for Ashlyn at the time, everything moving forward frame by frame, Lori pulling the trigger, Craig falling to the ground, Rob Kearns jumping out of the way, Ashlyn hearing the boom of the gun going off in her hands, not realizing Lori had gotten another shot off until she saw Kearns on the ground after Lori fell. . . .

By the time the questioning was over, she'd given up trying to wipe away the tears. Finally, the man put his pen down. "You're quite upset about this."

Ashlyn blinked, her mouth hanging open. "Is that a question?"

"Officers have to be prepared to handle life-and-death situations all the time without getting distraught to the point where they can't function."

"I'm not on the street. I'm in a hospital, where I've been for hours, and nobody will even tell me how my partner is."

The man pushed his frames up on his nose. "You were here last night, weren't you?"

She nodded.

"You shot a suspect in another case."

Ashlyn nodded again.

"How is that suspect?"

"He died." Ashlyn paused, and then she shook her head. "He jumped out a window and broke his neck."

"In the past twenty-four hours, you've been involved in two high-profile arrests where suspects have died, and on both occasions, you fired your gun. How much sleep did you get in the past forty-eight hours?"

Ashlyn stood, imagining she must look like a newborn fawn trying to stand for the first time. She reached for the table to support herself. "If you have any more questions, I expect to have counsel present."

She didn't have the energy to slam the door behind her, just concentrated on putting one foot in front of the other as she moved steadily back to the small room that had been cleared for police officers. Through the doorway, she could just see Daly and Tain, others gathering as well, before everything went black.

# AFTERWORD

"Did you go to see Ashlyn today?"

Alison nodded, poking at the food on her plate with her fork.

She did more poking than eating. Daly frowned, though it didn't feel like much of an effort for his face to slip into that expression. There hadn't been much to smile about in the past few days.

Questions, accusations, internal investigations, funeral arrangements. Never mind the grief. The regret. All the things he could have done, should have done differently.

He studied his wife's face for a moment, noting the way the corners of her eyes sagged, the droop of her shoulders. "She's not doing well?"

"I think she's lost some weight. Doesn't look like she's sleeping much either. Can you explain to me why she's still staying at the house?"

Daly groaned. "With everything going on, we never had a chance to get her moved back to her own place. And until they've finished the investigation, it's likely best not to do anything through the department."

"It's not like Craig would mind. But I can't imagine it's helping her right now."

"No, probably not."

"I tried to persuade her to move in with us for a while."

"Do you want me to talk to her?"

Alison shook her head. "We can let her know we're there for her, but that's about the best we can do. She's going to have to work through this on her own."

"I always thought of Ashlyn as being pretty tough and capable."

"Not invincible, though. She cares, Daly. Handles the guys like one of the pack, but she has a big heart."

"It would be a shame to lose someone with so much promise."

"Do you really think that could happen?"

Daly shook his head, pushing his plate aside.

Alison looked at him. "Since when does the department refuse to disclose whether an officer is alive or dead, anyway? The way this is being handled, I don't like it."

"Me neither. But there are a lot of things to consider."

"Like how Lori Price found out who the suspect was."

Daly nodded. "I'm being questioned this afternoon."

Her shoulders drooped even further, something he hadn't thought possible. "Why do I get the feeling there's something you haven't told me?"

"Because you have good instincts?"

"Where were they when I decided to marry a cop?"

Daly knew part of her was joking, but it was the other part of her, which was deadly serious, that had him worried.

Ashlyn opened the door. "I thought you were going away."

Tain shook his head. "I didn't want to be unreachable." He followed her inside. "I didn't think you were here. Your car . . ." He gestured to the empty driveway.

"I parked it in the garage," she said, offering no further explanation.

He followed her to the living room. "I thought you'd like to know about Rob Kearns."

She sank down on the sofa, hugging a pillow. "What about him?"

"They found all sorts of stuff on his computer. Security footage that he'd edited and made photographs from. Karen, Cindy, Stephanie, Nitara, Lori . . ." Tain swallowed. "You. And the reporter who covered that case years ago, he confirmed Rob was the teen arrested. Juvenile record wiped clean."

"Guess that should make it easier to tie up the loose ends." She mumbled the words as she leaned against the arm of the sofa, her feet tucked under her body.

"The department went public today. He died in the hospital."

She didn't respond.

"We do have some good news."

Ashlyn's eyes turned in his direction.

"Lindsay Eckert's in stable condition. Long-term prognosis is good."

"That's . . . that's great, Tain."

"We should go out, have a quiet dinner, just a few hours to clear your head and take your mind off things. What do you say?"

She didn't answer. Her mind seemed to go from an endless jumble of disconnected thought to blank.

"Ashlyn . . ."

"Nobody will tell me anything."

She could hear Tain blow out a deep breath.

"I do know something. Lori and Hawkins were having an affair, and she used it to find out where the rape suspect lived."

She looked up. "Is that why they're keeping such a tight lid on this?"

He shrugged. "I suppose it's as good a reason as any. There are rumors about internal reviews on all our procedures because of the whole mess."

Tain put his hand over hers and squeezed it gently. "It wasn't your fault, Ashlyn. There was no way you could have known Lori would find out the address and beat you there. The officers who were sent around back and deferred to her have a hell of a lot more to answer for than you do."

"I shot another cop, Tain." She pulled her hand back, rubbing her forehead as she squeezed her eyes shut. "That's something I've got to carry."

"And she shot your partner first. Nobody's going to forget that."

"I guess Lori has a lot to answer for."

When he didn't respond, she dropped her hand and opened her eyes. Tain wasn't looking at her; he was looking at the floor. She'd seen a lot of raw pain from him, a lot of concern for her. Avoidance wasn't something she was used to.

"Tain—"

"Ashlyn . . ." He looked up, looking like he was trying to find the right words. "Lori didn't make it."

"At what point did you become aware of the relationship between Inspector Hawkins and Constable Price?"

Daly cleared his throat. "When the results of Constable Price's rape kit were put into a report that I received."

"And why did you receive that information?"

"The officer on the case, Constable Nolan, was doing field work."

"You mean the undercover arrangement with Constable Hart?"

"That's correct," Daly said.

"What did you do with the report?"

"Nothing."

"Nothing?"

"I didn't inform Constable Nolan of the contents."

"Did you inform any of your commanding officers?"

"No."

"Why not?"

"As you know, we were in the middle of three very serious investigations. Lor . . . Constable Price had been taken off the case, and dealing with an affair didn't seem a high priority at that time."

"So you did not reveal your knowledge of this matter to anyone."

"Yes."

"You did disclose the results of the kit?"

Daly nodded. "It came to my attention that Constable Price was still trying to get back on the rape case. I told her that if she continued to pursue an involvement with the rape case that I would disclose the results of the rape kit."

"There's one thing I'd like to be clear on," one of the

women said. "How was it that Inspector Hawkins's DNA came to be on file with our crime lab?"

"A few years ago he was involved in a case where he was injured. There were several blood samples taken at the scene, and his DNA was taken for elimination purposes in the investigation."

"Shouldn't it have been deleted from the system?"

Daly shrugged. "I can't explain why it wasn't. All I know is that when I confronted Constable Price, she didn't deny it."

"Did you have any other supporting evidence in your possession that confirmed the affair?"

"No, sir."

The questioning continued, covering his working relationship with all the officers involved. . . .

When it was over, Daly went to his office, locked everything away, took his few personal photos down from the shelves, put them in his briefcase, and went to hand in his badge and gun.

He unlocked the door and stepped inside. The night was already unusually dark because of the growing storm clouds, but he didn't turn any lights on.

No matter how many times he was questioned, he found it hard to believe that the case was being handled the way it was. No telephone, limited access to a select group of people. . . . All this time and he still didn't even know exactly what had happened. From the moment he'd hit the pavement everything was hazy or nonexistent. There were so many gaps, so many questions.

And he'd had a hell of a fight to get released from the hospital. They'd tried to persuade him to wait until morning, but he'd pushed back hard, arguing over the merits of a good night's sleep in his own bed.

Now, as he stood there, listening to the sound of nothing, his anticipation of being home was overshadowed with the new reality. Finally, he could get some answers. He swallowed, wondering if he really wanted to hear what he dreaded, what he feared most.

Nobody would answer him when he'd asked about Ashlyn. The way their eyes had skirted away from his gaze, the slight tensing of the facial muscles . . .

He leaned against the wall, closing his eyes as the image of her walking into the kitchen in her pajamas, taunting Tain, flashed through his mind. He rubbed his forehead, thinking about the first night she'd slept there, sitting in bed with a book in her hands, the way she'd glared at him when he made her move over. . . .

Those moments when they'd talked over the case, and the moments in between, when they didn't have to say anything at all.

The clock ticked softly as he stood there, coming to terms with the fact that he was going upstairs to an empty bedroom, not knowing whether it was too late to tell her how he felt.

Craig trudged up the stairs and walked down the hall. He paused. The warm orange glow of the fire shimmered on the walls of his bedroom.

He stepped inside the room and turned toward the walkthrough closet. He felt a lump rise in his throat and swallowed hard.

She had a loose robe pulled around her, and her eyes were focused on the ground, as though something was pushing her head down. Then, as if she could feel his gaze, she looked up.

Ashlyn's eyes widened, her hand covering her mouth as she gasped, and then her whole face lit up with a smile, despite the tears that started trickling down her cheeks.

"You're okay?" he asked her.

"Me?" She brushed the tears from her face. "I was . . . I didn't . . . They wouldn't let me see you."

He tried to give her a reassuring smile. "Nobody would tell me anything, either."

"Tain came by, said they got enough evidence to seal the case against Rob Kearns."

Craig nodded. "That's good. I, uh . . ." He scratched his head. "I didn't think you'd be here."

Her smile lingered despite a shadow that had passed behind her eyes, her relief at seeing him giving way to uncertainty as she tried to explain why she was still in his house. "Guess they were too busy with the inquisition to worry about moving me out."

"I'm just sorry you had to handle things without me. I guess they were keeping me sealed off to make sure they could set the record straight."

"They've been interviewing you?"

"Relentlessly for the past week. How do you think I got my strength back?"

She gave him a thin smile. "Not strictly motivated by hospital food?"

His gaze drifted over her form, her pale skin, recalling the hollow cheeks that had stood out starkly before she set eyes on him and smiled. "You look like you haven't eaten at all."

She shrugged, only the ghost of a smile remaining on her face as she turned away from him.

He moved toward her, standing just behind her and slightly to her left side, brushing his fingers against her arm. "Ashlyn . . ."

The images were cloudy, like a fog had been over his brain when it was happening so he couldn't pull the memory into focus, but he could hear her words, hear her telling him to hold on, telling him she'd be right there.

There were fleeting seconds where he could remember her face, the look in her eyes that made him think he wouldn't be foolish to hope.

Or was it all just jumbled impressions that had been distorted through the mix of fear and painkillers?

She'd started to cry again, her shoulders trembling, her hands covering her face.

"Hey, everything is going to be okay."

"I know," she said as she wiped her cheeks again. "I'm just so relieved. The more time passed . . ."

He tilted her chin up with his fingers. "What happened wasn't your fault."

She turned, reached up and put her arms around his neck

gently, kissing his cheek. He felt her silky hair brush against his skin. "I was so worried, Craig."

Ashlyn held him for a moment, and then he felt her slipping away as his heart pounded against his chest. He wrapped his arms around her.

"All they would tell me was that another officer had died. When nobody would tell me how you were . . ." he said.

"Don't you remember anything?"

"Hazy images that I wasn't sure I hadn't dreamed."

They stood looking at each other for a moment, Craig's grip on her loosening.

"Here you are, worrying about me when you've just been released from the hospital. I'll sleep on the couch."

"You don't have to do that."

"If I'd known you were being released, I would have gone home."

"I'm glad you're here."

"Why? So you can enjoy the comfort of your own home and still get breakfast in bed?"

He smiled back at her, running his fingers across her cheek. "That would be a first." He took a deep breath. "Do you know what the worst thing about this case was? Lying beside you and knowing you could be so close, but I couldn't really be with you."

Ashlyn's eyes expanded for a second, and then she shook her head. "You're unbelievable. All this time, and I could never figure out . . ."

"I didn't know you were investing a lot of energy into that."

"Be serious."

His expression sobered. "I am, Ashlyn."

They stood for a moment, both staring at each other. Craig finally gave her a wry smile. He released his hold on her and turned away, moving toward the bed as he unbuttoned his shirt and started to maneuver his arm out of his sleeve, struggling to pull it around with his one arm, avoiding the use of his injured shoulder.

He almost cursed as he stretched a bit beyond what was

comfortable, and then he felt her hands, guiding his arm to relax as she pulled the shirt back carefully, avoiding the bandages as she pushed it down his arms and to the floor.

Craig turned as she moved to face him. His skin tingled as she touched his arm. Her eyes glistened as she reached up, pushed his hair back and kissed him, hesitantly at first, her lips lingering a few millimeters from his own before they pressed against his with intensity as she moved to close the gap between their bodies. As he reached to tighten his hold on her, she moved her arm, bumping his shoulder, and he groaned.

She pulled back. "I guess I should go easy on you."

He shook his head, reached down, tugged on the cord that held her robe in place and slid it off her shoulders, his breath catching as he felt her smooth skin against his own. He bent down and with his good arm lifted her up and put her down on the bed as he felt her arms reach around him, her lips pressing against his own.

# JIM KELLY

# THE FIRE BABY

An American plane crashes into a remote farm on England's Cambridgeshire Fens. Out of the flames walks a young woman, Maggie Beck, with a baby in her arms—the only two survivors. Now, twenty-seven years later, Maggie is dying. As she lies in the hospital, she gives a startling deathbed confession to the patient in the bed next to hers, Laura, a woman slowly awakening from a coma. The confession would blow open the murder case that Laura's husband, reporter Philip Dryden, is covering…if only Laura could communicate the shocking secrets she's learned.

ISBN 13: 978-0-8439-6001-3

# ☐ **YES!**

Sign me up for the Leisure Thriller Book Club and send my FREE BOOKS! If I choose to stay in the club, I will pay only $8.50* each month, a savings of $7.48!

NAME: _____

ADDRESS: _____

TELEPHONE: _____

EMAIL: _____

☐ I want to pay by credit card.

☐ **VISA**     ☐ **MasterCard**     ☐ **DISCOVER**

ACCOUNT #: _____

EXPIRATION DATE: _____

SIGNATURE: _____

Mail this page along with $2.00 shipping and handling to:
**Leisure Thriller Book Club**
**PO Box 6640**
**Wayne, PA 19087**
Or fax (must include credit card information) to:
**610-995-9274**
You can also sign up online at **www.dorchesterpub.com**.
*Plus $2.00 for shipping. Offer open to residents of the U.S. and Canada only. Canadian residents please call 1-800-481-9191 for pricing information.
If under 18, a parent or guardian must sign. Terms, prices and conditions subject to change. Subscription subject to acceptance. Dorchester Publishing reserves the right to reject any order or cancel any subscription.